THE PILGRIM CONSPIRACY

Dutch anthropologist Jeroen Windmeijer (1969) writes thrillers in which Roman and biblical history and the history of his hometown, Leiden, are brought together. His first book was very well received by both the press and booksellers, in the Netherlands and beyond. With *The Pilgrim Conspiracy* he claims his place among the great storytellers. Jeroen's thrillers are plot driven, smart and authentic.

Also by Jeroen Windmeijer

St Paul's Labyrinth

The Pilgrim Conspiracy

Jeroen Windmeijer

OneMoreChapter

One More Chapter
an imprint of HarperCollins*Publishers* Ltd
1 London Bridge Street
London SE1 9GF

www.harpercollins.co.uk

This paperback edition 2020

First published in Great Britain in ebook format by HarperCollins*Publishers* 2020

First published in Holland in 2018 by HarperCollins Holland, as *Het Pilgrim Fathers Complot*

A catalogue record for this book
is available from the British Library

ISBN: 978-0-00-837918-6

Set in Birka by
Palimpsest Book Production Limited, Falkirk, Stirlingshire

Printed and bound in Great Britain by
CPI Group (UK) Ltd, Croydon CR0 4YY

To Dünya

After Moses and Aaron arrived, they told Pharaoh, 'This is what the LORD God of Israel says: "'Let my people go so they may make a pilgrimage for me in the desert."'

Exodus 5:1

Preface

In the spring of 2017, linguist Piet van Vliet found a unique manuscript in the archives of Leiden's Heritage Organisation. It offers a rare glimpse into the lives and minds of the Mayflower Pilgrims. Seeking a home where they would be free to practise their faith, these Puritan English Protestants came to Leiden in 1609. No longer safe or welcome in England under King James I, they stayed in the relatively tolerant Netherlands for eleven years. In 1620, part of the group boarded the *Mayflower* and set sail for the New World where they became the original founders of the United States of America. They took with them many seventeenth-century Dutch ideas that we might think of as being modern, such as the separation of church and state, civil marriage, freedom of religion, freedom of speech and freedom of the press.

Principally, the manuscript tells the story we already know about the Separatist Christians who were persecuted for their faith. Nonetheless, its discovery is sure to generate great excitement in academic circles – and far beyond. Any manuscript written by an ordinary citizen reporting on historical events in a personal way is a valuable resource for historians, providing insights into how major events affected the lives of common people. Often, such documents paint a different picture to the

one that we see in the historiography. But this personal document
– the writings of an anonymous chronicler of the Leiden Pilgrims'
daily lives – is much more than that. It not only contains crucial
information that will allow historians to add nuance to some of
the assumptions that have been made about the Leiden Pilgrims
in the past, but it also brings to light new details that could
explain why one part of the group eventually chose to emigrate
to America while the majority stayed behind in the Netherlands.
As a result, it is likely that the history books will, at least partially,
need to be rewritten.

It is not immediately apparent who the intended audience
for this document might have been. It is obviously not a journal.
Did the author want to record the Pilgrims' trials and tribula-
tions for posterity? Was it intended for personal use? Was he
the group's historian? There are large gaps between entries, often
spanning many years, and it seems probable that the author's
accounts of the intervening episodes have been lost.

But the discovery of a manuscript hidden for almost four
centuries is the stuff of adventure tales, a find that every historian hopes to make at least once in his life. In their documentary,
New Light on the Pilgrim Fathers, Leiden TV's Lisette Schouten
and Guido Marsman have created a fascinating reconstruction
of this extraordinary story. It is a story that I will explore in
detail later in my book.

Does this manuscript answer all our questions? Can we now
write a definitive history of the Mayflower Pilgrims?

The answer is . . . no.

What is certain to frustrate anyone with even a passing interest
in the Pilgrims, from the academics at home and abroad who
specialise in the period to the curious layman, is that the final
pages of the document appear to be missing. Did the author

omit them intentionally? Or did someone else decide that we could read up to this point and no further?

The author makes a promise on the last pages – the last pages that we know to exist – that certain secrets will soon be revealed. The idea so appeals to our curiosity and imagination that we can safely assume that the dust that has literally been stirred up by this ancient manuscript is unlikely to settle any time soon.

The translation from old English and Dutch has been executed by the inimitable Piet van Vliet himself. Thanks to his smooth conversion into modern language, we feel as though we are being addressed from the distant past by a fellow human being who, with all his quotidian worries and ordinary cares, is more like us than we could ever have thought possible.

The resulting document was the inspiration for this novel in which I have attempted to fill in the gaps of history in a plausible way. I am extraordinarily grateful to Piet van Vliet for choosing this novel as the platform for his manuscript. After all, an article in a historical journal would only be read by a few specialists, but now, the information contained in this unique text can be made available to a wider audience.

Jeroen Windmeijer

PART ONE
THE OLD WORLD

LEIDEN

Chapter 1

Peter de Haan gripped the handle of the door that led to the lodge room, as the Freemasons called their meeting place or temple. The open evening at which the lodge's chairman, Worshipful Master Coen Zoutman, had told visitors about 'his' lodge, Loge Ishtar, was drawing to a close. After his presentation, guests and lodge members had gathered at the drinks reception in the function room downstairs while the chairman himself had stayed upstairs in the temple to answer the questions of curious visitors. The event had, after all, been a unique opportunity for outsiders to see inside the Masonic Hall on the Steenschuur canal, a building that was usually shrouded in mystery.

Peter and his girlfriend Fay Spežamor were ready to leave, but Fay didn't want to go without saying goodbye to Coen. Fay had been a member of Loge Ishtar since its foundation in 2014. As a lodge made up of both male and female Masons, Ishtar was very unusual at a time when Freemasonry was still almost exclusively male and had only recently started to accept female members.

A sudden feeling of dread washed over Peter, making him reluctant to push down on the door handle.

Fay, who was right behind him and not expecting him to stop, bumped into his back. 'What's wrong?' she asked, startled.

'I don't know,' Peter answered. Then, very slowly, he opened the door.

The main lights in the temple had been switched off. A single spotlight blazed in the darkness.

Peter and Fay followed the widening ray of light.

Suddenly, they both held their breath as though they had just jumped into the freezing water of an ice-cold river together.

In front of them, perfectly illuminated on the black and white tiles like a toppled king on a chessboard, lay the body of the Worshipful Master.

Fay let out a scream then immediately clapped her hand over her mouth to stifle it.

Peter ran over to the chairman. His head was surrounded by a pool of blood. On the tiled floor next to him was a gavel, bloody and covered in hair. Sticking out of his chest was a set square that looked like it had been put there with tremendous force. But strangest of all was the pair of compasses that had been stabbed through his clasped hands.

Although he knew it was pointless, Peter pressed the index and middle finger of his right hand to the man's neck. There was no sign of life.

Peter turned to Fay who stood motionless in the doorway, her eyes wide and her hand still pressed over her mouth. In a daze, he shook his head, then stood up and took his phone out of his pocket to call 112.

Do I ask for the police or an ambulance, he thought.

He keyed in 112, and the screen lit up. The call was answered on the first ring.

'Do you require police, fire or ambulance?' The voice was friendly but slightly brusque.

'Police,' said Peter. 'In Leiden.'

He was transferred immediately.

'Leiden Police,' said a female voice a few seconds later. 'What's your emergency?'

He hesitated for a moment and then said, 'Hello. This is Peter de Haan. I, uh . . . Someone has been murdered . . . I . . .'

'Sorry, could you repeat that please?'

Peter composed himself. 'We need the police, and I think we need an ambulance as well, but the victim is already dead.'

'Where are you now, sir?'

'I'm . . . We're in Leiden, on the Steenschuur. Steenschuur number 6.'

'Hold the line please while I request those services. They should arrive within the next ten minutes.'

There was a short silence.

Then the woman asked, 'Can you tell me what's happened?'

'We're in the Masonic Hall. There was an open evening. I'm with my girlfriend in one of the rooms, the temple, and the chairman of the lodge is lying on his back on the floor. It looks like he's been attacked with a large Masonic gavel.'

'You're sure he's not alive?'

'Yes. I checked his pulse. There's no sign of life.'

Peter stared down at the man whose friendly face had looked out over this room just a short while ago. He walked slowly backwards towards Fay, keeping his gaze fixed on Coen's lifeless body.

'What's the victim's name?'

He reached Fay's side, and she put her hand lightly on his back.

'He's called Coen . . .' He looked at Fay enquiringly.

'. . . Zoutman,' she said.

'Zoutman,' Peter said. 'Coen Zoutman. Coen with a "C".'

He heard the staccato rattle of a keyboard.

'The police will be with you shortly, Meneer De Haan,' the woman said. 'Please don't touch anything, and make sure that nobody else enters the room. Are you listening, Meneer De Haan?'

'Yes, yes,' Peter replied distractedly.

'There's an ambulance on the way too, sir,' the operator said. 'Again, don't touch anything, and don't let anyone else into the room. Do you understand?'

'I understand.'

'When assistance arrives, I'll disconnect this call. Is that clear?'

'Yes.'

'The number you're calling from, is that your own phone?'

'Yes, it's mine. Peter de Haan.'

She asked him for his address, and he told it to her.

'Could you please also make sure that no one leaves the building?' she asked abruptly.

'Lots of people have left already,' Peter said. 'But I'll let everyone else know.'

The other end of the line was quiet for so long that Peter began to wonder if the operator was still there at all.

Then she spoke again. 'I've just received a report that the police are outside Steenschuur 6. They'll take over from here.' She said goodbye and hung up.

Peter stared blankly at the phone in his hand as though he

hoped that it could provide answers to the tornado of questions in his head.

'Let's go,' he said to Fay, who still hadn't spoken.

Fay left her hand on Peter's back even as they left the temple as if she was afraid she might fall if she let go.

Just as he closed the door behind them, the doorbell rang in the hall below.

'Come on. Let's go back downstairs,' Peter said.

Fay nodded and moved her hand away. The warm spot where it had been cooled instantly.

'Peter?' she asked him.

He turned towards her, and she put her arms around him. 'This . . . is . . . crazy,' she said shakily.

They let go of each other and went downstairs.

The bell rang again, more insistently this time.

Peter opened the door.

Two young police officers – one male, one female – stood in front of him. They were visibly nervous.

'Good evening,' the policewoman said. 'My name's Dijkstra, Leiden Police. Are you Meneer De Haan?'

'Yes.'

'You reported that you found a body. Where's the victim?'

'Upstairs, in the temple.'

Without waiting to be invited in, the two police officers entered the front hall.

'Van Hal,' the male officer said as Peter politely shook his hand.

They went upstairs.

'I'll be with you shortly,' Peter called after them. 'I'm just taking my girlfriend into the other room.'

Neither of the police officers responded.

Fay stood perfectly still. She only seemed to come to life again when Peter gently touched her. She smiled at him vacantly, as if she was trying to remember who he was.

Peter held her tightly as they walked into the function room together. Everyone in the room lifted their heads to look at them, sensing that something unusual was going on. The chatter stopped abruptly as if the sound had been muted with a remote control.

Peter settled Fay onto a chair and brought her a glass of water which she drank with tiny sips. Then he addressed the group that had gathered in a semi-circle around him. 'Ladies and gentlemen,' he said, 'I'm Peter de Haan, Fay's boyfriend. I'm afraid something terrible has happened. A few minutes ago, Fay and I went upstairs to say goodbye to the Worshipful Master. We found him lying on the floor. He's dead.'

Cries of horror filled the room. A few people started to cry.

'I've called 112. There are already two police officers upstairs in the temple. I'm going to go up to talk to them now, but until we hear otherwise, no one is allowed to leave the building.'

Peter wanted to check on Fay first, but she appeared to be in good hands. Some of her Masonic brothers and sisters had gathered around her like a protective shell.

Back upstairs, he hesitated in the temple doorway.

When she saw him hovering there, the female police officer, who was crouched down beside Coen Zoutman's body, got up. Her male colleague was talking into his radio.

'So you were the one who found him?' she asked as she walked towards Peter.

Her blue plastic shoe covers rustled on the tiles.

'That's right,' Peter said. 'Me and my partner, my girlfriend. You just saw her. Fay Spežamor. I was a guest here tonight. There was an open evening. The chairman gave a talk, an introduction to Freemasonry. After it finished, we went downstairs. That was at about ten o'clock, I think. There was a reception down in the function room, but he spent the rest of the evening up here, talking to people and answering questions. Fay and I wanted to say goodbye to him before we went home. That's why we came back up.'

'Do you know who saw him alive last?'

'No . . . There was a big group of people still up here waiting to talk to the Worshipful Master after we'd gone downstairs.'

'The Worshipful Master?'

'I mean the lodge chairman. Sorry. Coen Zoutman. Inside this building, he's addressed as "the Worshipful Master". But . . . look, there were a lot of people coming and going up here. Downstairs too. It was an open evening. I think it's going to be very difficult to—'

'The Duty Officer has been informed,' the policeman said, interrupting him.

'He's calling in the Forensic Investigations Unit. They'll be here in about fifteen minutes.'

'Right then,' said the woman who had introduced herself as Dijkstra. 'We'll get this lot cordoned off here and outside as well. Nobody will be allowed to leave the building until we've taken everyone's name and address.'

Peter looked up at the All-Seeing Eye above the chair where Coen Zoutman had sat earlier that evening, so relaxed and completely absorbed in his role.

Was the All-Seeing Eye the only witness to this murder? How ironic.

'No security cameras here?' Dijkstra asked. It sounded more like a statement than a question.

'I doubt it,' Peter said. 'Only initiates are allowed to see the rituals that are performed in here.'

'That sounds creepy,' Van Hal said. 'Secret rituals . . . in Leiden of all places.'

'There's nothing else we can do here for now,' Dijkstra said. 'We'll go down and cordon everything off.'

Peter needed some fresh air. He followed the two officers outside. While Dijkstra and Van Hal were blocking off both ends of the street with red and white tape, two more police cars arrived, followed by an ambulance and a car from the coroner's office.

Behind them was a large SUV that pulled up outside the Masonic Hall and parked on the kerb. Two men dressed in civilian clothes got out. One of them was an older man with short, grey hair and a neatly trimmed moustache, and the other a younger man who was completely bald.

Dijkstra strode over to the two men to report her findings. She looked over her shoulder at Peter, and he heard her saying his name.

The three of them approached him.

'Detective Chief Inspector Rijsbergen,' the man with the moustache said, shaking Peter's hand. 'Willem Rijsbergen. This young man here is my "partner", as we're apparently calling them these days.'

The younger detective introduced himself. 'Van de Kooij. That's just my surname, not where I'm from,' he added with a grin, referring to De Kooi, a neighbourhood in Leiden Noord that was known for its colourful character and salt-of-the-earth residents.

'Right, well . . .' said Rijsbergen, rolling his eyes. He had clearly heard this 'joke' many times before.

'Willem!' someone shouted. It was a slim man in his fifties with dark curls and narrow, trendy-looking glasses.

'Ah, here comes Anton,' Rijsbergen said to no one in particular. 'Anton Dalhuizen.' He turned to Peter. 'Dalhuizen is the forensic physician from the Public Health Department. In cases of unnatural death, which is what we appear to have here, they perform the autopsy.'

Dalhuizen jogged over to join them, clutching an old-fashioned black doctor's bag.

'I understand there are still people inside the building?' Rijsbergen asked.

'There are still some visitors downstairs,' Peter said. 'There was an open evening tonight, and it was very busy. But quite a few people have already left.'

'Guestlist?'

'I don't think there is one. There were at least sixty or seventy guests. I'm not sure exactly. There were about twenty members of the lodge, so forty, maybe even fifty people were non-Masons.'

'And you're a member?'

'No, I'm not a Mason. My girlfriend is. I came with her.'

'Excellent,' Rijsbergen said under his breath. It wasn't clear to Peter whether this was meant ironically; there was absolutely nothing about this situation that could be described as 'excellent'.

They went into the function room.

'Right,' Rijsbergen said to Dijkstra. 'If you and Van Hal get started with taking the names of the people who are still here, we'll have a look upstairs.'

Peter followed them, but once he reached the landing, he wondered why he was there. Right now, what he wanted more than anything was to go home with Fay, get into bed next to her and hold her tight.

Dalhuizen produced some blue plastic covers from his bag, which he, Rijsbergen and Van de Kooij pulled over their shoes.

'Dear God,' Rijsbergen exclaimed when they opened the temple door and saw Coen Zoutman lying on the floor.

'It looks just like a film set,' Dalhuizen remarked.

They lingered at the door for a few moments, like they actually were afraid that they might be interrupting a take on a film set.

Van de Kooij entered the room first. 'See if you can put the lights on, Curly,' Rijsbergen told him, and Van de Kooij felt along the wall for a switch. He soon found it, and the whole temple was flooded with bright light.

The staged lighting had seemed to cast an eerie enchantment over the temple. Now the spell was instantly broken.

Dalhuizen crouched next to the body and felt Coen Zoutman's neck with his index and middle fingers, just as Peter had done earlier.

'The manner of death looks pretty clear to me,' he said, loud enough for Peter to hear. 'Severe blunt force trauma to the back of the head caused by a heavy object – presumably, this mallet here. I expect the victim would have been killed instantly. Whoever did it . . .' Rijsbergen and Van de Kooij moved closer to the body '. . . would probably have had to make an incision with a knife before they could insert this set square into the heart. You wouldn't be able to get it through the bone and muscle tissue otherwise. The same goes for the compass through the hands . . . And even then, they would have had to use considerable force. But anyway . . .' Dalhuizen stood up. 'That's my initial assessment. I'll leave the rest to the pathologist. My job's done. I've confirmed his death, and there's nothing else for me to do here.'

They returned to the landing where Peter was still hovering.

'Thanks, Anton,' Rijsbergen said.

Dalhuizen pulled the blue covers from his shoes, crumpled them up and put them in his bag.

'You can dismiss the ambulance crew when you get back downstairs. And send someone in to block these stairs off, if you don't mind.'

Dalhuizen gave them a thumbs up. 'Gentlemen,' he said by way of goodbye before he left.

'I don't think it's going to be easy,' Peter said. 'So many people in one place.'

'Right,' Rijsbergen said. 'We'll wait for forensics. They'll be here soon. Van de Kooij, could you give the public prosecutor a call?'

Peter had seen enough Dutch true crime shows to know that the public prosecutor – the *officier van justitie* – was officially responsible for leading the preliminary criminal investigation. The police worked in close consultation with them, and their permission had to be obtained before the police could use more serious investigative tools like phone taps.

Peter was about to go over to Fay when Rijsbergen asked abruptly, 'Would anyone be able to confirm that you were both downstairs all evening? And that you only went upstairs when this gentleman was already dead?'

Peter hesitated before answering. The thought had struck him that he might be an obvious suspect. 'Um . . . Yes, of course. Lots of people saw me. Saw us. Fay and me. When we came upstairs, he was already dead.'

'How much time was there between you discovering the body and calling 112?'

'That was . . . That can't have been more than a minute.'

'All right,' Rijsbergen said. 'The time of the call will have been logged, naturally, and the conversation will have been recorded. The problem, Meneer De Haan, is that the pathologist will shortly establish a time of death. That's always going to be an estimate, so we'll never know the time to the minute. But it's clear that he died somewhere between the presentation finishing at about ten o'clock this evening and about eleven o'clock when you made the call.'

'Yes, but . . .' said Peter, who was not only beginning to get angry now but also growing increasingly concerned by how easy it was to follow the detective's logic. 'You surely aren't suggesting that you suspect Fay and me of . . .'

A smile appeared on Rijsbergen's face that seemed to be an attempt to convey both fatherly reassurance and incredulity at Peter's apparent naivety. 'Don't take it personally, Meneer De Haan,' he said. 'At this stage, as I'm sure you'll understand, we can't rule anything or anyone out.'

'Shall I have them taken to the station?' Van de Kooij cut in eagerly.

'Just take it easy, Van de Kooij. No need to be hasty.'

'I'm not a suspect, am I?' Peter asked.

'It would be a very devious murderer who called the police,' Rijsbergen said, 'but I've seen stranger things.'

Peter didn't find this answer particularly reassuring.

'You and your girlfriend found the victim, so . . .' He left the rest of the sentence hanging. 'Let's not get ahead of ourselves, Meneer De Haan,' he said wearily. 'As I said, at this stage, we need to consider all possible theories.'

Suspects? Us? Thoroughly unsettled, Peter shook his head. He could imagine how the idea would seem reasonable from a policeman's point of view, but to him, the mere thought of it was too absurd for words.

But not even I could say that I knew where Fay was for the entire evening.

He heard movement on the staircase.

Two men and two women came up the stairs, each carrying a briefcase-sized evidence kit. They wore baggy white crime scene suits made of a thin, papery material. All four had pulled the hoods of their suits over their heads and covered their mouths with face masks.

'We're going in,' the woman at the front said curtly before pushing past them.

'Hey, Dexter,' Van de Kooij greeted the man at the back who raised his free hand in a salute.

Rijsbergen sighed.

'I think, perhaps, that it might be a good idea to do what my colleague suggested.'

He looked at Peter almost triumphantly, like he was ready to slap the handcuffs around his wrists there and then.

'What do you m-mean?' Peter stammered.

'I think we ought to have you and your girlfriend taken to the station. Separately.'

Peter was dumbfounded.

'Until then, the pair of you are not to speak to each other.'

Chapter 2

Earlier that day

Despite being turned up to full blast, the space heater didn't give off much heat. By the time Peter had managed to warm up one side of his body, the opposite side had already cooled down, and he had to twist around to warm it up again. And so he sat, uncomfortably turning this way and that while he tried to read a copy of *Mayflower*, Christopher Hilton's comprehensive history of the Pilgrims. The situation hardly lent itself to quiet study, but Leiden's American Pilgrim Museum was far from busy that afternoon, and there wasn't much else for him to do.

Peter had met the museum's director Jeffrey Banks some time back, an American with a dark sense of humour and a slightly wry smile that seemed to play permanently on his lips. This veritable walking encyclopaedia had originally been an art historian, but now he delighted in showing visitors around the little museum that was really just two rooms: the 'living room' and the 'kitchen'.

In anticipation of the upcoming four-hundredth anniversary of the English Pilgrims' journey from Leiden to America, Jeffrey wanted to expand the museum's opening hours beyond its current limited schedule of 1 p.m. to 5 p.m. on Wednesday and Saturday afternoons. Peter had volunteered to cover two afternoons a month, and that was why he now found himself sitting here, surrounded by original seventeenth-century furniture and other objects in the museum's living room. Visitors to the modest little museum could almost literally step back into the 1600s – with the obvious exception of the space heater, of course.

The only entrance to the living room was via a stable door that opened onto the street. The top half could be opened independently if someone rang the bell or knocked on the window.

The room had a terracotta flagstone floor and was dominated by a large table covered in history books about the American Pilgrims. Several wicker chairs, all from the seventeenth century, were arranged around the table.

In front of the window was another table stacked with more books, one of which had been left open. A chair had been pushed back from the table at an angle, making it look as though the book's reader had just popped out on an errand and would be back at any moment.

The sturdy, thick wooden beams on the ceiling and the original tiles that decorated the wall and box-bed all added to the rustic ambience.

There were moments when Peter imagined that he really had travelled back in time here, especially at the end of the afternoons when the daylight faded. Then he could sit in complete silence and let his eyes wander around the dim room that was lit by three large candles.

There had been a noticeable increase in the number of tourists streaming through the museum lately, more than half of them from the United States, the New World that the Pilgrims had set out for in 1620 after an eleven-year stay in Leiden.

But there were very few of them in today.

Jeroen Windmeijer

Peter de Haan, fifty-eight years old, lecturer in Archaeology and History, had – if you counted his time as a student – been at the University of Leiden for exactly forty years. Two years ago, he had missed out on a professorship after the sudden death of his boss, Arnold van Tiegem. The board had chosen another candidate over Peter, just as they had done years earlier when his old mentor Pieter Hoogers had retired. He knew that some people looked on him with a certain amount of pity because of this, but he had never actually been very interested in a professorship at all.

However, after the snub, Peter had decided to work one day a week less, which gave him more time for volunteering, and, more importantly, time for the great love of his life.

Fay Spežamor.

He and Fay had met in the National Museum of Antiquities. Fay complemented her work as a lecturer in Greek and Latin Language and Culture at the university with the post of Curator of Roman and Etruscan Art at the museum. They had formed a friendship which, to their mutual surprise, had blossomed into romance.

Fay had been widowed when her husband had died of cancer shortly after the birth of their daughter, Agapé. She was an extraordinarily vivacious woman in her early fifties who had an inexhaustible fascination for everything related to the classical era. Her shoulder-length hair was more grey than black, and she had a petite frame and unmistakably Slavic features with a narrow face and eyes that blazed fiercely whenever she was trying to make a point. Those same eyes could smoulder with love when she looked at Peter, a love that neither of them, after so many years of being alone, had ever expected to find.

Peter shivered.

Although spring had officially arrived almost a month ago, it was still cold, especially in this old building with its single-pane windows where the sun's rays never quite reached.

There was a knock on the window.

Peter turned the heater down, tucked the ribbon marker into his book and put it aside. He stood up, and a twinge of pain in his shoulders made him realise how awkwardly he had been sitting in the wicker chair for the last hour. He hobbled stiffly over to the door and opened the top half.

Willem Hogendoorn's cheerful face beamed back at him.

'A very good afternoon to you, Peter,' he said.

A small group of people was waiting behind him.

Peter had got to know Willem quite well. He was a tall man, almost entirely bald except for a wispy ring of hair around his skull. His open face had the healthy glow of someone who spent much of his life outdoors. After his retirement, the former detective had devoted his time to providing guided walks around the city, and he regularly called in at the museum with his tour groups. He had devised the walks himself, and they covered a wide variety of themes. The Pilgrims tour started at the museum, and it was enjoying an increasing popularity.

'Come on in,' said Peter, opening the bottom half of the door.

The visitors each paid the five-euro entrance fee, and Peter dropped the money into a tin on the table.

The group of eight, including Peter and Willem, was really the maximum number of people that the tiny museum could accommodate – in such a small space, visitors soon found themselves bumping into each other.

'This house, ladies and gentlemen,' Willem said, launching straight into his talk, 'is furnished as it would have been in the time of the Pilgrims. The building itself is from the fourteenth century and was built between 1365 and 1370. It's been rebuilt and remodelled over the years, but everything you see here is authentic. Every chair, table and cabinet dates from the seventeenth century.'

Willem took a couple of steps away from the group and stood next to the historical map of Leiden that was hanging on the wall above the desk.

'In the sixteenth century, there were various Puritan groups in England who thought that the Anglican Church hadn't taken the Reformation far enough. To put it simply, they felt that England wasn't Protestant enough. The whole hierarchical system of bishops and archbishops was still in place with all its incense and robes and so on. So they wanted to separate themselves from all of that, become their own, autonomous religious community.'

'That was in the time of King James, wasn't it?' one of the tourists asked.

The slightly mousy woman spoke Dutch, but she had the typical accent of someone who had lived in an English-speaking country for a long time.

In response to her question, the man next to her began to nod enthusiastically. He had a full, grey beard and an enormous belly upon which rested an expensive-looking camera that was hanging from a strap around his neck.

'Exactly,' Willem confirmed. 'That was in the time of King James I. Or *Koning Jacobus*, as we called him in Dutch. *Jacobus de Eerste*, to be precise. After his accession to the throne in 1603, the situation in England became unbearable for the Puritans. King James was very much against the separation, and he began to persecute them.'

'Puritans,' the fat man said with a smile. 'Music to my ears, that word.'

Peter raised his eyebrows slightly, but Willem ignored the man's comment and continued.

'It became difficult for them to find work,' he said. 'Travel was forbidden unless you had official permission, and it was quite common for people to be accused of crimes they hadn't committed. In 1608, a group of Puritans from Scrooby in Nottinghamshire decided to leave England. These people, who later became known as the Pilgrims or Pilgrim Fathers, fled in secret and went to Amsterdam. The Netherlands was a land of religious tolerance, and it was also increasingly prosperous. Above all, there had been a truce between the Spanish and the Dutch for twelve years, so it was a peaceful country too. After a short while . . .' Willem tapped the old city map with his right hand '. . . the group's religious leader, John Robinson, decided they should move from Amsterdam to Leiden. There was a lot of work available in the textile industry here, and you could get a job even if you had no previous experience. All you needed was physical strength. They lived here . . .' he circled his hand over the map '. . . around the Pieterskerk, including the area where the Pesijnhofje is now. It's a little courtyard with almshouses around it. We'll be visiting that later.'

The tourists, who had arranged themselves in a semi-circle around the table, were spellbound.

'They stayed here for eleven years. During those eleven years, they worked hard and saved hard. Then, part of the group decided to go to America. Most of the group stayed here, so in Leiden, you'll still meet people who are descended from those Pilgrims in one way or another. They have typical Leiden names like Cooke, Cooper and Turner.'

'Are we allowed to take photos?' someone asked Peter, who nodded in reply.

Evidently, this was the moment the visitors had been waiting for; they immediately took out their cameras and were soon busily absorbed in taking photographs. In such a small museum, it was almost impossible to take pictures with no other people on them, so a complicated choreography of stepping aside and squashing together had to be performed to give everyone room.

'The kitchen is next door,' Willem said. 'We'll have to go outside to get there because there's no connecting door between the two rooms.'

He nodded at Peter, who took some keys from a drawer and handed them to Willem.

'Follow me,' said Willem.

'So what made them leave Leiden?' Peter heard another woman ask when they were outside.

Peter smiled.

They always asked the same questions. It was understandable, of course. He could probably have given a guided tour himself by now, just based on everything he'd picked up from Willem's answers.

'That's an excellent question,' Willem said to the woman, whose face lit up at the compliment. 'There were lots of reasons. It was clear that the English king would punish them for leaving England, so there was a fear that they would be prosecuted, even here. In addition to that, the truce with Spain was coming to an end, and there was already growing unrest in the Netherlands. What else might have played a role is that some members of the group didn't want to integrate into Dutch society. They wanted to stay pure, not mix. There were religious disputes, too complicated to go into now, but they didn't want to get involved in them. All sorts of things played a role, actually. Many of the Pilgrims just wanted to make a fresh start in a new country without any interference from others, so that they could practise their religion the way they thought was right.'

'Very good,' the fat man butted in again. 'That's why apartheid was a great system for us,' he said, his words a jumble of Dutch and Afrikaans. 'It's a great pity that this is over. You see, South Africa is a mess now.'

An awkward silence fell over the group.

His wife looked around the room, her face grim, like she was preparing herself for a discussion that she'd had many times before.

'If you'd all like to come with me,' Willem said, breaking the impasse.

With apparent relief, the others followed their guide to the second entrance on the corner of the street.

'Am I right in thinking that you're from South Africa?' Peter asked the couple, who had now dropped to the back of the group. They looked like they weren't sure if they wanted to go on with the tour.

'Yes, of course, we're from South Africa. At home, we speak Afrikaans, but I've always spoken Hollands too. This is very important.'

'Your ancestors—' Peter began to ask, but the man didn't allow him to finish the question.

'More than a hundred and fifty years ago, my own ancestors went to South Africa. They were Huguenots. That is why we're here, to find our roots. They were *Voortrekkers*, pioneers. My *oupa's oupa* was one of the founders of the Orange Free State. They left the Cape Colony with the other Boers when the English came. That was the Great Trek. They were also like Pilgrims.'

Peter nodded. Although the man's earlier comment had made him feel uncomfortable, as a historian, he always found it interesting to talk to people whose ideas were radically different from his own.

'That's why we live in Orania now. It's independent and *slegs vir blankes*, whites only,' the man said, unabashed. 'We have made our own free state, like my *oupa's oupa*. We have our own money, our own school, our own judges. Nobody tells us what to do. We also want to stay pure.'

'It's . . .' Peter began and then realised that he didn't have a clue how he should react to this last statement.

'Just like those Pilgrims,' the man continued. 'They also wanted to stay pure. They also left and went to a new land, a land full of savages, to make a fresh start as true Christians. But they did this better than us. They got rid of the natives, like Joshua in the promised land.'

'I don't think we . . .' Peter began hesitantly. 'In the Netherlands, we see that differently. We think . . .'

The man stared at him. He tilted his head upwards and stuck out his bottom lip as if he had already formulated an answer to what Peter was about to say.

'Come on, let's join the others,' Peter said, cutting the conversation short.

They would only find themselves mired in a pointless argument if he responded to the man's comments – although now he felt like he had merely chosen the path of least resistance.

'Yes, good,' the woman said.

The man looked like it had just dawned on him that the conversation – on this particular topic at least – was over.

Peter and the two South African tourists joined the rest of the group who were already in the other side of the museum. They entered a narrow hallway where a set of stone steps led to the kitchen about a metre and a half below street level. An assortment of items like tools and kitchen utensils had been laid out on a long, rough wooden table. Next to them was a large, antique Bible with decorative metalwork corners and clasps.

There were logs and large turves of peat stacked in the corner of the kitchen and in the hearth. Hanging over the ashes in the fireplace was an old cooking pot. It was empty, but it looked like it was still perfectly usable.

'The English colonies,' they heard Willem explaining to the group, 'had very high mortality rates caused by hunger and disease, and there weren't enough new people arriving to replace those who died. So the Pilgrims were more than welcome in America. As I said, not all the Pilgrims left Leiden – only those who were brave enough and healthy enough, and who had enough money for the journey. They had one last meal together in the home of their leader, Pastor John Robinson. Then, on July 21st, 1620, they travelled to Delfshaven, where a small ship, the *Speedwell*, was waiting for them in the harbour. The men, women and children sailed to Plymouth in England, and from there, they started the long crossing to America with the *Mayflower*.'

Peter walked over to the fireplace.

'This is clever,' he said, putting his hand on the hook that the cooking pot was hanging from. 'You can hang a pot on this pothook by its handle on these things sticking out here. Then you can raise it and lower it. As you might imagine, metal hanging above a fire would get extremely hot. So hot that you wouldn't be able to touch it. So, in Dutch, we say something is a *heet hangijzer* – a "hot pothook" – when it's a sensitive issue, like the Dutch slave trade or war crimes in Indonesia . . . or apartheid in South Africa.'

The South African couple's expressions remained blank, but the other members of the group smiled at the sly jibe.

'Anyway,' Willem said. 'As I was saying, on September the 6th, 1620, the *Mayflower* left England with fifty-seven people from Leiden on board. The journey was beset by problems, and it was only two months later, on November the 6th, that the passengers saw land again. On November the 11th, after a few reconnaissance expeditions, the Pilgrims found a suitable area for their settlement in New England. They called their new home Plymouth Colony. It would become the first permanently inhabited colony in America.'

'True pioneers,' said the South African man.

'Indeed,' Peter agreed, 'but without help from the natives, they would all have died within the first few weeks. It was winter when they arrived, and they couldn't find enough food. The severe frost and snow made it impossible for them to build houses. In those conditions, the weaker and younger ones were especially vulnerable, and half of the passengers and crew died. But their fortunes changed when the Wampanoag tribe helped them. They brought the Pilgrims food and tools and showed them which plants could be cultivated and where they could catch fish. But we all know how the colonists repaid those Native Americans for their help because—'

'Right,' said the South African man, who had now clearly had enough. 'We'll be off now. Thanks, that was very interesting.' He extended his shovel-sized palm and shook Willem's hand. Then he pumped Peter's, hand squeezing much harder and longer than was necessary.

Peter tried to hide his annoyance, but he was deeply irritated by the way the visitor seemed to be trying to exact some sort of revenge.

'*Baie dankie, seun*,' the man said with a grin. 'Thank you very much.'

'*Baie dankie*,' said his wife, avoiding shaking Peter's hand.

Without waiting for a reply or saying goodbye, they went up the steps and left the building.

As soon as the door was closed behind them, a few of the visitors let out audible sighs.

'Goodness, what horrible people. I'm glad they've gone,' said the woman who had asked a question earlier. The rest of the group nodded in agreement.

Willem gave them another opportunity to take photos, which they all gratefully made use of.

After the group had left, Peter returned to the living room and reinstalled himself next to the space heater, turning up the heat as far as it would go.

He rubbed the sore spot on his right hand.

They also wanted to stay pure. Peter mulled over the South African man's words. *But they did this better than us . . .*

Fragment 1 – Flight from England (January 1609)

We made it. We're safe.

For now.

In the year of our Lord 1608, John (Robinson – Piet van Vliet) and William (Brewster – Piet van Vliet) led us to freedom. We cried out 'Let my people go!' but it did not soften the hardened heart of the king. And so we were forced to leave our beloved England, creeping away in secret, like thieves in the night. True, the seas did not part for us, and the king's soldiers were not drowned, but we were able to escape on a ship sent by God. However, at first, it was only the men who escaped.

We had been betrayed a year earlier. We had paid an enormous sum to an English captain to take us to the Netherlands, a country where religious liberty still prevails. To avoid drawing attention to ourselves, we walked in small groups from Scrooby to Boston on the east coast. Once we were on the ship, we found out that we had thrown in our lot with a monstrous man. The devil take him! We had barely even set sail before a ship of the king's fleet appeared. The captain had reported us. They arrested all sixty of us, the men, the women and even the little children. To amuse the public – and, I am quite certain, to also make them afraid – we were made to walk through the city in a long procession. The crowds pelted us with rotten fruit and eggs . . . They threw us into prison, a dark, filthy dungeon infested with rats. The bread they gave us to eat there was mouldy, and the water they gave us to drink was foul, but even there, we gave each other strength. Even there, we found comfort in singing and prayer.

John spoke so beautifully when he quoted Paul's famous words, saying to us: 'But God chose what is foolish in the world to shame the wise; God chose what is weak in the world to shame the strong; God chose what is low and despised in the world, things that are not, to reduce to nothing things that are.'

After a month, it was decided that we had been sufficiently punished. We were sent home, burdened with shame and bereft of all else.

But if they had thought that this defeat had put an end to our desire to leave, they were wrong.

A year later, in the year of our Lord 1608, we tried again. Our group had grown and now numbered at least one hundred souls. The blessing of the Lord was upon our work.

Or so it seemed.

We men went on foot. We started in Scrooby in Nottinghamshire and went over the border to the neighbouring county of Lincolnshire and the stretch of shore between Grimsby and Hull that we had chosen for its remoteness. The nearest settlements, Immingham and Killingholme, were no more than a few farm cottages. We were so vulnerable, all too visible to anyone who was paying attention. Leaving the country without permission was forbidden, and a watchful shepherd boy or farmhand pausing to rest could easily have brought an end to our second attempt to escape. On the way, we drank from streams, catching the water in our cupped hands, and we ate the meagre rations that we had brought with us.

It had been arranged that the women and children would make the journey by water. Their boat, with all our possessions on board, arrived before us. But it ran aground in the shallows, and they were forced to spend the night on shore.

When we were reunited with our families early the next morning, we saw the Dutch captain's ship sailing into the estuary. But the tide was too low for him to reach us, and time was running out. As many people as possible were ferried to the ship by boat. The men went first, a decision that we came to regret because no sooner had we boarded the ship, a company of soldiers came rushing along the beach towards us. How we despaired, we men, when we saw our women and children being dragged away by the merciless soldiers of King James' army. We could only watch from the deck as our ship was tossed about on the surf. One man wanted to jump overboard to rescue his wife and children, but he would surely have been drowned by the powerful waves. And what could he have done if he had reached the shore? One man against the might of so many soldiers, all armed to the teeth?

I write 'men', but there was also a boy among us. He was under the special protection of Josh Nunn, one of the other leaders of our group. The boy never left Josh's side, often keeping tight hold of his hand – and when that was not possible, he held onto his coat.

The captain ignored our pleas and weighed anchor. And so, cowards that we were, we watched our wives and children being roughly led away as the ship sailed towards the open sea.

Not long afterwards, we were caught in the most horrendous storm. Many of us were convinced that this was where our story would end. We were blown adrift almost as far as Norway, and our journey took two weeks instead of the two days that the crossing should have taken.

All of us on board were despondent, praying, sick, nauseous, vomiting incessantly, growing weaker each day, roaming like ghosts over the deck and through the holds while our little ship was at the mercy of the elements. We had not brought enough supplies for such a long crossing. Our salvation was that there were fewer of us on board than we had initially planned.

Josh shared his food with the boy, the same scanty ration that had been given to the rest of us, which made the lad the best-fed passenger on the whole ship. No one knew who the child was, and no one dared to ask where he had come from. We knew that he was an orphan and that just like Josh, he did not have another living soul in the world, but we knew no more than that.

They often retreated to a quiet spot belowdecks where Josh talked to the boy endlessly, like a seller on a market stall persuading a customer to buy his wares. The boy appeared to repeat his words, nodding his head earnestly as he spoke.

Then, after our terrible journey, we finally arrived in Amsterdam. News of what had happened to our women and children eventually reached us: they had been dragged from prison to prison because nobody had been able to decide what should be done with them. After all, hadn't their only crime been a desire to be with their husbands and fathers? So, at long last, they were given permission to leave England and allowed to join us.

By August 1608, we were all together again, around one hundred and fifty men, women and children. In Amsterdam, we joined John Smyth, a good friend of our own John. You see, we are not the first Separatists to flee England because of James I. But our peace was short-lived; here too, we found discord. John Smyth felt increasingly drawn to the ideas of the Mennonites, who only baptised adults and not children, and he wanted to impose these ideas on us.

'Our' John decided that it was time to go, to leave Amsterdam behind us. He wrote a letter to the council of the city of Leiden.

The year of our Lord 1609 had only just begun.

Chapter 3

Peter closed the museum and went to the Lipsius Building to get a coffee and something to eat in the university's restaurant. Then he took a slow bike ride to the Jean Pesijnhofje near the Pieterskerk where Fay opened the massive courtyard door just as he arrived.

'Hey, sweetheart,' she said, her voice warm, as always. She brushed his cheek lightly with her lips, like a butterfly's kiss, and put her arms around him. 'I'm so glad you're going with me tonight,' she said.

He locked his bike, and they headed for the Rapenburg canal, arm in arm.

They were going to the open evening that night at Loge Ishtar, a Masonic lodge that accepted both men and women. Fay had joined the lodge three years ago. Every two weeks, its members met in the Masonic Hall on the Steenschuur canal where they not only learned to understand themselves better, Fay had explained to Peter, but also guided each other on a path of contemplation, reflection and self-improvement. Together, they thought about how they related to each other and to the world around them.

Peter knew that Fay had felt a sense of belonging in this community right from the start. She had told him about its members' genuine commitment to each other, and their shared desire to work on their own personal development and use this as a foundation from which to help create a better, more beautiful world.

'I had a very odd visitor in the museum today,' Peter said.

'Another direct descendant of the Pilgrims?' Fay asked wryly.

'No, actually,' Peter replied, laughing. 'This one was actually descended from a Huguenot from Leiden who emigrated to South Africa in the nineteenth century.'

The Huguenots were Calvinists, Protestant followers of the Swiss religious reformer John Calvin. They were persecuted on a massive scale in sixteenth-century France. After the horrific St Bartholomew's Day Massacre on the night of August 23rd and 24th in 1572 when countless Huguenots were murdered, a great number of Calvinists fled France. Many of them settled in the Netherlands, where names like Montanje, Parmentier and Labuschagne are still common in Leiden.

'Do tell,' Fay said invitingly.

'Like I said, it was very odd,' Peter went on. 'Willem Hogendoorn came in with a group of tourists. There was a South African couple with them who come from Orania. I googled it on my phone when they left. It's a sort of free state that was set up by whites after apartheid ended. Black people are absolutely not welcome there. They have their own money, schools, newspapers, legal system, their own local government, you name it. His *oupa's oupa*, as he said – his grandfather's grandfather – left Leiden in the early nineteenth century. He was one of the original founders of the Orange Free State, which was similar to what Orania is now. And he saw a lot of that same pioneer spirit in the Pilgrims, people who move somewhere else to make a fresh start and build their own community in a place that they believe God has chosen for them.'

'Well, that's not so unusual, is it?'

They walked along the Rapenburg. The evening was still light, and the air was crisp. Reflections of the trees and grand townhouses shimmered in the tranquil water of the broad canal.

'No, that's not really what was unusual,' Peter said. 'It was that the man was so blatantly racist . . . He said it was a shame that apartheid had ended because South Africa was a mess now. And that the Pilgrims and the other American colonists had gone about things in a much better way than the South African colonists because they had wiped out the indigenous people there.'

'You're right, that *is* unusual. You don't often hear people say that sort of thing quite so brazenly.'

'*That's* what surprised me,' Peter said. 'Of course, I know that there are people who think like that, but I was quite shocked, to be honest, that he had no qualms about saying it so candidly, especially to someone he'd only just met.'

'I'm sure there are plenty of people who really do still think like that,' said Fay.

'Anyway . . . I didn't call him out on it. I suppose I was a bit of a coward, but I didn't want to get into a pointless argument with him.'

'That was very sensible, darling,' Fay said, giving his arm a gentle squeeze.

They passed the Van de Werfpark and crossed the canal via the Groenebrug before turning left onto the Steenschuur, where the door of the Masonic Hall stood invitingly open.

The building was also home to an all-male Freemason's lodge. Loge La Vertu, or the Virtue. It had been established in 1757, making it one of the oldest groups of Freemasons in the Netherlands. The lodge's national serial number was 7. The lodge with serial number 1 was the oldest in the Netherlands, L'Union Royal in The Hague, founded in 1734.

An elderly man was waiting in the open doorway to greet them. Dressed in a black suit with a white shirt and a red bow tie, with a neat grey goatee, he looked every inch the proper gentleman. All that was missing was a monocle.

Fay gave him a quick hug. The gesture seemed a little over the top to Peter, but once they were inside, he realised that this was how the lodge members usually greeted their Masonic brothers and sisters.

They hung up their coats in the entrance hall and went into the spacious function room. The room was painted the mint green of a hospital ward. Mounted on the walls were display cases containing awards and insignia, along with objects that Peter couldn't even recognise let alone guess what they might be used for. Pride of place had been given to a large official portrait of King Willem-Alexander.

The room looked dated and old-fashioned, like a 1980s-era social club. Simple tables had been arranged in groups with a doily and two freshly cut carnations in a small vase in the middle of each one. Plain but functional chairs had been placed around them, as though ready for the imminent arrival of a bridge club.

Peter got two cups of coffee from a small bar in the corner. He carefully carried them over to Fay, keeping his eyes on the tray like a child taking part in an egg and spoon race.

He handed a cup and saucer to Fay, who was chatting to some of the other visitors. Since he'd so far not had a chance to smoke his daily cigarillo, he decided to take the opportunity to slip outside for a few minutes.

The double doors that led to a tiled-over back garden were

open. A few people were smoking under a large, sloping glass roof that looked a little like a conservatory without walls.

Sven, one of Peter's students, was standing among them. He was wearing a T-shirt with the words WE WILL NOT DANCE ON THE GRAVES OF OUR FATHERS printed in faded letters over an image of a stern-looking Indian. Every now and then, he pushed a pair of diminutive but showy, round spectacles back up the bridge of his nose. He was accompanied by a larger young man whose undersized shirt strained across his muscular torso.

The two young men crossed over to Peter. Sven looked ill at ease, as if he was in no mood for a conversation just then but realised that he couldn't ignore his lecturer.

'Hello, sir,' said Sven. 'Are you a member here?'

'No, I'm not a member. My girlfriend is. I just came along with her tonight out of curiosity. What about you two?'

'Just curiosity for us, too,' Sven replied and then introduced his friend in the same breath. 'This is Erik, by the way. We're both in the Catena student society.'

Without being asked, Sven took the cup and saucer from Peter's hand so that he could light his cigarillo.

The man standing next to them appeared to be lost in thought, as if he was mentally preparing himself for what was about to come. When the first wisps of smoke from Peter's cigar curled past the man's face, he gave Peter a brief sideways look.

'Is the smoke bothering you?' Peter asked, quickly taking a couple of steps away from him.

The man looked at him amiably enough, but he clearly had no idea what Peter had just said. He was very tall, well-built and looked to be in his fifties. His hair was remarkably long for his age and curled out from under a Boston Red Sox baseball cap. His face was so smooth that it looked like he had shaved only minutes earlier.

He said 'Hello' in English with an unmistakably American accent and shook Peter, Sven and Erik's hands with the enthusiasm of someone at a high school reunion greeting old classmates from half a lifetime ago. 'I'm Tony. Anthony Vanderhoop, to be precise.'

He pronounced his name the Americanised way, as 'Venderhoop'.

'But you can call me Tony. And you are?'

'I'm Peter de Haan, and this is Sven, and this is Erik.'

It must be great to be able to speak your own language wherever you are in the world, Peter thought.

'You don't speak Dutch?' Sven asked. 'Everything will be in Dutch tonight, won't it?'

'No, I don't speak Dutch, sadly. But my family goes all the way back to the very first Dutch colonists who went to America. One of my uncles researched it all. The way our last name is pronounced has changed over time.'

'We would pronounce it "fon-der-hope",' Erik said, overemphasising each syllable.

'Yes, just like that,' Tony said, but when he tried to repeat what Erik had said, it still came out as 'Venderhoop'.

'I'm from Boston,' Tony continued, 'I'm a member of a Freemasons' lodge there. We're a worldwide fraternity, as I'm sure you know, so whenever I'm abroad, I like to visit my brothers . . . and these days, my sisters too.'

When he said the word 'sisters', his mocking smile suggested that he did not entirely approve of female Masons.

'But will you be able to understand what's being said later?' Peter asked.

'Not entirely,' said Tony. 'But I still enjoy meeting my fellow Freemasons. I don't understand everything that's being said, but the words and phrases in the rituals are more or less the same, and I know all the gestures and actions too. I understand the meaning behind them, so the words aren't so important. If you're a Catholic, you can take part in a mass in a language you don't know and still understand what's going on in front of you. In your heart, you still feel like you're a part of it all.'

Peter, Sven and Erik all nodded.

'Well,' Tony said, suddenly bringing the conversation to an end. 'It was nice meeting you guys. I hope you enjoy the rest of the evening.'

He turned around and went over a group of people who looked like they had been waiting for him. As soon as he joined them, they all started to make their way back inside.

'Ladies and gentlemen,' said a loud voice. 'We're about to begin.'

Standing in the open doorway was a tall, strikingly beautiful woman with short, straight hair, slicked neatly to one side.

'If you'd all like to come inside, then we can begin.'

Once he was inside, Peter saw that many more people had arrived while he had been in the garden. He had trouble finding an unoccupied chair.

Fay and some of her Masonic brothers and sisters were sitting on a row of tall stools next to the bar.

Fay had told Peter that one of the items on the evening's programme would be a series of interviews with lodge members, talking about their backgrounds and their reasons for joining the Freemasons. The organisers had found a good mix of members, not only of different ages but also from the different degrees of Freemasonry: Entered Apprentice, Fellow Craft and Master Mason.

When they were asked why they had joined the Freemasons, they all spoke of a strong feeling of comradeship. Working on yourself as part of a group – 'the Craft' as they called it – was what created a bond between them.

Peter found the atmosphere extraordinarily warm and friendly but, at the same time, a little oppressive too.

It was all so very . . . nice.

It made him think of an evening in his student days and a service he had attended at a Baptist church. A study partner he'd since lost touch with had converted to Christianity. As part of their preparation for baptism, he and some of the other new members had had to introduce themselves to their congregation. He had asked Peter to provide moral support, which Peter had provided by sitting in a pew at the back of the church. When it was his friend's turn to step forward, he had made eye contact with Peter, and Peter had given him an encouraging thumbs up. There had been many stories that evening, told by people who spoke, often too candidly, about their personal journeys. They revealed the mistakes they'd made – complete with clichéd accounts of addictions to drink and drugs, how they had found the way to Jesus at last, and how the church had become their haven of peace. One by one, they opened up about their feelings of being immersed in a warm bath, of coming home, of finally being able to be themselves, of no longer having to wear a mask . . .

The very same atmosphere hung over this evening, and there was even the obligatory addiction story.

Naturally, Peter paid the most attention when it was Fay's turn to speak. She talked about her background in the Orthodox Church, a story that Peter already knew. She said that what she liked about Loge Ishtar was that nobody was asked to renounce their religious beliefs. One member's guiding principles might come from the Universal Declaration of Human Rights, while another's might be based on the Bible, the Torah or the Quran. And there were even people for whom nature was the greatest source of inspiration.

Eventually, the Worshipful Master – as the chairman of the lodge, Coen Zoutman, was officially addressed – spoke to the audience. He likened his brothers and sisters to travelling companions. Each of them took their own steps on their journeys, but the others gave them support where the path was difficult, and so they made the journey together. He sincerely invited everyone present to travel with them and join them as fellow pilgrims.

'Well then, ladies and gentlemen,' he began, but he was interrupted by a woman who suddenly jumped up from her chair. She bumped into the table in front of her, sending her coffee cup clattering to the floor.

She was a tall, heavy-set woman with long hair scraped back into a ponytail, accentuating the roundness of her pudgy face. There were red spots around her neck that had spread up to her chin and cheeks, and there was an embittered look on her face.

A man on the chair next to her raised himself half out of his seat and tugged at her arm in a desperate attempt to make her sit down again.

The whole room seemed to hold its breath.

The Worshipful Master looked at the scene with thinly veiled irritation. Before the woman could say a word, he said, 'I don't think this is the right moment, Jenny.'

The man managed to get the woman back onto her seat. She looked around her, appearing to be confused, as if she couldn't remember why she had been standing up. Her face had turned completely red.

Her companion leaned over to her and spoke in what looked like a gentle but stern voice.

The woman's shoulders sagged, and she bowed her head, like an athlete who had just lost a race.

'Ladies and gentlemen,' the Worshipful Master began again, in a tone that was no less calm than the one he had used before. 'The moment has arrived that I'm sure many of you have come here for tonight: a visit to our temple.'

Peter smiled. This had indeed been his main reason for coming with Fay: the opportunity to look inside the Masonic temple that was still a place of such mystery to him.

Because however you looked at it, although the Freemasons might no longer have been a secret society, they were still a society with secrets.

Chapter 4

A broad, winding staircase took the visitors up to the first floor of the Masonic Hall. The landing was too small to accommodate them all at once, and a few people had to stand on the stairs. An expectant hush fell over the group.

In the hallway, three loud knocks sounded on a tall door. It opened almost immediately, swinging outwards and forcing the people on the landing to squeeze even closer together. Shortly afterwards, the hallway emptied as they all surged through the door, like water flowing from a bath after the plug has been pulled.

Peter walked into the long hall.

Inside, a man and a woman sat at triangular tables placed on either side of the door. A candle on a tall stand stood in front of each table. A third stand was placed a few metres away, just in front of a large, cube-shaped object that Peter knew was referred to by the Freemasons as the 'Perfect Ashlar'.

Fay had told him that the Freemasons spoke of God as the Master Builder of the whole universe. They saw themselves as rough building blocks that needed to be smoothed and dressed so that they could become part of the Temple of the Great Architect of the Universe. The Freemasons' entire philosophy was based on the pursuit of self-improvement.

Lying on top of the cube was an old book – a Bible, Peter assumed – on top of which was what looked like a carpenter's set square, and a pair of compasses. On the floor, which was divided into black and white squares like a giant chequerboard, were a rough block of stone and what looked like a heavy mallet.

Running along both sides of the hall was a double row of chairs where the guests sat with their backs to the wall, facing the open space in the middle of the room.

Peter chose a chair on the front row so that he would have an unobstructed view of the proceedings. Before he sat down, he picked up the evening's programme that had been printed out on A4 paper and placed on the seat.

Because Fay was taking part in the ritual that was going to be performed that evening, she wouldn't be able to sit next to him. Peter saw her come into the temple, but she was staring straight ahead so intently that he couldn't make eye contact.

Classical choral music filled the room, which, according to the programme, was an excerpt from *The Magic Flute* by Mozart.

Zum Ziele führt dich diese Bahn,
Doch musst du, Jüngling, männlich siegen.
Drum höre unsre Lehre an:
Sei standhaft, duldsam und verschwiegen.

Sitting directly opposite Peter were Sven and Erik, and a few chairs away from them was Tony Vanderhoop, who had taken off his cap.

Above them, tiny, subtle lights had been inserted into holes pricked in the vaulted ceiling. The room's walls were panelled in wood and painted green, and the signs of the zodiac had been painted on them at regular intervals.

Peter's eye was drawn to the motto painted over the door, KNOW THYSELF, the Ancient Greek maxim that was inscribed over the entrance of the Temple of Apollo in Delphi. The concept behind it was that all humans possess innate wisdom: you already know everything that you need to know, but you would only find that knowledge by looking inside yourself.

The woman next to him whispered – a little too loudly, as though she wanted everyone to know that she was already very well-informed about Freemasonry – that the man and woman next to the entrance were the Senior and Junior Warden who acted as the Worshipful Master's left and right hand.

At the far end of the temple, another table and a chair stood on a platform where the Worshipful Master had taken his seat. The All-Seeing Eye was carved in relief on the wall behind him.

Like a king sitting on his throne, he stared impassively out over the temple, occasionally stroking his full, grey beard with his right hand.

Just before the doors were closed, the lady who had caused the commotion downstairs came into the temple followed by the man who had calmed her down again. They sat on the chairs furthest away from the chairman, near the door.

The music faded gently away, and the chatter in the hall died down.

The lights were dimmed, transforming the ceiling and its little lights into a starry night sky.

That would look good in my bedroom, Peter thought.

He recognised the constellations Orion and Ursa Major. It reminded him of a night he had spent on the banks of the Sea of Galilee with a group of backpackers he had met in Jerusalem. It had been much colder than he had been expecting and he had slept badly. Even with all his clothes on, he had shivered in his damp sleeping bag. He hadn't been able to sleep for more than fifteen minutes at a time, but what a view he'd had of the night sky and its countless stars. It had been an almost mystical experience.

The Worshipful Master opened the meeting with a sombre rap of his ceremonial gavel, which was immediately followed by raps in turn from the gavels of the Senior and Junior Wardens.

Worshipful Master: 'I give notice that I am about to open this lodge. All rise. Brothers and sisters, adopt the sign of fidelity.'

The members of the lodge stood up and placed their right hands over their hearts.

Worshipful Master: 'Brother Senior Warden, why have we come together this evening?'

Senior Warden: 'Worshipful Master, you have convened us with our guests for this special meeting, this special lodge.'

Worshipful Master: 'Brother Senior Warden, on what basis are we gathered tonight?'

Senior Warden: 'On that of mutual respect and that of Brotherhood, Worshipful Master.'

Worshipful Master: 'Sister Junior Warden, for what reason have we invited our guests?'

Junior Warden: 'Our wish is to make them aware of our Craft.'

Worshipful Master: 'Sister Junior Warden, what does our Craft entail?'

Junior Warden: 'Continuous work on the self in order to develop as a harmonious person truly fit to become a living stone in the Temple of Humanity.'

Worshipful Master: 'With these thoughts in mind, let us work together to make this evening a fruitful one. Brother Senior Warden, Sister Junior Warden, assist me in supporting this work by lighting the Three Lesser Lights and allowing the Three Great Lights to shine.'

Worshipful Master: 'Wardens and Director of Ceremonies.'

The wardens and Fay, who was the Director of Ceremonies, stood up and walked towards the Worshipful Master, who lit a taper on the Master's Light and gave it to her. This would be used by the 'Triangle' – the Worshipful Master and the two wardens – to light the three candles, known as the three Lesser Lights, one by one.

Fay had gone over the basics of the ritual with Peter the night before, so he was already familiar with some of the Masonic terminology.

The Junior Warden lit the first candle, the Pillar of Wisdom.

Junior Warden: 'May Wisdom guide the construction.'

The Senior Warden lit the second candle, the Pillar of Strength.

Senior Warden: 'May the temple be established in Strength.'

The Worshipful Master lit the third candle, the Pillar of Beauty.

Worshipful Master: 'May it be adorned in Beauty.'

Then the Worshipful Master, the two wardens and the Director of Ceremonies gathered next to the Perfect Ashlar on top of which lay the square and compasses. The Worshipful Master opened the book and placed the square and compasses on its pages.

Peter knew that the compasses symbolised the spirit and that the square represented the material world. The position of the compasses indicated the different degrees within Freemasonry. When the lodge was working in the first degree, Entered Apprentice, the compasses lay underneath the square: man's spiritual nature was still hidden by physical matter, trapped in the material world. At the second degree, Fellow Craft, one arm of the compasses was placed under the square: man's spirit was overcoming his physical nature, wrestling itself free from the material world. During the third degree, Master Mason, the compasses lay on top of the square: the spirit now reigned over the physical and had separated itself from the material world.

Worshipful Master: 'I thank you, brothers and sisters. With this gavel, I duly declare this special lodge open.'

Once again, the rap of the Worshipful Master's gavel was echoed by both wardens.

Worshipful Master: 'This lodge is now open. You may all be seated.'

The eagerness in this room to hear what's about to be said is almost tangible, Peter thought.

He looked at Fay. The look of concentration she had worn as she carried out her duties was still visible on her face. She stared down at the floor like she was afraid a spell would be broken if she looked at anyone.

The music started again. Peter recognised it as baroque. It was a beautiful piece, the sort of music he could play on Spotify while he was working without being distracted by what he was listening to.

When the last notes of the music had died away, the Worshipful Master spoke again.

'Esteemed brothers and sisters, honoured guests, dear people . . .' he began. 'What a pleasure it is to be able to speak to you this evening. I must be perfectly honest with you and tell you that I feel that I have been charged with no small task tonight. Let me explain. When we, as brothers and sisters, were preparing for this open evening, we decided that the programme should include a concise introduction to some of the symbols we work with as Freemasons. Of course, that's a very nice idea in principle, but in practice, not quite so simple. And why is that? Because what characterises Freemasonry is its use of a very wide range of symbols. It would be quite a challenge to choose just a few of those to give you an initial impression of Freemasonry, while still honouring the rich diversity of symbols that are important to us. Nevertheless, I hope that we have succeeded in creating a meaningful selection that will lift the veil a little for you and hopefully pique your curiosity. May it lead to the planting of a seed that spurs you to further exploration. And if it indeed does, please know that we would be delighted to assist you as you discover the possible meanings behind this wonderful symbolism.'

Fay looked up at last. She smiled at Peter, and an intense feeling of love flowed through him.

'However, I shall refrain from launching straight into a description of the major symbols,' the Worshipful Master continued. 'To begin, I would like to speak briefly about meanings and interpretations. I've given this presentation a title, and with good reason. The title is: "Wisdom, Strength and Beauty: Feeling with your mind, thinking with your soul . . ." Certainly, Freemasonry has a rich tradition of symbols. I can share the meanings behind some of them with you and, of course, I will do just that, but I would first like to make you aware of the fact that Freemasonry has no dogmas. Freemasonry gives everyone complete freedom to carry out the search for meaning in their own way. And while Freemasonry provides tools and symbolic sustenance for the journey, it has no universal truth or truths. The search for meaning is entirely personal. It's up to us as individuals to find the meaning or meanings that will help us to achieve deeper insight – into ourselves, into the world around us and into what moves us, especially in our interactions with others. The search for meaning is a challenge that requires bravery. Perhaps it requires a disposition and an openness that we rarely achieve in our daily lives, too. It might also ask us to take a different approach from what we are used to. That is why I speak of feeling with your mind and thinking with your soul. Because *that* is how we might be able to reach other, deeper layers. Layers which are still uncharted territory – terra incognita – but within which we may well find insights that will help us to become better people . . .'

The absence of dogmas was precisely what had initially attracted Fay to Freemasonry. Peter could understand why. She had been raised in the Eastern Orthodox Church, a branch of Catholicism based entirely on doctrines that had been set in stone centuries ago.

Her father and pregnant mother had fled to the Netherlands during the Prague Spring and brought their ancestral faith with them. Fay had struggled to leave her Orthodox upbringing behind her. The agonising suffering and eventual death of her husband Petr had been the final push she had needed to be able to let go.

'Does this mean that, as Freemasons, we stand utterly alone?' the chairman asked, looking out over the room. 'Certainly not. We are part of our lodge, part of a close-knit community of brothers and sisters who travel with us, who search with us, and who join together to try, little by little, to make the world a better place. We are part of what we like to think of as a universal chain of brothers and sisters that spans the entire globe.'

The Worshipful Master gave a friendly nod to Tony Vanderhoop, who smiled and nodded back.

'Each of us is a unique and, at the same time, essential link in the chain,' he continued. 'And so ultimately, we form a whole that is many times greater than the sum of its parts. Please keep this in mind later when you hear me speak about symbols. Perhaps my words will be the prelude to a personal search for what they might mean to you. And before I begin, let me give you one more piece of context. I'm sure you already know that we work with and within a threefold progressive degree system of Entered Apprentice, Fellow Craft and Master Mason. When a Freemason has made enough progress on their journey in the Craft, they're allowed to advance to a higher degree. I would like to emphasise that this is a process of continuous development. By no means is it so that the Master Mason possesses absolute wisdom and can end their search once they have been raised to the third degree. We remind ourselves constantly that we must never stop learning. This means that the process of finding meaning in the symbols we work with can be a unique, ongoing, and ever-expanding developmental path. That might be one of the most wonderful aspects of becoming and being a Freemason . . .'

Peter saw that a few people were smiling like they couldn't wait to join the Freemasons' ranks. Or perhaps they were already members of the lodge.

Fay often spoke in glowing terms about the brotherhood and sisterhood of Freemasons, but Peter imagined that you would feel a similar sense of belonging in any other community that you were enthusiastic about and dedicated to, like a sports association or a chess club.

In his speech, the chairman expounded on the meaning of some of the Masonic symbols, although he was very careful to reiterate more than once that everyone was always free to interpret them in their own way.

'What we're actually trying to do is chisel away at the rough stone to free the perfect block from within, to reveal it in all its glory.'

Peter thought that this was a beautiful idea. *How did that famous quote from Michelangelo go again*, he wondered. *When he was asked how he created such magnificent sculptures from marble, he replied, 'Every block of stone has a statue inside it, and it is the task of the sculptor to discover it . . .'*

The act of freeing oneself from unnecessary ballast in order to find out what really mattered . . . or to find God. That was a recurring theme in all belief systems, from Hinduism to Buddhism to the Abrahamic religions.

Hadn't Jesus told people not to store up treasure for themselves on earth? 'Where moth and rust consume and where thieves break in and steal; but store up for yourselves treasures in heaven, where neither moth nor rust consumes and where thieves do not break in and steal. For where your treasure is, there your heart will be also.'

Ultimately, it wasn't about the physical world, nor about the earthly possessions that you couldn't take with you, but about your immortal soul that needed to be freed from the mire of material things.

Peter was suddenly startled by the music that came unexpectedly from hidden loudspeakers, and he realised that he must have been lost in thought for quite some time.

When the music ended – *Maurerische Trauermusik* in C minor (K. 477) by Mozart – the Worshipful Master concluded his talk.

'And so, we reach the end of this short presentation. I have, of course, only been able to touch on a just a few points, give you only a brief insight into a much larger subject. But I hope that I have given you an impression of all the wonderful tools that Freemasonry can offer. And of course, I would be delighted if it has left you wanting more. I'd like to thank you for coming along and listening this evening. After this lodge has closed, you'll have an opportunity to share your questions, thoughts and insights with us and with each other. Allow me to end this talk in the traditional way: so mote it be – I have spoken.'

The Worshipful Master let his gavel fall, which was echoed by the Senior and Junior Wardens.

A third piece of music was played. A magnificent choir singing in what sounded like French. Peter recognised the tune and could even hum along. He looked at the programme and saw that it was *Pavane, Op. 50* by Fauré. He closed his eyes. The power and intensity of the music rose to a crescendo and then ebbed away. The sound washed over him like the waves of a calm ocean. It was hypnotic.

When the music ended, the Worshipful Master spoke again.

Worshipful Master: 'I give notice that I am about to close this lodge. All rise. Brothers and sisters, adopt the sign of fidelity.'

The members of the lodge stood up to make the sign of fidelity. The Worshipful Master and the two wardens closed the book and placed the square back on top of it.

Junior Warden (She extinguished the candle on the Pillar of Wisdom): 'May Wisdom guide us.'

Senior Warden (He extinguished the candle on the Pillar of Strength): 'May Strength support us.'

Worshipful Master (He extinguished the candle on the Pillar of Beauty): 'May Beauty reside in our hearts.'

They all returned to their former positions.

Worshipful Master: 'Thank you, Brothers and Sisters. How should Masons meet, act and part?'

Junior Warden: 'By the principles of the level, the plumb and the square, Worshipful Master.'

Worshipful Master: 'What are these principles, Brother Junior Warden?'

Junior Warden: 'To meet in harmony, to act according to the highest law, and to part as equals, Worshipful Master.'

Worshipful Master: 'So should we ever meet, act and part, so that our labours may progress. Brother Senior Warden, have we come closer to our goal?'

Senior Warden: 'Our desire was to share knowledge with our guests and that the evening would be fruitful. It was good.'

Worshipful Master: 'Then let us return, well contented, to whence we came. With this gavel, I declare this special lodge duly closed.'

The rap of his gavel was repeated by the wardens.

Worshipful Master: 'This lodge is now closed. I wish our guests a safe journey home.'

After a moment of hesitation – it appeared that no one wanted to be the first to leave – a few people all stood up at once.

Soon, ten or fifteen people had gathered around the Worshipful Master's chair, waiting to ask him questions.

Peter saw his student Sven among them, together with his brawny friend who had been in the garden earlier that evening. They hung back from the others but looked like they were listening in on the conversation. The American visitor, Tony, was there too, patiently waiting his turn.

The only people still in their seats were the man and woman who had come into the temple after everyone else.

One by one, the visitors shuffled out of the room. Someone gave Peter's hand a gentle squeeze. It was Fay. He hadn't noticed that she had come to stand next to him.

'And?' she asked softly.

'You did brilliantly,' Peter said. 'And I thought it was wonderful, really special.' He decided that it would better to keep the fact that he had drifted off for some of it to himself.

Chapter 5

Downstairs, a handful of guests were already putting on their coats – a bitterly cold wind gusted through the entrance hall each time one of them opened the door to leave – but most of the people who had come to the open evening stayed for the drinks reception in the function room.

In the cramped space behind the bar, four volunteers bustled around, smiling and apologising every time they bumped into each other. Peter eventually managed to order two glasses of red wine.

Fay's cheeks were flushed, but Peter couldn't tell whether it was from the warmth of the room or from relief that she had acquitted herself well.

He took a sip of wine.

It was of an exceptionally good quality, something he hadn't expected at such a simple event.

Noticing the look of pleasure on his face, Fay said, 'The Worshipful Master is a wine expert. He's won prizes in international wine tastings. He's even beaten renowned French tasters. The wine here is always excellent.'

'I am the true vine,' Peter said, quoting the words of Jesus from the Gospel According to John, 'and my Father is the vine-grower.' He took a second sip of the wine, swirling it around in his mouth appreciatively, like an experienced connoisseur.

'Yes,' Fay said, 'Jesus did rather like a tipple.'

Peter smiled.

'He removes every branch in me that bears no fruit. Every branch that bears fruit, he prunes to make it bear more fruit,' he said, finishing off the quotation. 'It would be a good motto for the Freemasons.'

'It could be,' Fay said. 'That scripture is about examining yourself critically, getting rid of your bad character traits, of your nasty habits, of your ballast. Pruning here and there so you can reach your full potential and really thrive. But if I recall correctly, there's a bit that comes after those verses that's about the punishment for people who don't follow Jesus, isn't there?'

'There is,' said Peter. 'It goes on to say: "Whoever does not abide in me is thrown away like a branch and withers; such branches are gathered, thrown into the fire, and burned."'

'Yes, exactly,' Fay said. 'That's what I meant. And that's why I never felt like I belonged in the Christian Church. That idea that you deserve eternal punishment for not following *someone else* in the right way. And the fact that other people are allowed to point out your faults, to tell you that you're doing it wrong, and then shove a book in your face and show you a passage that explains how you haven't been acting in accordance with doctrine. What I like about Freemasonry is that everyone can give their own meaning to the symbols. Nobody ever says to you, "Look, you've got it all wrong, and actually, it's like this or that." That's why I feel so comfortable here. There's no judgement.'

The room was still busy with clusters of people standing here and there, all talking animatedly to each other. The American Tony Vanderhoop was at the centre of a small group that appeared to be hanging on his every word. Jenny was sitting in a far corner, engaged in what looked like a serious conversation with the people around her.

'What did you think of it?' Fay asked.

'It was really interesting, amazing to watch,' he answered. 'How do you think it went?'

'It went okay, mostly. My part, I mean. I only made a couple of little mistakes.'

'Mistakes?'

'Hardly worth mentioning, really. I took too many steps here and not enough steps there. It wasn't quite right. Concentrating too hard, I think. There was one bit where I presented the candle a moment too soon, but it's all minor details. I'm not unhappy with how I did, but I want to do it better next time.'

'I thought it was fascinating,' Peter said. 'I realised that I knew much more about it all than I thought I did, because of you. I hardly heard anything new tonight, but I still enjoyed listening to the chairman's talk. I mean the Worshipful Master's, sorry. He explained everything clearly, made it easy to understand.'

Peter saw Sven and Erik come into the room. They went to the bar and then headed straight for the garden with their beers.

'Would you be interested in becoming a—' Fay began, but she didn't get a chance to finish her question.

The man with the bow tie who had greeted them at the front door came over and stood next to them.

'So,' he said simply, and then went silent.

Not exactly the best opener, thought Peter.

He gave Peter a friendly look, like a teacher patiently waiting for a pupil to answer his question.

'Hi, Johan,' Fay said. 'Let me introduce you to my boyfriend, Peter.'

The two men shook hands.

'Have you been a member for long?' Peter asked eventually.

'More than twenty-five years now. Not at this lodge, but Loge La Vertu, the boys' club, you might call it. Not that I've anything against women joining, you understand, but I do prefer being able to talk man to man, now and then. I think you have different conversations with each other when there are women around.'

'*Slegs vir mannen,*' said Fay, glancing at Peter and grinning.

'I was just talking to the American visitor,' Peter said, changing the subject. He had noticed Fay's irritation when Johan admitted his preference for unmixed lodges.

'Ah,' Fay said, 'the gentleman from Boston?' She laughed at Peter's apparent surprise. 'I just talked to him. But we knew he was coming; we were told about it at the meeting last week. He sent an email asking if he could come to a lodge meeting, and the open evening seemed like the perfect opportunity. He's from the grand lodge of Massachusetts in Boston. They say they're the third oldest lodge in the world, after the one in England that was founded in 1717 and the one started in Ireland in 1725. Their lodge was set up in 1733, so they seem to be right, on paper at least.'

'That's right,' Johan said. 'But Peter, I'm sure you're familiar with the stories about how the Freemasons originated with the Knights Templar, or to give them their proper name, the Poor Fellow-Soldiers of Christ and of the Temple of Solomon. They were a Christian military order, Knights of the Cross. You'll come across that fable very often in books and on websites about conspiracy theories. In the time of the Crusades, the Templars were one of the military units in the Holy War against the Muslims in the Holy Land. Some conspiracy theorists go even further back, all the way to 1000 BCE, to King Solomon and his architect Hiram Abiff, the man who built the first Temple in

Jerusalem. Solomon's master architect was thought to have secret knowledge, and it's believed that he hid it in his buildings. Some say that this knowledge was then passed down from generation to generation all through the centuries. And people think that the Freemasons hid secret messages and codes in cathedrals, like Chartres in France, or the Rosslyn Chapel near Edinburgh, messages that would only be understood by its initiates. But, dear Peter, I can assure you that this is all utter hogwash. People who believe that sort of thing are just a few steps away from believing that there's a secret government out for total domination over the entire world.'

For someone who started with such an unspectacular opener, Johan is quite the chatterbox, Peter thought.

'It's a subject that's close to my heart, Peter,' Johan continued. 'If you only knew how often I've had to listen to that drivel, how often I've had to *defend* my membership of the Freemasons. Yes, *that's* how it *feels*. We Freemasons are simply descended from the masons' guilds from five hundred years ago. That's all. There's nothing out of the ordinary about it. Those masons were free to travel from town to town throughout Europe so that they could build cathedrals. Yes, they did have secret handshakes, and they did have passwords, but that was simply their way of proving that someone was a member of the guild. The masons invited other people to join them, and they gradually formed a brotherhood. It was only during the Enlightenment that Freemasonry became a more philosophical movement. They were probably the first group to organise themselves separately from any religion, without, by the way, actually renouncing their religious beliefs. That really is the most remarkable thing about them: they were free thinkers and tolerant of opinions that were different from their own. That was unusual.'

Peter listened to Johan in wonder. He was amazed by the man's ability to tell such a coherent story off the top of his head.

'Thank you, Johan,' Fay said, 'for that clear and comprehensive explanation.'

Little laughter lines crinkled at the corners of her eyes. It looked like she had forgiven Johan for his earlier remarks about single-sex lodges.

'Well, anyway, Peter,' Johan said. 'It was good to see you here this evening. Perhaps we'll meet again. In any case, you are always very welcome. And it doesn't matter if you join a mixed lodge like Ishtar or one that's "*slegs vir mannen*".' He gave them both a twinkling smile and said goodbye.

The room was growing quieter now. Peter saw Sven and Erik leaving. Shortly afterwards, Jenny, the woman who had caused such a commotion earlier in the evening, left with the man who had been with her. Tony and his group had gone without Peter noticing them leave.

'Do you want to go soon?' Fay asked. 'Or stay a bit longer?'

'Let's stay,' said Peter. 'I'm going to get another glass of wine. Shall I get you one?'

Fay shook her head. 'I'm just going to pop to the loo. But I don't want to stay too late, okay?'

'That's fine. We'll leave soon.'

Peter went to the bar and picked up a glass of wine from a tray. He took a few sips, then absent-mindedly crammed three handfuls of peanuts into his mouth. He was filled with instant regret. He had been paying more attention to his weight since meeting Fay, which had led to him losing a few pounds.

He had also been playing water polo for a couple of years. It wasn't a sport he'd ever considered trying until he'd seen some water polo players practising at his local pool, De Zijl, while he was doing lengths. After seeing the way they combined playing a game with intensive physical training, he had been keen to give it a go.

At the moment, two glasses of wine a day were his only sin – and, not to forget, his daily cigarillo.

Fay came back from the toilet in the corridor and walked over to Peter, hugging people here and there on the way. 'Hey, darling,' she said when she eventually reached him. 'Do you mind if we go now?'

She suddenly looked exhausted, like she had just realised that she'd had quite enough of smiling and being friendly with everyone.

'Of course,' Peter said and drained his wine glass.

'I just want to say goodbye to the Worshipful Master,' Fay said. 'Do you think he's still in the temple? I haven't seen him down here.'

'Why don't we check upstairs?'

'Come, let us return to the West and prove ourselves to be Freemasons.'

This was one of the often-used phrases in Dutch Freemasonry, Fay had told him. When the Worshipful Master closed a lodge, he always ended the meeting by saying: 'Return to the West and prove yourself to be a Freemason.' The West was society, the material world, as opposed to the East, the spiritual or intellectual world, where wisdom came from. It was a reminder that Masons should apply the lessons they had learned in the lodge to their lives outside it, so that they could make a contribution, however modest, to building a better world.

Fay said goodbye to a few more people.

'I'll go to the loo, too,' Peter said.

'I'm so glad you came, Peter.'

'I was happy to come, darling,' he said. 'It was an interesting evening.'

'And who knows, maybe we'll find ourselves here together more often,' she said hopefully.

I suppose it's quite an inspiring place, Peter thought. *I'm sure it's easier to have decent conversations with people here than it is in the outside world.*

'Who knows, darling,' he said.

Peter left the function room and went to the toilets, a shabby area with dated tiling that was desperately in need of refurbishment. It was cold and smelled unpleasant, like the men's toilets in a student union bar. He tried to breathe through his nose so that he would take in as little of the foul air as possible. He washed his hands and went back out into the corridor where Fay was waiting for him.

They went upstairs.

A sudden feeling of dread washed over Peter, making him reluctant to push down on the door handle.

Fay, who was right behind him and not expecting him to stop, bumped into his back. 'What's wrong?' she asked, startled.

'I don't know,' Peter answered.

Fragment 2 – From Amsterdam to Leiden (spring 1609)

Our group had now shrunk to about one hundred souls. John Robinson wrote a letter to Leiden's council on our behalf asking for permission to settle in their beautiful city. We only wanted to be left in peace, he said, and he promised that we would cause no trouble. To our immense joy, the council decided in our favour on February 12th. For the second time in two years, we packed up our few possessions and prepared to resettle somewhere new. The council's only conditions were that we would behave honestly and obey all the laws and ordinances of Leiden. The city had surely never received a group of new residents more prepared to respect these conditions.

The foxes have holes, and the birds have nests, but will we ever have a place to rest our heads?

During the last service before we left Amsterdam, John gave an inspiring sermon urging us to stay on the right path. He cited the words in 1 Peter: 'Beloved, I beseech you as aliens and exiles to abstain from the passions of the flesh that wage war against your soul. Conduct yourselves honourably among the Gentiles, so that, though they malign you as evildoers, they may see your honourable deeds and glorify God when he comes to judge. For the Lord's sake, accept the authority of every human institution, whether of the emperor as supreme, or of governors, as sent by him to punish those who do wrong and to praise those who do right.'

Strengthened by these words, we said goodbye to the friends we had made, and with joy in our hearts, we went on our way, relieved and happy to leave the squabbles and infighting of this great city behind us.

We knew that the English ambassador had immediately submitted an official protest on behalf of King James I when he heard that the city of Leiden had agreed to take us in. So it was not without a measure of unease that we set off on our journey. We English had provided much support to the Netherlands during their heroic resistance against the

Catholic oppressors from Spain. The Dutch would therefore not want to offend our king. There had been a twelve-year truce with the Spanish, but of what value were the promises of godless, untrustworthy Catholics? And might the Netherlands once more need English support, perhaps much earlier than expected? But the city of Leiden, which had survived the Spanish Fury less than thirty-five years earlier with such heroism and great loss of human life – a third of the city had died in the Spanish Siege of Leiden – lived up to its motto: Haec Libertatis Ergo (All for the sake of Liberty – PvV). And hadn't the university, the reward that Prince William of Orange had given to the courageous people of Leiden to thank them for their efforts in the struggle for independence, chosen as its motto: Praesidium Libertatis? (Bastion of Liberty – PvV). The city council therefore decided not to give in to pressure from the English, proving that these mottos were not just hollow words. They would be honoured!

Leiden is like a city built on a hill that cannot be hidden!

When we arrived in Leiden, we learned that the city's magistrates had been so bold as to not allow the ambassador's protest to go unanswered. They wrote him a letter explaining that no one was refused entry to the city as long as they behaved honestly and obeyed all its laws and ordinances. However, they also expressed the hope that this position would not lead to a deterioration in their relationship with England.

As I wrote earlier, never had a more grateful group sailed into the city of Leiden! We moored our little ship on the wharf outside the Weigh House, and that is where we first set foot in this true bastion of liberty. And what a splendid city Leiden is!

We saw its splendour immediately. Leiden is a city all

bustling with activity and trade. Everyone seems to be in motion, on their way from here to there, dragging huge loads on carts. Boats sail up and down the canals laden almost to the point of sinking with grain, peat, hay and all manner of things. We see the city's wealth in her citizens who wear fine clothes and love to show them off. The textile industry which has brought Leiden such great prosperity is a blessing to us. There is so much work on offer, and all you need is strength and a willingness to work hard. There's no real need to speak the language – the heavy work can be done without words – although most of us are growing more fluent by the day. But for us, of equal importance is that we are free to practise our religion in our own way, just like many others who have fled persecution and found a safe haven here. We have seen Walloon Protestants, other Separatists from England, Huguenots from France, Mennonites, Baptists, Lutherans and even Jews. We are told that a third of the city's population is made up of people who have fled to Leiden from elsewhere.

This will be our home. At least, for now.

I do not believe that even Leiden is meant to be our final destination.

Chapter 6

Naturally, the murder of the chairman of the local Masonic lodge was the talk of the small university town – and beyond. In a short item on the national news, a journalist stood on the Steenschuur to report 'the mysterious death of Lodge Chairman Coen Zoutman, a man known for his warm and friendly character'. The Masonic Hall could be seen in the background; the street was cordoned off, and two police cars were parked at an angle on the kerb.

According to the reporter, the police were utterly in the dark as to both the identity and motive of whoever had committed the murder. As yet, no details had been released, but it was rumoured to have been a savage and brutal killing. One of the investigators' immediate priorities was to compile a list of everyone who had been at the lodge that evening.

Anyone who had attended the open evening was asked to make themselves known. There was also a general appeal for anyone who had seen anything in the vicinity of the lodge that night, no matter how inconsequential it might have seemed, to come forward.

The police force was on high alert. Although the constabulary in the usually quiet town of Leiden had little experience in dealing with murders, they knew that the first twenty-four hours after the crime were of vital importance.

Detective Chief Inspector Rijsbergen clicked the *X* on the browser window in which he'd just watched the news report on the broadcaster's catch-up service.

The chief inspector was a remarkably calm man, with short, grey, wiry hair and a well-maintained moustache. His carefully shaven face with its strong jawline was on the lean side. Combined with his toned, muscular body, it gave him a somewhat martial appearance, more like that of a professional soldier than a police officer.

Now he sat at his desk in his well-ordered office, where earlier that morning he had written a brief report of the murder. He stared at his computer screen.

Peter de Haan had not been amused when he and his girlfriend Fay Spežamor had been separated and taken to the station to be interviewed. Hadn't they been the ones who called the police after they'd found Coen Zoutman's lifeless body, De Haan had repeatedly asked on the way there. But Rijsbergen knew no one could be ruled out at this stage.

Although it had been close to midnight, Rijsbergen had decided to question them straight away. Peter de Haan had, understandably, looked tired when Rijsbergen and Van de Kooij interviewed him.

Peter had told them that he had met Coen Zoutman a few times. These occasions had always been chance encounters on the street when he had been with Fay Spežamor.

He had spoken calmly, telling them that he'd gone to the open evening with his girlfriend. That Coen Zoutman had given a talk about Freemasonry. That after the presentation, he and most of the other people present had gone downstairs to the drinks reception.

He had told them about everyone he had seen or spoken to

that evening: his student Sven who was there with his friend Erik, and the American man, Tony Vanderhoop, who had come to Leiden with some other Americans who were making preparations for Mayflower 400.

It was estimated that between sixty and seventy people had been in the lodge building when Coen Zoutman was murdered, and moreover, the front door had been unlocked the entire time.

We must put the little grey cells to work, Rijsbergen had thought. Despite the horrific nature of the murder, he was looking forward to solving the puzzle before him.

They had taken Fay Spežamor's statement next, and her account had been almost identical to that of her co-suspect except that she showed no trace of irritation at being questioned at all. She had appeared to accept the situation she had found herself in.

But a veil of immense grief had seemed to hang over her, a sadness that had spoken silently from her red-rimmed eyes. She'd sat in the interview room like a pitiful little bird, sometimes speaking so softly that Rijsbergen and Van de Kooij had barely been able to make out what she was saying.

She had talked about Coen Zoutman only in superlatives: he was the wisest man she had ever met, with the strongest and most loveable of characters and a great sense of humour. She had praised his encyclopaedic knowledge that he had gained not only from books but also from his many travels all over the world. Fay had told them about his retreats to a monastery where he often went to study and meditate for weeks at a time.

She had burst into tears several times during her interview. These were either the two most cunning villains that Rijsbergen had ever encountered – so cunning that they had managed to perfectly align their stories in the short amount of time between committing their heinous crime and being bundled into separate police cars – or they were completely innocent citizens who had had been in the wrong place at the wrong time but had done the right thing by immediately calling the police.

Strictly speaking, there were insufficient grounds to hold them any longer, so they were both taken home after midnight, this time in the same car. It had been made very clear to them before they left that they were not to reveal to anyone the details of their discovery of Coen Zoutman's body.

Rijsbergen shut down his computer. He'd only had a couple of hours' sleep. His wife Corinne had still been sleeping when he'd left the house to come back to work this morning. But, strangely, he didn't feel tired at all. There was a large, steaming mug of coffee next to his keyboard, already his second one of the day.

He drank his coffee pensively, blowing over the edge of the mug before each sip to cool it down.

Peter de Haan and Fay Spežamor's interviews had not yielded much.

Mevrouw Spežamor's white blouse and Meneer De Haan's pale blue shirt had been spotless, as if they had just come from the dry cleaners. Their hands and nails had been clean with no lingering scent of soap – although they had both looked at Rijsbergen strangely when he'd asked if he could smell their hands.

The only possible lead is Fay's casual comment about Coen Zoutman's election to the chair, Rijsbergen thought. *Might the election have created bad blood between Zoutman and one of the other candidates?*

Rijsbergen planned to speak to both her and Peter de Haan again later that day to see if a night's sleep had helped them to remember something they hadn't mentioned in their interviews.

A forensics unit had been at the scene all night taking photographs and collecting evidence. They hadn't finished their work until the early hours of the morning. Rijsbergen expected the report of their findings to appear on his desk at any moment.

He wanted to visit the Masonic Hall again before the body was removed from the temple and taken to the morgue. After that, a team of specialists would move in to clean up the crime scene.

There was a knock on the matte wired glass window of his office door.

The door opened before he'd had a chance to say 'Come in.'

'Are we going out?' Van de Kooij asked eagerly, as though they were about to go on a staff outing.

Detective Sergeant Van de Kooij, his right-hand man, was a balding thirty-something, a whole head shorter than the oak-like Rijsbergen.

'Yes, all right, Goldilocks,' said Rijsbergen, draining his mug in two overlarge gulps. He enjoyed teasing Van de Kooij about his premature baldness, mostly because his colleague's usual easy wit always failed him at such moments, and he seemed to resign himself to being the butt of Rijsbergen's jokes.

They went out to the car park behind the police station and got into Van de Kooij's car. Van de Kooij was a keen driver, and they often took his car whenever they went anywhere together. It was a somewhat oversized SUV that resembled a small Hummer. Rijsbergen always felt a bit silly sitting in it as it drove smoothly over the well-maintained Dutch roads, but he had to admit that it was comfortable. Its height meant that you could look down on the other motorists around you with a certain feeling of superiority. In Rijsbergen's opinion, that was the real reason his colleague had bought it.

'I want to go and see De Haan later, and that woman with the unpronounceable name, Fay,' Rijsbergen said as they arrived at their destination.

'Fay Spežamor.'

'Precisely. She said something yesterday about Zoutman being elected chairman of the lodge. There might be something in that. We need to find out who the other candidates were, what happened, who supported who . . . That sort of thing.'

With the street blocked off, they were able to park right in front of the door.

'Inspector.' The officer who was guarding the door greeted them and tapped his hat in a salute. He held up the red and white tape that was blocking the entrance so that Rijsbergen and Van de Kooij could step under it and into the building.

They took the winding staircase upstairs. The door to the temple was closed but not locked. Inside, they found the room exactly as they had left it.

But now, Zoutman's lifeless body lay under a white sheet.

They approached the victim but stopped a few metres away.

Rijsbergen crouched down, and Van de Kooij immediately crouched down next to him.

'They'll never get those bloodstains off the white tiles, you know,' Van de Kooij remarked.

Rijsbergen nodded absently, as if he hadn't heard what his partner had said. 'It's not . . .' he began. 'This murder wasn't committed in the heat of the moment. I think someone came here intending to take his life. It wasn't done on impulse or in a fit of rage. It wasn't an argument that got out of hand. The blow to his skull alone would have been enough to kill him. They didn't need to put that set square through his heart or the compasses through his hands.'

'Dexter said that Zoutman was already dead when that was done,' said Van de Kooij.

'Dexter' was the blood spatter analyst attached to the forensic investigation unit. His real name was Martin Garens, but everyone called him 'Dexter'. Few people in the force actually knew what he was really called.

Rijsbergen himself had never watched *Dexter*, the American TV show about the FBI blood spatter analyst who moonlighted as a serial killer.

'I just called Dexter for an initial update,' Van de Kooij said. 'Zoutman was hit on the back of the head with a huge amount of force. He would have been killed instantly.'

'Exactly what Dalhuizen concluded,' said Rijsbergen. 'So to ram the set square into his chest afterwards . . . And then go to the trouble of forcing those compasses through his hands. Making the incisions with a knife beforehand . . . Those were all gratuitous acts. Or at least, they weren't necessary to make him deader than he already was, and they weren't used to torture something out of him either.'

Rijsbergen stood up, stroking his chin with his right hand. 'It must be something symbolic,' he thought out loud. 'Maybe there's someone in this club who can tell us more about it. Have you heard anything else?'

'Yes, that it's not looking good evidence-wise. They said there were no fingerprints on the gavel or the compasses or the square. Looks like they've been wiped completely clean.'

'Hmm,' Rijsbergen muttered. 'That was to be expected. Or the murderer wore gloves. Or murderers, of course. One keeps him talking, the other one sneaks up behind him.'

'And something else . . .' Van de Kooij said. 'They found loads of shoeprints, obviously, but they're essentially useless because there were dozens of people walking around in here yesterday. It's completely impossible to get anything from them. The murderer's prints are bound to be among them, but they can't identify them. There were no hairs found in the blood and no accidental footprints left in it either, so none of it leads anywhere.'

'No cameras, obviously,' said Rijsbergen. 'No photos taken . . . Nobody who knows who was in the building when, or who spoke to Zoutman last. We don't actually know who was in the building at all. So all we can do now is talk to everyone whose name we have. See if anyone noticed anything.'

They returned to the landing as two men and a woman came up the stairs carrying a stretcher.

'Is it all right if we take him now?' the woman at the front asked.

'Go ahead,' Van de Kooij said. 'We're finished here.'

They manoeuvred the stretcher past them and into the temple.

Rijsbergen and Van de Kooij watched from a distance as they removed the white plastic sheet, coldly exposing the dead man's corpse.

There was no privacy in death.

The woman closed Coen Zoutman's eyes, but his mouth still gaped half open. He looked like a drunkard who had passed out on the floor.

They carefully moved his body onto the stretcher. Left behind on the tiles where his head had lain was a semi-circle of blood spatters, like a diabolical halo.

To meet your end like this, Rijsbergen thought. *To have gained all that wisdom, studied all those books, travelled half the globe, only to end up in a little hall in Leiden with your brains smashed in.*

'Chief Inspector!' A shout came from downstairs. 'Could you come here a moment, please?'

'We're on our way down!' Van de Kooij replied on his behalf.

The two men and the woman zipped up the black body bag containing Coen Zoutman's body. They strapped it onto the stretcher and carried it out of the temple with careful, shuffling steps.

Rijsbergen took a last look at the body shrouded in black.

It looked like they were carrying the giant cocoon of some strange insect. An insect that would eventually hatch out and reappear in an entirely new form.

Chapter 7

Peter let the heavy door of the Jean Pesijnhofje fall closed behind him, something that always made him feel like he was leaving an oasis of peace and calm. The original meaning of the word 'paradise' came from the old Iranian word '*pairidaeza*' – 'walled garden' – and this small, enclosed courtyard illustrated that perfectly. Beyond its walls was the big, bad world, the West, as the Freemasons called it, with all its problems, jealousy, greed and deceit.

Occasionally, he managed to hold onto the feeling of serenity for a while, but more often than not, it vanished before he reached the end of the street. Either a cyclist brushing past him, furiously ringing their bell, or an idiot on a noisy moped barely avoiding mowing him down, or sometimes just a cold, miserable drizzle would bring him abruptly back to the here and now.

He went left and walked around the Pieterskerk.

After the police had brought them home, Peter and Fay had sat on the sofa for a while. They had sipped at their tea without saying very much to each other.

Fay and her twelve-year-old daughter Agapé shared their home with Fay's mother, Alena. She had come downstairs in her old-fashioned nightdress and sleepily asked them what they were doing up so late. Fay told her she would explain everything in the morning.

Coen Zoutman's murder had naturally affected Fay more than it had Peter. She had spent so much time in his company, had so many conversations with him, and heard him speak so often at the lodge's fortnightly meetings. He had been her mentor.

'Who would do something like this?' she'd asked herself out loud, again and again. 'Such a lovely man. Such a *lovely* man.'

When they'd gone to bed, Fay had lain awake in Peter's arms for a long time. Her tears had left a large damp patch on his T-shirt. Peter hadn't been able to erase the image of Coen Zoutman's shattered skull from his mind, nor that of the man's hands, pierced clean through like a modern-day Christ.

Peter had been woken by the familiar sound of Alena pottering in the kitchen. As usual, she had been up early, making coffee and setting the table. Very carefully, so as not to wake Fay who was still fast asleep, he had crept out of bed and gone downstairs.

He had told Alena about the dramatic events of the previous night. As he spoke, unfolding the story of their grisly discovery in the temple, she'd had to sit down. She had perched on the edge of the sofa, fidgeting with the tea towel in her lap, and suddenly, she'd looked very old, as though the lines around her mouth had grown deeper.

Agapé had come downstairs too and soon lightened the mood with her cheerful chatter.

While Peter was drinking his coffee, a message arrived from Jeffrey Banks, the director of the Leiden American Pilgrim Museum, asking if he had time to come to the museum that day. He was expecting a visit from a delegation of Americans who were organising events around the upcoming four hundredth anniversary of the Pilgrims' arrival in America.

That must be Tony Vanderhoop and his group, Peter thought. *Who else would it be?*

In a small place like Leiden, coincidences like this happened all the time, and paths crossed with surprising frequency. During the forty years he had lived in the town, Peter had found that, sooner or later, every new person he met would reveal that they had an acquaintance in common.

There was just one lecture on his schedule that afternoon, so he had sent a message back to say that he would be happy to drop by.

Even if it's just to take my mind off last night, he had thought to himself.

Peter walked along the Pieterskerkhof and into the narrow alleyway of the Pieterskerk-Choorsteeg.

My God, I'm so tired, he thought.

He'd had very little sleep, understandably, but he never really felt fully rested after spending the night at Fay's anyway.

Fay's bedroom was too small for an actual double bed, so they'd bought a trundle bed at IKEA in Delft. It had turned out to be so uncomfortable that staying at Fay's always felt like being at a teenage sleepover.

Fay's mother, who had spent her entire working life teaching classical languages at a high school, also had a room in the little almshouse. After the death of Fay's husband, Alena had moved in with her and Agapé, making it a household of three generations of women.

They had worked out the perfect arrangement with each other. Alena was there when her granddaughter came home from school. She cooked dinner and made sure the house was clean and tidy when Fay finished work at around five. And if Fay spontaneously decided that she wanted to go out, she never had the hassle of trying to find a babysitter at the last minute.

The third bedroom in the house belonged to Agapé. Her name

was the Greek word for 'love'. But hardly anyone ever pronounced her name correctly and most people simply shortened it 'Aggie' or 'Aagje' – 'little Agatha'. She was a bright, lively girl who had inherited her mother's beauty and intelligence.

Peter walked along the Breestraat, past the imposing Stadhuis. The town hall's façade was bathed in golden, springtime light.

He turned left into Koornbrugsteeg and crossed the Nieuwe Rijn canal via the roofed bridge. Then he immediately turned right and took a left into the Beschuitsteeg.

As soon as he rounded the corner into the lane, he saw a group of people gathered by the museum door. Among them, he spotted the tall form of Tony Vanderhoop wearing his ever-present baseball cap.

Jeffrey was there too, standing between the group and the front door like a bouncer who hadn't yet decided if he was going to let people inside.

Peter and Jeffrey never socialised with each other outside the museum, but they had developed a good rapport. While not quite friends, their relationship was something that resembled a friendship.

Jeffrey had once confessed to Peter that, although he welcomed the increasing interest in the Pilgrims and Mayflower 400, he had strong objections to the way in which the English colonists' history had been mythologised. He was a scientist and preferred to concentrate on the verifiable facts. True, they weren't the stuff on which nations were usually built, but they were closer to what had actually happened. He rejected the oversimplified image of the Pilgrims as courageous men and women who had left Leiden and gone to America because they were afraid of losing their identity, heroes who started out with nothing and built their ideal of a pure, Christian community from the ground up.

Tony raised his eyebrows when he saw Peter coming towards him, but he smiled and looked genuinely pleased to see him again.

Up close, Peter recognised some of the other members of Tony's group, two men and three women, but none of them gave any indication of remembering having seen him at the Masonic Hall.

Jeffrey's face lit up. He was clearly relieved that he wouldn't be giving the tour on his own.

Peter shook hands with everyone.

'What a terrible business that was yesterday,' Tony said. 'Coen's death . . . Please accept my condolences.'

'Thanks,' said Peter. 'I didn't know Coen very well myself, but my girlfriend Fay is a member of the lodge, and she's devastated.'

'I can imagine,' Tony replied. 'I've been pretty shaken up by it myself. We Freemasons are all brothers and sisters. Even if we've never met each other, we are *one*.' He fell silent, as if the subject was something he'd rather not talk about for now.

'Come on,' said Peter. 'Let's go inside.'

They entered the room that had been set up as a living room.

'What a lovely place this is,' said a woman whose name Peter couldn't remember. 'This should definitely be one of the highlights of our programme.'

None of the Pilgrims ever lived here, Peter almost blurted out before deciding that it was Jeffrey's job to reveal that sort of information.

'As you probably know already, they're hard at work in Plymouth, Massachusetts, restoring the *Mayflower II*, a replica that was built during 1955 and 1956. If it's declared seaworthy again, they hope it'll be able to sail to England's Plymouth and to Delfshaven in the Netherlands in 2020.'

'And that's just one of the many things that are being planned,' the woman next to him continued. 'The list of events taking place in Leiden, Boston and Plymouth is huge. The list of events that are still at the planning stage is possibly even longer. And there's going to be quite a big celebration around the opening of the new research centre. Well, "research centre" might be over-stating it a little, but there will be a research department dedicated exclusively to the history of the Pilgrims. It's going to be a branch of the Leiden Heritage Organisation.'

This last detail appeared to be news to Jeffrey. He looked around the group with a delighted expression, as if he had actu-ally been the one to reveal it. Now that he knew that he had something real and long-lasting to look forward to as a result of the delegation's visit, he immediately appeared more at ease.

'And of course,' the woman went on, 'Jeffrey will have a vital role to play.'

A boy unwrapping the most longed-for item on his birthday wish list could not have looked happier.

Jeffrey went around the circle and shook everyone's hand enthusiastically, which they all tolerated with weak smiles.

They visited both rooms briefly, and since the American visi-tors were already well-versed in the history of the Pilgrims, Jeffrey focused on the history of the building itself.

After the requisite photos had been taken, the group went back outside.

'Are you coming with us, Peter?' Jeffrey asked. 'We're going to take a short walk around town and see some of the other places that are associated with the Pilgrims. It shouldn't take more than an hour.'

Peter looked at his watch. He still had plenty of time before his lecture was due to start. 'Yes, all right, Jeffrey,' he said.

They walked along the Nieuwstraat and past the public library towards the Burcht, which always made a huge impression on everyone who saw it for the first time.

The town centre was dominated by the Burcht. It was an enormous ninth-century motte, a man-made hill that rose twelve metres above ground level. On top of it was a tall shell keep with a circular, crenellated stone wall that was six metres high. Inside, a wooden walkway had been constructed along the castle's battlements, giving visitors fantastic views out over the city with its medieval houses, churches and narrow streets.

The Americans took photos of the castle with the eagerness of photography students who had been told to capture every detail of the building's construction.

Afterwards, they crossed the Oude Rijn canal and walked along the Haarlemmerstraat to the Vrouwekerkhof where the remaining walls of the Gothic Vrouwekerk still stood. Before it was renamed after the Reformation, this church had been called the *Onze Lieve Vrouwekerk*, or Church of our Lady.

Jeffrey told the group that ruins of the church, which had been attended by the Pilgrims, had almost been demolished by an overzealous city council. One phone call to the American State Department had been enough to have the plans to bulldoze it cancelled.

Philippe de la Noye had been baptised here in 1603. A Huguenot born in Leiden, he had sailed to America on the second Pilgrim ship, the *Fortune*. His descendants had anglicised their name to Delano, and one of them would eventually become the President of the United States of America: Franklin Delano Roosevelt.

On the little square in front of the remaining walls of the church, Jeffrey pointed out the long, dark stones laid out in a geometric pattern representing the graves that would have been there centuries ago.

They went back to the Harlemmerstraat and crossed the canal via the renovated Catharinabrug at the point where the Oude Rijn and Nieuwe Rijn rivers meet. They paused in front of the *Waag*, the seventeenth-century weigh house built in the Dutch baroque style where goods were once weighed for the market.

According to legend, the Pilgrims had first set foot in Leiden near the Waag. Jeffrey pointed out the exact spot opposite the building, and the members of the group all took turns to pose for photographs.

It's really all just a matter of faith, Peter thought. *As long as you say it convincingly enough and often enough, you can tell people that anything happened anywhere, and eventually, everyone will believe you. After a while, nobody will dare to question whether or not the story is true.*

As they were making their way along the narrow Mandenmakerssteeg towards the busy Breestraat, Tony began to slow down, apparently on purpose. Peter slowed his pace to match Tony's so that he wouldn't be left alone at the back of the group.

'You know, Peter,' Tony said when they were out of earshot of the rest of the group, 'Coen Zoutman's murder last night . . . His death has shocked me in so many ways. It's not just because it was so brutal and so unexpected. I feel like I've lost a friend, which is absurd, I know. I only met him for the first time yesterday.'

Peter nodded sympathetically.

'I can only imagine how awful it must be for you. And for your girlfriend.'

'It's such a tragedy. As I said earlier, I didn't know him well myself, but I'm shocked by how violent the murder was.'

Tony had grabbed Peter's arm as if he thought he might be

about to walk away. It created a physical intimacy between them that made Peter feel uncomfortable.

'But I mean, you were the one who found him, right? That's what I heard this morning.'

It's astonishing how quickly news like this gets around.

'That's right. Fay and I found him. It was horrible, a nightmare. I don't know how else to describe it.'

Tony shook his head in a way that suggested that he would have preferred it if Peter didn't describe it at all.

Then Tony said something in a whisper. Peter had to incline his head and lean sideways towards him to hear it.

'We've been the target of an increasing number of . . . threats, lately. The Freemasons, I mean . . . In the States too. I often wonder . . . Our grand lodge in Boston has been getting anonymous letters and emails. Sometimes, Peter, it feels like we're in a movie. We get letters in the mail where the words have all been cut out of newspapers, very old-school. We don't know who's behind it all.'

'And do you think it might be connected to what happened here?'

'I don't know. That's for the police to figure out, I guess.'

'Have you told the Dutch police about all of this yet?'

'I'll go to the police station this afternoon. The police want to talk to us, but we're flying back to the States tonight.'

At last, Tony let go of Peter's arm.

'There are a lot of crazy people around, especially back home, as I'm sure you know,' Tony said, and he smiled. 'There are conspiracy theorists who think that the Freemasons have been involved in pretty much all the evil in the world. They think we had a hand in 9/11, that we're responsible for just about every financial crisis there's ever been, that we started the French

Revolution, that we were behind the attack on Pearl Harbor, you name it. The Illuminati, Novus ordo seclorum, the so-called New World Order, all the Masonic symbols on the dollar bill, the All-Seeing Eye and the unfinished pyramid. Oh, I'm sure you know all the stories. I'd probably think it was funny if it wasn't so pathetic.'

The group stopped on the Langebrug, the five-hundred-metre-long street that had once been a canal. The famous painter Jan Steen had lived here. It was also the street where Rembrandt van Rijn had taken his first painting lessons with Jacob van Swanenburg.

Jeffrey told the group the story of James Chilton, a Pilgrim who was pelted with rocks by a group of boys in 1619 because they thought that he had been holding Remonstrant church services at his home. The Remonstrants were a group of mostly Protestant Christians who disagreed with the doctrine of the Dutch Reformed Church, the prevailing church in the Dutch Republic at the time.

So the much-vaunted Dutch tolerance wasn't really all it was cracked up to be, Peter thought. This was something he regularly tried to impress upon his students. The myth of total religious liberty was so deeply ingrained in the story that the Netherlands told about itself that it would be an uphill battle to convince anybody that it wasn't true.

'But why now?' Peter asked Tony. 'Why are the Freemasons getting so many threats right now?'

'Why now? We live in strange times. People feel like they don't understand the world any more. They feel powerless. Maybe the world has just gotten too big. We're bombarded with terrible news every day, on the internet, on our smartphones. Whenever people suffered in the past, they could blame the gods for every sickness, every bad harvest, every child's death, every shipwreck. People of faith were actually the first conspiracy theorists. Something didn't just happen. Someone *made* it happen, someone with a set plan. It was punishment for not following God's rules, or because a sacrifice hadn't been made, or even because two gods were warring with each other or whatever. But terrible things still happen in the world, utterly senseless, random disasters that have absolutely no purpose. If you don't believe in God, then the only possible cause of all these awful events is man. And the most convenient culprits are secret societies who are all hellbent on world domination.'

'And you think it has something to do with all that?'

Tony shrugged and stuck out his bottom lip to show that he didn't know.

They stopped at the former Stinksteeg, an alleyway that was now called the William Brewstersteeg after the Pilgrim whose printing shop had been here. The shop was closed down, Jeffrey explained, by none other than the English King James I, who was furious about a pamphlet Brewster had printed called *Perth Assembly*. Brewster fled to Leiderdorp, where he stayed until his departure for America. All this upheaval and disruption eventually led to the Pilgrims deciding to seek refuge elsewhere.

The group made its way along a winding route through streets and alleyways to the Lokhorststraat. They stopped at the Latin school where, Jeffrey told them, Rembrandt had studied as a young boy.

Rembrandt was three years old when the Pilgrims arrived and fourteen when they left again, so he was very likely to have bumped into John Robinson and the other Pilgrims in Leiden's small town centre at some point – a detail that seemed to delight the American visitors.

Walking ahead of the group, the expert guide led them to the Gerecht square. They turned left into the Muskadelsteeg and then left again around the Pieterskerk towards the Jean Pesijnhofje, where Fay lived.

I'll pop in and say hello to Fay, Peter thought. *Make sure she's okay.*

'We'll visit the Pieterskerk on the way back,' Jeffrey said. 'We can stop for coffee in the café there, but I want to show you a few other things first.' He opened the large, heavy door that led into the *hofje*. The Americans gasped in surprise as they went through the vestibule and realised that it led to an inner court-yard with a garden surrounded by what looked like little fairy-tale houses.

'John Robinson lived here, as did many of the other Pilgrims,' Jeffrey told them. 'Sadly, the original compound was demolished, but it stood on this exact spot.'

Peter noticed that Fay's bike was gone.

Maybe she's gone to her office at the university after all.

When they returned to the street, Jeffrey pointed towards the Pieterskerk. 'You might be interested to know,' he said, 'that they recently opened an escape room in the Pieterskerk.'

'Oh, with puzzles?' one of the women in the group asked. 'I love those!'

'Yes, exactly. But the fun thing about this one is that it has a Pilgrims theme. I've done it myself, and I must say it's quite ingenious. And the fact that it's such an old building adds to the whole experience, of course.'

'And did you manage to escape?' the woman wanted to know.

'I think that's for me to know and you to wonder about,' Jeffrey said, laughing. 'But I will tell you that I can highly recommend it. You should have a go if you have time. They have an English version, so we could ask if they have any slots available later. The theme changes every year or two, but for now, it's the Pilgrims.'

They moved on to a famous spot on the Rapenburg canal. It was here in front of the old university library in 1620 that the Pilgrims boarded boats bound for Delfshaven, where they would eventually set sail for England.

The tour ended on the Vliet, the canal where the Pilgrims finally left Leiden forever. A statue of a man waving a final farewell to the travellers had been erected on the canalside.

The group walked back towards the Pieterskerk.

Peter's conversation with Tony had left him feeling unsettled – as if their conversation had been unfinished.

'Tony, getting back to what we were talking about earlier,' said Peter, 'do you really have no idea where these threats are coming from? And why do you think that they might be connected to what happened here?'

'It's just a hunch,' Tony said. 'I don't know. I'll tell the police this afternoon. But you know, and this is just speculation, really, but maybe they should be looking at the Catholic Church. There are plenty of orthodox Catholics who still haven't accepted that Rome's word is no longer law. They see us Masons as godless devil-worshippers. But the States are home to an enormous number of different groups. We've got radical evangelists, trigger-happy born-again Christians who would happily annihilate everyone who isn't pro-life. We've got fascist white supremacist militias. And we've got tree-hugging hippies who see the Pilgrims – and maybe the Freemasons too – as the start of where it all went wrong in America, the beginning of the end for the indigenous population. I could go on, I really could. It's no wonder the Freemasons are usually the first organisation that dictatorships decide to ban.'

'Who could say?' Peter mumbled to himself. 'Who could say?'

But that's all in the USA, he thought. *How on earth can events over there be linked to Coen Zoutman's tragic death here?*

They reached the university's Academy Building near the Nonnenbrug Bridge.

Although he'd not actually spoken to any of them, Peter said goodbye and shook hands with everyone in the group. He waved at Jeffrey.

'Well, Peter,' Tony said. 'I'm sorry our meeting was in such unpleasant circumstances. But I hope that we'll meet again in better ones someday.'

'I hope so too.'

'If you ever decide to attempt the "great crossing" yourself,' Tony said, 'feel free to come visit me. Or us.' He gave Peter his business card.

Peter smiled. According to one of his colleagues who had lived in the States for a while, it was advisable to take such remarks with a grain of salt. 'You can visit me anytime' was more polite small talk than an invitation to actually visit someone.

But who knows, Peter thought.

Before Peter left, Tony gave him the sort of brotherly bear hug that Americans were famous for.

As he walked away, Peter wondered why Tony had taken him aside to tell him what he had told him, but it would have looked odd to go back and ask him.

I suppose you're inclined to be more candid than usual when you're talking to people you think you're never going to see again. It can be cathartic to tell your story to an outsider, someone who'll listen to you like a confessor.

Peter couldn't quite put his finger on it, but he had a strange feeling that something else had been going on, something that transcended the simple conversation they'd had. Like he'd been watching a subtitled film in which the lines spoken by the actors had been entirely different from the words on the screen.

Chapter 8

Rijsbergen and Van de Kooij followed the coroner's team as they carried Coen Zoutman's body down the stairs.

The building manager, Frank Koers, was waiting for them in the function room. He had spread out a floor plan of the building on one of the tables and placed glasses on the four corners to stop it from rolling back up.

They stood around the table like generals studying a terrain map to devise a plan of attack.

Frank traced a finger over the floor plan. 'As you can see,' he said, 'in the temple itself there's only one way in and out: this door here. No hidden escape routes, no secret tunnels or doors. The city architect, Jan Neysingh, designed an initiation chamber that was added to the first floor in 1950.'

Rijsbergen nodded. He blinked slowly, like he was taking a mental photograph of the plans in front of him.

'And here,' Frank Koers said, sliding his finger over the paper again, 'on the ground floor, we have the main entrance, the hall with the toilets. Then the entrance to this room with . . .' he pointed with his left hand at a door in the corner of the room '. . . a smaller room next door. That room leads to a large extension that runs the length of the garden. These doors . . .' he pointed to the two sets of double doors at the end of the function room '. . . take you outside to the garden. It's an enclosed yard with high walls. Not easy to get over.'

'But what if you *did* manage to climb over them?' asked Van de Kooij, who was furiously scribbling notes. 'Where would you end up?'

'Then you'd come out in the back gardens belonging to the houses on this block,' Frank said. 'And if you climbed over all of their walls, eventually you'd end up behind the synagogue on the Levendaal. But I've never gone beyond the garden myself. You'd have to take a look for yourself.'

'Well, let's do that then,' Van de Kooij said eagerly as he emphatically underlined the last few words on his notes.

Rijsbergen rolled his eyes, just briefly enough for his partner not to notice.

They opened the garden doors and went into the back yard. It was clear that it was rarely used. The tiles were edged in moss, the plastic chairs were coated in green algae, and there was a pile of sand in which a few overgrown but withered weeds had taken root. A metre-wide border ran along the wall, filled with little more than soil, and covered for the most part with a thin layer of moss.

'Your technical team was in here yesterday with floodlights,' Koers said. 'They took a lot of photos, so if someone left shoe-prints, I'm sure they'll have found them. But I think you'll see straight away . . .' he pointed to the strip of soil '. . . that nobody has set foot there for a very long time.'

'But if you were a bit of an athletic type, you could get over that easily, couldn't you?' Van de Kooij said to no one in particular. To demonstrate that he fit this description himself, he took off his jacket.

'Stop right there, Spider-Man,' said Rijsbergen.

'It doesn't seem likely that the killer left the building this way,' said Koers. 'It would attract too much attention, and you wouldn't get very far anyway because there's another garden behind here with yet another wall. The only way to get back onto the street is by going through a house. And that's what this person has done; they've simply left the building through the front door.'

'I suppose so,' said Van de Kooij. He put his jacket on the ground and took a run at the wall. With one enormous stride, he leapt over the border and grabbed onto the top of the wall with both hands. He used the bricks that stuck out here and there as footholds, like a free climber gripping onto a cliff face.

He managed to reach the top of the wall surprisingly quickly. He looked down at the other two men triumphantly before turning around to assess the area behind the wall.

'Yep,' he said. 'I can see gardens.'

'Come on, get down,' Rijsbergen said.

He smiled at Frank Koers, silently apologising for his colleague's behaviour.

Van de Kooij gave the impression that he would gladly tackle the walls in all the other gardens on the block to hunt for possible clues. He looked behind him one more time, like a general on horseback surveying the battlefield, and then he jumped down.

They went back inside.

'We'll knock on some doors on this block,' Rijsbergen said, an announcement that seemed to be intended for both Koers and Van de Kooij. 'And they'll all get an official letter from the police asking them to contact us if they've seen anything unusual. Will you still be here later?'

'Yes, it'll take me a while to tidy up here. Your colleagues have been through everything, emptied the bins, taken even more photos. They weren't pleased that we had washed all the crockery and glasses. But yes, I've enough to keep me busy here all morning.'

They said goodbye to the building manager. Once they were back outside, they walked along the Steenschuur towards the Korevaarstraat where they turned right.

There was no one home at most of the houses they called at. The handful of people who did open their front doors claimed not to have seen or heard anything. Some of them hadn't even been aware that a murder had taken place so close to their homes.

One resident allowed them to take a look in her back garden, which only confirmed Rijsbergen's opinion that the murderer could not have escaped that way.

'Let's go back to the station,' he said.

They exchanged very few words as they walked back to the car on the Steenschuur.

Just as Van de Kooij was about to drive away, the door to number 6 flew open.

Frank Koers ran towards the car and knocked urgently on the window, which Van de Kooij immediately opened.

'I thought I heard your car. I was waiting for you. Can you come back inside? I've found something.'

Van de Kooij parked the car again.

Koers waited for them in the doorway, hopping impatiently from foot to foot.

He led them back into the function room where everything had been put back in its place, and went over to the building plan that was still unfurled on the table. As they got closer, Rijsbergen noticed a creased napkin made of thick, almost linen-like paper on the table that hadn't been there earlier.

'Here,' Koers said. 'They must have missed this when they were going through the bins. It was crumpled up in a ball.'

Rijsbergen leaned forwards to examine what was on the smoothed-out napkin.

'I was going to throw it away, but then I suddenly saw . . .' Koers pointed at a corner of the napkin '. . . that there was something on it. I opened it up and . . . look!'

They found themselves staring at what looked like a hastily sketched map with the names of various rooms written on it in tiny letters.

It was a map of the Masonic Hall.

Chapter 9

The long walk had made Peter hungry. He decided to have lunch in the university restaurant in the Lipsius Building on the Cleveringaplaats.

He had just one lecture on his schedule that afternoon, 'An Introduction to the History of the Golden Age'. It was actually more of a seminar than a lecture, one of a series of twelve sessions in which Peter delivered a mini-lecture introducing the theme, and then, after a short break, gave the floor to two students who took over the session and explored the material in a practical way. They were free to do this however they chose: a debate with controversial propositions, a game, or perhaps a discussion of a current event related to the contents of the lecture.

Many of his students dreaded having to coordinate the second half of the session. Some of them were so wracked by nerves that they blushed from the neck up. But afterwards, they always admitted that it hadn't been as difficult as they'd thought it would be.

The Archaeology department had recently moved to the Bio Science Park, a nondescript and rather dull site on the outskirts of town. The faculty shared the park with several businesses linked to the university, including many pharmaceutical companies.

Peter had the good fortune to be associated with two faculties, one of them being Humanities, which included the History department. This had allowed him to take an office in the building that housed the History department, although he made sure that he showed his face in the Archaeology department a couple of times a week.

To describe the view from his new office window as less attractive than the one he had previously enjoyed would have been something of an understatement. The window faced a solid brick wall that belonged to the Botanical Gardens. But the many advantages of working in the centre of town – close to the university library and the Lipsius restaurant, and near to where Fay, Judith and Mark worked – made up for the uninspiring view.

Peter had met Judith Cherev more than twenty years ago when he had supervised her PhD thesis on Judaism in Leiden. She had been a student in her early twenties, and he had been a lecturer nearing forty. In the years since, they had developed a close friendship. These days, Judith worked at the University of Leiden's Religious Studies department as a lecturer in Judaism, and she freelanced as a researcher for the Jewish Historical Museum in Amsterdam.

Her partner Mark Labuschagne was a professor in New Testament Studies who specialised in early Christianity, but he was equally at home in the study of ancient religions. He read Greek, Latin and Aramaic with the same ease that most mere mortals read English. His own history included multiple stays in a secure ward in Endegeest psychiatric hospital in Oegstgeest. As was often the case with brilliant minds, the line between his genius and his madness was thin.

Peter, who for an atheist had an unusually keen interest in

Christianity and more than a passing knowledge of the Bible, enjoyed talking to Mark about anything that was related to the Christian faith.

Judith and Mark lived in a little house in the Groot Sionshof, one of the dozens of courtyards in Leiden, green oases of tranquillity in the urban desert of stone and concrete.

Peter's new office was the same size as his old one, which meant he had been able to set it up in exactly the same way. The bookcases, his desk, the long sofa and the coffee table all stood in their usual places, and the same three pictures that he had always had in his office hung on the walls here too: Pope John Paul II in his popemobile; Gustave Wappers' painting of Burgomaster Van der Werff suggesting to the starving citizens during the Spanish Siege of Leiden that they kill him and eat him rather than surrender; and a reproduction of *The Last Supper* by Leonardo da Vinci.

Peter greeted a few students as they passed by. He didn't actually know any of them, but since they appeared to recognise him, he returned their hellos.

He ate lunch in the Lipsius restaurant – soup with a bread roll and a salad – reading the university's weekly newspaper, the *Mare*, as he ate.

He had been at the university for so long now that he knew many of the people featured in its pages.

Peter glanced at his watch and realised with alarm that it was almost one o'clock. His lecture was officially supposed to start in just a minute or two. Luckily, he could fall back on the tradition of the 'academic quarter', which meant that a lecture always began fifteen minutes after the hour, but even so, he still needed to hurry.

He cleared his tray away and went to the History department

next door to the Lipsius Building to drop by his office and pick up everything he needed for the lecture.

When he checked his phone, he saw that he had missed a call. The caller had left a voicemail.

He listened to the message as he jogged back to the Lipsius Building, where the lecture rooms were located on the first floor.

'Hello, Meneer de Haan.' Peter was surprised to hear the voice of the police detective he'd met at the Masonic Hall the night before. 'This is Detective Chief Inspector Rijsbergen. We'd like to come by this afternoon to speak to you and your partner.'

Rijsbergen left his telephone number and asked Peter to call him as soon as possible. Peter shoved his phone into his pocket. He didn't have time to call him back now.

The corridor was deserted when he arrived. He grumbled under his breath, thinking that the students would all have left as soon as they had realised he wasn't there. But when he looked through the window next to the door, he saw that they were all patiently waiting inside the lecture theatre. He muttered a brief apology, and not wanting to lose any more time, jumped straight into his lecture, shrugging off his jacket, taking his things out of his bag and turning on the computer as he talked.

Peter spoke from memory, broadly outlining the early history of the VOC, the Dutch East India Company, while the students industriously typed his words on their keyboards. Or at least, that was what he hoped they were doing. Almost all of them took notes on their laptops, and usually, all he could see were the backs of their screens, row upon row of them like black gravestones.

They could be chatting on Facebook or watching their favourite series on Netflix for all I know.

He briefly went over the history of the Dutch West India Company or WIC, which was organised similarly to the VOC.

He explained that, in the sixteenth and seventeenth centuries, the WIC had a state-sanctioned monopoly on trade and shipping in West Africa south of the Tropic of Cancer, and in the Americas, and on all the islands between Newfoundland and the Strait of Magellan.

After the coffee break, two students took over the session. One of them was Sven, the student who had been at the Freemasons' open evening.

He was wearing the same T-shirt he'd worn the night before. Peter again noticed that he repeatedly pushed his glasses up the bridge of his nose with the index finger of his right hand. Peter couldn't tell whether this was out of necessity or if it was just a tic he had developed.

The young man next to him had shoulder-length hair, and he was wearing a faded black T-shirt with the name of a band on it that Peter had never heard of.

'Today, Stefan and I have decided not to focus on the Dutch West India Company's despicable slave trade, which was the source of the money that built all the grand canal houses in Amsterdam,' Sven said, pulling no punches as he started his presentation. 'We all know that story well enough already.'

'In our presentation,' Stefan continued, taking over from Sven, 'we want to focus on how the colonists' arrival in both North and South America had disastrous consequences for the native people there. The T-shirt that Sven is wearing today refers to the Native Nations' protests on the five hundredth anniversary of Columbus's landing in the Bahamas in 1492. They oppose the celebration of this event because, in the five hundred years since his arrival, the indigenous population has been decimated. That's why they chose "We will not dance on the graves of our fathers" as their motto.'

'But ultimately, the blame lies with all colonists,' Sven said. 'The French, the English, the Dutch and the WIC, the Irish . . . everyone who went to the Americas to steal the land and dispossess the indigenous populations – with no other purpose than to line their own pockets. That's why Stefan and I have joined a protest group dedicated to drawing attention to the history of the North American Indians during the four hundredth Anniversary of the Pilgrims' arrival in America.'

'In our opinion,' Stefan continued, 'the American Indians were the victims of an act of genocide. It was a deliberate attempt to eradicate what was considered to be an inferior race. This genocide, which was largely successful, was given a biblical justification. America was seen as the new promised land.'

There was murmuring and shuffling at the word 'genocide'.

'Obviously, we'd like to hear your opinions on this,' Sven went on, 'but I already know that some of you will say: "But they didn't set up concentration camps. They didn't have a conference where they decided on a Final Solution." However, we cannot discuss the settlers without also addressing the devastating effect they had on the Native American population, America's original inhabitants. The history books describe these colonists as intrepid pioneers, bravely seeking a place where they would be free to follow their faith. But the liberty they were seeking – the liberty to practise their own religion, to have self-determination free from state interference, to no longer fear for their lives, liberty that they eventually found there – came at the cost of the lives and liberties of hundreds of thousands, even millions of other people. American history books cultivate the myth of the empty frontier, the promised land, as I just said, that had only been waiting for the God-fearing Pilgrims to flee persecution in Europe and come and exploit it.'

Stefan took over.

'As Sven just mentioned, the idea of it being empty was a myth. In fact, it had been inhabited for thousands of years. The indigenous Americans hadn't built cities or cultivated vast swathes of land. They didn't even have the concept of land ownership as we know it. But there were territories that tribes believed they had a right to, and there were wars over them – there's no need to portray them as noble savages – but they didn't build fences around them. They hunted, but only killed what they needed for their own immediate use. They lived in harmony with nature. They didn't exhaust her resources. In his famous speech in response to President Franklin Pierce's call for the purchase of tribal lands, Chief Seattle, the chief of the Sioux Indians, said . . .'

He looked down at his notes. '"How can you buy or sell the sky – the warmth of the land? The idea is strange to us. Yet we do not own the freshness of the air or the sparkle of the water. How can you buy them from us? Every part of this earth is sacred to my people. Every shining pine needle, every sandy shore, every mist in the dark woods, every clearing and humming insect is holy in the memory and experience of my people."'

Stefan looked back up at the room.

'And that's why—' he said, but he didn't get a chance to finish the sentence.

'Sorry, but I'm going to have to stop you there for a moment,' Peter said. 'We can discuss the serious subject of genocide shortly, but let me just say this. It's very noble, that Chief Seattle speech, but as a historian, I want to make sure you're aware of something. Or were you already planning to tell us that it's highly unlikely that Chief Seattle ever said those words?'

'No, uh . . . what do you mean?' Stefan asked, slumping his shoulders.

'Listen, Stefan,' said Peter, getting up. 'I looked into this once when I was supervising a student's dissertation. It's like this, and I'll try to make it brief. Chief Seattle actually did make a speech in 1854, but it's doubtful whether anyone wrote it down at the time. A journalist who was there, Dr Henry A. Smith, wrote a report about it in his newspaper in 1887, almost thirty-three years later. Yes, that's thirty-three years later. In principle, nobody really doubts that a speech was made, but it would have been made in the language of Seattle's tribe, Salish, and that was not a language that Smith was familiar with.'

Out of the corner of his eye, Peter saw that some of the students were looking at him with obvious admiration.

'You can carry on shortly. But I wanted to interrupt you because this is a valuable lesson for you as historians. Smith didn't understand Seattle's language, so someone else must have told him about the contents of the speech. He didn't publish anything until thirty-three years after the event. Then, in the 1960s, the poet William Arrowsmith brought out another version of the speech based on the one published by Smith. He copied large parts of it, but he added some of his own ideas. Another version emerged in the 1980s, which is the version you've just quoted from, the one that you'll see most often on the internet and on those beautiful posters. That version bears little resemblance to the words originally spoken by Chief Seattle. It was written by Ted Perry, a teacher in Texas, and it was originally intended to be used in a film about ecology. The text he wrote struck a chord with the growing number of people interested in the environment, people who believed that the Indians were the original protectors of Mother Earth. It was a romantic image that easily caught on with environmentalists. So I have no problem with you quoting Chief Seattle. It's an inspiring speech.

Even I think it's an inspiring speech. But I would advise you to bear in mind that you should take those words with a grain of salt and ask yourself how likely it is that they were spoken by an Indian chief.'

Peter sat down again.

Stefan suddenly looked lost. He stood with his little sheet of notes in his hand like a disappointed customer in a newsagent's clutching a losing lottery ticket.

'But even so,' one of the other students said, putting her hand up as she spoke, clearly more for form's sake than actual politeness, 'the chief probably did say something like that. Maybe not in so many words, but we know that the contents of the speech reflect the Native American view of the world in which everything in nature is believed to be alive, to have a spirit. So does it really matter, in principle, what his exact words were?'

'Right,' Sven said. 'It's about the power of stories. It doesn't matter if a story is true or not as long as people believe it could be true.'

'That's a very interesting point, Sven,' Peter said. 'But then you're getting away from historiography and entering the completely different area of mythology or the world of alternative facts.'

Some of the students grinned at his use of the phrase 'alternative facts'.

'Yes, but,' Sven said, 'isn't that an equally legitimate field of study? Or am I mistaken? Haven't entire nations been built on a combination of truth and fable? In Leiden, we have the story of Burgomaster Van der Werff offering his body to the people of Leiden during the Spanish Siege. Or you could take another story from the same period: Cornelis Joppenszoon, the orphan boy who found a still-warm cooking pot filled with *hutspot* in the Spanish army's deserted army camp here on the Lammenschansweg at the end of the siege of Leiden, and realised that the Spaniards had fled from the Sea Beggars. Stories like these are obvious fabrications, but they've always been important for creating a feeling of unity in a society.'

'That's true,' Peter said.

'In the end, the majority decides whether a story is believable enough to be passed on,' Stefan said. 'History is always written by the victors, right?'

'But still,' Peter argued, 'it's up to the historian, to us as historians, to separate fact from fiction, truth from fabrication.'

'But that . . .' said Sven, clearly pleased to have found a segue that led back to what he wanted to say, '*that* is what Stefan and I were going to talk about. On the one hand, you've got the story of the winners, like the one told by the colonists—'

'Could you maybe explain,' said the female student who had spoken earlier, 'what you meant when you used the word "genocide"? That seems like quite a strong word to use.'

'It is,' Sven said. 'And it's justified. The United Nations defines genocide as "a denial of the right of existence of entire human groups". There are reliable estimates that the number of Native Americans decreased from about twelve million in 1500 to about two hundred and fifty thousand in 1900, making it the biggest mass extermination in the history of mankind. Of course, many Indians died from sicknesses because they were exposed to germs that they weren't resistant to, but many more died as a result of direct confrontations with the whites. We cannot go on talking about the history of the WIC without talking about its significant dark side.'

Peter stood back from the discussion that followed, but he listened to his students with a measure of satisfaction.

The argument about genocide was unsophisticated, but it had led to a lively exchange of ideas.

It was now just gone three o'clock, and a few of the students were starting to pack up their things. Peter put away his notes too. He would turn them into a short report to use in the students' assessment interviews at the end of the course. Alongside their exam grade, they would be given a checkmark for having delivered successful presentations.

When he looked up again, Peter realised that everyone had left except for Sven and Stefan. They were looking at him expectantly.

'Your presentation was fine. Perhaps a bit on the reductive side here and there, but that can sometimes lead to interesting discussions. It was good to talk about fact and fiction and our noble task as historians to differentiate between the two.'

They nodded.

'If you like,' Sven said, 'you could come along to one of our meetings. On the Haagweg.'

'Ah, yes,' said Peter. 'Your protest group.' He smiled. 'I don't mean this to sound disparaging, but I think I can guess how your group's discussions go. In my experience, the discussions in groups like yours tend to be a bit unsophisticated. There's rarely anyone who's prepared to offer an opposing point of view or who really understands the topic that's being discussed. I'm sorry, Stefan, but the way you brought up Chief Seattle's speech without having looked into its background . . . It's not such a huge problem when you do that here. I mean, you're here to learn. But a protest group, well that's real life, and the combination of emotions and a lack of knowledge can be a dangerous one.'

Sven and Stefan looked genuinely offended.

'But . . .' Sven began, clearly trying to come up with a way of saying what he wanted to say without seeming disrespectful. 'I'm sure you'll see that it's not as bad as you think. And you can hardly make a judgement about it when you've not seen it for yourself, can you? You could be the one to voice that opposing point of view.'

'Exactly,' Stefan continued. 'Then we could spar with you in a proper debate. Ultimately, what we want to do is gag our critics with the power of our arguments. To try to muzzle them any other way would be a sign of weakness.'

'Well, maybe, gentlemen. Who knows?' Peter said, attempting to end the conversation.

'It was horrible, wasn't it?'

Peter looked at him quizzically.

'That business yesterday, I mean,' Sven said, surprised that Peter hadn't instantly understood what he meant. 'At the Freemasons, the chairman's murder.'

'Oh, yes, absolutely. Awful,' said Peter.

Sven had been there too, of course.

Sometimes Peter was inclined to compartmentalise all the worlds he lived in – the university, home, his relationship with Fay, the city – as separate things with no connection to each other. When the different worlds collided, it gave him the same feeling he got when he saw someone he only knew from, say, the ticket office at the cinema, and didn't quite recognise them outside of their usual environment.

'I saw it on the news this morning,' Sven said. 'Erik and I had already left by the time the police came.'

'Ah, okay. We were still there. Yes, it was all very distressing. A great tragedy, of course.'

Sven nodded.

'Shall we get going?' Stefan said, tugging at Sven's jacket. 'We said we'd go for a drink.'

When they were gone, Peter tucked his bag under his arm and walked back to his office.

Stefan's words about gagging and muzzling their critics throbbed in his head like the nagging pain of a slowly emerging toothache.

Fragment 3 – The Pilgrims as citizens of Leiden (summer 1611)

The last three years have been difficult ones. Our two attempts to escape from England stripped most of us of every last penny we had, so we came to Leiden with little more than the clothes we were wearing and the few belongings that we could carry.

We have been fortunate that there is no shortage of work here, and that we were able to find lodgings quickly, albeit in the rougher parts of town and having to cram many families under one roof. Daylight struggled to make its way into the first homes we had here, but the same cannot be said of the rainwater, nor the countless rats, mice, lice and who knows what other vermin we shared our dwellings with. Walking through the narrow streets regularly led to the loss of a shoe in the thick mud.

Most of us are employed in the textile factories. It is filthy, backbreaking work. Our paltry wages must pay for the food in our bellies as well as the roofs over our heads. Others work in the city's brewery, or as opticians, joiners, pipe-makers. Some do well, very well, and have set up their own businesses, or even, in one case, teach at the university.

Nicholas (Claverly – PvV) is making a name for himself as a pipemaker, and William has developed a method for teaching people English. Students from Germany, France, Denmark, Belgium and the Netherlands are queuing up to take lessons from him. It is marvellous to hear people from all four corners of Europe speaking to each other in the language that we learned at our mothers' knees. The ease with which people master English using William's system is most impressive. How convenient it would be if the whole world spoke English one day! How much easier it would be to converse with each other. There would surely be many fewer misunderstandings, fewer conflicts and perhaps even fewer wars. Latin is for scholars, but anyone of average intelligence can learn to speak our English!

We try to assemble at John's house every Sunday, whatever else may be going on in our lives. A short time ago, he bought a house in the Kloksteeg, opposite the Pieterskerk, together with some other members of our group. The house has been converted into a home – for John and his family – and a meeting room and church for our congregation. Out of the goodness of his heart, John has had twenty little houses built in the garden for the poorest among those who originally came with him from Scrooby. I am not ashamed to say that my family and I belong to this group. For us, the move to the Netherlands was even more of a wrench than it was for the families with whom we share the garden. I received a good education in England. My family and I were not wealthy, but neither were we without means. We had a house, land, cattle, servants . . . We had some capital. I had a secure job as a town clerk. But we lost everything we owned. Our own hands are all that we have left now, and with these, we try to earn our daily bread. Did we make too great a sacrifice? Do we regret our decision to leave behind our life in England? No, of course we do not! We left hearth and home so that we could finally be free, truly free to lead our lives as we wished and to serve our God as we wished!

There is such an enormous difference between our first home in Leiden and where we live now. Instead of the gloom of a leaky house in one of the city's dark alleys, now I am sitting at a table as I write this, in front of a house set in an enclosed garden with green all around me. We work just as hard as before but coming home afterwards is very different now.

This is where we go to church too. As Separatists, we do not belong in the Reformed Church, and we are not welcome in the other churches in Leiden. This means that we mix less with the rest of Leiden's citizens, but I wonder whether that is such a very bad thing after all. A handful of people from our group have applied for 'poorterschap' which allows them to become official burghers of Leiden. Burghers have more rights and more opportunities, which makes life here easier, especially since poorterschap is compulsory for merchants. But we prefer to remain English subjects, like children sent away by a hard-hearted father, ever hopeful that we might one day return to his good graces.

We have two services on Sundays. The first service is very early in the morning before we have broken our fast. We do not take communion every Sunday, but when we do, we make sure that the sacramental bread, the body of our Lord and Saviour, and the wine, his precious blood that takes away the sins of the world, do not mix with the profane food in our stomachs. We begin by saying a long prayer together. We do this standing up, like loyal subjects standing out of respect for their king. We enjoy singing psalms, without the accompaniment of any instruments. The words soar from our hearts and rise up to God. John reads a passage from the Bible and interprets it for us. He gives us advice and encouragement about how to live a good life. Because choosing the right path is not always easy. He always knows how to find just the right words to send us out of church feeling stronger than when we arrived. Sometimes we feel like sheep among the wolves who need to be as wise as serpents and as innocent as doves. Because even here in Leiden there are quarrels, the same quarrels that we thought we had left behind in Amsterdam! The arguments about predestination – has God already set down the fate of every man in the Book of Life, or can we still control our own destinies? – usually go over my head. Tensions sometimes run high, but I hope that we might be kept out of it all.

Afterwards, we eat a meal together as brothers and sisters. This is the best meal of the week for many of us, although some would be ashamed to admit it. We contribute food for the table according to our means, just as each of us contributes what he can to our shared funds. None of us thinks of it as private property. The smallest coin from a poor widow means as much to us as a larger sum of money from the richest man in the group!

John has prepared us for the possibility that this may not be where we belong, that the day may come when we leave this city. There are other places, other worlds where we could go, must go, if we are to be free, freer than we are here.

We hold a second service in the afternoons. This service

has a different character. Naturally, it opens with prayer, followed by a reading from the Bible with commentary and explanations, but afterwards, we have the opportunity to share our thoughts and concerns with each other as equals. What has been happening? What are our difficulties and worries? Are we all still able to afford food? Does everyone have work? Is anyone struggling with the language? Have there been confrontations with other believers? The women listen to these conversations so that they can learn from what the men discuss with each other. There are no secrets between us.

Sometimes we welcome guests from outside our group. We want them to know that we have nothing to hide. On the contrary, in fact! Occasionally, someone from the university will come to speak to us. And several people have joined our congregation already! The Walloons – the people of the Southern Netherlands – feel especially at home with us.

The little fellow who seemed to be particularly favoured by Josh Nunn is growing into a boy who rarely speaks in public but who seems to increase in confidence by the day. He is a member of Josh's household. Although he still stays close to Nunn's side, I have recently seen him walking through town, usually alone. Sometimes he joins the other boys, but he walks apart from them. The boy's private instruction continues unabated. Perhaps Josh sees in him a future leader of our community and is preparing him for that role.

Chapter 10

The surface of Chief Inspector Rijsbergen's desk was awash with paper: neat stacks of A4, lists of the names of people who were at the Masonic Hall on the Steenschuur on the day of the murder, the building plans, some printouts of the Masonic Hall's website and Wikipedia pages about the Freemasons, and, neatly stored in a clear plastic sleeve, a copy of the napkin that the building manager Frank Koers had found.

Rijsbergen picked the napkin up to take another close look at it. It showed the layout of the Masonic Hall sketched in pen and drawn with such untidy lines that it must have been done in great haste. Thicker lines marked the front and back doors. The almost indecipherable numbers on it appeared to denote distances.

There were actually two drawings: rough outlines of each of the two floors. The temple itself had been drawn in great detail. It showed exactly where everything in the room was, with the correct name scribbled next to it. The nib of the pen had pierced through the paper here and there like it had been resting on something soft.

Like someone's lap?

There were question marks next to some of the places where a door had been drawn; the draftsman probably hadn't been able to access whatever was behind them.

He stared at the napkin, wondering what on earth the drawing could mean.

The sketch was thrown away during the open evening, but that doesn't necessarily mean it was made that same evening, Rijsbergen thought, putting it back on his desk.

The Masonic Hall was kept locked when it wasn't in use, and only a small number of people had a key to the front door.

Anyone who did have a key would be free to come and go as they chose. There would be no need for them to draw a map of the building, quickly and in secret – only to throw it in the bin afterwards . . . So who would make a sketch like this? Why would they emphasise the front and back entrances – as possible escape routes – so clearly? And why would they dispose of it so carelessly when it could be used as evidence? It didn't make sense.

The original sketch had been sent to the lab to be tested for traces of DNA. It was obviously a long shot, but it might lead to some usable evidence. As a last resort, they could take a cheek swab from everyone who had been in the building. That might reveal the identity of the mapmaker.

It's a shame we didn't find the map ourselves before the building manager had a chance to smooth it out so carefully and smear his DNA all over it.

Rijsbergen shook his head as the cogs in his brain whirred. What if the killer – or killers – had had the map in their hands? Throwing it away afterwards would be evidence of an unbelievable level of stupidity. Criminals often did stupid things, of course. For some, it was the DNA on a casually discarded cigarette butt that led to their capture. For others, it was the analysis of bite marks on an apple core found near the scene of a crime. But this? Wasn't it just as easy to shove a paper napkin in your pocket as it was to throw it in the bin? Had they panicked? Had someone seen them doing something?

Rijsbergen could make neither head nor tail of it.

The best they could hope for was that there would be traces of DNA on the napkin, even the smallest amount. On TV trace evidence was enough to put the murderer behind bars in the space of a fifty-minute episode, including the adverts. So these days, it wasn't always easy to make the general public or the victims and their relatives understand why a criminal was still on the loose a week after a crime.

But even if they did find the person the DNA belonged to, they still had to prove that they had drawn the map. Their DNA could have been transferred to the napkin in all sorts of ways. And they also had to prove that the map had been left behind by the suspect rather than by someone else who had been trying to set them up.

He turned on his monitor to reread the notes he had made during his conversation with Tony Vanderhoop earlier that afternoon.

Van de Kooij and some of their colleagues had spoken to the other members of the American delegation. They hadn't been formal interviews, just conversations that were part of the standard procedure of talking to everyone present at the crime scene. Vanderhoop and the others were flying back to Boston that evening.

Vanderhoop had walked into Rijsbergen's office with an air of confidence that seemed typical of Americans. 'Good afternoon,' he had said brightly, shaking Rijsbergen's hand for far longer than was necessary, like he was trying to give an unseen photographer ample opportunity to capture the moment on film.

They took their seats, and Rijsbergen got straight down to business.

'Did you notice anything unusual yesterday?' he asked. 'Anything that might help us with our enquiries?'

Vanderhoop considered the question seriously for a moment, pausing exaggeratedly like an actor who had been directed to look grave and contemplative.

'No, not really,' he said at last. 'We've talked to a lot of people. I've been introduced to a lot of brothers and sisters. Of course, I've forgotten most of their names already. I'm afraid I might not be of much help to you, but . . .'

'But what?'

'But you should know that there have been a lot of threats made to the Boston lodges recently, specifically aimed at the Freemasons. Perhaps it's worth looking into whether something similar is going on here?'

Rijsbergen made a note of this, but he didn't see how threats made so far away could have anything to do with something that had happened here in Leiden. Then his gaze fell on the plastic sleeve with the map inside. He picked it up and showed it to Vanderhoop, who indulged him by examining it but appeared not to recognise it.

'I understand from my colleague that you were in the back garden with several other people on the night in question. Is that correct?'

'That is . . . correct,' said Vanderhoop, on his guard suddenly, like he was considering his answer carefully to avoid walking into a trap. 'We were in the garden talking to people. As I just said, I've forgotten most of their names. I might recognise some of their faces, but I couldn't tell you everyone who was there. It was a pretty big group. Some of them were smoking. Filthy habit . . . I chatted to Peter de Haan. He was with two young men, but I don't remember their names. We went back outside again after the presentation.'

Rijsbergen paused, allowing a meaningful silence to fall

between them, giving the impression that he was on to something but wanted to play his cards close to his chest.

'But what are we looking at here exactly?' said Vanderhoop, who had regained his earlier self-confidence.

'A paper napkin with a map of the building on it. It appears to have been drawn in great haste. The building manager at the Masonic Hall found it in a bin in the refectory.'

'Someone drew a map of the building and then threw it in the trash?'

'That's what it looks like, yes.'

'That's weird, don't you think? Why would someone make this and then throw it away?'

'You tell me.'

Vanderhoop had been staring at the napkin intently, but now he looked up abruptly, as if he had smelled something unpleasant. 'What are you suggesting?' he asked. There was a sudden edge to his voice.

'I'm not suggesting anything at all,' Rijsbergen replied calmly.

'No. Sorry. I'm drawing a total blank here. As I've already said, we were outside drinking coffee with a bunch of other people. After that, we went inside for the presentation. Some of the brothers and sisters talked about why they became Freemasons. Well, according to what I was told afterwards, because obviously the whole thing was in Dutch. I didn't notice anything odd about any of it.'

He stared at the map again.

'No, I'm sorry,' he said. 'I really can't help you.'

Vanderhoop and Rijsbergen had parted warmly in the way you might say goodbye to someone you've met on holiday – with a certain detached cordiality that comes from being confident that you'll never see each other again.

Vanderhoop had given Rijsbergen his business card which the detective had taken carefully between his thumb and fore-finger. The moment Vanderhoop had left the room, the detective pushed the card into a plastic evidence bag with his pen. He sealed the bag and attached a label with the date and the name 'Tony Vanderhoop'.

When the Americans had left, Van de Kooij had come into Rijsbergen's office with some sheets of paper in his hand. He'd yanked out the chair that Vanderhoop had been sitting on and perched on the edge of the seat like he was trying to avoid sitting on the warm spot left by Vanderhoop's backside.

'Are you any the wiser after talking to him?' he asked. 'Do you think he had something to do with it?'

'Who? Vanderhoop?' Rijsbergen asked in reply. 'I don't know. I think he's a bit of an oddball, but that's not much to go on. The only thing he's really got going against him is that he was in the Masonic Hall last night. But so were sixty or seventy other people. I've yet to see anything that looks like a motive. So at the minute, we only know enough to be able to speculate. The same goes for that Peter de Haan fellow and Fay Spežamor . . . it looks like they were just in the wrong place at the wrong time. But who knows what might still turn up? Anyway . . .'

He made a few notes and then put down his pen.

'What about you? Are you any wiser?'

'No, not really,' Van de Kooij replied. 'They were all very nice people, very helpful. Couldn't tell us anything we didn't know already. Took down all their details, obviously, made copies of their passports and so on.'

'Good. How many names do we have now?'

'About sixty, I think. That means we still need to find ten, maybe twenty of them.'

'Well, that's great progress. There's not much more we can do now than go down the list and talk to the people whose names we do have. We'll start with Peter de Haan and his partner. You and I will do them and a couple of others, and you can give the other names to the rest of the team. If we all do five or six, then we'll get through everyone in two or three days. And we'll have the test results for the map back from forensics either tomorrow or the day after.'

Van de Kooij jumped up from the chair. 'Great. I'll get that organised then.'

At least there was one person who was enthusiastic about the task that lay ahead of them.

Chapter 11

Peter sat in his office. Although it was strictly forbidden, he'd lit one of the five cigarillos he habitually smoked each week. Every Sunday evening, he put five of them in a silver-coloured cigar case, one for each weekday. He'd opened the window wide, and now he sat on the windowsill, blowing the smoke outside. It was a pointless exercise because as soon as he blew the smoke out, the wind blew it right back in. But he hoped it would fool the smoke alarm on the ceiling above him.

He mulled over that afternoon's lecture. His response to the use of the term 'genocide' should probably have been more rigorous. Although you could certainly call what happened to the indigenous population a decimation, the word 'genocide' was problematic because it suggested a deliberate plan.

He took a drag on his cigar, held the smoke in his mouth and blew it out through his pursed lips in a long streak.

He was pleased that the other side of the story would also be presented as part of the commemoration of the Pilgrims' departure from Leiden four hundred years ago. It was an opportunity to show the uglier side of history and to highlight the conditions that the Native Americans were living under now.

Peter had called Chief Inspector Rijsbergen as soon as he'd got back to his office.

Rijsbergen had told him that he would be visiting Fay between five and six and that it would be most convenient if Peter could be there at the same time.

It was almost half past three. Peter usually worked until around six, but right now, he couldn't focus at all. He felt an over-whelming need to be with Fay.

There was a knock at the door. It opened before he could answer.

Peter hurled the stub of his cigarillo outside and grabbed the aerosol that was on the windowsill. He always sprayed a few puffs of air freshener around the room to mask the smell after he'd had a cigar.

When the door was fully open, Peter froze with the aerosol still in his hand, like a graffiti artist caught red-handed by the police.

It was Mark. He burst out laughing. 'You know you can smell that cigar smoke all the way down the other end of the corridor, don't you?' he said. 'That air freshener is useless.' He closed the door behind him. 'I just came by to see how you were doing. I heard about what happened last night. Judith told me you and Fay went to that open evening.'

'Thanks, Mark. That's very thoughtful of you.'

There was a three-seater sofa in Peter's office that gave it a homely feel. Mark sat down on it.

'It was awful,' Peter said. 'In one word, awful.'

'Bizarre, too. A murder committed at an open evening with so many visitors.'

'You're right, it was bizarre, but . . . Did you know that Fay and I were the ones who found him?'

'Seriously? Wow!' Mark, who had been sitting on the edge of the sofa, fell backwards so that he ended up looking oddly slumped. 'That's awful,' he said. 'Fay knew him quite well, didn't she?'

'Yes, she did. He was the chairman of her lodge, so she'd spent a lot of time talking to him. I only met him a couple of times myself, but still . . . To find him like that . . .'

Stop talking, Peter told himself sternly.

But Mark didn't seem very interested in hearing about how he and Fay had found Coen Zoutman.

'How's Fay doing?'

'Oh, just as you'd expect.' Peter said. 'Badly, of course. It's really shaken her. She's got no idea who could have done it. A good man, Zoutman. He wouldn't have hurt the proverbial fly.'

'So it's a mystery.'

Peter told him about the Americans he'd met at the American Pilgrim Museum.

'I came straight back here after the tour. Apart from that man, I haven't talked to anyone about it . . . Actually, that's not entirely true. One of my students was there yesterday too. I talked to him about it, but only briefly.'

'And what are you going to do now?'

'Now? I'm going to head home. Well, to Fay's. See how she's doing.' Peter went over to his desk chair to put on his jacket. 'How about you?'

'Back to the office, do an hour there, and then I'll go home too, I think. I want to do a bit of work at home, and then it's my turn to make dinner. Judith cooked last night.'

Peter was very happy with Fay, but even after all these years, he couldn't help feeling a hot, almost visceral stab of jealousy at moments like this. He could try all he wanted to resist it, try to reason the feeling away, bring to mind the cosy domesticity he enjoyed with Fay, sitting outside together in front of her house with glasses of wine in their hands, watching Agapé play with a ball in the little courtyard . . .

But despite all of that, at moments like this, when Mark spoke so easily of cooking for Judith, Peter saw himself in Mark's place, stirring various pans on the hob with a cold beer next to him on the kitchen counter, condensation glistening on the glass. And Judith, coming in rosy-cheeked from the cool air outside, wrapping her arms around him and leaning into his back, tenderly kissing his neck . . .

But anyway . . .

Mark started to get up, but just then, his mobile rang, and he crashed back onto the sofa. He leaned to one side so that he could fish his phone out of his trouser pocket.

'Hello,' he said. Then he listened to the person on the other end of the line for what seemed like an unusually long time.

'Yes, that's right,' Peter heard him say.

'Hmm . . . of course. The Sionshof . . . Yes, that's where I live.' He looked at Peter with furrowed eyebrows, not sure where the conversation was heading. 'What?' he said suddenly, raising his voice. 'They've *what?*' He listened again as the person explained, then said, 'Right. I'm on my way.'

'What was that about?' Peter asked when Mark hung up.

'There was something . . . Uh . . . It was someone from the housing association that manages the complex. I'm their contact person for the Sionshof residents.' He paused. 'Someone's daubed red paint on the outside wall.'

'You're kidding.'

'No. But it's not just that. That would just be a random act of vandalism. This is something else.'

'Meaning?'

'They've turned the word "Zion" over the doorway into "Zionists", and above that, they've written "Death to the".'

'Where's the sense in doing that?'

'It doesn't make any sense, of course. It's called the Groot Sionshof, for heaven's sake.' Mark hissed the first 's', like a snake. 'Supposedly, the stonemason who was supposed to chisel the name over the door made a mistake, and that's why it's written with a "z"' rather than an "s". If protestors wanted to make a point about Israel, doing this makes no sense at all. The Sionshof's got nothing to do with Jews. There's nothing Jewish about it.'

Then they looked at each other in horror. They had both just had exactly the same terrible thought. So it was no surprise when they both said the same name.

Chapter 12

'Judith!' Mark screamed when she answered her phone. He jumped from the sofa with an anxious look in his eyes and put his left hand over his heart like he thought that it might calm it. 'Where are you?' he asked, his voice still much too loud.

Peter, who had been watching Mark anxiously, felt his shoulders drop.

'She's at her office!' Mark shouted, as if Peter was standing on the other side of a town square. 'It's okay, darling,' he said, calmer now. 'I'm so relieved.'

He told Judith what had been done to the doorway of their *hofje*. Judging from his reaction, Peter got the impression that Judith wasn't the slightest bit worried that the stunt might have been directed at her in any way. Mark made one or two half-hearted attempts to connect the vandalism to the fact that she lived there, but the more he tried to convince her, the less likely the link started to seem.

'I'm coming over, darling,' Mark said.

Peter couldn't hear Judith's reply, but it was obvious that she was protesting.

'No, I'm not overreacting,' said Mark. 'I just want to see you. This has given me a fright. I'd rather we went home together.'

Peter heard him say that he would set off immediately. Judith had apparently relented.

'She's at the office,' Mark said again, entirely unnecessarily. He held up his hand and left Peter's office without another word.

Peter sighed deeply, relieved that their panic about Judith had turned out to be a storm in a teacup.

These are strange days, he thought. *It's no wonder my nerves are shot.*

He called Fay.

'Hey,' she said, sounding like she had just woken up from a deep sleep.

'How are you doing, darling?'

'Oh, you know . . . It's just all so sad.'

'I'm coming over, all right?'

'All right,' she said.

'Are Alena and Agapé with you?'

'They've gone to the Antiquities museum. They were going to go for pancakes afterwards.'

'Ah, that's nice.'

'Yes,' Fay said flatly. 'But I ought to go and get dressed. I've got to pick my bike up. I left it at the office yesterday. Oh, never mind. It can wait until tomorrow.'

When Peter arrived at the little house, he heard the shower running. The living room and kitchen were perfectly neat and tidy. Alena had probably had something to do with that.

Although most men would be less than thrilled at the idea of spending so much time with their mother-in-law, Peter got on well with Alena. She was well read, interested in current affairs and able to give her opinions on them in a pleasant, level-headed way.

Fay had been cautious about introducing Peter to Agapé. Her

daughter had only been a few months old when her father had died, and she had no memory of him at all. Fay had been reluctant to bring a new 'father' into her life without being confident that the relationship would last. But there had been a natural easiness between Peter and Agapé from the very beginning. Agapé called Peter by his first name, although Fay had once revealed that she told the other children at school that he was 'sort of like a new dad'.

Two glasses stood invitingly on the kitchen counter next to an opened bottle of red wine.

Peter heard Fay turn off the shower, and less than five minutes later, she was downstairs.

She hugged him, and he pressed his face to her damp, sweet-smelling hair.

'Come on,' she said. 'Let's have a drink.'

She went over to the counter and poured them both a glass of wine.

Once they had settled on the sofa, Peter told her about the paint that had been daubed on the wall of the Sionshof. 'They're so horrible, those anti-Semitic slogans,' she said. 'And so stupid as well. The Sionshof has nothing to do with Zionism at all.'

Fay sighed irritably.

'And no sign of the culprits, I bet,' she said.

'None, I'm afraid. Mark was really worried about Judith. He was scared that someone might have been targeting her.'

'I don't think that's very likely. Do you?'

'No, I'm sure it was just some stupid protestors, and it'll turn out to be nothing. But it's still a rotten thing to do. It doesn't make any sense. It's so pointless.'

'And cowardly.'

As Peter took a second sip of his wine, he noticed that Fay's glass was already empty. She went back to the kitchen to pour herself a second. She knocked it back standing next to the kitchen counter, and then poured a third, filling the glass to the brim.

'Steady on, darling,' Peter said.

'Sorry,' Fay apologised. 'I think I just need something to calm me down.' She carefully carried her wine back to the sofa, watching the glass to make sure she didn't spill any. 'That detective called again,' she told him. 'He was trying to get hold of you, but when he couldn't, he called me. He's coming here with his colleague tonight to speak to us.'

'Yes, I know. We spoke earlier. But why's he coming?' Peter said. 'Didn't we tell him everything yesterday already?'

'He wants to speak to us again, anyway. And he wants to know more about Coen winning the election for the chairmanship. Maybe they think it's got something to do with his murder.'

'Do you think it might?'

'I don't know. There was some . . .' She lowered her voice as if she was afraid that someone was listening. 'The lodge isn't *always* perfectly harmonious. There was some resistance to him becoming chairman.'

'You've never told me that.'

'No, because it was just bickering. Some people were annoyed at yet another man claiming the chair despite us finally having a co-Masonic lodge. Others thought he was too liberal. Some people need more authority, they need a Worshipful Master who's more—'

The harsh clang of the doorbell interrupted her.

Hanging outside next to Fay's front door was a large, old-fashioned bell, a bronze contraption that was rung by pulling on a chain. Each time he heard it, Peter was reminded of play-times at primary school, when that week's bell monitor would ring one just like it to let the children know that it was time to go back indoors.

Peter got up to open the door.

Rijsbergen and Van de Kooij were waiting outside.

'Ah,' said Rijsbergen. 'You're here too. Good.'

They stepped into the living room and sat down. They had both unbuttoned their coats but left them on.

'Would you like something to drink?' Fay asked.

'No, thank you,' Rijsbergen replied. 'We won't keep you long. We just wanted to have another quick chat with you, particularly about the election that you mentioned yesterday. I'd like you to tell us more about that.' He took out a small notebook and opened it on his lap.

'All right,' Fay said.

She spoke with a steady voice, but Peter knew her well enough to tell that she was making an effort not to sound tipsy. She had downed two glasses of wine in less than five minutes.

'I don't have any new information, but there is ... How should I put it?' She took a large gulp of wine. 'Coen was the chairman ...' she began hesitantly. 'He was the first chairman, the first Worshipful Master, since our lodge, the first mixed-sex lodge in Leiden, was established. But his appointment was a bit controversial. There were other candidates at the time, of course, that goes without saying, but Coen won the election. Although "election" is probably too big a word for it. But he won it by a landslide. The overwhelming majority of the members supported him.'

'How was that done, the election?' Rijsbergen wanted to know. 'Did people raise their hands? Did you put votes in a ballot box?'

'That last one, yes,' said Fay.

'Then that would make it just a normal election, wouldn't it?'

'Yes, although there wasn't any campaigning, no election posters and so on. But you need to find out which candidate has the most support. The members rejected the idea of raising hands because it wasn't anonymous, obviously. So a secret ballot made the most sense. Then there's no trouble afterwards, nobody giving other members dirty looks for not supporting them.'

'Well,' Rijsbergen said. 'That may be true, but people will still try to guess who did or didn't vote for them. But anyway, Zoutman won?'

'Yes. He got nearly two-thirds of the votes if I remember correctly. That would have been about forty votes. The two other candidates got about ten votes each.'

'So he would have been able to count on most of the members to support him?'

Fay nodded.

'Do *you* think,' Van de Kooij asked, 'that we should be looking at the people who stood against him?'

'It wasn't really about the position of chairman, as such,' Fay pondered. 'To a certain extent, it's an honorary title. But even so, the Worshipful Master is still first among equals.'

'*Primus inter pares,*' Van de Kooij said, rolling the 'r' of his Leiden accent even more deliberately than usual, Rijsbergen thought.

'That's right,' Fay agreed. 'The Worshipful Master doesn't dictate what we do or anything. But he leads our discussions. And, in a way, he's the face of the lodge to the outside world. He's the one who speaks for us when it comes to things like the open evening. If the lodge is asked for interviews, he's our spokesman. But there was a certain . . .' She was clearly choosing her words carefully. 'There was a certain amount of conflict about how the Worshipful Master should give us guidance. You might not expect that of the Freemasons, but we're only human, after all.'

'What do you mean by that?' Rijsbergen said, taking over from Van de Kooij.

'Freemasons are proud of the fact that we're not dogmatic,' Fay explained, 'and that we give each other room to express points of view that might be different from our own. Everything is open to discussion. Nothing's set in stone. Not even the symbols we use. I think Coen said something about that at the open evening. He was talking about the All-Seeing Eye on the wall behind him. He told us about his own understanding of that symbol, what it meant to him personally, and that other people's interpretations of it could be entirely different, and that was absolutely fine. But there were people with less . . .' She hesitated again. 'I can only describe them as less-enlightened minds. And they weren't content with that. They'd say: "The All-Seeing Eye is the Eye of God that sees all. It provides an incentive to be good even when you're alone, even when there's nobody else around to witness your actions. No other explanation needed. Period. End of discussion."'

'And that's precisely the opposite of the whole spirit of Freemasonry, isn't it?' Peter chipped in.

'You said there was some conflict?' Rijsbergen asked. 'Between?'

'Well, what I just said. Between people who work from a belief in a fixed and indisputable history, that stories should be taken literally, that symbols are one-dimensional, which is a contradiction in terms of course . . .' Fay rolled her 'r's exaggeratedly too, giving Van de Kooij an impertinent sideways glance '. . . because the meanings of symbols can change depending on who's looking at them. Or even *when* they're looking at them, the stage they're at in their life. And on the other side of the conflict, there are people like Coen and like me who focus less on the literal nature of our traditional stories and more on their allegorical meaning, the message behind them, the undercurrents of meaning. And I say "less-enlightened minds"' because to let go of those rigid interpretations takes guts. It takes wisdom and life experience.'

Peter could see a parallel with the way Jesus always told the common people parables, and then he revealed their true meanings to his disciples in the evenings. Ordinary people like farmers and labourers would be content with the simple story and its literal meaning – which could also be said of most people of faith today, too – but those at a higher level, the initiates, could cope with more.

'I don't know if this clash between the two cultures, if you can call it that, would be enough to make someone beat poor Coen to death with a gavel,' Fay said in conclusion. 'But I'm assuming that you don't want to rule out anyone or anything just yet, do you?'

'Yes, correct,' Rijsbergen said. He closed his notebook. 'Right,' he said, in a tone that made clear that, as far as he was concerned, the conversation was over. 'That's all for now.'

'Not entirely,' Fay said.

Peter possibly looked even more astonished than Rijsbergen and Van de Kooij.

'What do you mean?' Rijsbergen asked, opening his notebook again.

'I think . . .' Fay paused for a moment, which had a dramatic effect '. . . that I can explain why they killed Coen the way they did.'

Fragment 4 – John Robinson and the spiritual life of the
Pilgrims (1617)

*I have had the privilege of knowing our spiritual leader, John
Robinson, from the very beginning. Let me tell you more
about him.*

*He was born in 1576 in Sturton le Steeple, a village not far
from Scrooby. He earned a degree in theology at Corpus
Christi College in Cambridge when he was only twenty years
old! It was here that John first became acquainted with
Puritan ideas. He felt an immediate affinity with them.
Elizabeth I was our queen in those days, and you were not
likely to find yourself in trouble if you held beliefs that devi-
ated from those of the Mother Church as long as you did
not stray too far from the path that had been set by Rome.
And all was well until James I – the Dutch call him Jacobus
– ascended the throne. The relative liberty that we had previously enjoyed – although they would laugh here at what we
thought of as 'liberty' – was over. The clergy was brought to
heel almost overnight, and they were forbidden to interpret
the Gospel in their own way. Our John, who had by now
become a pastor, openly preached Puritan ideas from his
pulpit. In the year of our Lord 1603, John was removed from
his position, and it was made clear to him that under no
circumstances was he ever to preach again.*

*However, John was not prepared to abandon what he
believed to be the truth. 'If I were to remain silent, the very
stones would cry out,' he told me.*

*And did he give up? Did he return to his old master like a
whipped dog? No! And that is how we eventually found in him
a marvellous leader, a new Moses to lead us out of our slavery.*

It was not long before he joined the ranks of the Separatists, first elsewhere, but then after a year, he came to our congregation in Scrooby. He soon became one of our leaders. Looking back, John was actually behind many of the decisions that would determine the fate of our group: establishing the Scrooby Church, the flight from England to the Netherlands and the move from Amsterdam to Leiden.

When our original pastor stayed behind in Amsterdam, John became the spiritual leader of the group in Leiden. In 1615, he entered the University of Leiden as a student of theology. John is a seeker of truth. In fact, he has been a seeker of truth his whole life. He rejects nothing, is always open to new ideas. He tests all things and holds fast to what is good. He believes that everything can be discussed, that there should be a free exchange of opinions. 'A discussion can be enlightening even when your opponent spouts blatant nonsense,' he once told me. When I looked at him a little stupidly, he explained to me that, although in the heat of the moment, you might not be able to find the right words to express them, your own ideas only become clear to you when you discuss them with other people, including those who espouse views that are different from your own.

We spend many hours conversing, sitting outside the little house that, because of his great generosity, I can call my home. Now, when I say 'conversing', I make it sound like an exchange of ideas on the same level, between equals, but that is actually not what it is at all. While I never, not for one moment, feel that I am unworthy or inferior, the relationship between us is that of a teacher and his pupil. We are not on the same level. Even after all these years, I can count on the fingers of two hands the number of times that I have been able to surprise him with an insight or answer. But I still glow with pride when I remember the few occasions when John has fallen silent and mumbled something like, 'My goodness, you're right,' or 'I've never looked at it that way,' or 'You've expressed that much better than I could have done.'

If I think back on our conversations, there are three things that we return to repeatedly in one way or another: liberty, equality, and democracy. These are the three principles in which he believes with his whole heart, soul and mind.

John once said to me: 'I hold these truths to be self-evident: that all men are created equal, that they are endowed by their Creator with certain unalienable rights, that among these are life, liberty, and the pursuit of happiness.' He repeated these words to me so that I could write them down because, when he said them the first time – entirely spontaneously, so it seemed to me – they touched my heart so.

He also told me that if we ever have the chance to leave Leiden and build a new society on virgin soil, these words should be the guiding principles upon which it is founded. It will be a modern-day Atlantis, a true Utopia, a new Promised Land. And part of this ideal of liberty that he so reveres and prizes is the freedom to find his own meaning in the Bible. Moreover, John believes that all churches should have liberty, and that they should be independent and free from interference by the state. And as I wrote above, John considers equality to be of the utmost importance because who you are and what you do for a living does not matter. He actively embodies these beliefs in his own life, just by spending time with me. He will discuss anything, without judgement, with me or anyone else who chooses to sit with us – although, secretly, I always hope that nobody else will have the time or opportunity to join us. 'Who are we to judge others?' he once said. 'Only God can decide who will be saved at the Last Judgement.' The third pillar of his philosophy is democracy because the members of the congregation decide for themselves who should lead them. Of course, we also have elders, men who have been elevated to positions above the 'ordinary' members of our congregation, but they are no more than the representatives who regulate our day-to-day affairs. The congregation chooses these elders, and every adult man is eligible to become one. Where could you find more equality than we have here? The congregation can also remove the elders if they fail to discharge their duties satisfactorily.

Sometimes John tries to educate me – and the people who have gathered around us – about the fierce debate taking place within the Dutch Calvinist faith. To be honest, the finer points of it go over my head, yet even the simplest of minds can see that the row, which started with a quarrel between two professors, Gomarus and Arminius, is no longer confined to the Academy but has spilled out beyond its walls and is going on everywhere. From what I am able to understand, according to Gomarus, God judged each of us even before the creation, so we can have no influence over our fate. At most, our actions might give some indication of what awaits us in the hereafter. In contrast, according to Arminius, man can choose whether to follow God's path or not. He gives us free will and the means to make the right choice, but He already knows what our choice will be before we make it. John has confessed to me that on some evenings, when he comes home after the public debates at the university, he is so fired up and agitated that he lies awake for hours, unable to fall asleep. John agrees with Gomarus – a position that clearly curries no favour here in Leiden.

The adopted 'son', as everyone thinks of the boy whom Josh Nunn has taken under his wing, has grown into a handsome, bright young man, a fully fledged member of our congregation. Sometimes he speaks at Sunday worship, which some members tolerate with a measure of reluctance. Or is it jealousy? People object because he has no formal training in preaching God's word and correctly explaining His Scriptures. They never do this openly, of course, but only when they think they are not being observed. A more serious objection is that the boy sometimes has the tendency to interpret things too liberally, as though he is looking for the story that might be hidden behind a story. As though he has found an obscure meaning that, to us mere mortals, remains invisible.

Chapter 13

'What do you mean?' Rijsbergen asked, narrowing his eyes. 'You can explain why they killed Coen the way they did?'

'I have an idea about the murder itself, not about who did it. The symbolism used in the Worshipful Master's murder was unmistakable. But I was still too overwhelmed and tired to realise it the first time we spoke to each other.'

Now she had the detectives' undivided attention. Van de Kooij narrowed his eyes, just as his senior colleague had done.

Peter looked at Fay in surprise. *Why hasn't she told me this*, he thought.

'And which symbols would you say the killer has used?' Rijsbergen asked.

'They're blatantly obvious,' Fay said. 'If you'd not spoken to me today, someone else would probably have told you sooner or later. I'm sure you've seen the three pillars in the temple? They have candles on them that are lit during the ritual and then put out again afterwards.'

Rijsbergen nodded, quickly followed by a nod from Van de Kooij.

'They're the Three Great Pillars, and they're called Wisdom, Strength and Beauty. I could tell you much more about them, but I'll leave that for another day. We Masons say that Wisdom refers to mind or reason, Strength refers to the will, and Beauty refers to feeling or emotion. You could also say that the pillars represent our thoughts, actions and feelings.'

'That sounds logical,' Rijsbergen said.

'The killer was aware of this – or the killers, of course,' Fay continued. 'By the way, do you know yet if it was one killer or more than one?'

'We're still considering every eventual possibility at this stage of the investigation. But, obviously, I wouldn't be able to tell you even if I did know.'

'Of course, of course,' Fay said quickly. 'Right, so, thinking, acting and feeling. The killer bludgeoned the Worshipful Master's head to stop his thoughts. Or at least, that's my theory. They impaled his hands with the compasses so that he wouldn't be able to act; his hands are literally tied. And they destroyed his heart, the source of his emotions, so that he would never be able to feel again.'

While Rijsbergen was writing down Fay's words, Van de Kooij stared intently at his notebook if he wanted to make sure that they were being recorded accurately.

'That probably explains why the killer put so much effort into mutilating the victim,' Rijsbergen said after he had written everything down. 'But it doesn't necessarily mean that the perpetrator was deeply familiar with the symbolism. It's quite possible that the chairman had talked about those things in his presentation that evening. Or that they found out about them on the internet. It's not secret knowledge, is it?'

Rijsbergen had been unable to resist sounding slightly caustic when he said the word 'secret', but if Fay had noticed it, she wasn't letting it show.

'Not at all,' Fay answered calmly. 'That's basically open knowledge. I wouldn't be surprised if you could find that information just by clicking on the top link in a Google search. But you're right: the way the murder was committed only shows that the killer had some knowledge of the symbolism of the three pillars. It doesn't say anything about how long they'd had that knowledge or how they came by it.'

'Right, well, that seems to have cleared up the mystery of the bizarre staging,' Rijsbergen said. 'Let's hope it also brings us closer to solving the case.'

After exchanging a few pleasantries, the detectives left.

Alena and Agapé came home not long afterwards. Fay quickly tipped her wine into the sink and held her face under the kitchen tap to freshen up. Agapé was allowed to stay up for a while before Alena and Fay took her upstairs and put her to bed together, as they did every night.

Alena always told Agapé a bedtime story, never from a book, but always from memory, drawing on an incredible wealth of Greek myths and sagas, Czech folktales and European fairy tales and fables – often chosen according to the season or what was happening in the girl's own life. Alena had been a much-loved teacher once; even the rowdiest pupils would hang on her every word as soon as she began to tell one of her stories.

Peter often listened in on Alena's stories. She had the voice of an expert narrator, and in just a few words, she could conjure entire worlds filled with fairies, elves, abandoned orphan children, gods and heroes, and all of the exciting adventures they had. If she was telling the story for the second or third time, she invented new details or gave it a twist so that her audience was always enthralled.

Peter opened Fay's laptop to check his emails. She had left

her Outlook mail client open. Just as he was about to close it, he noticed the name Fay had given to one of the many folders that she'd made.

Fay was a very well-organised person. She always dealt with emails promptly, and her inbox never contained more than a couple of messages. She answered them immediately and either deleted the original email or filed it somewhere in one of many folders.

One of them was labelled 'Coen Zoutman'.

There was a (1) next to his name, which meant that it contained an unopened email. It looked like Fay had set up a filter so that his emails would be sent directly to this folder.

That's strange, Peter thought. *She never told me she'd been emailing him at all.*

He glanced at the stairwell to see if anyone was coming, but he couldn't hear anything. He opened the folder and saw that Fay and Coen had emailed each other frequently over the last few days.

Peter debated whether to open one of the emails. He decided against it, but the first line of each message was shown on the screen anyway.

Coen Zoutman

I hope we'll find a moment to talk face to face . . .

Coen Zoutman

You're right, Fay, as always . . . ☺ It's a delicate . . .

Coen Zoutman

Don't tell anyone what we have discussed Fay. It is . . .

Coen Zoutman

I understand that you're eager to find out exactly what I want you to . . .

Coen Zoutman

Don't be alarmed when you read this, but I have a strange feeling . . .

Peter sat frozen, frustrated by his own sense of integrity. He didn't want to betray Fay's trust. But when he moved the mouse to close the folder, he accidentally clicked on one of the unopened messages.

He cursed under his breath.

Coen Zoutman

That's fine, Fay. I'll see you this evening!
Regards, Coen

The mail had been sent the previous day, a few hours before the murder.

What should I do, Peter brooded, restlessly moving the cursor back and forth over the screen.

There are some other unopened emails in the inbox, so she mustn't have looked at her mail at all today. There's nothing important in this message. And if I leave it, she'll know that I've been reading her emails . . .

He heard footsteps at the top of the stairs.

He hastily clicked on the email to delete it, and then he opened the 'deleted messages' folder and deleted it permanently. He closed Outlook and opened his own mail client. Just as he saw Fay's lower legs appearing on the stairs, the Outlook website disappeared from the screen and was replaced by the Leiden University homepage.

'All work and no play makes Peter a dull boy,' Fay said with a smile when she got back downstairs.

Alena was still upstairs.

'What are you up to?' she asked.

'Nothing, I . . .' He logged into his work email. 'Just checking my email. But there's nothing important.' He quickly clicked on a random message before looking back up at Fay. 'How's Agapé?' he asked. 'Did it take her long to fall asleep?'

'No,' Fay said, smiling warmly at him. 'She was out almost before Mam had finished her story.' She sat next to Peter on the sofa, tucked her legs underneath her and leaned against him. He put his arm around her.

'This can all wait until tomorrow,' he said, closing the laptop and putting it on the coffee table.

'Good.' Fay kissed his neck and snuggled into him.

He usually treasured moments like these, but now he felt odd, like it wasn't his own, familiar Fay sitting next to him, but a stranger.

What are you hiding from me, he thought.

'I don't think it's all sunk in yet, everything that's happened,' said Fay. 'Poor Coen . . . I hope they find whoever did it soon.'

This isn't the time to ask about that long email conversation with Coen, Peter thought. *There'll be another opportunity to ask her about it soon enough.*

'Come on,' Fay said with what sounded like forced cheerfulness. 'Let's just watch a film. We could talk all night about what happened, but it won't do us any good.' She turned on the television and pressed play on a film they'd recorded a while ago.

Peter looked down at Fay now and then as they watched the film. She was focused so intently on the television that a little furrow of concentration had appeared between her eyebrows.

What are you not telling me, Peter wondered. *How well do I know you? How well can you ever know someone?*

When the film ended, Fay sat up and peeled herself away from him. She mumbled something that sounded like 'bed' and went upstairs.

Peter stayed behind on the sofa for a while. He pulled the laptop onto his knee and opened it.

Fay had just one password for all of her programs and accounts, a combination of her name and Agapé's and the year Agapé had been born.

I might as well read them, Peter thought. *She's not likely to find out, and I've already seen one of them anyway.*

He opened Outlook and clicked on the 'Coen Zoutman' folder.

His index finger hovered for at least a minute over the left mouse button that would open one of her emails with a single click.

But I don't want to be in the kind of relationship where you secretly read each other's emails. That's the beginning of the end.

He clicked everything away.

I'll ask her about it tomorrow. Then she'll be able to tell me about it herself. There's probably a simple explanation.

He gently closed the laptop again.

And why should lovers tell each other everything? Fay doesn't know everything about me, does she?

He was tired, and it would have been the easiest thing in the world to crawl into bed next to Fay, but he felt like he really needed to spend the night in his own bed. He wasn't sure he could bridge the distance he felt between himself and Fay now simply by lying next to her.

Standing at the kitchen table, he wrote a note telling her that he had an early start the next morning and had gone home because the books he needed were still at his place.

I'm not being entirely honest, he thought.

But neither is Fay.

Chapter 14

The next morning, Rijsbergen and Van de Kooij visited the morgue. There was no doubt about the cause of death in the Zoutman case, but Rijsbergen wanted to speak to the pathologist and get the latest update from the man himself. They were likely to have found items on the victim's body that would prove useful. Receipts, notes, business cards . . . in his pockets, in his wallet . . . No stone would be left unturned at this stage. Everything was potentially an important clue.

The investigation team had been able to speak to roughly half of the people on their list in a short amount of time. Although everyone on the list had had the opportunity to murder Coen – they had, after all, been in the building when he was killed – the team had been able to eliminate them as suspects with a reasonable amount of confidence. In general, they seemed to be ordinary, good-hearted people in their sixties and seventies. Most of them had gone downstairs to the drinks reception immediately after the Worshipful Master's talk. Those who had stayed upstairs to ask him questions had joined the others not long afterwards. It was difficult to imagine – although not entirely impossible – that one of these guests might have made some excuse, perhaps that they were going to the toilet, then gone back upstairs after the question and answer session, stove the Worshipful Master's skull in, bored through his hands and heart, and then calmly gone back downstairs to rejoin the other guests. Moreover, the extreme violence used in the murder would have demanded a physical strength that these older guests were unlikely to possess.

The whole thing was so chaotic. There were too many people involved. There had been too many people in the building that evening, people who all left behind their shoeprints, fingerprints and hairs.

Van de Kooij turned the car into the morgue's car park.

The reception desk was in a hall that was far too large for the purpose, and empty except for two sofas, a side table and the row of hooks where they hung up their coats. It had a glass roof that looked like it had been added after the morgue was built, perhaps in a desperate attempt to let some light into this realm of the dead.

Despite his long career, Rijsbergen had rarely dealt with murder cases in Leiden. He could count on one hand the number of times he'd been to the morgue. Like most people – or at least, he had always assumed that most people would share his feelings on this – he found visiting this building intensely unpleasant. It was difficult to understand why anyone would willingly study for so many years just so that they could then spend the rest of their lives cutting up people's bodies to find out how they had died.

Van de Kooij, on the other hand, was bouncing along next to Rijsbergen so energetically that he seemed almost thrilled at the prospect of seeing Zoutman's corpse again.

Pieter-Nicolaas van Eijk was waiting for them behind the security door. He was a cheerful man in his forties with a badly receding hairline and fashionable, black glasses with chunky frames. He wore bright orange sneakers and tight, new-looking jeans with a spotless white lab coat on top. Before he shook hands with them, he handed Rijsbergen and Van de Kooij identical lab coats.

'Here,' Van Eijk said. 'Put these on, and we'll go downstairs.'

They descended a wide staircase that led to a small hallway where several corridors met. Each corridor was sealed with a sliding glass door.

Why are these places always underground, Rijsbergen wondered.

Van Eijk punched a code into a small keypad next to one of the doors. It slid open with a gentle hum. A long corridor stretched out in front of them. The polished linoleum floor reflected the light from the evenly spaced, oblong florescent lamps on the ceiling. They passed a series of dark red doors, all of which could only be opened by entering a code into a keypad on the wall.

Framed posters had been hung on the walls at regular intervals. Rijsbergen realised with surprise that they were all Dutch poems on the theme of death. He noted with satisfaction that he was familiar with most of them.

At the end of the corridor, they went left. Van Eijk stopped so abruptly that Rijsbergen and Van de Kooij bumped into him.

Van Eijk pressed the buttons on the door lock, keeping it covered with his left hand. 'I don't think you'll be too surprised to hear that I haven't much to say about the cause of death,' he said as they entered the room.

Is it really colder here than it was in the corridor, Rijsbergen thought. *Or is it just my imagination?*

Inside, a long wall was neatly divided into ten silver-coloured squares with handles, behind each of which was a drawer containing a body. A tall, narrow metal table stood in the middle of the room laid out with instruments, knives, spatulas and shiny metal bowls in various sizes.

Van Eijk walked to the only drawer that had a label hanging from the handle. He pulled it open, and the bier behind it slid out smoothly, almost silently, revealing a corpse hidden under a white sheet.

'Could you tell us something about what you found, anyway?' Rijsbergen asked.

'Certainly,' Van Eijk replied. 'I'll give you a copy of the report shortly, but I can briefly summarise the cause of death. Penetrating skull fracture caused by two, perhaps three blows to the back of the head with a hard object. I have absolutely no doubt that he was dead before he hit the floor. It's obvious that whoever did this was very strong. It would have taken a huge amount of physical strength. Or rage . . . In any case, he – or she, we can't rule that out – was at least as large as the victim, possibly slightly larger. Probably someone right-handed otherwise they would have struck the other side of his head. Meneer Zoutman's blood would probably have spattered onto the killer's clothing. In my opinion, the initial blow would have been enough to kill him.'

'And the compass stabbed through the hands . . .' Van de Kooij began and then trailed off.

'Yes, that was done post-mortem, when the blood had already stopped circulating. Well, it's all in the report. We can at least be sure that Meneer Zoutman wasn't tortured before he was dealt the blow that killed him.'

'So they weren't trying to extract information from him,' Van de Kooij concluded. He was standing right next to the mortuary cabinet, like he was trying to prove that he was a hardened copper and not afraid of death.

Rijsbergen kept a few metres' distance.

'No, not very likely,' Van Eijk agreed. 'But that's your area of expertise, so I'll leave the interpretation of those injuries to you.'

Rijsbergen smiled. 'Unless you are good at guessing, it is not much use being a detective,' he said in English.

'Uh . . . I guess so,' Van Eijk said uncertainly.

'Stabbing the heart and the hands was an overtly symbolic act,' Rijsbergen said. 'Or so it's been explained to me. The Freemasons are concerned with thoughts, feelings and actions. The man who killed Coen Zoutman—'

'Or woman,' Van de Kooij butted in.

'The *man* who . . .' Rijsbergen continued irritably, but then thought better of it and paused. 'Or do you think that a woman would be capable of something like this?' he asked Van Eijk.

'We can't rule anything out,' Van Eijk replied. 'It would have to have been a damned strong woman, but they do exist.'

'Why did you open the drawer by the way?' Rijsbergen asked. 'Was there something you wanted us to see?'

'There is. I want to show you two things, actually. First, there's something on the body, a tattoo of something that I don't recognise.' He picked up a corner of the sheet. 'I'm going to pull back the cover,' he warned them, 'but just enough for you to be able to see the tattoo.'

'Yes, thanks. Much appreciated,' Rijsbergen said, but Van de Kooij was visibly having trouble hiding his disappointment.

Van Eijk folded the sheet back, revealing part of the left side of Zoutman's body. His arm, stretched out straight next to his body, was milky white.

Rijsbergen was overcome by a feeling of deep sorrow.

So this is where we all end up . . . he thought. *All our knowledge and experience, all our wisdom . . . What good does it do us? What do we take with us? What do we leave behind?*

Rijsbergen knew without touching the body that it was stone cold; it had the cool, hard look of carved marble.

Van Eijk took a thin, retractable rod from his breast pocket and pointed it at Zoutman's body next to his left breast where his armpit began. There was a tiny tattoo there, no bigger than a five- cent coin.

He walked away for a few moments then came back with a magnifying glass and gave it to Rijsbergen.

Holding the magnifying glass in front of his right eye, Rijsbergen leaned forward to examine the tattoo. It felt strange to look at another person's skin so closely, especially that of a dead person. The wrinkles, the little hairs, the moles and other imperfections were so clearly visible. It was a profoundly intimate act – one that the deceased was unable to object to.

The tattoo was of a triangle pointing upwards. Just above the base of the triangle, on the right and on the left, were two short, horizontal lines that led to the two sloping sides of an inner triangle positioned parallel to the outer edges of the larger triangle. It looked like a peak on a hospital heart monitor. A small circle had been drawn over the apex of the inner triangle.

'That is indeed . . . unusual,' Rijsbergen said slowly. He handed the magnifying glass to Van de Kooij, who was hopping impatiently from foot to foot.

'I've photographed it,' Van Eijk said. 'I've had it enlarged to make the detail easier to see when you show it to people.'

'Could you give me a piece of paper?'

'Sure. Come over here.'

Van Eijk walked over to an oak desk in the corner of the room. It was sturdy and old-fashioned and looked out of place in such sterile and utilitarian surroundings.

Rijsbergen made a sketch of the tattoo with a pencil, hoping that copying it might bring some knowledge or memory to the surface of his mind. He showed the drawing to Van Eijk.

Van Eijk nodded. 'It looks a bit like a pyramid,' he said.

'Yes, or . . .' Rijsbergen said thoughtfully 'Or *two* pyramids, one inside the other. Or two mountains with a . . . a sun in between them?'

'Yes, that's what it makes me think of too. A sun.'

'You really need to . . .' Rijsbergen started, still sounding irritated. He held the sketch of the tattoo at arm's length. 'It reminds me more of . . .' he continued, more calmly now. 'It reminds me of the All-Seeing Eye that we saw in the temple. Remember? It was on the wall behind Zoutman's chair. Anyway . . . we'll show it to the experts. Maybe they can tell us more.'

It was only now that he noticed the clothes rack in the room. It looked like it belonged in a dry cleaners – a free-standing rail with plastic covers on hangers dangling from it. The blood on Coen Zoutman's clothing was clearly visible, even through the plastic.

'And what was the other thing you wanted us to see?' Van de Kooij asked.

'Ah, that's in here,' Van Eijk said, and he picked up a heavy envelope from his desk. He opened it and removed a sealed plastic evidence bag.

'This is from his jacket, all found in different pockets. It looks like he wasn't carrying a wallet or a phone.'

He passed the bag to Rijsbergen who saw immediately that

as well as a business card, some bank cards and bits of paper, it contained a long, white envelope.

'Did you open the envelope?'

'No, it wasn't sealed. We read the letter inside. But it's not actually a letter. It's Bible stories. We found fingerprints on both the envelope and the paper, but they all belonged to the victim. The contents of the letter might be useful to you.'

'Maybe he wanted to give the envelope to someone that evening,' Van de Kooij suggested. 'But didn't. Or couldn't.'

Without removing it from the evidence bag, Rijsbergen looked closely at the business card that Coen Zoutman must have used as chairman of the lodge. It gave his name, his title, and the website and contact details of the Masonic Hall on the Steenschuur.

His attention was drawn to a sort of logo or symbol that filled the entire left half of the card.

He held his sketch of the tattoo next to the business card.

'They're similar, right?'

Van Eijk and Van de Kooij leaned forwards to study the two images.

'Yes, they are,' Van de Kooij admitted somewhat grudgingly.

'I see that they're both triangles, yes,' Van Eijk said. 'With circles inside them . . . It could be a variation on the same theme.'

'Yes,' said Rijsbergen.

He opened the evidence bag and shook the contents out onto a table: the business card, the bank cards, the pieces of paper and the envelope.

Van Eijk passed a box of latex gloves around, and they all pulled a pair on. He took the sheets of paper out of the envelope. The pages were densely covered in writing in an ornate, unmistakably old-fashioned hand.

Rijsbergen read out the text at the top of the page. It appeared to be a motto that Coen Zoutman had given to his writing, like an epigraph in a book.

> Do you still not perceive or understand? Are your hearts
> hardened? Do you have eyes, and fail to see? Do you
> have ears, and fail to hear?
>
> MARK 8:17–18

'This is . . .' Rijsbergen leafed through the rest of the pages. 'This is quite a lot of text. Could we get a copy?'

'There's a copy in the file that I'm going to give you,' Van Eijk said. 'Along with the autopsy report, photos of the tattoo, copies of the business card and the bank cards and so on. Everything's been scanned, so I'll send you everything via email later, too.'

'Thanks,' Rijsbergen said, giving the letter back to him. 'This only seems to deepen the mystery further, but there's a good chance that there's something in here that will help us to complete the puzzle at some point.' He took off the latex gloves.

Van Eijk handed Rijsbergen a folder.

They all walked back to the exit together.

'Those poems on the corridor . . .' Rijsbergen said. 'They're a nice touch.'

Van Eijk beamed.

'Yes,' he said brightly. 'My pet project. Poetry and love go hand in hand, but there's poetry in death too.'

Fragment 5 – William Brewster and the Pilgrim Press (1619)

The other person to whom I would like to dedicate a few pages in this account is William Brewster. He was born in Scrooby, so he knew everyone in the group, some literally from the day they were born. The same was true of his father. He was the postmaster in Scrooby, which meant that he knew all the families in Scrooby and the surrounding areas too.

The Brewster family lived in Scrooby Manor, a fortified manor house that had hosted kings on their journeys through England. The postmaster's job came with a generous salary, so Brewster Snr was able to send William and his brothers to a good university. William studied at the University of Cambridge, and by 1583, he had advanced to the position of personal assistant to Sir William Davidson, Queen Elizabeth's Secretary of State. William had already visited the Netherlands on diplomatic missions between 1584 and 1587. He also visited Leiden on those trips. So, when we were searching for a new home after our unhappy sojourn in Amsterdam, he was the first to suggest the city of Leiden.

He was always reluctant to speak of it, but his employer, Sir William Davidson, had somehow been involved in a failed plot to assassinate Mary Stuart. Whether this was the case or not, the suggestion alone was enough to cause Sir William to fall out of favour with Queen Elizabeth, who punished him by fining him so heavily that he was ruined.

Because of this, William lost his job as Davidson's assistant. He returned to us in Scrooby, where he was eventually able to succeed his father as postmaster. One of the rules imposed on every civil servant was the requirement to conform to the state religion, the Church of England. At first, William did so faithfully, or at least he kept up the appearance of doing so. But as time went on, he became increasingly troubled by it.

Our region was known to be sympathetic to the Puritan and Separatist ideas that William had learned about at Cambridge. It was at this time that I truly got to know him. Of course, I knew of him before then, but this was when he began to attend the sermons given by Separatist preachers. Eventually, he invited Reverend Richard (Clyfton – PvV) to visit him at Scrooby Manor.

Reverend Richard visited often, and this led to the manor house becoming the principal meeting place for all the Separatists in the area.

I also regularly attended the meetings at Scrooby Manor. Somewhat to our surprise, the authorities did not bother themselves with us for the first year or two. We did nothing to undermine the state, naturally. But William was still an official in the service of the government who was very conspicuously not observant of the state religion. Perhaps we should have been content with what we had. Perhaps we should have kept a low profile. But in 1606, motivated by our fervent desire to practise our faith in the way we saw fit, we established the Scrooby Separatist Church.

Unfortunately, the founding of our church coincided with the appointment of a new Archbishop of York. Like anyone in a new role, he was eager to demonstrate that he was the right man for the job. He made it his immediate mission to shut down all of the non-conforming churches.

When the closure of our church was announced, we realised that we could have no future in England. William told that there was freedom in the Netherlands and that the Dutch were tolerant of other faiths. We started to make plans to escape to the Low Countries.

The new archbishop summoned William before the ecclesiastical court for his role in founding our church. He failed to appear, but he could not have done so even if he had wanted to. He was in Boston prison after our first failed attempt to leave the country.

He was sentenced in absentia and ordered to pay a fine. A warrant was issued for his arrest. However, the officer charged with arresting William could not find him and had no idea where he was. Unbelievably, the authorities were not aware of the fact that William was already under lock and key!

When William was finally released, we made a second attempt to leave the country. This time, we succeeded.

William lives close by now. His front door is on the Stinksteeg, but his home is officially part of another house on the Pieterskerk-Choorsteeg. There is such a great shortage of housing in Leiden that the house where William lives was built right behind another house. The new part continues behind the house next door so that it is shaped like the letter 'L'. It is an unusual construction, but it has been most advantageous because, in 1616, William came up with the idea of setting up our own printing house, the Pilgrim Press. The building's odd shape meant that the press could be concealed away from prying eyes.

More and more people were asking John to set his ideas down on paper, which he eventually agreed to do. He could have had his book printed at one of the many presses here in Leiden instead of setting up his own. However, there was another reason for us to have our own printing house. Publishers in England are still subject to strict censorship laws, which makes it difficult to obtain books that contain non-conformist ideas.

If a government is afraid of ideas that are different from its own, surely that means that it is aware that its own ideas are wrong? That is what John always says. If they are so convinced that they alone have the truth, and that nothing is superior to their beliefs, then why are they afraid of us and what we believe? By definition, the absolute truth will always withstand any challenge from an idea that is less true, so wouldn't our false beliefs doom us to failure?

If our plan is of man, it will fail. But if it is of God, they will not be able to defeat us. In that case, they may even find themselves to be fighting against God. So where did this fear of us and of our ideas come from?

And so, we decided to start our own press. I write 'we', but my role in this operation is modest, of course. At the same time, the word is a sign of our group's unity and shows how much we all have an interest in the endeavours of each member of our community, whatever they might be.

Now that we have our own typesetting equipment, we can print books that are banned in England. Sometimes, not even Dutch printers will dare to publish the most inflammatory works. The Netherlands may be a liberal country, but printers must still include their name and address in everything they publish so that they can be called to account if necessary. And this is why the unusual construction of William Brewster's house is perfect for us. He gives his home address as the Stinksteeg, but his house is officially part of the house on the Pieterskerk-Choorsteeg, and that is where he has registered the Pilgrim Press. It won't fool many people in Leiden, but it will not be easy *for the authorities in England to find out who or what is behind the press.*

I have lost count now of how many books we have printed since we started the press. Somewhere between fifteen and eighteen, I think. They include volumes that anyone could have printed without calling trouble upon themselves, but there have also been works that would be seen as pernicious in England.

I think we may have overplayed our hand by publishing our last book, Perth Assembly by David Calderwood, which, put simply, gives a very different view of the Articles of Faith than the official view dictated by James I. This book could not have been printed in England, so David Calderwood came to us, or rather, to William. They eventually smuggled the book to Scotland in wine barrels, an adventure worthy of its own book! But when the English authorities found out that the book had been printed and distributed, the wrath of the king himself was brought down upon us. An investigation was launched to discover where the book had come from. It reached a dead end in England, but the trail soon led to the Netherlands, the usual suspect for any book of suspicious origin. I do not know how they discovered William so quickly, but I know that it did not take long for them to ask the Dutch authorities and then the Leiden city council to find him. We understand that this has created a huge dilemma for the Netherlands because they want their relationship with England to remain cordial. But at the same time, what is all their talk of freedom worth if they allow those freedoms to go by the board at the first sign of a storm? If they hand over a man who sailed to the free port of Leiden in search of those freedoms? Isn't the freedom to say and write and print and publish what you want of great importance to the Dutch? It is an essential part of who they are!

William's business partner, Thomas (Brewer – PvV), was summoned to the town hall. He told them honestly that William was in Leiden. The authorities asked William and Thomas if they would surrender themselves, to which the men agreed. They hoped that this would help to defuse the situation. Soon afterwards, they were voluntarily imprisoned in the town hall. They were prepared to suffer for a nobler, more worthy cause rather than deny their most deeply held beliefs purely to prolong their temporary existence here on earth by a few breaths.

And, yes, they did knowingly and wilfully disobey the law by not stating the name and address of the printer in the book. The Synod of Dordrecht (1618–1619 – PvV) brought an end to the absolute freedom of the press in the Netherlands: it was now forbidden to publish literature that was not in accordance with the official teachings of the Dutch Reformed Church. All of this ultimately led us making the decision, with pain in our hearts, that the Pilgrim Press must be shut down.

William asked the city's officials to allow him to end his voluntary detention. Permission was granted, but now he is in hiding, afraid that sooner or later, he will be extradited to England. He seems to have judged the situation very well; the English ambassador was beside himself when he learned that William had escaped his clutches. He even issued an official warrant for his arrest, but William remained untraceable.

The English government next focused its anger on Thomas, whom they held responsible for William's escape. To make the investigation into the affair easier for the English, the Dutch government was prepared to surrender him to England for questioning on the strict condition that he was to be returned to the Netherlands within two months. England agreed. The Netherlands offered more security to a subject of the English king than the English king himself was prepared to offer. We think that were it not for this agreement, Thomas would not have survived his stay in England.

It is clear that our time here is coming to an end . . .

Chapter 15

Peter looked at the clock radio. It was after eight o'clock. Whenever possible, he liked to start his working day at 8 a.m., so he usually got up at around seven.

He'd been staying at Fay's a lot recently, but now, for the first time in weeks, he'd had a good night's sleep.

Maybe I should spend the night in my own bed more often, he thought. *And it might actually be a good idea for me and Fay to give each other some space for a while.*

Spending so much time together in her little house was lovely, but with four people living there, it often felt crowded.

He grabbed his phone to see if he'd had any messages while he'd been asleep. He had sent Judith a WhatsApp message before he went to sleep, asking about the graffiti over the Sionshof door. Sometimes they texted each other in the mornings while they were both still in bed – Mark was usually downstairs working already or making coffee.

But Peter could see that she hadn't been online since the previous evening.

Just as he was about to put his phone down again, he noticed that the little checkmarks next to his message to Judith had turned blue. Her status changed from 'Last seen yesterday at 23:17' to 'Online' and then to 'Typing . . .'

It appeared that she had a lot to say because it took a while for her message to appear.

Judith

Hey! Good morning! Everything's fine here. Someone came to clean the wall. It turned out to be the sort of paint that's easy to remove, probably something water-based, but I wouldn't know. Police said that their chances of catching whoever did it are practically zero. They'll make some house-to-house inquiries, but none of the neighbours has a view of that door from their own houses. Someone passing by might have seen something, but the culprits will no doubt have had someone on the lookout.

                                                            8:04

Peter

Good morning, Gorgeous. ☺

                                                            8:04

Peter

Glad it's being taken care of. Still annoying, though. Worried?

                                                            8:04

Judith

Yes, it's just annoying, a stupid stunt like that . . . So no, not really worried. Fairly sure they wouldn't have known someone Jewish lives here.

Peter

No.

8:05

Judith

They want to make a statement about the Israeli occupation of Palestine? Fine. I'd probably agree with their arguments. But to vandalise a courtyard wall because it happens to have the word 'Zion' over the door is plain idiocy.

8:05

Judith was a member of Een Ander Joods Geluid, 'A Different Jewish Voice'. It was a Jewish organisation that focused on the Israeli-Palestinian conflict and the situation in Israel. Its members wanted Israel to cease its occupation and end its human rights violations, a stance that was unpopular with Jews both inside and outside Israel's borders.

Judith

Ugh. It's so annoying.

8:05

Peter

I know . . . But the police must be aware of any groups in Leiden that might do this sort of thing. Leiden really isn't big enough for there to be all sorts of political cells operating under the police's radar. ☺

8:05

Judith

I'm sure you're right. But anyway, I'm just going to assume it was a one-off. Mark was rattled. He's such a sweetie. He thought it was specifically aimed at me.

8:05

An icon appeared in the top left corner of his screen to tell him that he had another message.

That can wait, he thought, and he carried on typing.

Peter

That was my first thought too, you know.

8:06

Judith

And you're a sweetie too. xxx

8:06

He felt a stab of something between pain and pleasure in his abdomen.

Judith

I'm going to get up. Mark is already downstairs, and I can smell coffee . . . Maybe see you later today? Lunch? Much love.

8:06

Peter

Sure. I'm going to have a quick coffee and get going. 1 pm?

8:06

No reply came to his last message, no matter how many times he looked at his phone.

The other message was from Fay. She hadn't added any emoticons, but she hadn't needed to. Her anger was almost bursting out of the little screen.

Fay

Have you been reading my email?

8:05

Trouble in paradise . . . Peter thought.

He started to type a reply, but then he stopped. He knew he really ought to call her to clear the whole matter up, although he didn't understand why there was a matter that needed clearing up in the first place. Whenever he used her laptop to check his mail or read the news, Outlook had almost always been left open. Suddenly, he felt enormously irritated by her message and annoyed by the lack of trust it implied.

For goodness sake, she's the one who's been hiding things, he thought. *So who should be pointing fingers here?*

Now that she knew he had been looking at her emails, he actually regretted not reading them all.

Fay would know from the little blue ticks that he had read her WhatsApp message. She would also have seen that he had started to type a reply and then stopped.

You're angry, are you? Well, now I'm angry, Peter thought. He decided not to reply just yet. *It might be childish but let her stew for now.*

There were no more messages from her after that.

She'd be justified in seeing it as an admission of guilt if I don't reply, Peter realised. *But how does she even know that I was looking at her emails?*

A series of messages from Piet van Vliet arrived in quick succession. Piet was a linguistics specialist who worked for the heritage organisation Erfgoed Leiden en Omstreken whose premises were on the Boisotkade.

Peter waited until Piet had finished typing.

Piet

A very good morning to you, dear Peter! Can I pop by to see you today? I have something fantastic to show you!!!

8:06

Piet

As an expert on the history of Leiden, I'm sure you'll find it interesting. I thought of you straight away.

8:06

Piet

I've chanced upon a previously undiscovered manuscript written by one of the Pilgrims. A rare glimpse into the Pilgrims' world through the eyes of an insider.

8:08

Piet

It sheds new light on the time the Pilgrims spent in Leiden, but it raises lots of new questions too!

8:08

Piet

It's too much to write in a text. I'll drop by this morning. See you later, Piet.

8:10

Peter

I'll be at my office within the next hour. No appointments for the rest of the day except lunch with Judith. Come in any time, and I'll see you when you get there.

8:12

Piet

Great. Then I'll see you soon. I have to go to the library anyway. Give my fondest regards to the delightful Mevrouw Cherev!!

8:12

The delightful Mevrouw Cherev . . .

Judith was a regular visitor to the city archive. Piet had told Peter on more than one occasion that he enjoyed her visits enormously.

We're such old letches, Peter thought irritably.

He decided to completely turn off his phone.

I'll leave Fay hanging for a while, he thought. *What a strange state of affairs this all is . . . Tensions among the Masons because of an election? Fay having long email conversations with Coen that she never told me about?*

He took a shower and then drank a cup of tea in his tiny kitchen. He'd lived in his flat in the low-rise, three-storey apartment block that belonged to the University of Leiden for twenty-five years now. It was part of a large complex that took up a sizable part of the Boerhavenlaan and stretched around the corner onto the Van Swietenstraat. It was home to many of the academics from other countries who had temporary contracts with the university, and doctoral candidates and visiting professors, but also people like Peter who had carried on living there after finishing his PhD.

The flat was actually too big for him: a spacious living room, a bedroom, a study and even a guest room, although he couldn't remember the last time he had hosted a guest. Instead, it hosted a clothes airer permanently covered in drying laundry, and an ironing board where he ironed exactly one item of clothing at a time – whatever he was going to put on that day. Leaning against the guest bed was a racing bike that he'd bought on impulse because he'd thought he should get more exercise, but so far, he'd hardly used it at all.

His phone was still switched off when he walked down the long Boerhavenlaan towards the Rijnsburgerweg. As he strolled under the enormous rustling poplars that lined the whole street, he looked enviously at the huge townhouses at the end of the Boerhavenlaan, imagining what it would be like to live in one of them. But he would never be able to afford anything like that on his salary, and anyway, what would he do with three, or maybe even four times as much space?

He walked through the railway tunnel, negotiating the chaotic tangle of badly parked bikes, and headed towards Schuttersveld.

The sundial at the De Valk windmill had sadly been removed to make way for the redevelopment of the square and the addition of the deepest car park in Europe – a seven-storey underground lot that had been under construction for years.

This walk had become part of his morning routine over the last twenty-five years. He walked past the small dock on the Prinsessekade and onto the Rapenburg, the city's most beautiful canal, known as Leiden's *'Goudkust'* or 'Gold Coast'. At one time, he'd been in the habit of taking a photo here on the same spot at the same time each day. But after he'd forgotten a couple of times and cheated by taking a photograph on the way home or even the next day, he had eventually abandoned the project. He had planned to turn it into a time-lapse video showing the passing of time, the changing of the seasons . . .

Since he'd not eaten breakfast, he turned right onto the Groenhazengracht canal to buy bread rolls at the Frisian bakery. He had a mini fridge in his office that he kept stocked with things he could have for breakfast. There had been times in the past when he'd spent the night on the large sofa in the office, but that had stopped when he'd met Fay.

Maybe those times will return sooner than I ever could have imagined, he thought as he strolled onto the Doelengracht with the bag of warm bread rolls.

He passed the ornate arch of the Doelenpoort gate and glanced up at its statue of Saint George on horseback inflicting a fatal blow to the dragon that lay on its back under his horse's feet. The dragon symbolised the base desires that man had to overcome or 'kill' to prevent his soul from being dragged down into the quagmire of all that was worldly or even hellish.

He managed to work through a few emails as he ate his

breakfast at the computer, but his mind was elsewhere, brooding over the situation with Fay.

He was, however, curious about the manuscript that Piet van Vliet had found. Piet had started out as a linguist, but his research had increasingly led him into the field of history. He was often asked to help decipher manuscripts from the sixteenth and seventeenth centuries, his area of particular expertise.

Peter got up from his chair, frustrated by his inability to concentrate on his work.

What is Fay hiding, he wondered. *If you had any information at all that could help solve something as serious as a murder case, why wouldn't you share it? Why on earth would she keep it to herself that she and Coen had been having a long email conversation shortly before he was killed? Should I confront her about it? I haven't actually read the emails – I didn't lie about that – but I couldn't help reading the first lines.*

He needed a cigar. He took out his cigar case, removed one of the slim cigars and put it in his mouth before going outside to sit on a low wall next to the bike rack.

He felt himself grow calmer with each drag on the cigar.

When he looked up, he saw Piet van Vliet walking towards him. It was easy to recognise him from the characteristic spring in his step, the gait of a man who strode cheerfully through life. Piet started waving at him when he was still quite far away, something that Peter always found difficult to deal with. He could never decide whether to keep looking at the person walking towards him – and what sort of expression should you adopt during those fifteen or twenty seconds? – or to casually look away like something else had caught his eye until the person was closer.

He decided to concentrate on finishing his cigar. He threw the stub at the base of a nearby tree.

Piet stopped at arm's length from him.

'Peter,' he said, shaking his hand wildly. 'Long time no see. Good of you to find time for me. How are things?'

Peter stood up. 'Good, good. Thanks, Piet. I'm curious about what you want to tell me.'

'Yes, I think you're going to like it. I . . .' Piet looked around skittishly. 'Shall we go to your office? We can talk more easily there.'

'Yes, uh . . . yes, of course,' said Peter, suddenly realising that Piet was being far more secretive about his discovery than he had been in his messages earlier that morning. 'Is it a secret then? Something we can't talk about out here?'

'No, no,' Piet said and laughed. 'It's more . . . Well, perhaps a bit of a secret, but there are fewer distractions indoors. It just makes conversation a bit easier. And it means I can show you something on your computer.'

Once they were in Peter's office, Piet sat straight down at the computer without asking permission. Their relationship was a friendly one, but Peter felt himself bristle at his presumptuousness.

Piet opened his own email client, scrolled through a few messages and double-clicked on the one he had been looking for. He whirled the chair around with a flourish to face Peter, who had ended up sitting on the sofa as if he was the visitor in the room.

'So as I told you earlier, I've found a manuscript from the time of the Pilgrims,' Piet said. 'It's a tremendous document, quite unique. Someone who was there right from the start during their flight from England to Amsterdam, the move to Leiden, and eventually on the crossing to America. An ordinary man, well-educated, but not a prominent member of the Separatist community. It's someone who's writing an account of the everyday events, the quarrels . . . But it's not a diary. There are gaps between entries that last for years . . . Some parts of the manuscript might have been lost. We don't know. And there are some cryptic references that we're not sure about, but those might become clearer at some point. We're translating it into Dutch now. And that's no easy task because the handwriting is almost illegible. On top of that, it's seventeenth-century English peppered with seventeenth-century Dutch words. We're attacking it sentence by sentence, line by line. Sometimes a single phrase takes hours to decipher. It isn't easy, but I have someone who's a specialist in this area helping me, so we're making steady progress.'

'That sounds amazing, Piet,' said Peter, genuinely glad for him, but also glad for the distraction this news brought from the strange tide of recent events. 'But why hadn't anyone found this manuscript before now?'

'That's the best part of this story. Really, you could turn it into a movie. Imagine the opening scene: it's just another day at the office for the dashingly handsome linguist-slash-historian, examining manuscripts, making notes about what he finds. In the gloom of the archives, ancient dust dances in the shafts of sunlight that fall through the high windows.'

'But there aren't any windows in the archives, are there? And you have all those fluorescent lights.'

'Yes, yes, of course, but it's a film, isn't it? I'm not dashingly handsome either,' he said, chuckling.

Get on with it, Peter thought. 'Go on.'

'And then, suddenly . . .' Piet continued, 'the background music stops, and the viewer knows something is about to happen. The researcher reaches for an old book, but he fumbles.'

Piet was on his feet now, totally absorbed in his role.

'The book falls – I'm seeing it in slow motion – and the researcher desperately tries to catch the valuable tome before it hits the ground and suffers irreparable damage. Such a terrible black mark on his professional reputation! But the book tumbles to the floor. He can't stop it. It falls open, its ancient pages exposed to the cruel sunlight. And then . . . We zoom in on the text. The camera glides slowly over the book and stops at the corner of the page. We notice that the paper curls at the edges, just slightly, and then we see it! This is no ordinary page, but two pages cunningly stuck together. What secret has been hidden here for hundreds of years? Why did someone go to the trouble of hiding it so ingeniously?'

'Is that really how it happened?' Peter asked, impressed by Piet's storytelling.

'That's exactly how it happened, Peter,' Piet said, sitting down again. 'I picked the book up and realised that some of the pages had been stuck together. It's been done so cleverly that you can't actually see it, so it's quite possible that anyone who handled the book before now just never noticed. But to make a long story even longer . . . We examined the book thoroughly, and it turned out that there were other pages just like it. We separated them under lab conditions using tiny surgical scalpels. The book was damaged, of course, but only very lightly. We found almost twenty of these small pages, all densely covered in writing. It's amazing.'

'Wow, Piet, that really is fantastic. Congratulations.'

'Thanks,' Piet said, trying to compose his face in a humble expression and failing completely. 'But, naturally, I thought of you straight away, our city historian . . . You're interested in the Pilgrims too, right?'

'Yes, I am,' Peter said. 'It's not the main focus of my research, but if you're a historian with a particular interest in Leiden, you can't really avoid it.'

'And you volunteer in Jeffrey's museum?'

'That's right. You've done your homework.'

'That's why I wanted to let you know about it. If you like, I could send you updates about the translation as we go along.'

'Yes, I would like that!' Peter replied eagerly. 'That would be great. What sort of impression have you got from it so far?'

'We've translated six of the fragments. I've got them as attachments in my email. I'll forward them to you now. As I said, no secrecy. I'm a firm believer in sharing sources and information. That's how science should be, in my opinion.' He turned around, asked Peter for his email address and then forwarded the attachments.

The message arrived with a ping.

'Well then,' Piet said, standing up to give Peter his chair back. 'I won't keep you any longer. I was on my way to the library to pick up some books I'd ordered. The translation is proving to be a devil of a job. As I said, the handwriting is often illegible, and there are a lot of words we don't recognise. We don't just want to translate it. We want it to be a modern text that's easy to read so that when you read it, you'll think: hey, this could almost have been written by someone today.'

'Yes, that's always a wonderful thing,' Peter agreed. 'When people from the distant past speak to us in a way that we can understand, we can see that they're just ordinary people like us.'

'Precisely,' said Piet. 'What's extraordinary here is that we have an original text from the time, an eyewitness account that was never read by anyone else after it was written. It's quite exceptional. There's nothing particularly remarkable about the text itself. Most of it was already known from other sources, but there is something strange about it. The author frequently mentions a boy under the care of a Josh Nunn, someone we've not come across before. The boy appears to be Nunn's protégé, a pupil with special status. It doesn't seem to have been clear to the other people around him at the time exactly what the boy's role was, either. He went to America in the end, and this Josh stayed behind.'

Piet paused for a moment, like he was deciding whether to tell Peter more.

'And in the sixth fragment . . . Well, actually, you know, I'm sure you'll see it for yourself. We're hoping that more information will emerge as we go along. We've translated more than eighty per cent of what we've found.'

'That all sounds fascinating,' Peter said. He couldn't wait to start reading.

When Piet was gone, Peter sat at his desk and clicked on the first attachment in the email Piet had just sent him.

He started to read.

Fragment 1 – Flight from England (January 1609)

We made it. We're safe.

For now.

Chapter 16

Rijsbergen sat at his desk, looking through the folder that the pathologist Pieter-Nicolaas van Eijk had given him. He had skimmed through the autopsy report, but it had revealed nothing new.

The scraps of paper found in Zoutman's pockets were trivial notes, things like a shopping list for 'butter, cheese, eggs'. The receipts were from the supermarket, the dry cleaners and a bookshop. He'd recently purchased a copy of *The Sources of Western Esotericism* by Jacob Slavenburg from Boekhandel De Kler. 'The esoteric tradition can be better understood if one has knowledge of the archetypal imagery of the creation myths,' Rijsbergen had read on the author's website, which told him precisely nothing.

The only thing in the file that might provide some sort of clue was the envelope with the handwritten Old Testament stories inside. Rijsbergen had contacted the Religious Studies department at Leiden University, and they had put him in touch with Professor Mark Labuschagne. Rijsbergen hoped that the Bible expert might be able to shed some light on Zoutman's motives for writing these stories out by hand. He would ask about them at the Masonic Hall too. Perhaps the stories were for a lecture he'd wanted to give?

Rijsbergen put everything back in the folder, closed it, and went to the interview suite where two young men were waiting in separate rooms: Sven Koopman and Erik Laman, who had both been at the Freemasons' open evening.

Officers from the investigation team had brought the two students in shortly after Rijsbergen and Van de Kooij had returned from the morgue. The inspectors had been working their way through the list, visiting people one by one, and what had initially been a routine visit to the first student, Sven, had taken an unexpected turn.

Sven had broken out in a sweat and started to stutter when asked even the most straightforward questions. He had contradicted himself, said he wanted to speak to a solicitor, and then changed his mind. He had immediately implicated his acquaintance Erik without any prompting from the detectives.

This had been sufficient grounds for the detectives to bring Sven in for questioning and to send some colleagues to pick up Erik too.

The detectives had told Rijsbergen that Sven studied History at the university, and that, intriguingly, a certain Peter de Haan was one of his lecturers. It was a coincidence but hardly unusual in a small town like Leiden.

When Rijsbergen and Van de Kooij entered the interview room, they found Sven sitting with his head bowed as though in prayer. The interview room was simple, nothing like a Hollywood interrogation room – there was no large mirror concealing a team of cops and psychologists ready to analyse even the slightest change in the suspect's tone of voice. The windows were latticed with wired glass, but they were transparent enough that anyone looking in would be able to see that everything was being done by the book.

However, a camera had been installed near the ceiling in one of the corners to record interviews, a measure designed to protect both the suspect and the police. Whatever either party said in this room, there was no possibility of their words being twisted later. How those words should be interpreted was another story, one for the judges and lawyers to tell in the courtroom.

Rijsbergen introduced himself and Van de Kooij and then explained the purpose of the conversation they were about to have. He asked Sven about his degree course and his background, and then, in a gentle tone, he asked his first question. 'Why were you so nervous with my colleagues, Sven?'

'No reason in particular,' Sven said. 'I've never had anything to do with the police in my life.'

'But then you've got nothing to be worried about, have you?' said Rijsbergen. 'What could have made you stutter, turn red and contradict yourself?' he asked, reading out the words from the report that his colleagues had written after visiting Sven.

'Or ask for a solicitor?' Van de Kooij added, much less patiently. 'Is there something you want to tell us? We'll get it out of you eventually so you might as well tell us now. We can keep you in custody for three days, and then we can get an extension for another three days if we need to. And after that, we have the option of putting you on remand. Do you know how long you can be on remand for, Sven?'

Sven shook his head.

'More than a hundred and ten days, Sven. That's more than three months. I reckon that will make you talk. So you're better off—'

'I don't think that's necessary,' Rijsbergen cut in. 'Sven looks like a reasonable young man to me, sensible too. Never had anything to do with the police. Of course he wants to co-operate with us. I'm sure he thinks it's awful that Meneer Zoutman was murdered, too.'

'I didn't have anything to do with *that*,' Sven said, aggressively at first, but then his emotions got the better of him, and he choked on the last word. 'I didn't have anything to do with *that*,' he said again, swallowing hard as he gulped back his tears. 'There are witnesses,' he said, calmer now. 'We were outside with some other people after Meneer Zoutman's talk. We were still out there having a beer when the police came.'

'I believe you, Sven,' Rijsbergen said. His voice was warm and paternal. 'I believe you.'

Sven straightened himself up and smiled, as though this was an oral exam at school, and he had just been told he had passed. 'Thank you,' he said.

'But then there's still something you need to tell me about, Sven,' Rijsbergen went on. 'Just now, you said: "I didn't have anything to do with *that*." I think that's quite interesting. Don't you, Van de Kooij?'

Van de Kooij nodded. 'I didn't have anything to do with *that*,' he said, imitating Sven's voice mockingly.

Rijsbergen furrowed his brow and stared at his colleague. 'You see, Sven, that leaves us with another question,' he said. 'You and your friend weren't involved with the murder. So what *were* you involved with?'

Sven slumped in his chair.

'*What* were you involved with, Sven?' Rijsbergen asked.

'Think about those one hundred and ten days in prison, Sven,' Van de Kooij said, goading him. 'Some of the big guys in there would just love to get their hands on a lovely boy like you.'

Rijsbergen couldn't help laughing. He lifted his left hand up from the table a fraction to silence Van de Kooij. 'I'm afraid my colleague has been watching too many American TV shows, Sven. But he does have a point. It would be better for you if you were honest with us.'

Sven buried his face in his hands, like a child hoping it would make him invisible. 'We were just trying to get our bearings,' he said at last.

'Ah, now we're getting somewhere, Sven. I'm so glad,' Rijsbergen said. 'And where, exactly, were you trying to get your bearings?'

Van de Kooij reached over for the file on the table next to Rijsbergen. He took out the plastic sleeve containing the map that had been found the previous day and showed the sketch to Sven. Sven closed his eyes but then immediately opened them again.

'Was it something to do with this?' Van de Kooij asked him.

'Yes,' Sven admitted. 'I drew that. But . . . How did you get it?'

'We're not at liberty to reveal those details,' Van de Kooij said seriously. 'But a more interesting question, Sven, is what might it be?'

'It's a map.'

'A map,' Van de Kooij repeated, like a foreigner practising his Dutch vocabulary. 'We can see that.'

'Yeah, a map.'

'Why did you draw a map of the Masonic Hall, Sven?' Rijsbergen asked genially.

Sven took the map from Van de Kooij.

'Why did you draw a map of the Masonic Hall, Sven?' Rijsbergen asked again. 'And why did you throw it away afterwards? That's what I find most puzzling about all of this. You make this fantastic map, really put your heart and soul into it . . . And then you throw it away!'

Van de Kooij laughed and shook his head as though his colleague had just said something astonishing.

'Me and my, uh . . . friend, Erik,' Sven said. 'He's not really a friend, more of an acquaintance. I know him from the protest groups in Leiden.'

'Protest groups?'

'You know . . . Anti-globalisation groups, environmental activists, the Vrijplaats Leiden cultural and social centre on the Middelstegracht, the *Fabel van de Illegaal* organisation that works with refugees and illegal immigrants . . . That sort of thing.'

Rijsbergen nodded to show that he understood.

'We had a meeting last week on the Haagweg. You know it? Haagweg 4, the cultural centre. It was to coordinate the Mayflower 400 protests. There are going be to huge events here and in America and England to commemorate the four-hundredth anniversary of the Pilgrims setting sail from Leiden. Now, the thing about it is . . . Well, what it boils down to is that we think the tone of these events is too positive. The Pilgrims' arrival in America more or less led to the obliteration of the indigenous culture, the obliteration of the Indians who were living there. We want to see more emphasis on the negative effects of colonisation, on the darker side of its history.' As Sven spoke, he visibly regained his confidence, sitting up straight, almost on the edge of the chair. 'I'm telling you all this to put everything in the right context,' he said, with an obnoxious air of intellectual superiority.

'So there's this protest group,' he continued, 'that Erik and I are part of. And Erik wanted . . . He's really deeply into this stuff. The Pilgrims are generally considered to be the founders of what eventually became the United States of America. But Erik is convinced that the Freemasons played a crucial role in

America's history as well. He says there's a clear link between the Freemasons and the foundation of the United States. Lots of the Founding Fathers like George Washington and Benjamin Franklin were Freemasons. So if you really want to understand the ideas that the USA is based on, you need to get an understanding of the way the Freemasons think.'

'And *then* what, Sven?' Rijsbergen said, less patiently this time. 'You were planning to learn all about the Freemasons for the *Mayflower* anniversary?'

'Like I said,' said Sven, sounding like he had lost some of his earlier confidence. 'Erik said we needed to look at the bigger picture. The Freemasons play a central role in loads of conspiracy theories . . .'

'That's all well and good, Sven,' said Rijsbergen, 'But I still don't see . . . I was reading about the Masons on Wikipedia yesterday. The first lodge wasn't set up until the start of the eighteenth century if I remember correctly. The Pilgrims left Leiden in—'

'1620,' Sven interjected.

'Right,' Rijsbergen said, massaging his forehead with his fingertips. 'So that's about a hundred years earlier. And in Leiden—'

'That's right,' Sven said, like a teacher complimenting a pupil for giving a correct answer. 'The seventh Dutch lodge, Loge La Vertu, was established in Leiden in 1757. The first English lodge opened in 1717. Actually, to be more precise, it was the first grand lodge because it was made up of several smaller lodges that decided to unify.'

'I'm sorry, Sven, but I'm afraid that we're straying from the subject at hand,' Rijsbergen said, cutting him off.

'Just tell us what you were both doing there,' said Van de Kooij, obviously running out of patience.

Rijsbergen nodded approvingly. 'You still haven't answered our first question, Sven,' he said. 'Why did you draw the map?'

'I drew the map,' Sven said, 'because we wanted to go back to the Masonic Hall again. Erik was hoping we could have a look around without anyone bothering us. He thought we might find something we would help us. It all sounds a bit stupid now, but—'

'And what then? *Hasta la victoria siempre?* Ever onward to victory? That does indeed all sound a bit stupid, Sven,' Rijsbergen said testily. Based on his gut feeling, which rarely failed him, he 'knew' that Sven was telling the truth about why they had made the map.

What a waste of our time and energy this is, he thought

'Yes, that's why,' Sven said defensively. 'It was so we'd be well-prepared when we went back. The idea wasn't just to show all the rooms but to show where the cupboards and cabinets and things are. We might have been able to find something in the temple or see inside the closed rooms.'

'But *then* what?' Rijsbergen said, slamming the palm of his hand down on the desk in frustration.

Sven shrank back like a scolded child.

'What did you think you'd find if you broke in, Sherlock?' Rijsbergen asked, raising his voice. 'A cupboard that said: ALL THE FREEMASONS SECRETS? With a warning on it in big red letters: TOP SECRET! NOT TO BE READ BY THE UNINITIATED?'

Sven smiled sheepishly, as if now, he too could see that the whole idea had been ludicrous from the start. 'I don't know what we . . .' he protested weakly, 'or what Erik was trying to find. It was his idea, really. I just made the map. I think he genuinely believed he was going to find an archive or something that was kept hidden from outsiders, only meant for members

. . . But given what happened that night, when you put it like that, I suppose it does sound a bit . . . strange, yes.'

'One last question then,' said Rijsbergen. 'I just want to know why you drew the map and then threw it in the bin.'

'I did that when the police arrived,' Sven said, 'after the chairman's body had been found. Erik and I were in the back garden with some of the other guests. Someone came and told us what had happened, and they said we all had to come inside. I panicked. I knew how strange it was going to look if you saw me with the map. I thought we would all be searched before we left. I threw it away for the exact same reason I'm sitting here now. Because having a map of the building where someone had just been murdered would look suspicious. I hung around in the garden until everyone else had gone inside, then I crumpled it up and threw it in a bin. I wasn't really thinking about it. I was just glad to be rid of it. Until the police arrived this afternoon. Then I suddenly had this horrible vision of my map being found.'

'Indeed,' Van de Kooij said triumphantly.

'And then I thought: I want to explain everything, *can* explain everything because I had nothing to do with the murder, but I do want a solicitor. I've read too many stories in the papers about detectives who have blinkers on when they're interviewing people, like in the Schiedammer Park murder case. But at the same time, I figured I won't need a solicitor because I have absolutely nothing to hide.'

Rijsbergen nodded and smiled ruefully.

It sounds plausible, he thought. *And if there'd been no murder, they'd probably never have used the map anyway. Wild plans like theirs are almost always too childish to ever actually be put into action.*

Rijsbergen and Van de Kooij's interview with Erik was considerably shorter; it was little more than a verification of the information that Sven had already given them.

Erik's account corroborated Sven's entirely. He made a half-hearted attempt to justify his plan to break into the Freemasons' building, but then, just like Sven, he foundered when he tried to explain what he thought he might have found there.

Out of nowhere, Erik started to talk about the graffiti on the Sionshof. He suggested that the police would find the perpetrators at Haagweg 4. He gave them the names of three activists who were especially passionate about what they saw as Israel's illegal occupation of the Palestinian territories.

Erik had heard about their plans to vandalise the Sionshof through the grapevine. It had seemed utterly stupid to him from the start. Although these young men were unmistakably left-wing, the language they used to discuss their hatred of Israel was almost identical to that of the anti-Semites on the extreme right. Erik despised them for it and had decided he should give their names to the police.

Rijsbergen had noted down the names so he could pass them on to another department who would pay the young men a visit.

Eventually, Sven and Erik were sent home.

Neither of them spoke to each other when they left. Rijsbergen watched them through the glass doors of the police station entrance as one turned left onto the Langegracht and the other went right.

They hadn't even said goodbye to each other.

Rijsbergen returned to his office. He took the copies of Zoutman's handwritten Bible stories out of the folder to give to Mark Labuschagne later.

'Exodus,' the chairman had written on the first page. 'The story in a nutshell'.

Fragment 6 – From Leiden to America (1620)

We are going to America.

Although, not 'we' exactly. Most of us will stay behind in Leiden. Some of our group have already returned to England. Life in Holland was much harder than they were able to bear, and they chose to go back to Scrooby. Life is not easy there either, but it will at least be familiar. Not even the risk of being thrown in jail as soon as they set foot on shore was enough to persuade them to stay here.

We help each other as much as we can here, but there are limits to what you can do for other people. Many of us only barely manage to keep our own heads above water. Of course, some of the people staying here in Leiden stay because they cannot afford to make the great crossing, even though John and William say that something could always be worked out to make it possible for them. They could borrow the money for the voyage and pay it back once they were in America.

Our group is also ageing. While we have welcomed new members and new babies, it is not enough to support the healthy growth of our group. If we remain here, within a few years, our group will fall apart, and its members will disappear into the wider Leiden community. We see it happening now. We are forced to send our children out to work from such a tender age. Their families need the extra income they bring in, but it has led to them becoming more and more involved in a life that we would rather protect them from. Roughhousing in the street, gambling and drinking all have an allure that is almost impossible for our young ones to resist.

We strive to honour God's commandment to observe the Sabbath, but it is of little consequence to the people of Leiden. It is becoming increasingly difficult for us to impress upon our young ones the importance of observing Sunday as a day of rest. But try stopping your twenty-year-old son when his friends meet him at work and drag him off to the inn to get drunk and do heaven knows what other sinful things. There are women of low morals . . . A day's wages are soon spent in such a den of iniquity! And if your son has grown tired of the heavy work in the shipyard or blacksmith's, try forbidding him to join the navy or the army.

Enter through the narrow gate; for the gate is wide and the road is easy that leads to destruction, and there are many who take it. For the gate is narrow and the road is hard that leads to life, and there are few who find it.

And so, together, we have decided that it is time for us to move on. Pilgrims are we on the paths of righteousness. We know that America is a land of promise. It could be our promised land. We can bring the good news of our Lord and Saviour to the godless heathens who live there. They have been heading for eternal torture in hell since time immemorial, but now we will tell them that He died for them, for the remission of their sins. And we will finally be free there. No more looking over our shoulders, no more fear that the English will demand our extradition. We will be able to read what we want, preach what we want, and freely discuss what we want with each other. And at the same time, we will be able to save the pitch-black souls of the ignorant savages there who walk about in darkness!

We live in the year of our Lord 1620. The Twelve Years' Truce that was agreed between the Netherlands and Spain in 1609 is coming to an end. There is already heavy fighting in Germany. (This was the start of the Thirty Years' War – PvV.)

For most of us, returning to England is not an option. We have managed to preserve our Englishness here and have proudly held onto our own way of life, but we have no desire to go back.

And yet, something troubles me, especially when I read back over what I have written today. It is all true: our desire to practise our own faith, the fear that our group will disappear into the Leiden population, the concern for the souls of our children who are constantly exposed to and sullied by the wickedest sins and temptations that the Devil can contrive to divert them from the path that leads to Salvation. The poverty, the toil, the theological disputes that we find ourselves entangled in, but . . . This applies to all of us. We all find ourselves in the same plight.

And yet, John has chosen to stay here.

I will write it again.

John Robinson is to stay here.

John has gathered an inner circle around himself to which I sadly do not belong. They will also remain here. These people could afford to travel to America and even have enough money to take others with them.

It is difficult to understand why. Impossible, in fact. All the reasons I have mentioned for leaving here make perfect sense, and few would argue with them. If they make sense for the rest of us, then surely they must make sense for John and the people around him too – possibly even more so!

So what reason do they have for staying behind?

An obvious division has formed between those who are leaving and those who have decided to stay. The latter group also includes people who do not have enough money to emigrate now but may be able to make the journey in a year or two.

Although it pains me greatly, my family and I are among those who are unable to find the means to make the great crossing.

What concerns me is that there is a group of people who could easily pay for their crossing but still choose to stay, despite all the problems we have here.

Why do they not leave?

I am not privy to whatever has caused it, but I can see that the group has split in two. There is no crystal-clear dividing line that makes it clear to outsiders who belongs to which group. Nor are there two distinct factions who stand opposite each other or sit apart from each other during worship. It seems to be much more subtle than that. There is one group around Josh Nunn and another around William Brewster. However, the two groups do not appear to be firmly fixed, and I have been unable to discern who is on each 'side'. William has often openly and vehemently expressed his revulsion for what he sees as an overly liberal interpretation of scripture. People who share this opinion have gravitated towards him. These are the people who are determined to leave Leiden and go to America. Those who have gravitated towards Josh Nunn – many of whom work in the building trade, stonemasons and so on – he that hath ears to hear, let him hear – have chosen to stay in Leiden. Josh has done well for himself and has his own private loge box at the theatre. The men at the core of his group meet there often and discuss things with each other during the intervals.

Josh has now taken a new boy under his wing. He seems to be starting anew with the same process as before: they withdraw together to speak in private. It is obvious that Josh does most of the talking – I see them sometimes, sitting together in our shared garden – and the boy nods as earnestly as his predecessor did ten years ago.

And here is the most astonishing thing of all: that – former? – apple of Josh's eye, the young lad who is now a grown man in the prime of his life. The boy who spent the last ten or eleven years as Josh's inseparable shadow. The boy upon whom Josh looked with fatherly pride, nodding in approval when he spoke in church – to the increasing vexation of the members of the other faction. That boy . . .

That boy is going to America.

Chapter 17

Peter had read the translated fragments that Piet van Vliet had sent him twice now.

He read them in a rush the first time, scanning them like someone quickly reading through a love letter to get the gist of it.

Then he read them a second time, calmly, carefully, forcing himself to take a moment now and then to make notes. It was exactly as Piet had told him: in broad terms, the fragments contained nothing very different from what they already knew. The flight from England, the brief stay in Amsterdam, the eleven years of poverty and religious quarrels in Leiden.

He wasn't sure what to make of the business with the young boy who seemed to be under the protection of a character called Josh Nunn. He noticed that his first thoughts were of some sort of non-platonic relationship, but it was no doubt a sensibility peculiar to modern times that made him jump to such a conclusion.

Peter had never heard about disagreements or discord within the group before.

Might there have been other reasons, reasons that aren't already widely known, that would explain why more than half the group eventually chose to stay behind in Leiden, he mused. *And if so, what do they have to do with the group around Josh Nunn?*

An email from Mark arrived. He had been approached by Detective Chief Inspector Rijsbergen who had asked him to visit him at the police station at three that afternoon. Apparently, Coen Zoutman had had an envelope full of biblical texts in his pocket on the night he was murdered. He hoped that Mark, being a professor, would be able to offer some insight into the case. 'Two heads are better than one,' Mark had written, 'so I wanted to ask if you'd mind coming with me.'

Peter emailed him back to say that he would be happy to help.

He realised with a start that it was already a quarter to one. He turned on his phone to see if he had missed any messages. There was just one, from Judith, agreeing to meet for lunch.

It looked like Fay was as determined to keep up the radio silence as he was.

Irritated by it nevertheless, he rushed over to the Lipsius Building, as the LAK had been renamed years earlier.

Judith was rarely punctual, so he ended up waiting for her in the atrium for a while.

The hall was a hive of activity. The long couches and chairs were all occupied, and there were students everywhere, many of them eating and working at their laptops.

Eventually, Judith arrived, and as she walked towards him, the soft rays of midday light that fell through the high windows illuminated her long, black hair that was gathered messily in a large hair clip. She was wearing a blouse that, from a distance, looked like a batik print, with a denim jacket, a flowing flower-print skirt and knee-high black leather boots.

Her face lit up when she saw him. She kissed him, as she always did, lightly on the cheek.

He breathed in the smell of her hair and closed his eyes for a moment.

'You okay?' she asked. She was smiling, but her tone was serious.

'Oh, yes,' he said. 'I'm fine. It's just been crazy lately.'

'I know, honey. It's all so *much*.'

After they had each put together a lunch at the various food stations in the canteen, they took their trays into the dining area. Almost every table was occupied, but they spotted two people leaving seats by the windows that looked out onto the Witte Singel, the old city moat.

'How are you both doing?' Judith asked. 'You must be really shaken by it all.'

'Yes, we are. It was awful . . . That poor man. And it's even worse for Fay. She knew him so well, much better than I did, of course. This has obviously all had a much bigger impact on her.'

'Oh, poor Fay,' Judith said. 'It's good that you have each other, though.'

I'm not so sure about that, Peter thought.

'Do they know anything more about the murder yet?' Judith asked.

'Not really, no. I don't get the impression that they're making much progress.'

He told Judith about the conversation that he and Fay had had with the police the day before and what the current situation was.

'I'm going to the station with Mark this afternoon,' Peter said. 'They want us to look at some texts that Coen Zoutman had in his pocket when he was murdered. Biblical texts. That's why they've asked Mark.'

He took a couple of spoonfuls of soup. 'How about you? All ready to leave on Sunday?'

Judith had been given a grant to spend three months doing research at Harvard University.

'Just about. There are a few loose ends to tie up here and there, things I need to finish before I go. I made a list this morning and got a bit of a fright when I saw how long it was. Calls to make, papers to mark, appointments with students before I leave so they can get on with their dissertations while I'm away. Everything I'll be taking with me is laid out ready to be packed at home. I just need to sort out some books to take, although I expect I'll be so busy there that I won't have much time to read them. The time will fly by, but I'll miss everyone. I'll miss you.'

Peter smiled. 'Time always seems to pass more slowly for the people left behind. The person who goes away is usually so busy processing all the new experiences they're having that it flies by.'

'That's true,' she said. 'And Mark will be coming over halfway through, so that will split the time up nicely. But my invitation still stands, you know. I'd love you to come and visit me there – or you and Fay together.'

Peter wondered if he should tell Judith about what had happened between him and Fay, about the emails to Coen Zoutman that she'd not told him about and the angry texts that morning.

'Actually . . .' he began, but then decided not to finish the sentence.

I'm not going to bother Judith with our relationship problems, he thought.

Instead, he spent far longer than was necessary blowing on the soup on his spoon before he ate it.

Why shouldn't I go? A break might be just what I need.

He could feel Judith watching him, but he concentrated on his soup.

Maybe it would be a good idea to get away from everything for a while. See new things, enjoy new experiences . . .

He put down his spoon and looked at Judith. She was staring at him, just as he'd suspected. 'I'll do it!' he said. 'Why not do something crazy for once?'

The smile on Judith's face could hardly have been wider. 'Do you really mean it?' she asked. Her cheeks flushed pink.

'Yes, I really mean it.'

She stood up and leaned across the table. Peter tried to stand up, but there wasn't enough room behind him to move his chair back properly and he got awkwardly stuck halfway.

Judith put her hand on the back of his head and kissed him on the cheek. 'I'm so glad,' she said. She was still beaming at him after they had both sat down again.

'You know,' Peter said, 'in three weeks, I'll be finished with lectures. And I haven't any other obligations to keep me here. I've got a few things that I still need to do. There are two articles that I ought to finish writing, but I don't need to be sitting at my desk here to do them.'

Judith nodded slowly, as though she couldn't quite believe it. 'Actually,' she said, 'I've been keeping it to myself but, secretly, I'm really dreading being away for three months. I've never been away from home on my own for so long before. Mark is coming after six weeks. Maybe you could come before then? Then I'll only be on my own for two or three weeks. I'd really like it if you could, Peter.'

'All right, Judith,' Peter said. 'It feels a bit impulsive, but it feels like a good decision too.'

'And Fay?'

'Oh, Fay will be fine. She's got a busy summer ahead of her. She'll be in the final stages of writing the book she's been working on. She'll probably be thrilled that she can completely devote herself to that without having to worry about me. Just the book, Agapé and her mother. I should think Fay will be quite happy.'

The prospect of spending two or three weeks in the United States, somewhere he'd only been twice before, was suddenly very appealing. 'I'll have to be quick if I want to book a flight and a hotel.'

'You won't need a hotel, silly. Harvard is giving me an apartment. I've seen the photos. It's quite big. There's a sofa bed in the living room, so it's been set up to accommodate more people than just the visiting researcher.'

'Won't Mark mind?'

'Mind? Why?' She looked genuinely surprised. 'Oh! No, of course not,' she said when she realised what Peter meant. 'Don't be silly. Mark's the least jealous person in the world – I don't think he even knows what jealousy is – and in your case, there's no reason for him to be jealous at all. Or do you think that Fay will mind?'

'No, I think that Fay will feel the same.'

'Well, then. That's perfect, isn't it? And I'm not assuming that you'll want to spend the whole time in Boston. You're welcome to, obviously, but you'll want to see other things too, I expect. New York isn't too far away. Oh, it's going to be great!'

Peter decided he would book a flight to Boston right after lunch.

I'm sure Fay will be less than pleased at first, but it might do us good to take a break from each other.

Judith and Peter ate the rest of their meal in companionable silence.

They looked at each other fleetingly from time to time –

anyone watching them might have thought they were a couple still caught up in the giddy first days of a romance.

When they had finished eating, Peter bought them a cup of coffee each so that he could make their time together last a little longer.

'Have you heard any more about the paint on the Sionshof wall?'

'No,' said Judith. 'I hope they can tell us something soon. That stunt was too stupid for words, but I'll still be glad if the police find whoever did it.'

'If only they knew that, as a member of Een Ander Joods Geluid, you'd probably actually agree with them.'

'Yes, indeed, I would. Not with the "death to . . ." part, naturally. But I would gladly talk to them if the police ever find them. It feels like everyone's completely lost the ability to be rational about the conflict, it really does. There's an attitude developing in Israel that says, "There's only room for us Jews here." All those colonists in the illegal settlements . . . It's just awful. And that Israeli soldier who shot a Palestinian detainee in the head, they've just given him an appallingly short sentence. The poor boy was already lying on the ground, wounded. He was defenceless.'

'Yes, I saw the video of that. But Een Ander Joods Geluid is trying to make people aware of this other side of the story, aren't they?'

'Yes. But I'm afraid that we're increasingly just a "voice crying out in the desert". Literally in the desert in this case.'

They had both finished their coffee now, and they got up from the table. They cleared their trays away, then said goodbye in the atrium.

'I'm planning to work in the café in the Pieterskerk for a bit tomorrow,' Peter said. 'So if you fancy a decent cup of coffee . . . And if you have time, of course.'

He wanted to have Judith to himself again, but somewhere quieter than here where they were surrounded by hundreds of people.

'I'd love to,' she said, smiling. 'And I'll always make time for you.' She hugged him, keeping her arms wrapped around him for a moment longer than usual.

Peter buried his face in her hair again and pressed a kiss onto the top of her head.

'I'm so glad you're going to come to America,' she said. 'You will really come, won't you? I'll be disappointed now if you change your mind.'

'No, no, I'm really coming. I promise,' he said.

As soon as he got back to his office, he booked a flight to Boston and paid for it with his credit card. He forwarded the booking confirmation to Judith's email address.

'I keep my promises . . .' he typed with a growing feeling of excitement.

The handful of appointments that were in his diary for the weeks he would be in Boston could be dealt with via email or Skype. Just one meeting would have to be brought forward – or even postponed. No doubt most of his students would be delighted that they'd all be getting extensions on their dissertation deadlines.

Although it wasn't absolutely necessary – outside of term time he could do with his time as he pleased to a large extent – he sent an email to the heads of the History and Archaeology departments and their administrators.

He sat on the sofa to read for a while before he went to the police station with Mark.

Now that the euphoria was subsiding, Peter began to feel guilty for making such a big decision without asking Fay. *Perhaps I have been a bit too impulsive,* he thought.

Chapter 18

Mark responded enthusiastically to the news that Peter had just booked a flight to Boston so that he could visit Judith.

'That's really great, Peter,' he said.

As they were cycling to the police station on the Langegracht, Mark put his hand on Peter's arm and left it there for a moment.

'This is going to make her feel so much less alone there. And your visit might overlap with mine. Send me your flight details later. I can't actually remember exactly when I'm going over there.'

'I will,' Peter said. 'I think she'll be on her own for three weeks, then I'll be there for three weeks, and then you'll be there for three weeks, and then she'll have three more weeks on her own.'

'Perfect.'

Mark took his hand off Peter's arm.

Peter spent the rest of their journey telling Mark about the manuscript Piet van Vliet had found, giving him a broad outline of the fragments he had read.

They parked their bikes in the racks outside the station. Inside, they reported at the front desk where Chief Inspector Rijsbergen came to meet them.

He seemed taken aback when he saw Peter.

'Mark is a good friend of mine,' Peter said. 'He asked me to come with him. I know a bit about the subject too.'

'And two heads are better than one,' said Mark.

Rijsbergen appeared to hesitate for a moment, but then he asked them both to follow him.

'There are two things that I'd like to show you,' Rijsbergen said as soon as they were all inside his office. 'The first concerns a letter that we found in the inside pocket of Coen Zoutman's jacket. It's not a letter as such ... It's stories from the Old Testament that he's written out by hand and added some commentary to. We'd very much like to know why Meneer Zoutman chose these stories in particular and why he had them on his person. That second question is more difficult to answer, but I think you might be able to help me with the first.'

'And the second thing?'

'That's more ...'

Rijsbergen produced a file and took out the photographs of the tattoo. He gave them to his visitors.

'The pathologist found this tattoo on Coen Zoutman's body, positioned between the left breast and the armpit.'

Peter and Mark studied the images, turning them around and holding them in various positions.

'It goes without saying that we'll be circulating this image among the Freemasons.'

'I'm sorry. I've never seen this before,' Mark admitted. 'The triangle itself is an ancient symbol. In Christianity, it represents the Father, the Son and the Holy Spirit. It can be a symbol for femininity as well because of ... well, I think it's clear why. But used in this combination?'

'It looks like two triangles,' Rijsbergen speculated. 'Or two mountains? Two pyramids?'

'And that little circle could be a sun?' Peter suggested.

'Or the circle denotes a place?' Mark chimed in.

'There's an image of the All-Seeing Eye in the Masonic temple. Could it be that?' Rijsbergen thought out loud.

He quickly typed something into his computer. When he had found what he was looking for, he turned the screen around towards Peter and Mark.

'That could be it, I suppose,' Mark said absently, holding the photo so that the triangle pointed upwards. 'But if it is, then I don't know what that smaller triangle is supposed to be.'

Rijsbergen showed them Coen Zoutman's business card.

Mark and Peter also noticed that the image on the card was similar to the tattoo and the line drawing of the All-Seeing Eye, but they weren't convinced.

'I'm sorry,' Mark said. 'I can't help you. What I can do is post the image on a forum about symbols and cryptology. Not this photograph, obviously, but a good drawing of it. It might give you something. Members often post requests about this sort of thing. It's worth a shot.'

'I'd appreciate that,' Rijsbergen said. 'Feel free to make a sketch of it to take home with you.'

'And the letter?' Peter asked.

'I have that here,' said Rijsbergen. 'It's a lot of text, but I'm sure you'll recognise the stories, so you'll be able to read it faster than I could.'

Mark took the sheets of paper from him and read the first few words aloud.

Do you still not perceive or understand? Are your hearts
hardened? Do you have eyes, and fail to see? Do you
have ears, and fail to hear?

MARK 8:17–18

'These are the words that Jesus spoke to his disciples,' Mark
explained. 'After the miracle where Jesus fed four thousand
people with seven loaves and two fish. When they'd all eaten
their fill, the disciples gathered up the leftover pieces of bread.
It was enough to fill seven baskets. Afterwards, Jesus and his
disciples got into a boat. But the disciples had only brought one
loaf of bread with them, and when Jesus realised this, he said:
"Why are you talking about having no bread?" Then Jesus speaks
the famous words that Meneer Zoutman has chosen as a sort
of epigraph for his letter.'

'And why would he . . .' Rijsbergen began to ask.

'It looks like he wants to tell people something that he
considers to be self-evident, but most people are blind to. They
have eyes but cannot see.'

Mark quickly read the first page and passed it to Peter.

The room fell silent.

Exodus:
The story in a nutshell

1

Everything begins with Abraham.

Commanded by a God unknown to him, Abram, as he was called then, was instructed to take his family and leave Haran, a town that today lies a little over forty kilometres from Şanlıurfa, a small town in the southeast of Turkey. Previously, his father, Terah, had left Chaldean Ur in what is now the southeast of Iraq, to live in Canaan, now the West Bank. They had never been beyond Haran before.

God promised Abram that He would make him the father of a great people and that He would give him the land of Canaan – to this day, this promise underpins the claims made by Jewish settlers about their right to build settlements on Palestinian territory.

It soon seemed that the promise of many offspring – 'I will indeed bless you, and I will make your offspring as numerous as the stars of heaven and as the sand that is on the seashore' – would come to nothing because of his wife Sarai's infertility. But one day God Himself visited Abram in the company of two angels. Sarai, which means 'royal', was now to be called Sarah, 'princess', and Abram was now called Abraham. The added letter, 'Hee', symbolised God's grace. Sarah baked bread for God and His heavenly companions, which they consumed with great relish.

God repeated his promise that He would give countless offspring to Abraham and ninety-year-old Sarah, who, understandably, laughed when she heard this. In the meantime, at Sarah's insistence, Abraham had taken a concubine, Hagar. She had a child, Ishmael, but this became a problem when Abraham and Sarah did indeed have their own child, Isaac, just as God had promised. They decided to send Hagar and Ishmael away into the wilderness. Miraculously, they survived, and according to tradition, Ishmael became the father of the Islamic peoples. God then told Abraham to sacrifice his only son Isaac on a mountain in the land of Moriah. He followed this command and set off with his son. After three days of travelling, he took the bundle of wood they had brought with them and tied his son to it. Just as he was about to cut his son's throat, they heard the bleating of a ram whose horns had become caught in a thorn bush. Instead of his son, Abraham sacrificed the ram – the Muslims celebrate this miracle every year at Eid al-Adha, the Festival of Sacrifice. For Christians, this story foreshadows the story of Jesus, God's only son, who is sacrificed by his Heavenly Father.

Imagine Abraham and Isaac on their journey back home. How would the son have looked at his father?

2

Isaac, in turn, had two sons: Esau and Jacob. Jacob cheated Esau of his birthright in exchange for a plate of lentils. Jacob took several wives and had twelve sons. One of them was Joseph, the apple of his eye, who had been born to his favourite wife, Rachel. Joseph possessed the gift of prophecy and the ability to interpret dreams. His eleven brothers were so jealous of Joseph's position as the favourite son that they sold him to passing merchants who then sold him on to Potiphar, a high-ranking servant of the pharaoh. Joseph quickly rose to great power. He interpreted the pharaoh's dream about seven skinny cows eating seven fat cows, predicting that seven years of abundance would be followed by seven years of famine and that the land's good harvests should be stored. As a reward, the pharaoh made him vizier of Egypt. His eleven brothers and their father Jacob were not so fortunate. Because of the famine, Joseph's brothers went to Egypt to beg for food at the court, not knowing that when they grovelled in the dust before the throne, the man sitting upon it was Joseph. To their shame, they eventually recognised him as the brother they had sold.

And this, according to the Bible, is how the people of Israel came to be in Egypt. After many years, the pharaoh, who had been so kind to them, died and memories of Joseph faded. The Hebrews, as they were called then, became slaves, forced to work in the mercilessly hot sun, making bricks of clay for the construction of Egyptian cities. Because the Hebrews were growing in number, the pharaoh ordered all their new-born boys to be killed. The baby Moses escaped certain death when his mother put him into the Nile in a bulrush basket sealed with tar. He was found by an Egyptian princess and brought up as a prince at court. Not until he was forty years old did he discover that he belonged to the enslaved people. One day he killed an Egyptian overseer who had mistreated a Hebrew slave. Moses fled to a place in the desert called Midian, where *he was taken in by the shepherd Jethro and his family. Moses married Jethro's daughter Zipporah, with whom he had two sons: Eliezer, 'God is my helper', and Gershom, 'stranger'. Moses explained his choice of the name Gershom with the words: 'I have been a stranger in a strange land.'*

After exactly forty years – he was eighty by then, and a shepherd – while out with his flock one day, he saw a bush that was burning yet not consumed by flames. From within the fire, the voice of God spoke to Moses for the first time, calling Himself 'I am who I am'. He told Moses to lead 'His' people out of Egypt.

Moses returned to Egypt, but ten times, the pharaoh refused to let the Hebrews go. Ten plagues came upon Egypt: water turned into blood; frogs infested the land; lice tormented both animals and humans; a swarm of flies drove people to madness; a plague broke out among the livestock; boils covered the skins of the Egyptians; a storm of hail and fire destroyed the harvest; locusts covered the whole land; there was darkness for three days, and finally, the first-born son in every family died. Each time, the Hebrews were spared. Before the last plague, they smeared their doorposts with the blood of a slaughtered lamb so that the Angel of Death knew to pass over that home.

When his own first-born son died, the pharaoh realised that he could not win. He allowed the Hebrews to leave. According to the Bible, there were six hundred thousand men, not including the women, children and slaves.

But soon the pharaoh regretted his decision and sent his army to recapture them.

Moses and the Hebrews had now arrived at the Red Sea and were trapped by the water on one side and the approaching army on the other. Upon God's command, Moses held his staff over the sea, and the waters parted. The Hebrews were able to walk across the bottom of the sea, but when the Egyptians tried to follow them, the waters closed again, and the pharaoh and his soldiers drowned.

3

Having barely escaped the murderous clutches of the Egyptians, the Hebrews began to complain about the lack of food and water. On God's command, Moses threw a piece of wood into a spring of bitter water, and the water instantly became sweet and drinkable. Manna fell from the sky every morning and stayed on the ground after the morning dew had evaporated. It looked like coriander seeds, but it was white and tasted like honey cake. It had to be collected immediately and eaten the same day because, the next day, the manna would be rotten and full of worms. On the day before the Sabbath, a double portion could be gathered – which would not spoil – because there would be no fresh manna on the Sabbath. The word manna literally means 'What is that?' This was what the Hebrews said when they saw the food for the first time. Large numbers of quails also fell from the sky for them to eat.

When the Hebrews arrived at Mount Sinai, God finally showed Himself to His people. They were afraid and asked Moses to relay God's messages for them. Moses went up the mountain and stayed there for forty days and forty nights without eating or drinking. God gave him the Ten Commandments on two stone tablets, along with many other laws by which the Hebrews were to live. God promised Moses *that He would help them remove the Canaanites from the Promised Land. He also gave precise instructions for the construction of a tabernacle, a portable tent that served as a place of worship for the Hebrews and a symbol of God's presence in their midst.*

When he came back down the mountain, Moses discovered that, under the leadership of his brother Aaron, the people had made a golden calf by melting down all of their gold jewellery so that they would have a visible god to worship. Furious, Moses smashed the stone tablets, ordered the execution of three thousand people, and went back up the mountain where he spent another forty days without eating or drinking. He received the Ten Commandments for a second time. When he left the mountain, the Hebrews made the tabernacle and the Ark of the Covenant, a wooden chest containing the stone tablets that was carried on two poles. God's presence dwelled in the Ark of the Covenant, and He would appear to His people in the form of a cloud. Wherever the cloud stood still, the Hebrews would stop and make camp. If the cloud carried on moving, the people would follow it.

And so Moses led them to the border of the Promised Land. Because of his own sin – he had struck a rock three times with a rod to make water appear when God had told him to strike it only once – Moses was able to see the Promised Land but not enter it. The Hebrews were punished for their sins by being made to stay in the desert for a total of forty years. They set up their tents opposite the city of Jericho on the banks of the river Jordan.

Moses died at the age of one hundred and twenty. He was buried by God Himself, with His own hands, in a place that is known to no one.

4

*When the Hebrews finally entered the Promised Land under
the leadership of Moses' successor Joshua, they slaughtered
many, many tens of thousands of people whose only crime
was that they already lived in the land that had been promised to the Hebrews. If we add up the deaths mentioned in
the Bible, we arrive at a total of at least six hundred thousand
people, all killed in the conquest of the Promised Land.*

I will end with three stories.

Numbers 31:7–18

Revenge on the Midianites and division of the spoils

*They (the Hebrews) did battle against Midian, as the Lord
had commanded Moses, and killed every male. They killed
the kings of Midian: Evi, Rekem, Zur, Hur, and Reba, the five
kings of Midian, in addition to others who were slain by
them; and they also killed Balaam son of Beor with the sword.
The Hebrews took the women of Midian and their little ones
captive; and they took all their cattle, their flocks, and all
their goods as booty. All their towns where they had settled,
and all their encampments, they burned, but they took all
the spoil and all the booty, both people and animals. Then
they brought the captives and the booty and the spoil to
Moses, to Eleazar the priest, and to the congregation of the
Hebrews, at the camp on the plains of Moab by the Jordan
at Jericho.*

*Moses, Eleazar the priest, and all the leaders of the congre-
gation went to meet them outside the camp. Moses became*

angry with the officers of the army, the commanders of thousands and the commanders of hundreds, who had come from service in the war. Moses said to them, 'Have you allowed all the women to live? These women here, on Balaam's advice, made the Hebrews act treacherously against the Lord in the affair of Peor, so that the plague came among the congregation of the Lord. Now therefore, kill every male among the little ones, and kill every woman who has known a man by sleeping with him. But all the young girls who have not known a man by sleeping with him, keep alive for yourselves.'

Deuteronomy 7: 1–3; 12; 16; 21–24

Dealing with other nations

When the Lord your God brings you into the land that you are about to enter and occupy, and He clears away many nations before you – the Hittites, the Girgashites, the Amorites, the Canaanites, the Perizzites, the Hivites, and the Jebusites, seven nations mightier and more numerous than you – and when the Lord your God gives them over to you and you defeat them, then you must utterly destroy them. Make no covenant with them and show them no mercy. Do not intermarry with them, giving your daughters to their sons or taking their daughters for your sons . . .

If you heed these ordinances, by diligently observing them, the Lord your God will maintain with you the covenant loyalty that He swore to your ancestors . . . You shall devour all the peoples that the Lord your God is giving over to you, showing them no pity; you shall not serve their gods, for that would be a snare to you . . . Have no dread of them, for the

Lord your God, who is present with you, is a great and awesome God. The Lord your God will clear away these nations before you little by little; you will not be able to make a quick end of them, otherwise the wild animals would become too numerous for you. But the Lord your God will give them over to you, and throw them into great panic, until they are destroyed. He will hand their kings over to you, and you shall blot out their name from under heaven; no one will be able to stand against you, until you have destroyed them.

2 Chronicles 25: 1–2; 11–12

The good king Amaziah

Amaziah was twenty-five years old when he began to reign, and he reigned for twenty-nine years in Jerusalem. His mother's name was Jehoaddan of Jerusalem. He did what was right in the sight of the Lord . . .

Amaziah took courage and led out his people; he went to the Valley of Salt and struck down ten thousand men of Seir. The people of Judah captured another ten thousand alive, took them to the top of Sela, and threw them down from the top of Sela so that all of them were dashed to pieces.

Mark passed the last page to Peter and waited for him to finish reading. Neither of them had needed much time to read the texts. There was nothing in them that they weren't already familiar with. Just as the title had announced, it was the story of the Exodus from Egypt in a nutshell – plus a brief outline of its prehistory. And they both knew the stories that Coen Zoutman had ended the letter with. They described how, with their God's help and approval, the Israelites had committed unimaginable atrocities when they conquered Canaan: how entire nations were wiped out, how only virgins were spared, how defeated cities were burned to the ground, and how the Israelites made off with the spoils, the cattle, the harvests. And how the ten thousand enemies who had survived the battles were thrown to their deaths from the top of a rock.

'Well?' Rijsbergen asked, hopefully. 'I mean, obviously, I've read them myself, and I already knew the basic stories, but . . . Do you have any idea why Meneer Zoutman has chosen these stories in particular?'

Peter put the pages on Rijsbergen's desk. 'No,' he said. 'Everything in that letter was written two and a half thousand years ago, so there's nothing new to be discovered from them.'

'Those stories at the end are quite strange,' Rijsbergen said. 'I mean, I'm from a Catholic family, and I'm reasonably familiar with the Bible, but I didn't recognise them. Is that really what it says in the Bible?'

Mark nodded, almost apologetically, like he had been caught in a lie that he would have preferred to keep covered up.

'I mean . . .' Rijsbergen said. 'The International Criminal Court in The Hague would have their hands full if those events were to take place today: invading a country, full-blown genocide, the destruction of entire peoples along with their culture and religion, razing their temples to the ground, murdering prisoners, carrying off virgin women as the spoils of war . . . all of those things would be classified as crimes against humanity these days. But that's all in the Bible?'

'Yes,' Mark said, 'it's all in the Bible, the book that many people still say should be our guide to leading a moral life in modern times . . . That claim doesn't seem to hold much water when you read those stories. But you know, Meneer Rijsbergen, the Exodus from Egypt . . .' He let out an ironic laugh, as if he was recalling some lark from his youth. 'It's always been a mystery to me why people still take that story literally.'

'I don't really believe it happened either, at least not exactly like that,' Peter said. 'But the story must contain a grain of truth. Maybe it was a smaller group of people or a few families that left Egypt. And later, they merged that story with other, older stories. Who can say?'

He glanced at Rijsbergen. This may not have been quite the right time or place to have this discussion, but Rijsbergen looked fascinated.

'Go on,' Rijsbergen said, nodding at Mark. 'It won't do me any harm to learn more about it, and you never know, you might tell me something that will help with the investigation.'

'That's good, because look . . .' Mark said. 'To start with, it couldn't have been six hundred thousand men. That's the number explicitly stated in the Book of Exodus. But when you include all the women and children, the old men and the servants – yes, the slaves apparently had their own staff – it soon adds up to two and a half million people. Other historians estimate that there were three or even four million. There weren't even that many people living in Egypt at the time! Surely there'd be evidence of such a massive depopulation in the Egyptian historiography. They were known for recording everything accurately. When the vanguard of those four million people reached the promised land, the rear guard would still have been in Egypt! Despite centuries of searching, there's not a scrap of archaeological evidence to support the presence of such a large group of people in the desert. And how did so many people survive in the hostile desert environment? Yes, manna fell from heaven, and they ate quails, but how much manna and how many tens of millions of quails would there have had to be to feed millions of people for forty years?'

'The manna and the quails, yes. Those are a bit problematic,' Peter admitted.

'Around the time of the supposed Exodus, there were only around two to two and a half million people living in Egypt,' Mark continued. 'That narrow strip of green along the Nile couldn't possibly sustain more people than that. So how could the Israelites grow enough food on an even smaller, much less fertile piece of land?'

Mark was well and truly on his soapbox now.

'And then there's the fact that the Promised Land they were "fleeing" to was actually occupied by the Egyptians. That would be like if a group of Jews were to escape Nazi Germany, and then, at the end of their arduous journey, heave a huge sigh of relief at having reached Nazi-occupied France! Where they then go on to murder everyone living there. With impunity!'

'That's why I say,' Peter repeated, 'that I don't think that's exactly how it happened. They're parables. It's not what we would consider to be a factual historical account.'

This is precisely what I was just talking to my students about, Peter thought.

'That's all well and good,' Mark said, 'but this parable is the story of Israel. The state of Israel was founded on it. Take that foundation away, and the whole thing collapses.'

Isn't that what Sven said, Peter thought. *'Haven't entire nations been built on a combination of truth and fable?' he'd said. 'Stories like these are obvious fabrications, but they've always been important for creating a feeling of unity in a society.'*

All three men were quiet for a moment.

'Is any of this useful?' Peter asked Inspector Rijsbergen.

'I find it interesting whether it's useful or not,' said Rijsbergen. 'Especially this idea of a story like this not being a literal account. I think that Mevrouw Spežamor mentioned something similar in our conversation yesterday when she was talking about the internal conflict at Loge Ishtar. You know, an investigation like this . . . In some ways, it's not so very different from the scientific research you do at the university. That can sometimes lead to dead ends too, can't it? At times, you might feel like you're on a road to nowhere, but then you'll unexpectedly get a positive result. So initially, everything is potentially relevant because you don't know what the scope of your investigation will be. I sometimes compare it to walking around in a place you're not familiar with: you don't know what the quickest route to your destination would have been until later.'

Peter and Mark both nodded.

'So . . .' said Rijsbergen. 'In summary, neither of you have any idea why Zoutman might have had these stories in his pocket? You don't think there's anything new in them? The stories haven't been retold in a particularly unusual way. Nothing has been left out or added to them?'

Peter and Mark shook their heads.

Just then, the telephone on Rijsbergen's desk rang.

He gestured for Mark and Peter to remain seated.

Peter picked the pages up again. He narrowed his eyes and looked at Coen's neat, regular handwriting, hoping he might discover a hidden message somehow, perhaps by focusing only on the initial letters of each sentence. But he couldn't see anything unusual in it.

'*What?*' Rijsbergen exclaimed. It almost sounded like a cry of despair. Then he listened as whoever was on the other end of the line spoke. He hung up, then sat in his chair with the telephone receiver in his hands.

'What is it?' Peter asked, alarmed. 'Has something bad happened?'

'Yes,' Rijsbergen said. 'This case has just become much more complicated.'

Chapter 19

A body had been found in the murky waters of the Galgewater canal. The victim's body had drifted against the wharf and been found floating halfway under the Rembrandt Bridge. His hands had been tied together.

Starting at the low wall around the De Put Windmill, tall white screens had been erected in a wide semi-circle around the scene to keep curious spectators away. A similar construction had been set up on the opposite side of the canal, near the place where Rembrandt had been born. However, it was impossible to prevent onlookers from videoing the scene from further along the wharf.

Who on earth would you want to show the video to, Rijsbergen thought irritably. *'Have you had fun today?' 'Oh, yes! There was a dead body in the canal, and I got a video of it. Look, it's got a hundred and fifty likes already!'*

Two officers were waiting in a police boat for further orders.

An ambulance was already at the scene when Rijsbergen and Van de Kooij arrived with a fleet of police cars.

Willem spotted Anton Dalhuizen, the Public Health Department's forensic physician who usually carried out the initial examination of the deceased in the event of a suspicious death.

They went to talk to the man who had found the body. His face was ashen. A dog sat waiting patiently at his feet in the middle of the pool of water that had formed around it.

The officer who had been speaking to the witness gave Rijsbergen and De Kooij a brief summary of events. The man had been standing on the lower section of the wharf throwing a tennis ball into the water for his dog. Usually, the dog would bring its ball straight back, but on the last throw, the ball had drifted a little. Instead of retrieving the ball, the dog had barked loudly and swum frantically back to his owner. When he saw what had upset it, the man had immediately called 112.

'What do you think?' Van de Kooij asked as they descended the steps to the wharf.

'It's very . . . unusual,' Rijsbergen said hesitantly. 'I mean, it's unusual to have two murders in Leiden in such a short time. You're automatically inclined to think . . .'

'That the two are connected.'

'Yes, precisely.'

The two police officers in the boat looked up at Rijsbergen and Van de Kooij, who seemed to tower above them like harbour masters.

'Get him out of the water, boys,' Rijsbergen told them.

They pushed the boat off from the side of the wharf. Its motor chugged softly as it moved towards the floating body.

'And for God's sake, get rid of that lot on the other side!' Rijsbergen shouted to nobody in particular. Five or six officers instantly jumped to attention, and within a few minutes they had cleared the area – although they had no control over the people peering from the windows of their own homes.

One of the officers in the boat grabbed the victim by his collar. The boat reversed, and they towed the body slowly along the canal to the wharf where their colleagues helped them to haul it out of the water.

'Look,' someone said. 'His legs have been tied together as well.'

'You'd think there would be witnesses,' Van de Kooij thought out loud. 'You couldn't do this without someone seeing you . . .'

'He could have drifted here from somewhere else,' Rijsbergen suggested. 'Or maybe he was dumped off a boat. You could probably do that without being noticed.' He sighed deeply.

Two members of the ambulance crew placed a stretcher on the ground and lifted the body onto it.

Dalhuizen joined the two detectives. 'The pathologist will have to establish whether he drowned or if he was already dead when he went into the water,' he said, kneeling down by the stretcher. For formality's sake, he pressed two fingers to the dead man's neck.

'Any idea how long he's been in the water?' Rijsbergen asked.

'Hard to say exactly . . . The skin looks fairly normal, no discolouration, no signs of blistering or slippage, no bloating, eyes still in the sockets. He can't have been dead for long. The hair follicles are still firmly attached . . . As an initial estimate, I'd say he's been dead less than twenty-four hours, so he's not been in the water any longer than that. Maybe less if he died elsewhere.' He stood up again. 'As I said, Van Eijk will give you a definitive answer on that, but I don't expect that he'll come to any conclusions that are spectacularly different from mine.' He pulled off his latex gloves.

'Thanks, Anton,' Rijsbergen said. He smiled. 'You've already been very helpful.'

'Gentlemen,' Dalhuizen said. Evidently, this cursory greeting was as far as Dalhuizen's cordiality extended; he went back to his car without another word.

Rijsbergen looked down at the body.

'Could you give me some gloves?' he asked one of the para-medics. The man produced a pair of latex gloves from his overalls and gave them to Rijsbergen.

Rijsbergen put them on and searched the victim's pockets. He pulled out a wallet, a smartphone, and another phone, a simple, old-fashioned Nokia.

Brown water streamed in a thin trickle from the wallet and phones and pooled on the ground.

Rijsbergen opened the wallet, looking for a driving licence or anything with the victim's photo on it.

There was a student card inside.

Rijsbergen removed it and held it up to his eyes to read the name on it. 'Y. *Falaina*,' he said slowly.

'Sounds like that Belgian footballer,' Van de Kooij said. 'Come on, what's he called again? Big, curly head on him.'

'Is this really important right now, Bergkamp?' Rijsbergen asked.

'Well, yes, maybe they share the same nationality.'

That's true, Rijsbergen thought.

'Fellaini,' Van de Kooij said. 'Marouane Fellaini. Plays for the Red Devils, Manchester United. His parents are Moroccan.'

North African . . . He does look like he could be North African. Or South European or maybe Middle Eastern.

'Well, anyway,' Rijsbergen said. 'We'll find out who he is, or rather . . . who he was. Go and get some evidence bags out of the car, and we'll take these things with us now. Forensics can deal with the phones, and we'll have a look at whatever's in the wallet when we get back to the station.'

Rijsbergen waited for Van de Kooij to return.

The paramedics strapped the body onto the stretcher and pulled a thick plastic cover over it.

An image flashed in Rijsbergen's mind's eye.

Might he also have . . .

'Wait!' he shouted.

He squatted down next to the stretcher and put the wallet and phones on the ground. Then he drew back the plastic sheet, carefully unzipped the man's jacket and unbuttoned his shirt. The young man was wearing a vest. Rijsbergen used both hands to pull the vest, shirt and jacket aside so that he could see the skin on the left side of the man's chest.

There, in exactly the same place that Coen Zoutman's tattoo had been, between the nipple and the armpit, a small section of skin about the size of a five-cent coin had been cut away.

'What can you see?' Van de Kooij asked impatiently.

'Something that's not there . . .' Rijsbergen said, straightening the victim's clothes up again. With a quick nod to the ambulance crew to let them know that they could take the victim away, he stood up again. He put the wallet and telephones in the bags that Van de Kooij held out for him.

They took a few paces backwards together, away from everyone else who was working on the crime scene.

'And?' Van de Kooij asked again.

'A piece of skin cut away from the same place where Zoutman had that tattoo,' Rijsbergen said in a half whisper.

'Bizarre,' was all that Van de Kooij managed to say. 'Just . . . Bizarre.'

'Let's go back,' Rijsbergen said. 'Tell the rest of the team to get started on the house-to-house straight away. Make sure they knock on every single door in the area. And have someone contact the media, Leidsch Dagblad, Leiden TV, TV West, Sleutelstad FM, et cetera. Keep the details vague, obviously, but have them appeal for witnesses on their websites, Facebook, radio, whatever. Anyone who saw anything unusual over the last twenty-four hours, around the Galgewater or anywhere else.'

'Will do,' Van de Kooij said, and bounded over to a group of police officers, clearly enjoying being in a position to give orders to other people for a change.

The police officers separated into teams and spread out over the neighbourhood as the paramedics quietly closed the ambulance doors.

Van de Kooij drove them back to the station. In the narrow streets around the Galgewater, his car seemed even more out of place than it did on the main roads.

The evidence bags containing the dead man's wallet and mobile phones lay in the footwell next to Rijsbergen's feet.

The tattoo and the excised skin clearly showed, without a shadow of a doubt, that Coen Zoutman and this Y. Falaina were connected in some way.

But how, Rijsbergen wondered. *Was this young man a Freemason too? Do the other Masons have the same tattoo? Or is this a special group of initiates?*

They drove over Oude Singel canal via the Blauwpoortsbrug and turned left onto the Turfmarkt. In the distance, the mighty De Valk windmill towered over the main route into the city centre.

When they arrived back at the station, Van de Kooij took the mobile phones to the digital forensics team. They didn't expect to encounter too many problems with unlocking them. Generally, only hardened criminals protected their devices with the sort of encryption that was nearly impossible to crack, and Rijsbergen surmised that this was unlikely to apply to the young man they'd fished out of the Galgewater. Water damage was more likely to be the issue.

Van de Kooij would contact the Leiden Freemasons to ask if they knew a Y. Falaina. And he would also search the police records to see if they already had information about him.

Back in his office, Rijsbergen spread the contents of the wallet out on a tray. As well as the student ID card, there was a debit card and a few loyalty cards, nothing unusual. There was a handful of loose change and a twenty-euro note but no receipts or anything else that might contain a clue.

Rijsbergen sat down and sighed deeply, then called the forensics team who promised they would send someone straight over to pick up the wallet and subject it to closer analysis, although he didn't expect them to find much. The murderer – or murderers or murderess – could have disposed of the wallet if they'd wanted to.

There were two brisk knocks on the office door.

Without waiting for a response, Van de Kooij burst in and immediately started to talk. He was holding a sheet of paper in his hand, but he didn't look at it as he spoke.

'Yona Falaina. That's what he's called. The surname is Greek, apparently. The first name is Hebrew – it means "dove". That's the only concrete information we've been able to turn up so far. Not much else otherwise, and nothing at all that's of any use to us. He's lived in the Netherlands for about fifteen years. He's legal. National insurance number checks out. He's got a valid passport and a valid residence permit, no criminal record, always paid his taxes on time, no speeding tickets or parking fines, nothing. If you google his name, all you'll find are pictures of women's shoes on eBay and really colourful fake nails – no idea what that's about. No family, no memberships, and I couldn't find a single photo of him. He's not on Facebook, doesn't seem to have had any paid work, and it looks like he was a ghost student, registered for classes but not attending them. But he must have had a source of income from somewhere – we're looking into whether that was from a job or capital of some sort – because he was renting a room in Leiden. There's a car on its way to that address now.'

Van de Kooij had delivered all this information to Rijsbergen at such speed that he was almost breathless. He made no effort to conceal his pride at having been able to discover so many details about someone who seemed to be almost undiscoverable.

'Well done, Sherlock,' said Rijsbergen. 'We should . . . We'll give the photos that were taken at the scene to a sketch artist so they can create a good likeness of him. We can circulate that and start by showing it to the Freemasons. I'm sure he must have known Coen Zoutman, the man who had the same tattoo as him. Or rather, had a tattoo in the same place . . . If Zoutman knew him, then the other Masons probably knew him too. And get the financial investigation unit to look at his bank account. Where was he getting his money from? What was he doing with it?'

'There was one more thing.' Van de Kooij held out the sheet of paper he had been holding in his hand.

There was a picture on it.

'What are we looking at?' Rijsbergen asked.

'The official symbol of the Freemasons: the square and compasses. I've just printed it out.'

'That does look like two triangles,' Rijsbergen said dubiously, 'with a small circle on top of one of them. But the triangles on the tattoo are arranged differently. And what about that G?'

'No, that G wasn't on the tattoo.'

'What does it stand for?'

'Could stand for all sorts of things,' Van de Kooij said. 'I've just been reading about it. Going from what we've heard so far, it seems typical of Freemasonry. By which I mean that it's left up to the individual Masons to fill in their own meaning for it. The G could stand for God, Gnosis, Goodness, Geometry, the Grand Geometer – for God as the Great Architect of the Universe.'

Rijsbergen looked at the image again. 'I'm not convinced,' he said, 'even if it does have two triangles and a circle in it. But let's keep it in mind. First, go and sort out the other business I was just talking about.'

Van de Kooij, visibly excited by the new tasks, turned around and left the room.

The telephone rang.

'Hey, Rijsbergen.' It was Michiel Kooman from the digital forensics department.

'Hello, Michiel,' Rijsbergen said. 'Have you got something for me?'

'Yes and no . . .' Michiel replied. 'Getting into the phones was a piece of cake. No security to speak of, just a normal PIN code, but we cracked that straight away. He didn't make any calls on the smartphone, but he didn't receive any either. He'd completely turned off the phone's location services and disabled Google's location history. He'd also disabled the function that allows apps to search for available wireless networks. I could go on, but what it comes down to is that he mainly used the phone at home for looking things up. Unfortunately, the search history was set up so that it was deleted regularly. But we might be able to recover it in some way.'

'That's all a bit odd, isn't it?'

'Very odd. He definitely didn't want anyone knowing where he was or where he'd been. And it looks like he took a large sum of money out of a cash machine every now and then and paid for everything in cash. We'll soon see.'

'And the other phone?'

'Actually, that's an even weirder story,' Michiel said, sounding surprised. 'It's a prepaid phone. He might have replaced them regularly because this one looks new.'

'And he used this one for making calls?'

'Correct,' Michiel said. 'And the strange thing is, the contacts list is completely empty. But two days ago, he was called multiple times by the same number, and he didn't pick up. It could be that he was already dead by then. The number was still in there.'

'And?' Rijsbergen said with a growing feeling of excitement.

'So we called the number, and it went to voicemail.'

'Whose voicemail?'

'Coen Zoutman's.'

Chapter 20

Peter and Mark arrived at the History department, still deep in discussion about what could have happened to make the case more complicated.

They hovered at the building's entrance, holding onto their bicycles, unsure what to do next.

'We could go for a coffee,' Mark suggested. 'And you can show me that Pilgrim manuscript. I'd really like to see it.'

'All right,' Peter said.

It would be nice to have some company just now.

'Strictly speaking, though, whoever wrote that document wasn't actually one of the Pilgrims because he stayed behind in Leiden.'

They went inside.

'What does Fay think about you going away for three weeks?' Mark asked once they were in Peter's office.

Peter busied himself with the coffee machine to give himself more time to compose his answer. 'To be honest . . .' he said, 'I still need to tell her. I haven't spoken to her yet.'

Mark narrowed his eyes.

'But, uh . . .' Peter said, 'I'm sure she won't have a problem with it. She's been working on that book for such a long time, and I know she wants to get it finished. She'll be glad to have me out of her hair for three weeks.'

He'd hoped this would sound light-hearted, but Mark didn't laugh.

'Things are all right with the two of you, aren't they?' Mark asked, sounding concerned. 'This trip isn't you running away from something, is it?'

Mark wasn't known for his keen sense of empathy, but this wasn't the first time he'd surprised Peter with this sort of insight. Every now and then, he would say something that defied everyone's expectations of him.

'No, there's nothing wrong,' Peter said hastily. 'Nothing to worry about, anyway. Every relationship has its ups and downs, right?'

'That's what they say, but Judith and I have never had a "down". Not as far as I'm aware of, anyway,' Mark said and smiled.

While the coffee brewed, Peter uncoupled his laptop from the docking station on the desk and sat down next to Mark on the sofa. He opened the files that Piet van Vliet had sent him.

'There's something interesting in the last fragment. You'll see it yourself when you read it. It looks like a group developed within the Leiden Separatists, and it specifically mentions that it was mostly builders, masons . . .'

'A group *inside* the English Puritans?'

'Yes. It's all a bit cryptic, really. You need to see it for yourself. But the author also says: "he that hath ears to hear, let him hear". Like a word to the wise. I think he's hinting at something, but he either doesn't dare say it or doesn't want to. And straight after that, there's a sentence about the key player in the group, Josh Nunn, who's got his own loge box at the theatre. His own *loge*.'

Mark looked at him in astonishment.

'Builders, masons . . .' Mark said slowly. 'And a loge? As in Loge La Vertu? Okay, he's writing about a loge in a theatre, but still . . . It surely can't be what I think it is.'

'You're thinking it's the Freemasons too, aren't you?'

'Absolutely,' Mark replied. 'Stonemasons meeting at a loge . . . . That would be incredible. This was about a hundred years before the first English lodge was established. If Piet can find a connection between the Freemasons and the English Puritans who stayed behind in the Netherlands and show that they were the forerunners of the Leiden lodge . . . . I mean, it seems far-fetched, but if he can find evidence to back it up and develop it into a hypothesis, I'd be very interested in seeing it.'

For years, Mark had been avidly compiling a collection of theories that could be filed under the category 'alternative science'. Many of these were sent to him unsolicited by people who believed that they had found a code in the Bible that had never been discovered before. They would attempt to back up their claims with complicated calculations that were impossible to follow. Often, these were about the Book of Revelation, the last and by far the most enigmatic book of the Bible, full of dark verses and apocalyptic predictions.

Mark had an acquaintance who was an Egyptologist. He regularly sent him large envelopes stuffed with densely written sheets of paper that he'd been given by people who thought they could prove that the conventional Egyptian chronology was incorrect, or that the pyramids had been built by aliens, or that there were long-forgotten energy sources – deliberately covered up by governments! – that could solve our current energy problems in an instant.

Mark planned to turn them into a book one day; he already had enough material to fill several volumes.

'But it's not very likely, is it?' said Peter.

'It's not likely at all, but it's not completely impossible either. It would be unscientific to just dismiss everything that doesn't fit with what we already know. Because there *could* have been Masonic groups before the first English grand lodge was established in 1717. That was a union of several English lodges, so they were clearly active before then. It's possible that there were similar groups in the Netherlands – or in Leiden. There's no way of knowing for sure. But if it's true, it's not recorded in any official histories. If the Pilgrims and the Freemasons were connected, we would have to revise history as we know it by more than a hundred years. The first Dutch loge was set up in The Hague in 1734 with help from English and French Masons, the Loge du Grand-Maître des Provinces Unies et du Ressort de la Généralité . . .' Mark pronounced the name with perfect French diction. 'Our Pilgrims went to America in 1620. The connection between them has never been made before.'

'But most of the Pilgrims stayed behind.'

'That's true, but even so . . . Look, nothing is impossible. This idea is just completely new.'

'It would clarify something that I've often wondered about,' Peter said.

'What's that?'

'It's simple, really. Whatever reasons the Pilgrims had for leaving, they must also have applied to the people who stayed behind, but most of them stayed here. Why didn't they *all* leave? It's an obvious question, isn't it?'

'Maybe they didn't have enough money for the crossing,' Mark said sensibly. 'Or maybe they fell in love with a beautiful Dutchwoman. They might have been afraid of spending weeks on a boat heading for a world they didn't know. It might have been their promised land, but it was full of dangers. I could think of a dozen other reasons. Staying here might have been the wisest choice in the end. Lots of passengers died before they even reached America, and half of those who survived the crossing died during that first winter. The ones who stayed in Leiden were probably smarter than the others.'

'Well, who knows? Their reasons could have been as banal as you suggest they were. But if it was their promised land as you say, wouldn't that have been like most of the Israelites deciding to stay in the desert rather than going to the promised land with Joshua?'

Mark laughed heartily, like he had just heard a brilliant joke. 'And that they thought,' he said, still laughing, '"Oh, this will do. We survived the Ten Plagues, we've wandered in the desert for forty years, the storm has passed. The manna's falling straight out of the sky and the quails are almost flying into our mouths. Let's just stay here, eh?"'

'Yes, pretty much,' said Peter, looking at Mark with amusement.

Mark put his glasses back on, still grinning.

Peter passed the laptop over to Mark and got up to pour the coffee. 'Oh! Sorry, I completely forgot to ask about the graffiti on the Sionshof wall. Has there been any news?'

'Oh, that?' said Mark, who was already intently focused on the screen. 'They solved that pretty quickly, actually, amazingly quickly. They've caught the people who did it. The police officer who called me sounded very surprised himself, like he couldn't believe how quickly they'd cracked the case.'

'That's very impressive. Did anyone see them?'

'No. The policeman was a bit of a pompous sort. He went on about good detective work and intelligence from the field, good sources and so on, but I got the impression that what really happened was that someone from their own circle snitched on them. It turns out they were protestors, objecting to the Israeli occupation of Palestinian land.'

'What about Judith?'

'She was relieved. But she knew it wasn't aimed at her, or at least, it wasn't likely to have been.'

'I'm glad it's been sorted out before she leaves on Sunday.'

'Me too,' Mark said. 'Right, let me read this.'

Peter opened the window and perched on the windowsill.

'Do you mind if I . . .' he began, but Mark was so absorbed in the text that Peter didn't need to bother asking. He lit his cigarillo, took a careful first drag and allowed the smoke to escape from his lips. He sipped his coffee slowly and allowed himself to relax for the first time that day. He closed his eyes and tried to focus, although he wasn't sure exactly what he should focus on.

Something that Mark just said? Or something in Coen's Bible stories?

Peter took another drag on his cigar, keeping his eyes closed, afraid that he would lose his train of thought if he opened them. He felt like he was on to something but couldn't put his finger on what it was. Often, when he was working on a paper, an idea would form in the back of his mind, but it was more of a hazy notion than something he could put into words.

A few moments later, he opened his eyes and looked at Mark. He was still engrossed in the manuscript.

I might as well light another cigar, Peter thought. *Mark's a fast reader, but this will take him a while.*

Peter gave up. Experience had taught him that it was pointless to try to focus on this vague feeling. It was better to leave it alone, like stewing a good cut of meat on a low heat without removing the lid so that the cooking process wouldn't be disturbed.

'Fascinating stuff,' Mark said excitedly when Peter had finished his second cigar. 'Really fascinating. Not much in it that we didn't already know, of course, but to have an insider's view . . . Fantastic.'

'Yes, most of it is just what we already know,' Peter said. 'But what was new for me was this idea that there were tensions within the group. I've never heard about that before. That could explain why more than half of them ended up staying in Leiden, couldn't it? And those references to a young boy . . . That's a bit odd too.'

'Isn't it? The idea that there was some sort of split, that really is new. Interesting. And the boy . . . Maybe he was meant to be the new leader? Was he being initiated? Who knows?'

Mark scrolled through the text until he found the passage that he was thinking of.

'This part is very unusual, Peter.' Mark let his index finger hover half a centimetre away from the screen, like someone just learning to read. 'Those who have gravitated towards Josh Nunn – many of whom work in the building trade, stonemasons and so on – he that hath ears to hear, let him hear – have chosen to stay in Leiden,' he read aloud. 'That explicit reference to Masons is striking.'

Peter sat back down next to Mark. 'And so is that quotation, "he that hath ears to hear, let him hear".'

'The emphasis on that specific trade is intriguing, especially because it's mentioned together with that scripture, which gives it even more emphasis.'

Mark moved to give the laptop back to Peter but then paused. 'Can you email it to me?'

'Sure, no problem. Piet is always saying that he's a great believer in sharing resources as much as possible.' Peter stood up and put the laptop back on his desk. 'I'm going to head home to Fay,' he said. 'It was good talking to you, Mark. We've covered a lot of ground, and something gives me the feeling that I'm getting closer to finding a solution. Even though I don't know what it's supposed to solve.'

'That sounds hopeful,' Mark said, smiling. 'Well, I'll be on my way. I'll see you at La Bota on Saturday.'

'See you then.'

Fay, Peter, Judith and Mark had planned a leaving dinner for Judith that Saturday.

I'm glad I'll get some time with Judith alone tomorrow though, Peter thought.

They went outside and said goodbye.

Peter turned right onto the Doelensteeg and headed for Fay's house. Mark went the other way towards his office on the Witte Singel.

Halfway across the bridge over the Rapenburg, Peter stopped and idled for a while, not sure that he wanted to go to Fay's house after all.

But I can't keep avoiding her.

He crossed the bridge and walked along the canalside, dragging his feet. The Dutch expression 'with lead in the shoes' suddenly felt very appropriate.

Fay's house was quiet and still.

He knew that Agapé was at korfball training, and Alena often went with her.

Maybe she's not at home, he thought hopefully. *Then I can at least say I came by*.

He went inside.

But I still need to tell her that I'm going to Boston in three weeks.

'Are you home, darling?' he said cautiously as he went into the living room. 'Fay?' He called out louder this time.

He had already turned to leave again when he heard Fay's voice coming from above him.

'I'm up here!' she called down.

He heard her coming down the stairs.

She stopped on the bottom step, like someone about to jump into a swimming pool but baulking at the thought of the chilly water.

'Why didn't you reply to my text?' Fay asked.

Peter froze in the doorway with his hand on the door handle as though he was on his way out and hadn't arrived just a few moments earlier.

'I wasn't sure what it was about,' he said, closing the door and going back into the living room.

'You weren't sure what it was *about*?' Fay parroted indignantly. 'You'd been reading my emails, hadn't you? You even opened one and deleted it afterwards!'

'But how—'

'I saw that there was a mail from Coen yesterday. All his emails automatically get sent to a folder. His are the only messages that go in there.'

'And why—'

'You were completely out of order, Peter. I don't owe anybody an explanation for what I do. Not even you. And not for this. It's none of anyone's business.'

Peter gulped.

People often underestimated Fay because of her friendly manner – even Peter sometimes misjudged her – and in discussions, they would frequently be surprised by how remarkably assertive she could be.

'Did you read any of the other emails?' she asked.

'No,' Peter replied.

I might as well be honest.

'Listen,' he said. 'Let's sit down, all right?'

Fay sat in the armchair and Peter took a seat on the sofa.

'I opened the laptop,' he said. 'Your mail client was open. I saw that there was a folder called "Coen Zoutman". I thought it was odd because you never told me that you emailed each other at all.'

'And I didn't *have* to tell you that.'

'You're right,' Peter said, holding up his hands defensively. 'I saw that there was a new message, and I clicked on the folder. But then, I realised that – and this is exactly how it went – that I shouldn't be looking at your emails. I meant to close the folder, but then I accidentally clicked on that new email. All it said was "I'll see you this evening." Nothing more. And then I thought . . . It was stupid of me, Fay. I'm sorry. But then I thought: there's nothing important in this email, so I'll delete it before Fay sees that I've opened it.'

'That was his very last email to me, Peter.'

'Yes, I know.'

'I knew he'd sent me an email, but I couldn't bring myself to look in that folder. I just slammed the laptop shut when I saw it. It really spooked me. It was irrational, I know, but I didn't dare to read what he had written to me. And it was like . . .' Her voice was suddenly stifled as she choked back tears.

Should I go over to her, Peter thought. 'Sorry, darling,' he said. 'It was stupid of me. I should have told you straight away.'

'It felt like . . .' Fay said, ignoring Peter's apology. 'It sounds mad, but it felt like I could make him still be alive by not reading that email. It's not . . . I know it's not rational. It even sounds crazy to me when I say it out loud.' She sniffled.

'When I finally got up the courage to read it this morning,

it was gone. But deleted emails stay in the trash folder for a while, so you still have a chance to recover them.'

I didn't think of that.

'So I found the email. And no, there was nothing out of the ordinary in it, but it was his last message to me. And apart from that, I really don't like you nosing around in my emails.' She glared at him. 'Are you sure you didn't read any of the others?'

'No, honestly I didn't,' Peter said. 'I wouldn't do that, would I? Not normally, anyway. It's a strange situation, a strange time . . . How many times have I worked on your computer? And how often do you just leave everything open? I always close it all without looking at it. You do trust me, don't you?'

Fay glared at him.

'Really, Fay, I'm sorry. I won't do it again.'

She appeared to have decided to let it go for now. There's little point in fighting an opponent who has already given in.

'You could easily have restored the message, you know. You can mark an email as unread. I would have been none the wiser.'

'Ah,' Peter said, with real surprise. 'I didn't know that.' He smiled at her. 'I'll keep that function in mind for next time,' he said jokingly. It was an attempt to clear the air, but Fay remained stone-faced.

'Good,' she said, and there was still a sharp edge to her voice.

'Is there something I should know?' Peter couldn't resist asking. 'Why are you so upset about this? I understand that it's not nice knowing someone's been reading your emails when you'd rather they didn't, but this reaction seems a little bit . . . Is there something you're worried I might have read? Something you're hiding from me?'

Fay shook her head vigorously.

She took a fraction of a second too long to deny it, Peter thought.

But right now, I'm not in a position to interrogate her about her
emails with Coen Zoutman.

'Good,' he said. 'Shall we leave it there, then?'

A silence hung over them, like the two actors in this scene
were waiting for instructions from a director.

'I'm over it already,' Fay said, breaking the impasse.

They both stood up. Fay went over to hug him, and he wrapped
his arms around her.

'I do have something to tell you, by the way,' he said.

Fay let go of him and took a step back. She looked like she
was on her guard. 'Go on,' she said, trying to sound light-hearted,
but she couldn't hide the tension in her voice.

'Judith's asked me to visit her in Boston. I've said yes . . .'

'Oh. Okay,' she said with visible relief. She smiled. 'That's . . .
great, right?'

'I'm staying for three weeks. Or rather, I'll be in America for
three weeks, and I'll spend some of it with her, a week maybe.
They're giving her a big apartment, she says.'

'Well, that's nice, isn't it? It'll be lovely for her, and for you too.
It's been ages since you last went travelling. It'll do you good.'

'I'm leaving in three weeks.'

'Oh.' She seemed taken aback. 'That's . . . soon.'

'I've just booked it.'

'Right, well . . . You don't waste any time, do you?'

'No,' Peter agreed. 'It was a spur-of-the-moment thing. She
asked, and I said yes. But it felt right. And anyway, you've got
your book to do.'

'That's true,' she said. 'I'll be busy. And it won't get in the way
of our holiday plans this summer. Better that you go now than
in the summer, right?'

A few months earlier, they had booked a three-week holiday

to the Greek island of Santorini. Apart from the odd long weekend they'd spent on the Dutch island of Texel, it was going to be their first real 'family' holiday.

'I'm so glad you don't mind, Fay.'

'It's fine, really. And you're right. I can work on my book, and you'll come back refreshed and full of energy.' Apparently having said all she wanted to say, she went over to the kitchen counter and opened a bottle of wine. She poured two glasses and took them back over to Peter. 'To Boston, then,' she said as they clinked their glasses.

'And to us . . .' Peter said, more hesitantly.

'And to us,' Fay said. 'Now, don't do anything I wouldn't do.' She took two large gulps of wine and went back to the kitchen. 'Are you going to visit the Freemasons while you're there?' she asked.

'That's a good idea, actually. Why not?'

'I'd love it if you called in at the grand lodge in Boston. Take some photos or a little video or something for me. I'm so curious to see what it looks like, an old lodge like that.'

'I will.'

Fay appeared to have decided that it was now time to empty the kitchen cupboards and give them a thorough clean.

Peter picked up her laptop. 'Just reading your emails,' he teased.

He was relieved to see that Fay could already laugh about it. 'I've moved them to a new super-secret program that nobody will ever get into,' she said.

Yeah, yeah . . . Peter thought. *It's all well and good that people have the right to keep some secrets in a relationship, but you're not being completely honest with me, Fay.*

When the laptop had started up, he saw that Fay's Outlook program was open, as though she wanted to make it abundantly clear that she trusted him.

But he could see at a glance that something had changed.

After a quick glance at Fay fanatically scrubbing in the kitchen, he looked at her email folders.

The 'Coen Zoutman' folder was gone.

Chapter 21

Peter and Fay usually made a point of going to bed at the same time, and they would lie next to each other, chatting about their day or reading. But tonight, Fay went upstairs alone.

When Peter undressed in the darkness of the bedroom later that night, he could tell from the way Fay was breathing that she wasn't asleep. But they didn't speak.

When Peter got up the next morning, Fay stayed in bed. Again, Peter was convinced that she was awake.

He left the house without eating breakfast. Agapé was already downstairs. He told her that he had to leave early because he had a busy day ahead.

It wasn't a lie – he really did have a lot to do. The decision to visit Judith had meant moving a lot of his work forward. He spent most of the morning at his desk marking a large stack of papers. Later that day, he was due to give a guest lecture for his colleague Job Westrate on the history of ideas in the seventeenth and eighteenth centuries.

He found it difficult to concentrate, and not just because of his spat with Fay. Coen Zoutman's death weighed heavily on his mind.

Peter had read on the Leidsch Dagblad's website that the body of a young man had been found in the Galgewater. Whether or not this second death was connected to Coen's murder, he found it deeply troubling that a body had been found so close by, under a bridge that he had crossed countless times.

In their initial press briefing, the police had emphasised that the death was suspicious, and not simply an unfortunate accident in which someone had fallen into the canal and drowned.

Peter had studied the artist's impression of the victim, but it didn't look like anyone he knew. And the name Yona Falaina didn't ring a bell. It gave him a strange feeling of relief – at least the victim wasn't one of his students.

He pushed the pile of unmarked papers aside.

Peter filled up the coffee machine and switched it on. While he waited for it to percolate, he took up his usual position on the windowsill and lit a cigar.

There must have been something in those emails, he thought. *Do I have anything on my computer that I definitely wouldn't want anyone to see?*

He couldn't think of anything.

Of course, nobody likes the idea of someone digging around in their emails without asking permission. I understand that. It's a question of privacy more than anything else.

He had noticed that whenever his students discussed the topic of privacy during their coffee breaks, most of them were worryingly apathetic. None of them seemed concerned that the government was about to introduce a law giving them increased powers to monitor their emails and telephone calls. 'I've got nothing to hide,' was the standard response. But if he asked them to give him their mobile phones so he could read their chats and text messages, they always refused.

I don't suppose I would like it if Fay read my texts and emails either, so she's hardly being unreasonable. What really bothers me is that I had no idea she and Coen had been emailing each other so much.

Peter smoked his cigar and let his mind wander until he was suddenly startled by a sharp pain. The stub of his cigarillo had become so short that the glowing ash stack had scorched his fingertips. He still hankered for one last puff, but there was too little left of the cigar now. With a pang of regret, he threw the stub outside.

He poured a cup of coffee and sat at his computer.

In just over three weeks, he would be following Judith out to Boston.

I could make good use of my time there by learning more about the Pilgrims, Peter thought. *I might find out something about the possible connection between the Pilgrims and the Freemasons if I visit the Boston grand lodge. I'm pretty familiar with the subject now. Maybe I'll get to talk to someone who shares my interest in it. It would be great to be able to tell the visitors in the Leiden American Pilgrim Museum some stories that are based on my own experiences.*

Peter opened the files that Piet van Vliet had sent him. He created a blank Word document, then he spent some time cutting and pasting until he had combined all the separate fragments into one continuous text.

Piet could turn this into a book one day, Peter thought, *although the audience for it would be quite small. Actually, this sort of material would make a great novel. It deserves a wider audience.*

He printed everything out and tucked all of the pages into a document wallet, like a student finishing off an assignment.

There were a few things in the manuscript that had stood out to him. First, the boys whom Josh had taken under his wing like protégés. One of them went to America on the *Mayflower*, but back in Leiden, he was immediately replaced by another boy. Secondly, the conflict or division that had developed within the group. And lastly, although it was more implied than explicit, the possible connection between the Pilgrims and the Freemasons. Might those three things be linked in a way that had – so far? – always remained hidden?

He pasted the relevant passages into another separate document and wrote a description above each section to remind himself which part of the manuscript they came from.

The men watch helplessly from the boat as the women and children are taken away by soldiers.

As soon as we had boarded the ship, we saw a company of soldiers rushing along the beach towards us.

I write 'men', but there was also a boy among us. He was under the special protection of Josh Nunn, one of the other leaders of our group. The boy never left Josh's side, often keeping tight hold of his hand – and when that was not possible, he held onto his coat.

The rough crossing from England to the Netherlands that takes much longer than planned.

Josh shared his food with the boy, the same scanty ration that had been given to the rest of us, which made the lad the best-fed passenger on the whole ship. No one knew who the child was, and no one dared to ask where he had come from. We knew that he was an orphan and that, just like Josh, he did not have another living soul in the world, but we knew no more than that. They often retreated to a quiet spot belowdecks where Josh talked to the boy endlessly, like a seller on a market stall persuading a customer to buy his wares. The boy appeared to repeat his words, nodding his head earnestly as he spoke.

After they have settled in Leiden.

The little fellow who seemed to be particularly favoured by Josh Nunn is growing into a boy who rarely speaks in public but who seems to increase in confidence by the day. He is a member of Josh's household. Although he still stays close to Nunn's side, I have recently seen him walking through town, usually alone. Sometimes he joins the other boys, but he walks apart from them. The boy's private instruction continues unabated. Perhaps Josh sees in him a future leader of our community and is preparing him for that role.

After a few years in Leiden.

The adopted 'son', as everyone thinks of the boy whom Josh Nunn has taken under his wing, has grown into a handsome, bright young man, a fully fledged member of our congregation. Sometimes he speaks at Sunday worship, which some members tolerate with a measure of reluctance. Or is it jealousy? People object because he has no formal training in preaching God's word and correctly explaining His Scriptures. They never do this openly, of course, but only when they think they are not being observed. A more serious objection is that the boy sometimes has the tendency to interpret things too liberally, as though he is looking for the story that might be hidden behind a story.

As though he has found an obscure meaning that to us mere mortals remains invisible.

The group separates.

We are going to America.

Although, not 'we' exactly. Most of us will stay behind in Leiden. Some of our group have already returned to England. Life in Holland was much harder than they were able to bear, and they chose to go back to Scrooby. Life is not easy there either, but it will at least be familiar. Not even the risk of being thrown in jail as soon as they set foot on shore was enough to persuade them to stay here.

Shortly afterwards, the author says:

I am not privy to whatever has caused it, but I can see that the group has split in two. There is no crystal-clear dividing line that might make it clear to outsiders who belongs to which group. Nor are there two distinct factions who stand opposite each other or sit apart from each other during worship . . .

Those who have gravitated towards Josh Nunn – many of whom work in the building trade, stonemasons and so on – he that hath ears to hear, let him hear – have chosen to stay in Leiden. Josh has done well for himself and has his own private loge box at the theatre. The men at the core of his group meet there often and discuss things with each other during the intervals.

Josh has now taken a new boy under his wing. He seems to be starting anew with the same process as before: they withdraw together to speak in private. It is obvious that Josh does most of the talking – I see them sometimes, sitting together in our shared garden – and the boy nods as earnestly as his predecessor did ten years ago.

And here is the most astonishing thing of all: that – former? – apple of Josh's eye, the young lad who is now a grown man in the prime of his life. The boy who spent the last ten or eleven years as Josh's inseparable shadow. The boy upon whom Josh looked with fatherly pride, nodding in approval when he spoke in church – to the increasing vexation of the members of the other faction. That boy . . .

That boy is going to America.

There was likely to be a simple explanation for it all. Josh might have intended for the boy to succeed him, and when that boy decided to go to America, Josh's eye fell on a new boy. And . . . Over time, splits often develop in groups – especially in religious groups like the Protestants where the absence of a central, papal authority means that members can interpret the scriptures in any way they wish. There are often people who want to return to the origins of their religion, who believe in strict conformity to the absolute fundamentals of the faith because they think that the divinely inspired texts are being interpreted too liberally. Other people believe that times change, and the way you engage with the ancient texts and their teachings should change too. After all, these days, no one still believes that you should be stoned for gathering wood on the Sabbath, just one of the many sins punishable by death according to the Old Testament.

Then there was the relationship between the Freemasons and the remnant congregation in Leiden. The evidence for it was scant, admittedly, but that 'he that hath ears to hear, let him hear' was intriguing.

There was also a logical explanation for the fact that such a large group chose not to go to America. The reasons were explained in the manuscript: the crossing was expensive and dangerous, some of the congregation had become official burghers of Leiden by obtaining *poorterschap*, which gave them a relatively large degree of liberty.

But for people who risked life and limb by coming to the Netherlands to escape religious persecution, they seem to have abandoned their fervent desire for religious freedom rather easily, Peter thought. *Did they choose the easier path instead? Make compromises and accept that this was the best they could do? Were they less devout than the people who went to the New World? And was the group that went to America made up of people who split away from the others? Fundamentalists who stood in opposition to the 'weak' ones who were left behind?*

Peter circled 'he that hath ears to hear, let him hear' in red pen.

He left his office and went to the lecture theatre in the Lipsius Building to give his guest lecture. His colleague, Job, was already waiting for him at the door. Job was a good-looking man in his early forties with a neat 'designer-stubble' beard. He was well-liked for his engaging teaching style and genuine interest in his students.

His eyes lit up when he saw Peter coming, as if he had been afraid that he wouldn't turn up.

'So glad you're here,' Job said, slapping a hand on Peter's back to steer him inside.

About twenty-five or thirty students sat waiting for the lecture to begin. Peter recognised some of them from his own lectures. Including Sven and Stefan.

Sven greeted Peter with a nervous smile that almost looked apologetic.

Job briefly introduced him, then Peter forged straight ahead with his lecture on Arminius and Gomarus. He spoke compellingly about the two professors and their heated debate in the early seventeenth century about the doctrine of predestination, man's free will – a debate that was to have a profound influence on the course of Dutch history.

Now and then, he wrote keywords on the old-fashioned blackboard with a stub of chalk. He wiped his chalky fingers on his trousers occasionally, creating a dusty smudge. It was a habit that Fay had always found quite endearing.

The students seemed to be mesmerised, nodding in agreement at certain moments and frowning in surprise at others.

'So, guys,' Peter said, 'on one side, we have Franciscus Gomarus in Groningen, a professor of theology who said that only God could decide if a person would be saved or not. Essentially, his idea was that everything has already been determined by God, and man can have no influence over His decisions. You can't achieve salvation by doing good works, by giving food to the hungry and water to the thirsty . . . I'm sure you're all familiar with the six acts of mercy?'

He paused for a moment and looked around the hall, where the students' vacant expressions told him that they were not, in fact, familiar with the six acts at all.

'You should give food to the hungry, water to the thirsty,' he answered for them. 'You should visit prisoners in jail, take care of the sick, welcome strangers, and clothe the naked. The Catholic Church has a bit of an obsession with the number seven, so they added 'bury the dead'. But Jesus only mentions six good works in Matthew 25. But I digress. What you do here on earth in the approximately twenty-six thousand days that the average person lives – in our time, that is, because people died younger in the seventeenth century – has no influence on God's decision about whether you'll be spending eternity in heaven or hell.'

'But that's really . . .' said one of the students, looking absolutely outraged. 'That's *really* . . .'

'Unfair?' Peter said.

'Yeah, if it doesn't matter what you do, then you might as well go wild and do whatever you want. If God's decision has already been made anyway.'

'Very good,' Peter said appreciatively. 'And that was also . . . Well, the idea is more that God is the sovereign Lord of all. He's so powerful that your insignificant human acts can have no influence on His decisions which, of course, are always wise and just. But Gomarus's opinion was aligned with that of Calvin. He said that God didn't completely absolve man of responsibility for his own actions. It's a thorny issue. Even though your fate is already decided, and you can't exercise any influence over it, you still have to follow God's moral laws, the Ten Commandments. Of course, this argument was partly a Protestant response to some of the more corrupt doctrines of the Catholic Church, doctrines that had no basis in scripture. You know about that, right? The Catholic Church taught that you could pay your way to heaven. Or rather, that you could shorten your time in limbo or purgatory – the awful waiting room where you're tormented before being admitted to heaven – by buying an indulgence. And that you could still earn your place in heaven anyway, like you can all earn your degrees by working hard. That idea, in particular, was seen to diminish the majestic divinity of God. You see, then it's like God is just an accountant who keeps a record of all your good and bad deeds. He tots it all up, makes the deductions, balances your book and then looks at the bottom line to decide whether you'll get to stay with Him forever in heaven, or whether you're going to the terrible place where there's no God, no love: hell. The Catholic Church had turned salvation into a "horse trade" where poor people would spend their last penny on indulgences, and unscrupulous priests lined their own pockets. According to Luther and others like him, that's not how God works. That describes a very small, human, all-too-human God. Moreover, there's nothing in the Bible about indulgences or buying forgiveness for your sins. Only your faith in God and His Son would save you. You could only be redeemed by the grace of God . . .'

He gave the students a chance to write everything down.

'And then on the other side of the argument, you had Arminius,' Peter went on. 'He was from Leiden. Actually, he lived quite close to here, opposite the Pieterskerk. He opposed Gomarus's view. Arminius thought that Gomarus's ideas about predestination were far too stringent. For example, in his view, man was free to choose whether or not he believed in God in the first place. So, to a large extent, redemption depended on the free will of each individual person. As I said earlier, these are thorny issues, guys. It's impossible for us to imagine today just how incredibly heated this debate became. But it was the issue of the day everywhere. Everyone had an opinion about it, and everyone was talking about it, not just in the university – on every street. Discussions often got out of hand and friendships were broken. Imagine going for lunch in the cafeteria after this lecture and finding that everyone there is engaged in a heated debate about theology, predestination in this case, and there are even people supporting their arguments by reciting long texts from memory. You're not likely to see anything like that today.

Imagine emotions and tempers running so high that some students have to be restrained because they're threatening to punch another student who doesn't share their opinions on man's foreordained fate.'

The students laughed.

'Different times, different times . . . But . . . anyway . . .' Peter felt his phone buzz in his trouser pocket. He was itching to check it, but he didn't dare. He was known around campus for being unusually intolerant of the use of mobile phones during his lectures. He usually left his own phone in his desk drawer to set a good example to his students and prove to them that life went on even when you were physically separated from your mobile devices. He regularly found himself with an empty battery and no charger, meaning that he would be out of reach for hours – something that this generation would find unthinkable.

He fished the phone out of his trouser pocket as nonchalantly as he could and dropped it into the inside pocket of his jacket that he had hung over the back of a chair. Now he wouldn't be distracted if the phone rang again.

He went on with the lecture, but the intense focus he'd had earlier in the session was gone. 'The official church of the Republic of the Seven United Netherlands was the Dutch Reformed Church. I think Meneer Westrate already covered this in an earlier lecture?'

The students and his colleague nodded in reply.

'After his death, Arminius's supporters tried to have his ideas adopted by the Reformed Church, the state church. They submitted a statement of opposition to the States-General, formulating their points of disagreement with Calvin's teachings which had been adopted by the church. This sort of statement is called a "remonstrance", and so they became known as the "Remonstrants".'

Peter erased the notes he had previously made from the blackboard and then, in large letters, wrote the words REMON-STRANTS – ARMINUS and CONTRA-REMONSTRANTS – GOMARUS – PRINCE MAURICE.

'This is the last thing I'd like to talk to you about today,' he said. 'And then I'm going to end with a clip from *God in de Lage Landen*, a rather underappreciated documentary series about the history of Christianity in the Netherlands. So, to continue . . . In 1619, a great synod, a church council, was convened in Dordrecht. It ultimately decided that Gomarus's teachings would become part of the official doctrine of the Dutch Reformed Church. Those who favoured Arminius's teachings, the Arminians or Remonstrants were given a choice between keeping quiet about their views or being persecuted by their opponents, the Contra-Remonstrants. The conflict intensified, and it took on a political dimension when Maurice, Prince of Orange, declared that the young Republic should only have one faith and chose to support the Contra-Remonstrants.'

While the faint rattle of dozens of fingers on the keyboards slowly but surely died away, Peter took a moment to find the section of the video that he wanted to play.

'Now we're going to watch a clip from this documentary, which, by the way, I wholeheartedly recommend you watch all the way through if you can. What's good about this is that the stories are told on location, so you're going to see a lot of well-known places in Leiden this video.'

For the next fifteen minutes, they watched as the presenter, Ernst Daniël Smid, told viewers about the Synod of Dort with all the eloquence and dramatic delivery of an actor, bringing history to life as he stood outside the house where Arminius had lived and walked past the stately townhouses on the Rapenburg canal.

Peter looked at the clock and saw that his time was almost up.

'I'll wrap this up now, guys,' he said and paused the video. 'As Meneer Smid explained, this led to an extreme intolerance towards other faiths in the Republic. Church services were only allowed to be conducted – in public at least – by the Reformed Church. If you wanted to hold public office, you had to conform to the Reformed Church, and swear an oath to that effect too. In reality, the hunger for prosecuting dissenting churches for holding religious services varied over time and depended on each city or region's governors. In the early days of the Republic, the main target was Roman Catholicism, the religion of the Spaniards who were the 'enemy'. In seventeenth-century Leiden, you could be fined two hundred guilders – an astronomical amount of money in those days – for allowing your house to be used for non-Reformed church services. You could even be banished from the city!'

There was a growing buzz of restlessness in the room, not so much because of this last eye-opening fact, but more because everyone was clearly ready for a coffee break.

'This was the time when *schuilkerken* were set up, clandestine churches where services were held in secret. There are a couple in Leiden,' Peter said, winding up the lecture. 'There's the Remonstrant church on the Hooglandse Kerkgracht and the Sint Lodewijkskerk on the Steenschuur. Well worth popping in, on Heritage Open Days for example. They were tolerated but not allowed to have a visible church façade on public streets, so they were often hidden inside houses.'

Job Westrate held up a hand to indicate that it was time for a break.

'Thank you very much, Professor De Haan,' he said sincerely. 'Let's stop there, and after a short break, I'll pick up exactly where you've left off, in 1620. We'll be looking at the radical Amsterdam Burgomaster Frederick de Vrij who demolished the stalls at a Sinterklaas market on Dam Square in an attempt to end the "popish" celebration of the Feast of Saint Nicholas, like a modern Christ in the Temple.'

Peter turned down Job's invitation to go for coffee with the excuse that he had another appointment.

As he walked back to his office, he took out his mobile phone There was a text from Fay.

It was short and simple.

Peter, we need to talk.

Chapter 22

A post-mortem conducted on the body in the Galgewater immediately after it was found had shown that the victim had been dead for somewhere between twelve and twenty-four hours, just as Dalhuizen had suspected.

That meant that Yona Falaina had been killed after Coen Zoutman.

Rather than having drowned, he had died before entering the water.

Everything pointed to death by suffocation. His neck showed no signs of strangulation. The absence of anyone else's DNA under his fingernails suggested that his hands had been tied together before he was killed.

Another twenty-four hours had passed since his body had been found, but the police were still essentially coming up empty-handed.

A check of the Interpol databases had turned up nothing useful in Greece. The man was registered nowhere, had broken no laws, had no debts, no irregularities in his documentation and didn't even have so much as a parking ticket in his name . . . he was a model citizen of the European Union. All that was left to do now was wait for a response from the Greek embassy who were looking into whether Yona Falaina had family who should be informed about his death.

Rijsbergen sat next to Van de Kooij in the car. A file on his lap contained a photograph of Yona Falaina taken from municipal records and the drawing of Coen Zoutman's tattoo. They would be showing both to key figures within the Freemasonry community.

The first name on their list was Jenny van der Lede, one of the two candidates who had stood against Coen Zoutman in the chairmanship election.

She lived in the Burgemeesterswijk, an expensive and popular 1930s neighbourhood in Leiden, just beyond the Zoeterwoudse Singel, part of the seventeenth-century ring canal that enclosed the centre of the city.

As they drove to her house, Van de Kooij excitedly told Rijsbergen about one of the true crime programmes he and his partner Sharon enjoyed watching on his favourite TV station, the Discovery Channel. You could easily fill an entire evening with *Homicide Hunter*, *or Deadly Women*, or *American Monsters*, or whatever they were called.

Van de Kooij had a boundless admiration for the tenacious American sleuths who always seemed to be haunted by that one, unsolved murder, even after years of retirement. What he liked most was that they used old-fashioned detective work. They were always thinking about possible motives or mulling over the inconsistencies in the testimonies of both suspects and witnesses, many of whom also took part in the show. He loved how they would comb through box after box of the dusty files that had been stored in warehouses for years, and how, eventually, they would join all of this evidence up in a logical way.

How disappointing it must be for him then, Rijsbergen thought, *that you get to do so little of that here in Leiden. And then when those sorts of cases do come your way, they're never as simple as they are on television.*

Because so far, every trail they had tried to follow had been a dead end.

The Dutch police successfully solved eighty per cent of murder cases. However, that figure included cases where there was no real case to solve because the murderer was apprehended at the crime scene or handed themselves in to the police. And, in eighty per cent of those cases, the killer was someone the victim knew – after all, you need a reason to kill someone – and sooner or later, detective work would lead to their door.

The murders that went unsolved were usually gangland executions in which organised criminals took out their rivals. They either carried out the hit themselves or flew in contract killers who were unconnected to the victim and disappeared again immediately after the murder.

Van de Kooij parked the car in front of Jenny van der Lede's neat front garden with its wooden bench that, judging from the moss growing on it, was more for decoration than actually sitting on.

They could see Jenny sitting in her living room. She greeted them with a friendly wave and came straight to the front door to let them in.

'Come in, come in,' she said, as though she was meeting up with old friends after much too long.

Jenny van der Lede was a large woman who had the sort of healthy glow that comes from spending a lot of time outdoors. Her bright eyes suggested a very keen interest in examining everything she saw and heard in the world around her.

'So, my colleagues have already been to see you,' Rijsbergen began as they sat down. He had politely refused her offer of coffee – he preferred to keep the tone of these conversations formal and businesslike.

Jenny nodded agreeably. She leaned back in her armchair and calmly waited to hear what Rijsbergen had to say.

'They spoke to you about the evening itself, of course, but also about the election that took place recently.'

'Oh, the election, yes . . .' she said. She crossed her legs, like someone settling in to tell a good story.

But then she said nothing.

'This is where you tell us about how the election went,' Van de Kooij said helpfully.

'Yes, right,' Jenny said. 'The election. Well, you know . . . There's not much to tell. We had three candidates: Coen and then two other candidates standing *against* him. Well, that's how it felt to me, anyway. We knew from the start that we'd have no chance of winning, and it turned out we were right. He won by a landslide.'

'So why did you stand in the election at all?' Rijsbergen asked.

'For the other candidate, it was purely a matter of principle,' Jenny said. 'He was worried that the election would just be a charade otherwise.'

'And what about you?'

'I . . .' Jenny said uncertainly. 'That was part of my motivation too. I wanted to provide some sort of opposition, a counter-weight, as it were. But it was more than that. I had two reasons for standing. And mine were principled reasons too. The first was very simple. The Freemasons have always been dominated by men, right from the very beginning. When Loge Ishtar was set up, we finally had a mixed lodge, one that women could join. And it really upset me that our first chairman was going to be another man. I thought: they've finally let us in, and we've *still* got a man at the helm.'

Rijsbergen nodded sympathetically.

'And the second reason?' Van de Kooij asked.

'The second reason,' Jenny said, folding her hands as though she was about to lead them in prayer. 'I think – or I thought, as I sadly must say now – that Coen was too permissive, if I can put it like that. I can't think of another word for it. It's hard to explain, but even we Freemasons . . . I mean, we're known for being free thinkers, for our tolerance towards others. We don't force our lifestyle on other people, we don't go from door to door trying to save souls, we don't damn people to eternal hell if they don't share our views.'

'But . . .' Van de Kooij said, keen to get to the point.

'But I found Coen's approach a bit too . . . a bit too permissive, as I said. If you give everyone absolute freedom in everything, then . . . Well then, everyone might as well just stay at home on their own and do as they please. You'd have nothing holding people together any more, would you? Yes, you'd have individual freedom, but if every individual person has total freedom, then there's no community. Then we're all just separate individuals. If you want to belong to a community, you have to surrender a part of yourself, give something up, sometimes you have to submit to something greater than yourself. So if you allow this extreme autonomy, this obsessive drive for independence where everyone has the right to come up with their own completely personal and individual meanings, how can we have any unity? And this is also – Coen and I often locked horns on exactly this point – this is why I had to stand against him. In my opinion, one explanation of a symbol or a ritual *can* be more valid than another. You should be able to say: "It's like this." Or: "Your interpretation isn't correct." This is a . . . I know this is a minority viewpoint. It's why I lost the election. But some people do agree with me.'

Jenny took a handkerchief out of the pocket of her cardigan

and mopped her reddened face with it. 'My point is, gentlemen . . .' she went on.

She spoke as though she was looking for the right words while she talked, but Rijsbergen's intuition told him that she had told this story many times before.

'In practice, something that's presented as tolerance can very easily become indifference. The line between the two is thinner than most people think. "I have my truth, and you have yours" looks like "Live and let live." But what you're actually saying is, "I'm not really interested. I don't care. I'm never going to be changed by anything you think because I'm not prepared to change my standpoint." Do you see? How can you have a connection with each other then? How can you have a community?'

'Then it looks to me like you don't really fit in there,' Rijsbergen said.

'Oh I do, I do,' Jenny said hastily. 'The fundamental ideas appeal to me. As does searching for the meaning of life without constantly being watched by a judgemental God. Those things have always spoken to me, but . . . the unrestrained freedom that Coen advocated, freedom for everyone to understand things in their own way, not to take any of it too literally . . .'

'Someone else I was speaking to,' Rijsbergen cut in, 'said that people like you – this person didn't name names, by the way – have "less-enlightened minds". They said that they're people who need a little more guidance. They aren't able to cope with so much latitude and need to have their hands held . . .'

'Oh, yes, I'm sure,' Jenny said, and she laughed disdainfully. 'Those people can be so patronising . . . But, in the end, what is it that we want?'

Jenny stood up. Her face was even ruddier now. She took out her handkerchief again and wiped her neck as well as her face.

'What is it that we actually want?' she said again. 'Do we want to live in a place where we all have individual freedom, but we have no connection to each other, nothing that we can share with each other? Where we're all separate atoms in a lonely universe, just occasionally bumping into each other? A place where someone can lie dead in their home for ten years before they're found? Or do we want to live in a place where people are engaged with each other, form a community? Where people look out for each other? Where someone will talk to you if they see that you're heading down the wrong path? Of course, this means giving up something of your freedom, as I said earlier, something of your individuality, and of course, it means compromising now and then, conforming, keeping your opinions to yourself, sometimes, for the greater good. Because when you disconnect from each other and allow everyone to just do whatever they want, you lose that safety and security. And you can't get it back. That's the indifference I'm talking about, that feeling that nobody is really bothered about anyone else.'

Jenny sat down again. 'Sometimes, one person just *is* more right than another. Not all opinions are equally valid,' she went on. 'And it's nothing to do with lacking maturity or being less enlightened or needing guidance. It's about how you want to live with each other – or not.'

This avalanche of words had left Rijsbergen and Van de Kooij speechless.

The sound of footsteps coming downstairs rumbled through the hall, and seconds later, a man appeared in the living room doorway. 'Sorry,' he said. 'Am I interrupting something?'

'This is my husband, Herman,' Jenny said before Rijsbergen and Van de Kooij had a chance to ask.

Herman walked over and shook their hands.

'Herman is a member of Loge Ishtar too,' Jenny said. 'He's one of the people who agrees with me about the things I was just telling you about.' She gave Herman a short summary of the conversation that had just taken place.

'Why don't you take a seat?' Rijsbergen said. Herman took a chair from under the dining table and put it beside Jenny's armchair.

Herman was a large man, perhaps a head taller than Jenny, but, sat next to her, he seemed much smaller.

It's like he's in her shadow, Rijsbergen thought. *He's even sitting hunched over so that he doesn't look bigger than her.*

'That's all well and good, Mevrouw van de Lede,' Rijsbergen said after a pause. 'But—'

'And of course I wouldn't kill someone over a difference of opinion,' Jenny said. 'Or condone someone else doing that either.'

It had been almost invisible, but Rijsbergen had seen it. It had lasted less than a fraction of a second, so tiny that it could have been a facial tic. Jenny had given Herman a fleeting, sideways glance.

Hmm, that was odd, Rijsbergen thought.

'I've already told your colleagues,' Jenny continued, 'that I have no idea who could be behind this. If they're from the lodge, then I must have been completely – and I mean *completely* – wrong about everyone I know there. And if that's true, then I can throw out everything I thought I'd learned about people over the last sixty years.'

Van de Kooij was about to say something, but Rijsbergen moved his hand subtly to warn him to keep quiet.

Why did she just look at her husband like that, Rijsbergen wondered. He recalled what Van Eijk, the pathologist had said: *It's obvious that whoever did this was very strong. It would have taken a huge amount of physical strength. Or rage. He – or she, we can't rule that out – was at least as large as the victim, possibly slightly larger. Probably someone right-handed.*

'Besides, everyone saw me that night,' Jenny said. 'After the presentation, I served behind the bar all evening, right up to the moment the police came. Even if I did have a motive . . .' There was that disdainful laugh again. '. . . I definitely didn't have the opportunity.'

Rijsbergen nodded.

He turned to Herman. 'And where were you?'

'Me?' Herman asked, sitting up straight. 'I came home shortly after the presentation ended. I had a glass of wine at the reception, but I was tired, so I didn't stay long.'

Rijsbergen looked Herman in the eye, and Herman met this with a steely glare as if the two men were daring each other to blink first.

'You wouldn't wish this on anybody,' Herman said at last. 'We disagreed with him, but this . . . This is just terrible.'

Rijsbergen took the photo of Yona Falaina out of the file and showed it to Jenny and Herman. 'As you've probably already heard,' he said, 'a body was found in the Galgewater yesterday. It was very quickly apparent that he had been murdered.'

Jenny and Herman looked at the photograph carefully, but they gave away nothing that indicated that they recognised the face on it.

'He was a young man, twenty-eight, probably from Greece originally. He lived in the town centre, just around the corner from the Masonic Hall.'

Herman hunched himself over again.

'No,' Jenny said firmly. 'I'm sure I've never seen him before. He has an unusual face, a bit like a monk or a priest. If you put him in one of those black cassocks that the Greek Orthodox priests wear, you'd believe he really was one. But why are you asking about him? Is his death connected to Coen Zoutman's murder somehow?'

'We don't know yet,' Rijsbergen said reticently. 'But I'm sure you understand that we're inclined to think that two murders committed in Leiden in quick succession could be connected.'

This answer didn't seem to satisfy Jenny, but she didn't question him further.

'Are either of you familiar with this symbol?' he asked, holding up the picture of Coen's tattoo. It was the sketch he'd made himself, which was larger and clearer than the autopsy photographs. No one needed to know where the image had actually come from.

Jenny and Herman obligingly looked at the triangle within a triangle with a small circle on top. They both shook their heads.

'No,' Jenny said. 'If it's related to Freemasonry, then the All-Seeing Eye would be the closest thing to it, but I've never seen it represented in that way.'

'I don't recognise it either,' said Herman. 'Where was it found?'

Van de Kooij flashed a look at Rijsbergen, and Rijsbergen blinked slowly, which Van de Kooij correctly understood as a sign that he should say nothing.

'We came across it during our investigation,' he said carefully.

'Well,' Jenny said in a tone that was clearly intended to let them know that, as far as she was concerned, the conversation was over. 'I get the impression that you're only telling me half the story, which I understand, of course. Police confidentiality and so on.'

They all stood up.

'I'm sorry I couldn't be more helpful,' Jenny said. 'It's a dreadful business. I've been wracking my brains over who could have done this. I'm sure it couldn't have been one of us. It's just not possible. I was the one who had the most difficulty with Coen. That was an open secret, I think. But otherwise . . . Obviously, there were a few people who took my side, but nobody who would go this far. No, I just can't believe that could be true.'

They walked into the front hall.

'No, absolutely, I completely agree with Jenny,' Herman said. 'The level of violence in the murder, and that business with the square and compa—'

Rijsbergen turned around, and before Herman had finished his sentence, said, very calmly, 'How do you know that?'

Herman gaped, his mouth opening and closing wordlessly.

Like a fish caught in a net.

Chapter 23

P eter arrived at the café in the Pieterskerk long before he was supposed to meet Judith. Classical music played softly in the background, and late-afternoon light shone through the stained-glass windows high above.

In two days, on Sunday, Judith would be flying out to Boston, and he'd be joining her three weeks later. There was a farewell dinner planned for Saturday, but Mark and Fay would be there, and today, Peter would have a chance to spend some time with her alone.

Peter often came to the church café to read the papers over a cup of coffee. Sometimes, if Fay's house felt too crowded at the weekend, he'd come here with his laptop and spend a few hours working rather than going back to his own home on the Boerhaavelaan.

The hushed atmosphere was disturbed only by the occasional hiss of the espresso machine or by tourists buying entrance tickets at the counter.

Frieke, the Pieterkserk's manageress whom Peter knew quite well now, often breezed through the café and stopped to talk to Peter. She told him about her new plans and new ideas in an endless stream of words that tumbled over each other. Peter always found her lively enthusiasm and positive can-do attitude inspiring.

Today, Peter was reading a printout of the speech Burgomaster Henri Freylink had given at the recent anniversary of the Old Leiden Historical Society.

I'm honoured to have this opportunity to talk to you about the identity of this fine city. Identity is a wonderfully vague concept, which means that you can make it whatever you want it to be. But today, let us talk about exactly what it is that makes Leiden, or in other words, what the character of the city actually is.

Freylink spoke at length about the anniversary of the Relief of Leiden on the 2nd and 3rd of October, 'When our love for the city is expressed in a rich variety of ways, including the modern tradition of wearing red and white.'

The city's identity has always been strongly connected to stories about its history – its heroic history, that is. Even the youngest nations use stories from a distant past to illustrate their greatness. This often goes hand in hand with 'invented traditions' which might not truly be very old at all. But they give the impression of being so. And that goes for Leiden too. Our 3 October Festival is full of them.

Peter was considering including the speech in his course on the history of Leiden with his second-year students. It gave a concise and clear overview of Leiden's history in fewer than twenty pages.

We talked just last week about stories and how they play a role in nation-building whether they're true or not.

Freylink, himself a historian, also emphasised the importance of the many immigrants who had made Leiden their home

throughout its history. 'Leiden, City of Refugees' had long been
the city's motto.

The population had clearly become less homogeneous after
the siege, and the question is, how did this population feel
about Leiden? Did they think of themselves as Leideners?
Were they proud of their city, proud of its past? It's impossible for us to know. In the hundred years after Leiden was
relieved, so many immigrants came into the city that they
were by far the largest demographic in its population. They
certainly would not have identified very much with Leiden
when they first arrived, and, to a large extent, how well
they integrated into Leiden's society was determined by
where they originally came from. There were many Flemish
people, but also Walloons, Germans, English and later,
Huguenots from France. For many years, the Flemings
married exclusively within their own circle, and there was
relatively little interaction with other groups . . . Of course,
most newcomers were simple labourers. After a while, they
would have started to form a bond with their new home.
The lovely carved stone plaque that can be seen on the
Nieuwe Beestenmarkt reflects this beautifully, depicting
Leiden as the 'The Land of Promises'.

Peter marked the margin next to this passage with two exclama-
tion points. He had seen the stone plaque many times. It dated
from 1611 and commemorated the expansion of the city that
started in that year. The image showed a scene from the Book

of Numbers. When the Israelites reached the border of the promised land, Moses dispatched twelve spies to find out how many people lived there and how strong they were. The spies were told to bring back fruits as proof of the land's fertility. When the spies returned, they brought with them a bunch of grapes so heavy that two men were needed to carry it.

The land of promises . . . Leiden as a promised land, Peter thought.

The sliding doors at the café entrance opened, and Judith walked in.

She was wearing her hair down, and it still looked damp, as though she had just showered. She was wearing a white sweater under her denim jacket, and, as usual, she was dressed in a flowing skirt and long boots. A Star of David pendant around her neck twinkled in the light from the fluorescent lamps above.

She sat next to Peter on the bench and gave him a sideways hug. As always, he buried his face in her hair for a moment. She smelled of shampoo, and of Magie Noire, the perfume she had worn since they'd met twenty years ago.

'It's so nice to be here,' she said.

They ordered an espresso each and then said nothing more until the little cups had appeared on the table in front of them.

'How did Fay react when you told her you were going to the States?'

'She was fairly positive about it,' Peter said. 'I think.'

'You don't sound sure.'

'Well, it did come out of the blue. And it's very soon, just three weeks away, so she was taken by surprise.'

'Yes, I imagine she would be. Mark was really pleased, by the way.'

'Yes, he said that yesterday. I saw him when we went to the police station.'

'Oh, yes, so you did.'

'But actually . . .' Peter sipped his coffee to give himself time to think.

Should I tell her about the emails to Coen that Fay was hiding from me? And is still hiding from me.

'Actually?' Judith probed.

It's really nothing, Peter decided. *Everyone has a right to keep secrets. Or at least the right to decide what other people know about them.*

'Actually, it'll work out well for her,' he decided to say. 'She wants to finish that book, and the three of us are going on holiday together this summer, to Greece.'

'Alena's not going with you?' Judith said, smiling mischievously.

'No, Alena's not going with us,' Peter said. 'She'll love having the house to herself for three weeks.'

'Have you heard anything else about Coen Zoutman's murder?'

'Not really. I haven't heard much more about it. But they've found another body.'

'I heard about that. The man in the Galgewater, right? Is it connected?'

'I don't know, to be honest. But two murders so close together, it's easy to think that they must be connected. But maybe it's just a coincidence. Who knows?'

A group of tourists came into the café and bought entrance tickets for the church at the counter.

'Shall we go in too?' Judith asked.

'All right,' said Peter.

Peter was a Friend of the Pieterskerk and had a lifetime membership that granted him free entry to the church whenever he wanted.

The church was accessed via a narrow passageway that brought the visitor out into a building that was always a breathtaking sight, no matter the season or time of day.

In this cavernous space with its colossal pillars, polished floor inlaid with tombstones, dazzling stained-glass windows, ornately carved wooden altar, and a golden pipe organ that almost covered an entire wall, everything indicated that this was hallowed ground and inspired a feeling of awe and reverence.

'When's Coen's funeral?' Judith asked.

'Next Wednesday. Fay's been selecting the readings for it this week with some of the other Ishtar members. They've got a wide range of holy books to choose from. Being Freemasons, they're not restricted to following just one set of religious traditions. As far as music goes, they've decided on classical instrumental pieces and one of Bach's cantatas.'

'Nice choice.'

'It is. Coen didn't have any family. He never married, and he didn't have children. And he was an only child whose parents were only children themselves. There wasn't another soul on earth who was related to him. The Freemasons were literally his only family.'

They wandered into a corner of the church where a permanent exhibition about the Pilgrims had been set up around John Robinson's grave. However, this wasn't his actual burial site. He had bought a plot in the Pieterskerk and been laid to rest there, but nobody knew exactly where his grave was. This tombstone was a memorial to him rather than his true final resting place.

Another invented tradition, Peter thought.

'Judith, do you ever wonder,' he said, 'what you would do if you could live your life all over again? Would you make different choices?'

Judith took some time to consider her answer. 'I don't think my choices would be very different,' she said. 'The finer details might change. Maybe I'd steer away from a certain boyfriend, or not go on holiday with a certain group of people. Maybe I'd go that Bruce Springsteen concert, after all. That sort of thing. But by and large, I'd make the same choices. Study history in Leiden, explore my Jewish background, be with Mark, live in the house I live in now. What about you?'

Even though he'd been the one to ask the question, Peter had to think before he could answer it. 'The same, actually,' he said after a pause. 'I'd change some of the details, just like you. But ultimately, I'd study history, write, live here in Leiden . . .'

'But sometimes . . .'

'What?'

'Sometimes I fantasise about starting all over again. Somewhere else, obviously, and with Mark of course, but somewhere far away from here, in a place where nobody knows me, where I wouldn't have any history, where I could be a blank page.'

'You'd take yourself with you, though.'

'Yes, naturally, you can't really be a blank page yourself, but if you were in a new environment . . . And I . . . Hey . . .' she stopped mid-thought. 'I've never actually read this before.'

Next to John Robinson's grave, the story of the Pilgrims and their connection with Leiden, and in particular with the Pieterskerk, was set out on large display boards.

REASONS TO EMIGRATE 1

For a small minority like the Pilgrims, it was difficult to maintain their own language, religion and habits. There were several marriages with Walloons, who had similar religious viewpoints. After many of the Pilgrims left for

America, it proved impossible to remain a clearly defined community. After their own preacher Robinson died, the people left behind in Leiden joined Dutch churches, and after 1630, the English Reformed Church. Finally, the group merged into the Leiden population.

'Maybe you can compare it to the Pilgrims,' Judith said pensively. 'I've always felt an affinity with their Puritanism. Rejecting material possessions, focusing on the spirit and on what's good, focusing on God. The idea that life is a journey, a pilgrimage. What they did, going to a new world to start all over again, is sometimes a very tempting idea.'

'That's true,' Peter agreed.

They walked down the central aisle of the church towards the exit.

'But the world they went to wasn't empty,' Judith said. 'The Pilgrims' so-called new beginning was the end of the world for the indigenous people who already lived there. Just like when the tribes of Israel arrived in Canaan after wandering in the desert for forty years. That land wasn't empty either. You know, that's a part of the Bible that I have a lot of trouble with. All those massacres, hundreds of thousands of people killed at once. Absolute barbarity. And when Joshua's men disobey him by sparing some of the men in a city, he orders them to push all their prisoners off a cliff to their deaths. Only the virgin girls were allowed to live. There's a bit in Deuteronomy, the first verses of chapter twelve that describe such unbelievable bigotry. I've read it so many times that I know it by heart now.'

That was precisely what those texts they found in Coen's pocket were about, Peter thought. *And the three stories at the end . . . They were all about the atrocities committed by the people of Israel when they conquered the promised land. Exodus seems to have been an important topic for him. But why?*

'"You shall surely destroy all the places where the nations whom you shall dispossess served their gods, upon the high mountains and upon the hills and under every green tree",' Judith recited from memory. '"You shall tear down their altars, and dash in pieces their pillars, and burn their Ashe'rim with fire; you shall hew down the graven images of their gods and destroy their name out of that place."'

'I suppose it was like a caliphate. Anyone who didn't follow the one true faith had to be killed,' Peter said. 'We're seeing something like that again now, aren't we? With ISIS? It's like you just said: they destroy all the images and idols from other religions and churches and take the women as sex slaves.'

'But it's happening in modern-day Israel too. Look at how they treat the Palestinians. Not that people are being shoved off cliffs of course, but they're increasingly being denied space. There are all those illegal settlements on the West Bank, and the entire Gaza Strip is like an open prison. And the Christian communities in Jerusalem's Old City are being put under more and more pressure ... Christians being spat at by Orthodox Jews ... There's less and less room for other faiths. That's something that ... Well, I'm finding it hard to reconcile myself to it all.'

They had arrived back in the café now, where Peter picked up his bag before they left the church.

'I'm going back to my office for a while,' Judith said. 'What about you?'

'I'm going to walk home.'

He took a moment to look at the memorial plaque for the Pilgrims that had been set into the wall.

During the Pilgrim Fathers' Leiden exile,
more than thirty family members died.
Many were buried in the Pieterskerk along with
their Leiden neighbours.

'BUT NOW WE ARE ALL, IN ALL PLACES
STRANGERS AND PILGRIMS, TRAVELERS
AND SOJOURNERS . . .'

Robert Cushman, Pilgrim Leader, 1622

Strangers and pilgrims, Peter thought. *Travelers and sojourners.*

Chapter 24

Peter, Fay, Judith and Mark sat around a table at the back of La Bota, a cosy 'brown café' in the Herensteeg, near the Pieterskerk. Peter had been a regular at the pub since his student days. The food was simple but good, and the prices were reasonable. The menu that was chalked on the wall had changed very little over the years. The garnish on every plate had always been the same too – a slaw of red or white cabbage with sultanas – but Peter had always found its predictability comforting. Your whole world could collapse around you, the years could fly by before you knew it, your life could be turned upside down or creep along with stupefying, quotidian dullness, but here, at least, you knew what to expect.

The owners greeted him like an old friend, even though they knew nothing more about each other than what they had gleaned from their brief chats over the years.

Shortly after Fay had sent Peter the text saying 'We need to talk', they'd had a long conversation.

In the end, it hadn't been about the – now vanished – email exchange between Fay and Coen Zoutman as he had been expecting.

Instead, Fay had told him that she'd realised that the murder had affected her so much that she felt she needed more time and space for herself. Naturally, the discussion had included the classic 'It's not you, it's me', which didn't just allow Fay to pre-emptively take all the blame herself; it also left Peter completely disarmed because now there was nothing left to discuss.

Fay's house was so tiny that she, Agapé and Alena felt like they were always on top of each other. It was entirely under-standable that she needed space.

But Peter still had the feeling that Fay was holding something back, that there was something else going on, something to do with her emails to Coen. But to ask her about it might risk damaging everything they had built together. He didn't dare. And, if he was honest, the prospect of having more time and space for himself was appealing.

This didn't mean that their relationship was over in any way; they were simply pressing pause. When the dust had settled, they would be able to press play again.

All in all, his spontaneous decision to visit Judith in Boston had worked out perfectly.

The food arrived, and the table filled with steaming plates.

Judith raised her glass for a toast.

'*L'chaim*,' she said.

'*L'chaim*,' they all replied.

To life.

For a while, the only sounds were of metal cutlery tapping on plates, ice cubes clinking in glasses, and pop music drifting from the speakers in the background.

'So you're just going to let him go?' Mark blurted to Fay.

Fay put down her knife and fork.

Peter gave her a sideways look, his fork hovering halfway between his plate and his mouth. Red wine jus dripped from the meat and splashed onto his plate, like drops of blood.

'We're not joined at the hip, you know,' she said. 'That's what I like about our relationship.' She picked up her knife and fork again and sliced off a piece of salmon. 'We're a couple, but that doesn't mean we need to know what the other person is up to every minute of every day.'

Peter smiled and nodded in agreement,

No, you're absolutely right, I don't know what you're up to, he thought.

'And it suits me, in a way,' Fay continued. 'I've been working on that book about Etruscan art forever and it's actually in its final stages now.'

Peter dunked a piece of steak into the jus, then ate it, relieved that they had avoided a potentially awkward scene.

'Has there been any news about that awful tragedy at the Freemasons' lodge?' said Mark, changing the subject.

'I don't think they've made much progress with the case,' Peter said, and he told them about the conversations he and Fay had had with the detectives, and about the body in the Galgewater. 'And what about that tattoo?' he asked Mark. 'Has anyone in your network been able to come up with anything?'

'No, nothing at all,' Mark replied. 'Most people suggest it's something to do with the All-Seeing Eye.'

Peter glanced at Fay.

But maybe you know what it is, he thought.

'We've all had an email about it,' Fay said. 'All the members of Loge Ishtar and Loge La Vertu, I mean. But nobody recognised the tattoo. And nobody knew the other man, either. Nobody has a clue why Coen Zoutman was carrying that summary of Exodus around with him. It's not a topic that's come up recently, so . . .'

'It's just all so strange,' Judith said.

'I've been giving a lot of thought to those notes that Coen

had with him,' Mark said, 'but I still don't understand why he chose to write about those particular stories.'

'It's just a very brief history of the Jewish people. Nothing more, nothing less,' Peter said. 'From Abraham to the Israelites' conquest of Palestine.'

'You know what's funny?' Mark said. He put down his knife and fork and looked around the table as if he was about to tell a joke. 'I've never really thought about it, but that story about baby Moses being put in a river in a basket sealed with pitch . . .'

'It's an exact copy of a much older Babylonian story about the king of Sargon, isn't it?' Judith said. 'Is that what you're thinking?'

'Yes, it is. Sargon's mother puts him in a basket and entrusts him to the waters of the Euphrates more than 2300 years before the birth of Christ. A gardener finds him and decides to raise him. Then the boy became the king's cupbearer, and he eventually manages to become king himself. But that's not actually what I was about to say. The funny thing is that if Moses' mother had really put him in the river in the place where the Bible says the Israelites lived, he would have drifted towards the Mediterranean Sea. The pharaoh lived in Memphis, and that was upstream. A little basket would have gone with the river's flow and not against it.'

Judith smiled.

'But that's what's so wonderful about the Old Testament, of course,' Mark said, in full flow now. 'We know the stories weren't written down until the sixth century BCE. Their authors borrowed liberally from other traditions and then added their own elements, creating something that was a mix of fact and fiction. In 587 BCE, the Babylonians occupied Judah under

Nebuchadnezzar II. They destroyed the city of Jerusalem and the Temple, took the Jews captive and deported them to Babylon. Half a century later, the Persian king Cyrus conquered the Babylonian Empire. He returned all the exiles to their homes, including the exiles from Judah. When the Jews returned to Judah in 538 BCE, they discovered that it wasn't an "empty land", as they might have expected, but a land populated by all sorts of people. That's when they started to write down the stories we find in the Old Testament. They used them to forge a mutual bond among the Israelites by creating a shared past. They took old folktales, historical sources and Babylonian myths and turned them into an epic saga about a people led by God that was brought out of Egypt and into the promised land – just like the people of Judah returning from exile in Babylon – and had to deal with the people who were already living there. You can see the similarities between the Jews' years as slaves in Egypt working on the pharaoh's huge building projects, and what the Jews freed by Cyrus had been through in Babylon: seventy years of exile and slavery working on huge construction projects for King Nebuchadnezzar. And then there are the similarities between the so-called Exodus from Egypt and the return of the exiles from Babylon.'

'You're right,' Fay said.

'But this sort of thing isn't confined to the past,' Mark said. 'The same sort of founding myth is being used again today. You can see the same elements in the Jewish people returning to the promised land of Israel, the myth of the empty land, the problem of how to deal with the people who already live there, and the old stories being used to justify the new invasion.'

Peter had stopped being amazed by how easy it was to debunk stories from the Bible once you started looking into them. The

Exodus story had gone on to form modern Israel's national myth. To a large extent, it was used to justify the state's existence: 'God promised this land to us. It says so in our Bible.' It was the ultimate mix of fact and fiction.

'Just one more thing,' Mark said, 'and then I'll shut up about it. As well as that weird thing about Moses and his basket, there's something else I'd not really given much thought to until recently: what about all the gold that these supposedly poor slaves were able to take out of Egypt and into the desert? I read in one of Maarten 't Hart's books that you'd need to melt down an incredible number of earrings to make a golden calf that was no bigger than a field mouse. And since the melting point of gold is a thousand and sixty-four degrees Celsius, you'd need a furnace to melt them. And then you'd need to make a mould of a calf to pour the molten gold into. Would the Israelites have had that sort of advanced technology in the desert? It's not something you could just make with a chisel! Afterwards, Moses grinds the golden calf into a powder, scatters it on the water and makes the Israelites drink it. How did Moses manage to grind the gold down to a dust so fine that it didn't sink?'

'Questions, questions . . . So many questions.' Judith laughed and topped up her wine glass. 'But anyway, everyone, whether we're supposed to take all those stories literally or not, I'm about to start a new chapter in my own story. And that's something you can all take literally.'

They all stood up, which gave the moment a note of solemnity that Judith hadn't intended.

'Well,' Judith said, 'today, we're saying a toast to life here, but tomorrow . . .' Before she continued, she took a drink from the wine in her overfull glass, spilling some of it onto the table. 'But tomorrow, I'll be toasting life in Boston.'

'*L'chaim.*'

To life.

Fay's phone had been pinging with messages all evening. 'Sorry, everyone,' she said. 'I'm getting so many messages. It's not usually like this.' She looked at her phone's screen. 'That's . . . odd,' she said.

'What is it?' Peter asked.

'A message about Jenny and her husband Herman,' she said, putting her phone back down on the table. 'Jenny's a member of Loge Ishtar too. So is her husband,' she explained. 'Do you remember them, Peter? There was a woman at the open evening who jumped up from her seat while we were doing the interviews.'

'Yes, I remember her.'

'When we were electing a new chairman,' she said to Mark and Judith, 'she was one of the candidates, but she wasn't elected. And now her husband, Herman . . .' She shook her head in disbelief.

'Go on,' Peter said. 'What about him?'

Fay regained her composure. 'It turns out that Herman was arrested yesterday. On suspicion of Coen's murder.'

PART TWO
THE NEW WORLD

PART TWO
THE NEW WORLD

BOSTON

Chapter 25

Judith had gone to the library, so Peter had the apartment to himself all morning. They had planned to meet up after lunch and finally do the Freedom Trail, a walking tour around downtown Boston. It passed by the local landmarks that were associated with the American War of Independence of 1775 to 1783.

Peter had been in America for almost three weeks – he was due to fly home in just two days – but this was the first chance they'd had to take the tour. He'd flown to Washington and stayed there for two days, but nothing had come of his plan to visit New York. He had enjoyed spending time in Judith's company so much that he hadn't wanted to leave.

As he tidied up the apartment, he listened to – more than he actually watched – a talk show on TV. He had noticed on his first day in Boston that Americans were absolutely crazy about talk shows. You could watch one at any time of the day if you wanted. A ticker running along the bottom of the screen kept you informed of the latest news. An endless stream of alerts, disasters, murders, shootings and traffic accidents flowed past the viewer on a bright yellow bar, like an overprotective mother constantly warning her children about every imaginable calamity.

Every fifteen minutes, a weatherman or woman would appear to give an update on recent meteorological developments. It was a constant bombardment of information that was regularly interrupted by commercials. According to the calculations Peter had made for his own amusement, the adverts lasted just as long and sometimes even longer than the programmes themselves.

The word 'apartment' was possibly too grand a description for Judith's open-plan kitchen and living room, bathroom and bedroom. But she had been lucky enough to get a place on the Harvard campus itself, in a building reserved for researchers from other countries. Although the units were clearly intended to be single occupancy, a blind eye was turned when visitors had guests to stay for a while. Peter slept in the living room on a sofa bed that he neatly made and folded away again each morning.

Judith always got up before him, taking a shower before going back to her bedroom, wrapped in a beach towel and surrounded by a cloud of steam. They had formed a tacit agreement on the day he'd arrived that Peter would wait until Judith was back in her room before he got up and took a shower himself. By the time he emerged from the bathroom and padded barefoot into the kitchen, Judith would be making coffee and topping slices of bread with cheese or ham. It had become a sort of polite ballet for grown-ups in which they carefully danced around each other without touching.

Judith spent most of her days in the cavernous Widener Library, a dream come true for any academic, whatever their field. It was the university's flagship library and housed more than three and a half million volumes on almost a hundred kilometres of shelving. Many of the books were housed in vast underground rooms that stretched beyond the walls and under the campus lawns outside.

Harry Elkins Widener, after whom the building was named, had been an avid book collector and a Harvard graduate. In the spring of 1912, he went to England with his parents to purchase rare books, but they had the misfortune of making the return journey on the *Titanic*. He and his father drowned in the icy waters of the North Atlantic Ocean. His mother survived and donated two million dollars, an unbelievable sum at the time, to Harvard for the construction of a library in their memory.

Judith had organised a visitor's pass for Peter, so over the last few weeks, he'd been able to spend time working next to her on his laptop in one of the reading rooms.

Back in Leiden, he had parted warmly with Fay, but an unmistakable feeling of distance had crept in between them, perhaps even a certain coldness. Neither of them had mentioned it, but Peter had known – and he was sure the same went for Fay – that these three weeks in the States would be decisive for their relationship.

How much will we miss each other, he had wondered. *What conclusions might we come to when we're away from each other for so long?*

They emailed and texted each other regularly throughout the day. Often, their messages were little more than businesslike reports of what they had been up to, but now and then, there was a glimpse of their relationship's former sparkle, the warmth and gentle teasing that they had taken for granted for so long.

Before he turned off the television, Peter sat down to watch a news report about two men who had disappeared while on a fishing trip in Plymouth Bay a few days earlier. Fishermen had found their empty boat bobbing in the sea. The sea had been calm that day, and according to the police, it was unlikely that the men had been swept overboard. They suspected foul play.

Footage of a large fishing vessel towing the little boat into Boston Harbor was shown over and over, like the trailer for an upcoming movie.

Peter closed the door to Judith's apartment behind him and then strolled along the paths that took him over the campus's perfectly manicured lawns. Students milled about all around him, hurrying to lectures with books under their arms, or studying and chatting on the innumerable chairs that seemed to be permanently set up outside. Joining the throng were hundreds of tourists trailing behind the students who were giving them guided tours of the campus.

Leiden is a great city to be a student, Peter thought as he watched the young people around him with a pang of envy, *but what a dream come true it would be to study here*.

He had arranged to meet Judith near the enormous statue of John Harvard, the university's founder. The statue's left shoe gleamed like gold, as though a fastidious shoeshine had spent decades concentrating on just that one spot. Countless people had touched the statue's foot over the years because it was thought to bring good luck. It was said that children who touched it would get a place at Harvard one day, so many visitors lifted up their little ones to perform the traditional ritual.

Peter arrived at the statue early and took a seat on one of

the nearby chairs. The walking tour would end at the campus, and afterwards, he had an appointment with the Freemasons who were based in an imposing building on the edge of Boston Common, the city's central park. Fay had got in touch with the lodge for him, and they had immediately offered to give him a tour.

He had arranged to meet up with Tony Vanderhoop the next day for a visit to Plimoth Plantation, an open-air museum where a seventeenth-century village had been recreated as it would have looked during the time of the Pilgrims.

He smelled her familiar perfume before he saw her.

Peter felt someone come up behind him and plant a kiss on his cheek.

Judith.

She laughed, delighted that she had been able to surprise him.

He grabbed her hand and squeezed it.

She was wearing a flower-print summer dress that showed off a hint of cleavage. Around her neck was the silver Star of David necklace that seemed to light up whenever it caught the sunlight.

'Come on,' she said. 'Let's go.'

They headed for the campus exit. According to tradition, students could only pass through the main gate twice: once on their first day as Harvard freshmen and a second time on graduation day. During the rest of their time at Harvard, they used the smaller gates on either side, as Peter and Judith did today.

Inside the subway station, people were posing for photographs under the HARVARD sign. Someone had put a pram underneath it to take a photo of their baby, as if the sign might have the power to preordain their child's future.

What would Arminius and Gomarus have said about this idea of predestination, Peter wondered with amusement.

South Station, Boston's central station, was just four stops away. They bought coffee at the Starbucks on the concourse.

'Have there been any developments in Leiden?' Judith asked. 'With the murder, I mean. I have to admit; I've barely given it a thought since I arrived.'

'Fay mentioned it in an email earlier this week, actually,' Peter said. 'Herman is still in custody, waiting for his trial. It's been about six weeks now. Apparently, he doesn't want to talk, so there haven't been any new developments as far as that goes.'

'Any sign of a motive?'

'There's speculation in the media that it could have been a crime of passion. Herman wanted to prove his love to Jenny by showing her that he'd do anything for her. That he'd even be willing to commit murder for her by assassinating the man who stopped her from becoming chairwoman.'

'That's not a very strong motive, is it?'

'People have been murdered for less. The media is saying that their marriage was in trouble. They're making it out to be the desperate act of a man who wanted to show how much he loves his wife. But who knows? It does sound absurd, but like I said, there are some who would need even less reason to murder someone.'

'Yes, I suppose that's true.'

'Because what's more . . . I think Herman is really the only concrete thing they have. They still don't know for certain who was there that evening. And it turns out that everyone they *do* know about has an alibi. They were all seen by someone.'

'People could be providing alibis for each other, of course.'

'Yes, that's possible too.'

They passed the sign for the Boston Tea Party Museum, which was entirely devoted to the American colonists' protest against the taxes imposed on them by the British government. On December 16th, 1773, sixty men, who would later come to be known as the Sons of Liberty, stormed the English cargo ships docked in Boston Harbor. The ships were full of tea imported from China, which they threw into the water. This was a pivotal moment in the American Revolution in which the United States fought for their independence from England.

Quite a revolutionary city, Boston, Peter thought as they made their way to the marina via the Rose Kennedy Greenway, a long park that curled around downtown Boston.

'So it was the perfect murder,' Judith said.

'The perfect *murders*. Because there was the young man in the Galgewater too. They'll find out who was behind it all, sooner or later. I'm sure they will. Although, I read a pretty comprehensive report about it in the Leidsch Dagblad that gave a bit of an update on developments in the case and it looks like all of their leads have been dead ends so far.'

They had reached the waterfront now. On Peter's first weekend in Boston, they had gone on a whale-watching cruise in a marine sanctuary where the whales came in search of food at this time of year. It had been awe-inspiring to see the mighty humpbacks rise ten to fifteen metres above the ocean then dive back beneath the waves, their broad tails languidly slapping the water's surface.

A mother and her calf had calmly swum past the exact place where he and Judith had been standing, as if they wanted to be admired. And, out of the blue, Peter had found himself welling up.

As he'd wiped away his tears with the back of his hand, Judith had put her arm around him.

'Now that's why I love you, Peter,' she had said. 'Such a big, strong man, crying at the sight of a whale.'

He had laughed and pulled her closer to him.

They walked to the Old North Church, which wasn't really the start of the Freedom Trail, but it was in a lovely Italian neighbourhood. Wandering through the narrow streets where the restaurants displayed their menus in Italian outside, they could easily imagine themselves in Italy.

The church was quiet. Apart from an attendant at the door, they were the only people inside.

The rows of seats on either side of the aisle were divided into low-walled wooden boxes like office cubicles. Judith took a photo of Peter in the pew that Teddy Roosevelt had once sat in, grinning like a football fan sitting in the team's dressing room on his favourite player's bench.

The church was famous for the role it had played in the mythologised story of Paul Revere. Revere was a silversmith and amateur dentist who had been relatively unknown in his own time. But the poet Henry Wadsworth Longfellow had immortalised him in the poem 'Paul Revere's Ride'. Written forty years after Revere's death, it told the story of how he had ridden out alone to warn the revolutionaries that the English were coming.

In the early days of the American Revolution, Revere helped to gather information about the British troops who were encamped in and around Boston. On the evening of April 18th, 1775, the sexton of the Old North Church hung two lanterns in the steeple to signal that the British troops were on their way to the towns of Lexington and Concord to confiscate the rebels' weapons. Revere had told him to hang one lantern if the troops were approaching by land, and two lanterns if they were coming by sea. Upon seeing two lanterns glowing in the church, Revere immediately mounted a borrowed horse and headed for Lexington and Concord with some of his comrades to warn the rebels. He made it to Lexington, but before he could reach Concord, he was intercepted and detained by the British. The other members of his party avoided capture and managed to reach Concord. Their warnings allowed the rebel militia to prepare for the first skirmishes in the American War of Independence.

Peter and Judith left the church and walked to the Paul Revere House. They decided not to go inside but spent some time browsing in the gift shop next door.

'I've always found the whole Paul Revere thing a bit baffling,' Peter said when they left the shop. 'Because there's just no truth at all in that story about him riding out alone to warn the rebels. I mean, he was stopped before he even got to Concord. His anonymous comrades were the ones who raised the alarm there, but they aren't mentioned anywhere in the poem. He didn't gallop from village to village shouting, "The British are coming! The British are coming!" He was just one of many messengers. And on top of that, they actually spread the news discreetly because not everyone in the villages was against the British.'

'But people still believe it.'

'Yes, and people continue to believe it even though it's demonstrably untrue. You've got to wonder why the myth is still being perpetuated.'

'A country needs myths. We talked about that when we had dinner at La Bota. Something to bring people together, a communal story. You need a foundation to build on, even if it's imaginary.'

'That's true, and I understand how it works, but it amazes me that they still teach this story to children at school. Look what we just saw in the gift shop: all the picture books, and quotes from the poem printed on mugs and t-shirts, even on the American flag.'

'Well, we *are* living in the age of alternative facts . . .' Judith said with a wry smile.

'Yes, you're right,' Peter said. 'But this has been going on forever. In the Netherlands, we've got Hans Brinker, who stuck his finger in a hole in a dyke and stayed there all day and all night, saving the entire country from the threat of flood with his bare hands. Or Jan van Speyk, the naval lieutenant who exploded his gunboat during the Belgian War of Independence rather than let it fall into rebel hands.'

'"I'd rather be blown up," he said, right?'

'Yes, exactly,' Peter confirmed. 'That's what he's supposed to have said. He stuck his lit cigar in a barrel of gunpowder and blasted the boat to smithereens. He's been venerated for centuries. There are even statues of him. But from a military standpoint, what he did was meaningless. Actually, it was completely pointless, because it didn't shorten the war at all, not even by a single day. Then there are the heroic Batavi who bravely revolted against the Roman Empire . . . Whenever you even scratch the surface of these stories, you find that there's nothing to them. National myths are quite harmless, really, and I'd put the Paul Revere story in that category. But when nations are founded on stories that turn out not to be true . . .'

They walked on, checking the map occasionally to make sure they were still following the route until a passer-by told them that all they had to do was follow the line of red bricks set into the pavement that marked out the entire trail.

When they reached the centre of town, they went into Faneuil Hall. The guidebook described it grandly as 'the home of free speech' and 'the cradle of liberty' because it had been the venue for the nation's very first Town Hall Meeting, a public event where politicians met with their voters. It was mostly given over to souvenir shops now.

A door on the other side of the hall brought them out onto the Marketplace, where three long buildings formed a bustling hub of cafés and restaurants.

Even though this was the first time that they had spent so much time together, being in Judith's company felt easy and natural. They always found plenty to talk about, and when they weren't chatting, their moments of silence were never awkward.

It was a glorious day, sunny but not too warm, which had brought lots of people outdoors.

They visited the Cheers bar, an accurate reconstruction of the bar from the TV series that Peter had once watched religiously every week. Peter wanted a photo of himself here too, sitting on the bar stool that the *Cheers* character Norm always sat on. A queue of people waiting to do the same formed behind Judith as she took the photograph.

It was still early, but they decided to order beers. Peter drained his glass with gusto and ordered another before Judith's glass was even half empty.

'I'll walk with you as far as the park,' Judith said. 'I can take the subway back to work from there.'

'All right,' Peter said, and he took a swig of beer to hide his disappointment. He had secretly hoped that she might duck out of work for the rest of the day so she could spend more time with him, but he knew that she had a lot to do in her short time in Boston.

They walked past the Old State House, which, according to the guide, had been an 'emblem of liberty' for more than three hundred years. It was a grand building with a stepped gable, and it had a white wooden tower on the roof. It so resembled a Dutch canal house that it wouldn't have looked out of place in Leiden. The Declaration of Independence was read to the people of Massachusetts for the first time from its balcony on July 18th, 1776. John Adams, the second President of the United States of America, would later declare: 'Then and there the child of independence was born.'

Peter and Judith followed the route that was marked out by the red bricks, but they had stopped reading about the buildings in the tour guide. Peter read out the name of each landmark as they went by, and that was enough for them both.

They spent some time wandering through the Granary Burying Ground where some of the heroes of the American Revolution were buried, including John Hancock, Samuel Adams and Robert Treat Paine – three of the signatories to the Declaration of Independence – James Otis, and, of course, the omnipresent Paul Revere.

Peter took a candid photograph of Judith as she stood under a tree, leaning over to read the inscription on a gravestone. She was half hidden in the shadow cast by the branches, but sunlight shimmered through the leaves and scattered dancing flecks of golden light all over her body. Her Magen David pendant glittered even more than usual. On the photo, the pendant itself vanished behind a ray of refracted light so brilliant that it looked like the silver star had become a tiny sun.

Many of the gravestones lacked the traditional religious imagery that would typically be found in cemeteries. The Puritans had been against the use of religious symbols like crosses, so the citizens of Boston expressed their belief in the afterlife in a more creative way. One of the most popular gravestone motifs was the Soul Effigy, a winged skull that represented the soul's ascent to heaven after death. They saw many images of the Grim Reaper and Father Time too.

They went down a short set of stone steps that led onto Tremont Street. They turned right, passing a group of tourists who were standing around a portly lady, dressed in a historical costume that reminded Peter of the fashions of the Dutch Golden Age. She twirled a stylish, pink linen parasol to protect herself from the sun.

Peter stopped when they reached Park Street Church so that he could read the entry in the tour guide to Judith.

'Listen,' he said. 'On this site, William Lloyd Garrison gave his first major speech against slavery. So it's an important site for abolitionists. And here on the steps, the American patriotic song "My Country 'Tis of Thee", was sung for the first time, a capella. It has the same melody as "God Save the Queen" and served as the unofficial American national anthem in the nineteenth century. The first verse goes:

> My country, 'tis of thee,
> Sweet land of liberty,
> Of thee I sing;
> Land where my fathers died,
> Land of the pilgrims' pride,
> From ev'ry mountainside
> Let freedom ring!

'Hey!' Judith said, 'isn't that last part in Martin Luther King's "'I have a dream" speech too?'

'Oh yes, now you mention it, it is,' Peter said. He closed the book and put it in his shoulder bag. 'Freedom is really the most important value to Americans, isn't it?'

'You think?' Judith chuckled.

'I know. It's not exactly a deep insight, but I've been here for almost three weeks now, and I feel like I've been bombarded with it everywhere I've gone. Freedom, freedom, freedom . . . "We fought for our freedoms. Our freedom is under threat . . ." But the fact is, this country was built on the back of slave labour, on unfair trade practices, on colonialism, the same things that made the Netherlands such a wealthy nation. Life is often still a struggle for those slaves' descendants, and the same goes for the Palestinians in Israel. The people who founded America and the Jews who went to Israel might have found freedom, but it was always at the expense of someone else's freedom. That's what's so hypocritical about the whole sto—'

'What?' Judith asked.

'I don't know. I feel like I just realised something. Could this be what Coen Zoutman's notes are about? He was telling the stories of Abraham and the other patriarchs, the journey out of Egypt . . . I was reminded of it when we were in the Pieterskerk, just before you came here.'

Judith raised her eyebrows.

'I can't see what those stories might have to do with . . .' she said hesitantly.

'No,' said Peter. 'Nor can I, actually.'

But for Peter, it was as if he had been standing in a dark room and someone had flashed the lights on and off: in that split second, he had seen the entire room as clear as day before the darkness had returned.

He closed his eyes and tried to recall what had brought the feeling on, the feeling that he was on to something. It was like hearing a snatch of a vaguely familiar tune that he couldn't quite recognise, but knew that he knew it.

And he knew that he knew this too.

No, he thought. *It's gone already.*

He opened his eyes again.

They had been standing on the corner of Park Street for a while now. They were on the edge of Boston Common. In the distance, Peter could see the grand Massachusetts State House, its golden dome shining in the sun as if lit from inside by a thousand lamps.

The park was busy. Mothers and young nannies pushed strollers and held the hands of small children as they made their way to Frog Pond, a long, shallow paddling pool with benches around it. People sat on the grass watching street performers, singers, jugglers and the ubiquitous living statues. Elderly gentlemen sat at small tables here and there playing chess.

A group of people, mostly African Americans, some naked from the waist up, congregated on the grass. They looked like they were homeless. Some sat outside improvised tents, while others lay on blankets or in sleeping bags. They were surrounded by empty beer cans and wine bottles, and Peter thought he could smell weed, although he could hardly believe that people would smoke it so openly in America. A man walked past him, talking loudly to himself in an obvious state of confusion.

'I really have to go now, honey,' Judith said. She said goodbye with a quick hug, then walked towards the subway station. Just before she reached the entrance, she turned around and waved at him.

In a film, this would be a dramatic scene, Peter thought. *The audience would be left wondering when – or if – these two characters would ever see each other again . . .*

Chapter 26

Willem Rijsbergen sat at home in his living room. A copy of a well-thumbed murder myster rested in his lap.

In his right hand, he held a tumbler into which he had poured himself a finger of whisky. He rolled the liquid around in the glass, focusing on the subtle changes in its golden yellow colour as it caught the light.

For years, Rijsbergen had toyed with the idea of turning his own experiences into stories after he retired. He could publish a new adventure every six months, like a Leiden version of Baantjer, the former policeman who had penned a hugely popular series of detective novels set in Amsterdam.

Customers in bookshops would eagerly ask, 'Is the new Rijsbergen out yet?'

He had always kept this ambition a secret – only his wife Corinne knew about it.

The series would be loosely based on his own life, although, because he had dealt with so few murders, he would have to invent a fictional crime for almost every book. But he could use the things he'd seen and done during his long career to add atmosphere to his stories and give them an air of authenticity.

But this case is different, he thought. *What title would I give this story? 'Master in Death', perhaps?*

He drained his glass and reached for the bottle of Lagavulin to pour himself another dram.

His thoughts turned back to the investigation. They had started by establishing who was innocent, crossing name after name off the long list that they had compiled at the beginning of the investigation: the non-members who had been at the open evening, Tony Vanderhoop and his delegation, the members of the lodge, and even the loosely affiliated members of the protest groups that Sven and Stefan were connected to.

Herman van der Lede had been in custody for six weeks now. He had appeared to misspeak when Rijsbergen and Van de Kooij had visited his wife, the only woman who had put herself forward as a candidate in the election of the new chair of Loge Ishtar.

Just before the detectives had left, Herman had mentioned the square and compasses, information that he almost certainly could not have had if he was innocent. Herman had refused to tell them how he knew about it. Even more telling was his refusal to say another word after he'd realised that he'd already said too much.

Herman's wife Jenny swore up and down that her husband couldn't have been involved in the murder. But she was also unable to explain how Herman could mention details that had not been made public, or why he'd remained tight-lipped ever since.

The investigation had – to use the bureaucratic term – been scaled back soon after Herman van der Lede's arrest. Most of the staff who had been working on the investigation had been reassigned to other, more urgent cases.

'You know as well as I do, Rijsbergen . . .' his boss had said to him. He hadn't looked at or spoken to Van de Kooij once during the exchange. '. . . It looks like we have our man, even if he's not saying anything. I can't justify keeping a big team on this case.'

Rijsbergen had wanted to make some sort of objection, more for formality's sake than out of any real sense of conviction. He knew that his boss was right, and that the argument was already lost. Herman was a strong suspect, not just because he knew things that he shouldn't have known, but also because he was refusing to say anything at all that might exonerate him.

'You and your partner can continue to work on this. Not full time, but you can follow every lead you get for the minute. That's if there are any because it looks like the case has already been solved.'

The Coen Zoutman case and the Yona Falaina case that was connected to it – although it was completely unclear what motive Herman might have had for killing Falaina – were unusually complicated. For a start, there had been a large number of people present at the Masonic Hall at the time of the murder. And then there was the lack of forensic evidence at the crime scene – or rather the excess of evidence, because so many of those people had been in the temple shortly before the murder and they had all left their shoeprints, hair, skin flakes, saliva and fingerprints behind.

Rijsbergen and his team had now spoken to everyone who, as far as the police had been able to establish, had definitely been at the open evening. However, the problem remained that they had been unable to name between ten and fifteen other people who had been there. And as time went on, it would only become even more difficult to find out who they were.

He and Van de Kooij had wanted to see Yona Falaina's room on the Korevaarstraat with their own eyes. When they got there, they discovered that it was almost as anonymous as a hotel room: a bed, a bedside cabinet, a desk with a chair, and a small bookcase that mostly contained books about religious and esoteric subjects. There were no photographs, no posters on the walls, no ornaments or knick-knacks, nothing that gave any clues as to who the man had been.

A young woman with remarkably pale skin had let them in. She had introduced herself as Rachel. 'There are five of us living here,' she explained as she took them up a grubby staircase. 'I've been here since my first year at uni.'

The stairs led to a landing where a bare bulb provided the only light. It was crammed full of boxes, empty wine bottles, a bicycle missing its front wheel, and bags full of clothes that were spilling their contents onto the floor. Two large, yellowing posters from a travel agency hung on the wall, one of a beach with palm trees and an azure-blue sea, and the other of a waterfall in a tropical forest. It smelled stale and damp, like a cellar.

'Sorry about the mess,' she apologised.

It only took a few minutes for them to look around Yona's room. Afterwards, they visited Rachel in her own room, which was very different from the stairs and landing. It was bright and airy, remarkably tidy, and it smelled clean and fresh, as though she had just lightly sprayed the room with perfume.

'I don't have much to do with my housemates,' she said. 'It was different when I first moved in. We used to eat together all the time, but those people have all left now. Like, with Yona, I only knew his first name and that he was from Greece. We've only shaken hands once. That was two years ago when he moved in. He never got any post either. He could have been lying dead in his room for weeks, and nobody would have noticed.'

'Oh, you'd have smelled that pretty quickly, you know,' Van de Kooij said. He started to laugh but stopped when Rijsbergen gave him an irritated look.

They stood in front of the large windows that ran from the sill all the way up to the ceiling and looked out onto the gardens behind the houses. Each plot seemed even more depressing than the one next to it, and they all looked gloomy, even in the middle of the day. It was obvious that none of the residents spent any time in them – there was no garden furniture to be seen. Everything looked sodden, the tiles were green with moss, the walls and fences overgrown with ivy and weeds.

'It's not a particularly uplifting view,' Rachel said. 'But it's cheap here. I'm doing a residency at the university hospital for my medical degree. Once that's done, I'll be leaving.'

Rijsbergen nodded sympathetically.

'Can I get you a cup of tea or something?'

'That's very kind of you, but no, thank you. We should get going.'

Rijsbergen suddenly felt sorry for her. She had looked disappointed when he had declined her offer of tea. He felt like he'd caught a brief glimpse of her loneliness, like seeing a single glove lying on a pavement.

He briefly considered accepting her offer, but he had so much to do that day that he decided against it.

'You're moving out?' he asked, trying to end the conversation on a different note. 'I imagine it's quite hard to find something affordable in Leiden. Have you found anywhere yet?'

'I'm emigrating,' she said. 'I'm going to Israel after my residency. I'm Jewish. My parents moved out there a few years ago. I'm trying hard to learn Hebrew, or Ivrit rather, the modern version.'

She pointed at a pile of books on her desk. *Learn Hebrew*, the cover of the book on the top of the pile read, *A Basic Course in Ivrit for Beginners*.

'That's a big step,' Van de Kooij said. 'Moving to another country. You'd be leaving behind everything you have here.'

'I'm not leaving that much behind, really,' she said, and she laughed unhappily. 'This doesn't feel like home any more. My parents felt the same way. The final straw came when my dad was surrounded by a group of boys on the Garenmarkt, and one of them spat in his face. It was *Shabbat*, and he was on his way to prayers at the synagogue just around the corner from here.'

'Did he report it?' Van de Kooij asked.

'Oh, there was no point. He wouldn't have been able to identify the one who did it anyway. Those boys thought they were supporting their Palestinian brothers by spitting in my father's face. It's just disgusting.'

'And that's why you—' Rijsbergen began, but she didn't give him the chance to finish.

Rachel's cheeks were flushed now. 'It's crazy, isn't it, that my dad is scared to walk down the street wearing his kippah? When was the war? Seventy years ago? And now we're all afraid again. I go to the synagogue too, but our community has almost disappeared here in Leiden. We even have to have Jewish men from The Hague come to our prayer services so that we have enough for the minyan.'

'Minyan?' Van de Kooij asked.

'Minyan,' Rachel repeated. 'There have to be at least ten men, a minyan, to hold a prayer service in a synagogue. We rarely manage that in Leiden, now. The Jewish community never really recovered after the Second World War. Almost all the Jews in Leiden were deported and killed. They took all the children from the Jewish orphanage, children who had fled here from Germany . . .'

'But now—' Rijsbergen began, but again, he wasn't given a chance to finish his sentence.

'My parents were so tired of it, and so was I. I want to live where I can hold my head high, where I can practise my faith, where I can belong to a community, where I can be free! A land where my father can walk down the street wearing his kippah without being scared that someone will spit in his face. Our synagogue is watched by CCTV cameras twenty-four/seven, and there's bullet-proof glass on the windows. For goodness sake, what sort of times are we living in?'

Rijsbergen wasn't sure what to say. 'I understand how awful that must be,' he decided to reply. 'I wish you success, Rachel, and good luck, too. I'm sure it will be good to spread your wings and move on.'

Rachel had given them a melancholy smile when they left.

The neighbours hadn't been able to tell them anything helpful, nor had the apartment's landlord. Some of the shop-keepers in the stores below the apartment had recognised Yona's face but knew nothing about him. The baker had told them that he often brought a loaf of bread and a small carton of milk from him, but that was as far as their interactions had gone.

Nobody seemed to have known the young man, and nobody appeared to have missed him after his death. He had moved through Leiden like a ghost.

Welcome to the twenty-first century, Rijsbergen thought bitterly. *We're connected to the rest of the world twenty-four hours a day, but we don't know our own neighbours. Yona could have been missing for months . . . As long as his rent was paid on time, who would have cared?*

Weeks after his murder, not a single witness had come forward. Apparently, not one person had seen any unusual activity on the wharves along the Leiden canals.

The Greek embassy had informed them that Yona had been an orphan with no family at all. There were no uncles, aunts, nephews or cousins. It looked like not a single soul had really known him except, perhaps, Coen Zoutman, if the tattoo they had in common was anything to go by. But the nature of their relationship still wasn't clear at all.

Van de Kooij had taken it upon himself to pay a visit to the synagogue on the Levendaal. They did have CCTV footage from the day of the murder, but there was nothing to see on it but empty back gardens.

Although he understood the chief superintendent's decision – and also respected it, of course – it frustrated Rijsbergen in a way that he couldn't put into words.

It was half-past ten, a good time to go to sleep. His wife Corinne had already gone upstairs and was reading in bed.

He had been sitting lost in thought for a while when the doorbell rang.

Before he had a chance to get up, Corinne called down the stairs, 'Did you hear that?'

Nobody ever comes to the door this late at night, Rijsbergen thought as he made his way to the front door. *They don't even deliver parcels after ten o'clock.*

He moved the curtain at the kitchen window aside to see who it was.

Van de Kooij. He was hopping impatiently from foot to foot and staring at the door. He reached out to ring the bell again.

Rijsbergen rushed over to the front door, but he was too late to prevent the piercing sound of the bell echoing through the hall a second time.

Corrine was standing at the top of the stairs. 'Who can that be at this time of night?' she asked anxiously. Her greatest fear was that, one day, one of the criminals her husband had arrested would turn up to exact their revenge.

'It's just Van de Kooij!' he called back to her. 'Nothing to worry about. Go to sleep, my love. I'll be up shortly.' Without waiting for her reply, he opened the door.

'I think I've found something,' Van de Kooij blurted out, ignoring the usual pleasantries.

'Something to do with Zoutman?'

'Yes, and Falaina,' he replied. Van de Kooij's neck was blotched red with excitement. 'Can I come in?'

'Uh . . . Yes, all right, but . . .' Rijsbergen opened the door wide and let his colleague in. As Van de Kooij brushed past him, Rijsbergen noticed the scent of Old Spice aftershave, something he had once associated with old men, but which was now inextricably linked to his partner.

He allowed Van de Kooij to walk ahead of him into the living room. He remembered the half-empty bottle of whisky and the glass next to it and felt ambushed, like an alcoholic getting a surprise visit from his AA buddy.

'Would you like a drink?' he asked as casually as he could manage. Van de Kooij declined, apparently too wound up to drink anything.

'So what was so urgent that it couldn't wait until tomorrow?' Rijsbergen asked when they had both sat down.

'I'll tell you, but first I want to show it to you,' Van de Kooij said. 'Have you got a computer down here?'

Rijsbergen reached over to the coffee table and took a laptop out of the large drawer underneath it. 'Here,' he said.

Van de Kooij opened the laptop, asked for the password, entered it and immediately started typing. He pressed the mouse button a few times, and then he picked up the laptop and brought it over to the sofa. He sat down so close to Rijsbergen that their thighs squashed against each other.

Rijsbergen edged away.

'There,' said Van de Kooij. 'Look at that.'

He clicked on a small triangle in the bottom left corner of the page, and the frozen image on the screen came to life.

Rijsbergen glanced at the words at the top of the screen.

Unsolved Murder Mysteries. Van de Kooij had selected an episode of one of the many Discovery Channel shows that he watched almost every night.

'Why are we watching—'

'Just watch,' Van de Kooij said, interrupting him with what sounded like both impatience and triumph.

The programme began with an aerial view of a city. Rijsbergen recognised it as Jerusalem from the gleaming golden cupola on the Dome of the Rock.

The camera soared over the Eternal City as though it was attached to a mighty eagle. The image zoomed in ever closer as an off-screen narrator delivered a typically American voiceover, pausing for dramatic effect on anything that even slightly hinted at excitement or intrigue.

'Four years ago . . . The eternal city of Jerusalem – the city where Jesus Christ once walked the earth . . . The city of the biblical kings Saul, David and Solomon was rocked by a series of brutal murders . . . that to this day, have never been solved . . . Will they ever be?'

A rapid series of images followed in which ancient symbols flashed on the screen, alternating with flickering glimpses of someone being beaten on the head with a gavel, an expanding pool of blood on the floor, slamming doors and flickering candles . . . Gregorian chants could be heard in the background.

Americans were masters in the creation of suspense, that much was clear.

For the next twenty-five minutes, Rijsbergen watched, mesmerised, as the four-year-old case of the brutal murders of two men in Jerusalem unfolded before him. The murderer had never been found.

Both men's heads had been pulverised with a Masonic gavel.

Both men had been single, with no other family . . . childless and the last in their family lines.

Both men had had a patch of skin, the size of a dime, about a centimetre-and-a-half across, removed from between their left breast and their armpit.

And both of them had been Freemasons.

Chapter 27

Peter turned around and set off for Boston Masonic Hall on Tremont Street. He made his way through Boston Common, passed Frog Pond on his left, and after a fifteen-minute walk, he reached the end of the park.

From here, he could already read the words inscribed on the building.

GRAND LODGE OF FREEMASONS IN MASSACHUSETTS

Below this, four large mosaics filled the spaces where windows must once have been. The murals depicted the sun, a square and compasses, a trowel, and pillars set against a background of elongated geometric shapes in different shades of blue.

The panel furthest to the right was taken up by the grand lodge's seal which featured two beavers on either side of a coat of arms. At the top was a dove with an olive branch in its beak, and below, 1733, the year the lodge was established, making it one of the oldest in the world. Above the date was a broad, scrolling ribbon with the motto: FOLLOW REASON.

Use your intellect . . .

Peter went inside. The handles on the front door were in the form of the Freemasonry symbol: a large, gold-coloured square and compasses with a 'G' in the middle. The seal with the two beavers that he had seen outside was repeated in a mosaic on the lobby's floor.

He reported to the uniformed security guard who ticked off Peter's name on a visitors' list and picked up the phone to announce his arrival.

'You can take the elevator to the second floor,' the man said and gave Peter a name badge, as though he was attending a conference.

When he stepped out of the lift, he was met by a rather stocky, moustachioed man with a long lock of hair combed over his bald pate.

'Mr De Haan!' the man said, greeting him like an old friend. 'Or may I call you Peter?' He smiled broadly, radiating the typically American positivity that Peter had encountered in so many people on his trip.

'Of course,' Peter replied.

They shook hands.

The man introduced himself. 'Walter L. Lunt. Come in, come in,' he beckoned.

He took Peter into a library where the walls were lined with bookcases that reached the ceiling. In the middle of the room were smaller bookcases at chest height. A wide variety of objects was displayed on top of them: photographs, books, certificates, building plans . . .

'I understand you're not a Freemason yourself?' Walter asked.

'No, but I'm very interested in Freemasonry,' Peter replied. 'My girlfriend is a member of a co-Masonic lodge where I live, in Leiden. When I told her that I was coming to Boston, she asked if I would visit the grand lodge. And take some photos for her if that was allowed.'

'Yes, yes, of course. No problem at all.'

Walter led Peter over to a display about the history of the Boston lodges. There were lots of black and white photos of men staring into the lens with sober expressions, photographs of the building itself and its predecessors, various certificates, and books opened at pertinent pages. Walter gave Peter a potted history of Freemasonry in the United States, describing how Freemasons had held meetings at the beginning of the eighteenth century even before they had been officially recognised and registered by the 'headquarters' in London. They had successfully petitioned the grand lodge in England for authorisation to become a grand lodge themselves and set up other lodges.

'I come from an evangelical background myself, Peter,' Walter said. 'I've struggled to break free from it for many years. The times we live in . . . I think it's more important than ever that we live according to our motto, "Follow Reason". We increasingly see the development of a bunker mentality among groups here in the USA. They're entrenched in the belief that they're right, clinging onto ideas that go back to their grandparents' time. For many people, the fact that an idea has been around for a long time is enough proof of its validity. But we Masons believe that we should test all things and hold fast to what is good. I'd be worried if I was still clinging onto the ideas I have now in ten years!'

They left the library and entered a long corridor. Doors on either side led to two enormous rooms, one even more opulent than the other. Peter felt like he had stepped back in time and that, at any moment, an eighteenth-century Freemason in full regalia might walk into the room.

Walter proudly pointed out various details like the walls which, at first glance, appeared to have been wallpapered, but which had in fact been meticulously painted. The intricate patterns had been painstakingly applied by hand.

'Several lodges meet in this building,' Walter explained in the third room after they had taken the stairs up to the next floor. 'I'm a member of the lodge that meets in this room.'

It was an extraordinarily stylish space. The Worshipful Master's tall, ornately carved dark wooden chair was flanked by two lower, but equally beautifully carved, seats. On the wall behind them was a golden letter 'G', surrounded by rays of sunlight. The semi-circular set of steps that led to the chairs looked like the rice paddy terraces on an Indonesian mountain.

One of the long walls was decorated with four paintings. Walter explained that they were allegorical representations of Solomon's Temple.

Each of the four paintings depicted the copper pillars of Boaz and Jachin. Boaz was one of the main characters in the Book of Ruth in the Old Testament, and Jachin was the first high priest of Solomon's Temple. The indomitable-looking pillars stood on a square in front of the Jewish Temple in Jerusalem, and the viewer looked through them onto the Holy of Holies.

On the opposite wall were paintings of men who were obviously previous chairmen of the lodge.

'This is where we perform the rituals of our Craft,' Walter said.

He took a seat on one of the chairs that had been arranged just as they were in the Masonic Hall on the Steenschuur with their backs to the wall so that everyone faced the large, open space in the middle of the room.

The relaxed way in which Walter sat down suggested that he was settling in to tell a long story.

'Sometimes, we refer to this room as a temple. That makes

sense, of course, when we realise that we're endeavouring to work on the symbolic Temple of Humanity. Our temple here is an allegorical representation of King Solomon's Temple. That's why these paintings of Solomon are displayed so prominently. The way we set the temple up depends on which degree the lodge is working in. We have a meeting tonight where we'll be using the symbols for the first degree, Entered Apprentice. What you see here is only a partial layout, by the way. Our work in this degree involves other tools, but we only bring them out when we're about to use them.'

Peter decided to sit down too, and just then, he noticed that the floor here had been laid with large, alternating black and white tiles, just like the temple in Leiden.

Walter looked at Peter expectantly in a way that suggested that he was waiting for Peter to ask him a good question.

Is Walter aware of what's happened in Leiden, Peter wondered. *Should I ask him about it later?*

'As well as the Three Great Lights, we have the Three Lesser Lights,' said Walter, impassively continuing his monologue.

His tone gave away the fact that he had given this talk many times before. Even the way he paused at certain moments seemed to be part of his performance.

'And we wear these . . .' he picked up an apron and a pair of gloves and gave them to Peter '. . . whenever we labour here together. How the apron is worn corresponds with the degree the member has achieved. An Entered Apprentice wears it in a different way to a Fellowcraft or Master. We tie the apron around our middle, and it symbolically separates the higher and lower parts of our natures. The white gloves signify that we want the work of our hands to be pure and unsullied.'

Peter handed the apron and gloves back.

'And finally,' Walter said, winding up his presentation, 'I'd like to draw your attention to the pattern of black and white squares on the floor. The chequerboard floor is sometimes called the mosaic pavement. This floor could represent the continuous chequered path of our lives in which opposites – good and evil, light and darkness, positive and negative and so on – exist alongside each other or combined with each other. It's also a floor that doesn't allow us to easily draw clear dividing lines. A floor, then, that forces us to see nuances, makes us come to the realisation that dividing the world into simplified boxes is probably not going to help any of us . . .'

Walter walked over to the edge of the floor.

'Around the outside of this challenging, confrontational and thought-provoking floor,' he said, pointing with his finger to make sure that Peter's attention was drawn to the detail, 'is a tessellated border with a toothed pattern. We Masons promise each other that everything we do, say and share will remain within this border, which is to say that we place mutual trust in each other, and we never betray that trust. Why? Not because we want to be part of a secret society but because we need to feel that we have a place where we can become – and be – our true selves. A sanctuary for self-reflection where we can be certain that whatever we share will stay inside this place so that we can be open with ourselves and with each other.'

Walter looked at Peter, visibly pleased with himself for having delivered yet another successful tour that covered all the core elements of Freemasonry.

They walked through the rest of the building, which appeared to contain several halls for other lodges, each decorated in a different way.

After they had looked around the last temple – or lodge

room – Peter asked Walter to take a photograph of him in a small, octagonal room where a real sword had been placed diagonally across a desk. Heavy velvet curtains hung at the windows which would have made the room completely dark when they were closed.

Walter explained that this was the room where members were initiated. It was also a space where people could retreat to be alone with their thoughts.

Peter looked at the photo: it could not have come out any better. He was looking at the camera with a resolute expression, like a man on a mission. He held the sword at an angle across his body with the blade's tip pointing upwards. The ray of sunlight that shone through the window fell precisely on the polished metal of the hilt, making the sword look like a *Star Wars* lightsabre.

Walter and Peter went back to the library.

Two large photographs stood on the mantelpiece, one of an older gentleman and one of a young man. A tealight had been lit in front of each picture. At first glance, the older gentleman looked stern, but the laughter lines around his eyes hinted at an outlook on life that was probably more cheerful than his portrait suggested. He had a large bald spot on the top of his head, but what remained of his silver-grey hair was long and thick and hung down to his shoulders. Together with his neatly trimmed ring beard, it gave him a somewhat eccentric appearance. It was easy to imagine him as a crusading knight in armour going into battle against the Muslims to win back Jerusalem for Christianity.

The young man had the face of someone whose life had already left its mark on him, who had experienced things that no one should ever experience, much less a man of his age.

'Who are they?' Peter asked. 'If you don't mind me asking.'

'Of course I don't mind,' Walter said, walking over to the fireplace. 'You might have heard about them on the news. Sam and George fell overboard on a fishing trip two days ago. At least, that's what the police think must have happened to them. Their bodies haven't been found yet.'

'Yes, I did see that on the news,' Peter said. 'But the sea was very calm that day, wasn't it?'

'Yes, that's what's so strange about it. Sam was – or still is, I should say – the Worshipful Master, our chairman. Neither of them had any family at all, so they'd become like father and son to each other. They were very close friends despite the age difference, even closer than a father and son, really. George was Sam's protégé. He could have succeeded him one day.'

Peter felt the hairs on his arms stand on end.

'And they don't know what happened to them?'

'No. It's a mystery. Maybe one of them fell overboard, and the other one tried to help him? But then you'd think he would have thrown the lifesaver to him, wouldn't you? Something's not right about it.'

'Could they have got into an argument? Or been kidnapped?'

'Or . . . maybe they went swimming. The sea can look deceptively calm. It wouldn't take long for you to get a cramp or for hypothermia to set in. These things do happen.'

Peter closed his eyes and shook his head in the hope that it would dislodge the idea that this might be connected to the double murder in Leiden.

Pure coincidence, he thought, trying to ignore a growing feeling of disquiet. *You can't go around seeing everything as a murder case, Peter. Nobody's skull was cracked open. Nobody's hands were*

*tied together. A likeness is not a link. Isn't that what you always
teach your students?*

'It's like a scene in a movie,' Peter said as they walked back
to the corridor.

'I hope they're still alive,' Walter said. 'I know it's hope against
hope, but I do. Some of our members were in favour of tempo-
rarily closing the lodge, but personally, it's made me want to be
here all the more. Showing visitors around the building makes
me forget what's happened for a little while.'

A book on the desk caught Peter's eye. The title was *A Song
in Stone*, and the name of the author printed on the cover was
Walter L. Lunt.

'You wrote that?' Peter asked, pleased to have found a way to
lighten the conversation.

'Yes,' Walter answered proudly.

'What sort of books do you write?'

'Historical fiction with a helping of religion and intrigue.
Knights Templar, that sort of thing.'

'Can you get them in bookstores?'

'You can buy one in the store here if you like,' Walter said
enthusiastically. 'I'll sign it for you too.'

'That would be great,' Peter said, curious to know what Walter
had written, and also impressed by his salesmanship.

He bought a copy of *A Song in Stone* in the lodge's small shop,
and, as promised, Walter signed it for him on the spot.

For Peter, my newfound friend from the Netherlands, he wrote
elaborately underneath the title on the first page of the book,
and then he added his name in swooping, cursive letters.

'Any questions?' Walter asked as they walked down the
corridor towards the lift.

Although he'd said this in a way that made it quite clear that

Peter wasn't actually supposed to ask any questions, there was something that Peter wanted to know.

'Earlier, you talked about testing all things and holding onto what's good. Or in other words, not immediately accepting something as truth.'

'That's right.'

'I was wondering . . . As you know, I'm from Leiden. There seems to be – or to have been – a debate among the Freemasons there. On one side, there are people like you who are strongly committed to the idea of there being "no dogma". They believe in giving individuals the freedom and responsibility of interpreting the symbols and stories for themselves. They seem to be in the majority.'

'That's the idea of Freemasonry, yes.'

'But then there's – or there was – another group who – how should I put this? Who prefer to rely on tradition. They believe in accepting someone else's explanations for things, in not asking too many questions, accepting the meanings given to you by other people, by higher minds. Standing on the shoulders of giants, or something like that. You could call them literalists.'

'Yes, I know what you mean.'

'It's as if there are two factions. One that takes the stories literally and wants to be part of a tradition where there's very little, perhaps even no room for personal meanings. And then another one that advocates for a more allegorical explanation of the stories and symbols.'

'I know what you mean, Peter,' Walter said again. 'That's something I'm aware of here too. But those people, the literalists, they all leave our ranks sooner or later because . . . well, because it goes against the whole spirit of Freemasonry, do you see? But we too have members with "unenlightened minds", as I call them.'

'There was a murder in Leiden six weeks ago,' Peter said. 'Actually, there were two murders. The Worshipful Master, Coen Zoutman, and then shortly afterwards, a young man. You might have heard about them.'

'Yes,' Walter said. 'I hadn't heard about the young man, but of course, we've heard about the murder of Coen Zoutman. Such an awful thing to happen. Just like in Jerusalem four years ago.'

'What?' Peter exclaimed. 'What happened in Jerusalem four years ago?'

Walter looked at him in astonishment.

'Four years ago? You don't know about it? It was a very high-profile case in Jerusalem. Two of our brothers were killed shortly after each other. They'd both had their skulls smashed with a gavel. The gavel that we use in our Craft, no less.'

'*What?*' was all that Peter could manage to say.

'They never found the killer – or killers. The bodies had been mutilated, although that might be overstating it. They'd both had a small piece of skin about the size of a coin cut out from between their left breast and their armpit.'

'But that's exactly what happened in Leiden! The killer used a gavel there too. Well, in the Worshipful Master's case at least. I don't know anything about skin being removed, but Coen Zoutman had a tattoo.'

'A tattoo?'

'Yes, a tattoo. Do you have a pen and paper?'

They went back to Walter's desk in the library.

Peter drew what he could remember of the tattoo that had been on Coen Zoutman's body.

Walter picked up the sheet of paper and held it up to his eyes, but then, after staring at it for twenty or thirty seconds, he put it back on the desk. 'No, I'm sorry,' he said. 'It doesn't look like anything I've ever seen before. It's vaguely reminiscent of the All-Seeing Eye, but I'm sure you've already considered that.'

'Yes, that's about as far as the police have got, too. But . . . that murder in Jerusalem, have you reported it to the police in Leiden?'

'Reported it? No, I've not reported it. None of us has, I think. We weren't even aware of the second murder in the Netherlands. But won't the Dutch police have made that connection themselves already? I would presume that the authorities all communicate with each other. Don't they have databases?'

'I don't think that they . . . I think they've mainly focused on Leiden. It's very possible that they don't know about the Jerusalem case and that they haven't established an international connection. But it looks like they've already found the murderer in Leiden.'

'And now . . . No, that's not possible.' Walter sat down at his desk and grabbed the edge of it with both hands. 'No, that's not possible,' he said again, as though he was trying, against reason, to convince himself.

'You're thinking what I'm thinking?' Peter asked.

'Well, you know . . .' Walter said. 'In poor Sam and George's case, we're still assuming it was a tragic accident. That's why I didn't make the connection with what happened in Jerusalem. And what's happened in Leiden. I don't think . . . What do you think, Peter?'

'It could just be a coincidence, but it is bizarre, isn't it?'

'I'll call the police later,' Walter said. 'So far, they've been treating it as a missing persons case, an accident, like I said. But what if there is a link between all these cases? It's the kind of thing I might put in one of my books, but the truth is sometimes stranger than fiction.'

I'll email Rijsbergen later, Peter thought. *It's gone five o'clock here, so it will be after eleven at night in Leiden. Rijsbergen might not read it until tomorrow morning, but this could be useful to the case.*

'We'll see,' he said. 'But I have a bad feeling about it.'

'I must say, so do I.'

They shook hands and went back to the corridor where Peter pushed one of the illuminated buttons on the lift. He felt like their shared concern had created a bond between them.

'Well, I hope you'll enjoy my book when you get back to your hotel,' Walter said, attempting to end their meeting on a positive note.

'Oh, I'm not staying in a hotel,' Peter said as they stepped into the lift. 'I'm staying with a friend. She's got a three-month research grant at Harvard, and she's staying on the campus. She's the only person I know here.'

A thought suddenly occurred to him. *Why didn't I ask about him earlier?* He put his hand over the sensor on the lift doors to stop them from closing. 'Do you know Tony Vanderhoop?' he asked.

Peter didn't need to be a body language expert to be able to tell from Walter's reaction that he did indeed know Tony – and that he didn't like being reminded of it.

'Yes, I know him,' he replied. 'Why?'

As if by magic, the friendly, open mood of the last two hours vanished.

Walter took a couple of steps towards Peter, blocking off the stairs. There was no point removing his hand from the sensor because the lift doors would take too long to close.

Peter waited to see what would happen next. He felt his muscles tense. *Fight or flight*, he thought.

Walter stepped closer, close enough to make Peter feel uncomfortable.

'How do you know him?' Walter asked. 'If you don't mind me asking.'

'He's . . . Tony . . . I don't know Mr Vanderhoop well,' Peter said, trying to downplay his connection to Tony. 'He was in Leiden about a month and a half ago with an American delegation organising some Mayflower 400 events. 2020 is the four-hundredth anniversary of the year the Pilgrims left Leiden and came to America. I only met Tony twice, very briefly. Since I was here in Boston visiting my friend, I thought it would be a good idea to meet up with him. But I hardly know him. Why? Do you have a problem with him?'

Walter said nothing, but Peter could tell that he was furiously turning this information over in his mind.

'I mean, as a Freemason, he's—' Peter began.

'A Freemason?' Walter scoffed.

Peter got the impression that if this exchange had been taking place outside, Walter would have spat on the ground.

'Did Tony tell you he was a Mason?'

'Yes, that's what he said,' Peter said.

Walter's shoulders slumped like he had just decided that Peter was 'good people' after all.

'Tony Vanderhoop was thrown out of the Masons years ago.'

Fragment 7 – From Leiden to America (November 1627)

I have been sent a letter. The first letter I have ever received.

I was so moved by it that it took me some time to regain control of my emotions. Just the thought that this little bundle of paper wrapped in nothing more than a simple envelope had travelled so far to reach me was enough to make me feel overcome. Who knows what dangers it met on its journey? It has crossed an entire ocean, but just a few words on the envelope – my name, my address and the name of the city – were enough to ensure that it reached its destination: the only place in God's great, wide world where I can be found.

Of course, this letter is not meant only for me but for our whole congregation. I will read it out at our next meeting.

Inside the envelope, there was another, smaller envelope with a letter inside. This was not addressed to me but to Josh.

This is not the first letter the congregation has received. We know that some letters are sent and never arrive, their contents forever unread, as if their writers were speaking only to themselves.

But this letter is from our man, Josh Nunn's first pupil, the little boy who clung to his side when our ship sailed from Plymouth to Amsterdam. Now he is like a sheep among wolves. I was surprised when he left us to go to America because he appeared to have aligned himself so clearly with the group that chose to stay in Leiden. But I was not privy to everything that was going on then, and there are still things that are hidden to me that have been revealed to others.

Much has happened there, and here too.

I will begin with there. In his letter, he tells us what has transpired over the last seven years. Much of what he writes was known to us, but he also tells us things that we did not know.

He describes the difficulties they faced in England. Deciding to go to America was one thing, but actually getting there proved to be difficult. The travellers were dependent on the will of the state, which grants trading companies the rights to establish colonies. Our group also had to ask permission to go to America because the land is under English rule. They were forced to acknowledge James I as head of the church. But what else could they have done? If they had refused, the entire venture would have been scuppered before their ship had weighed anchor. They also had to accept all the ecclesiastical appointments made by the king. Such a quandary! But just like Queen Esther, who saved her people by hiding her true faith when she married the Persian king Ahasuerus, the Pilgrims held fast to their own beliefs.

Once permission was granted, they had to find a trading company that was willing to take them to America. William Brewster was prepared to risk going back to England to find one, despite his previous problems with the Pilgrim Press. He negotiated on the group's behalf, which was no easy task. They eventually signed a contract with the Merchant Adventurers who financed the voyage. The Pilgrims had to promise them an almost impossible sum in return, but what choice did they have? And if the expedition failed, for whatever reason, not a penny of this sum would be refunded.

But does not the psalmist sing: 'The Lord looks down from heaven; he sees all humankind. From where he sits enthroned, he watches all the inhabitants of the earth – he who fashions the hearts of them all and observes all their deeds.'

Be assured, an evil man will not go unpunished, but those who are righteous will be delivered.

The group of one hundred people who had requested – and been granted – permission to settle in the beautiful city of Leiden had grown bigger, much bigger. The Lord had blessed our endeavour. Our group now numbered hundreds of souls.

Not everyone was able to go to America, of course, but then, not everyone wanted to. A split had developed in our group.

I know more now about what was going on then – I was a part of it too . . . But I'm getting ahead of myself. I will write more of this next time.

John was going to stay in Leiden, and William would lead the expedition to America in his stead.

The travellers pooled their resources and purchased a small ship, the Speedwell, to take them to the New World. It was in need of repair, but once this had been taken care of, they were ready to start their journey. When they got to America, the Speedwell would be used for fishing and visiting other colonies.

In July 1620, I and many members of our congregation travelled to Delfshaven to bid farewell to all those who were about to set sail on the good ship Speedwell. But the ship was overladen, and the captain refused to leave port. Some people would have to stay behind. Heart-breaking scenes played out on the quayside. Families were torn apart . . . Some of them were able to go while others had to wait here and hope that they would have another chance in the future. Eventually, sixty souls were able to board the ship. The others returned with us to Leiden.

You can imagine their disappointment. They must have felt like Moses when he saw the promised land but was forbidden to enter it.

In the letter addressed to me, he writes:

Finally, the ship weighed anchor! To see all those people standing on the quayside . . . I was leaving my old life behind me, bound for a new life, an unknown life. I would rather have stayed, but I had to go. Someone new has taken my *place in Josh Nunn's safe hands. And someone new will eventually take my place in America too.*

But even so, I was excited by the prospect of an adventure.

We set sail for Southampton with the wind in our hair, salt spray on our skin and joy in our hearts.

In my heart too!

The crossing went well. We went down to the sea in our ship and sailed the great water. We saw the deeds of the Lord, His wondrous works in the deep.

The Mayflower was waiting for us in the harbour with more passengers. Some of them shared our faith. Others did not, and these we named 'the Strangers'. They were poor people seeking prosperity in America.

However, it soon became clear that the repaired Speedwell would be able to carry us across the North Sea and no further. No sooner had we left Southampton than she began to take on water. We turned back, and after she was repaired in Dartmouth, we made a second attempt, but again she took on water. The Speedwell was not going to make it. Some of the passengers were transferred to the Mayflower, and yet another group was left behind, this time in England.

On the 6th of September, a hundred and two passengers, Pilgrims and Strangers, and twenty-five crewmen set sail for America.

The crossing was arduous. I could write a book about that alone. Storms rose up, so intense that we thought our final hour had come. The sea was so rough that it threatened to wreck the ship. The crew was afraid, and all cried out to God for help. We were worried that our prayers would never reach heaven; they were surely scattered on the wind as soon as we sent them up. Some wanted to throw the cargo into the sea to reduce the risk of sinking, but then what would we have had to eat? I went down into the hold of the ship and had lain down and was fast asleep. The captain came to me and said, 'What are you doing sound asleep? Get up, call on your god! Perhaps the god will spare us a thought so that we do not perish!' I was scared that the sailors would say to one another, 'Come, let us cast lots, so that we may know on whose account this calamity has come upon us.' And that the lot would fall on me. I was like a stowaway, even though everyone knew that I belonged to the group. The sea was growing more and more tempestuous, and I was afraid that I should answer: 'Pick me up and throw me into the sea; then the sea will quiet down for you; for I know it is because of me that this great storm has come upon you.' And that they would cry out to the Lord, saying 'Please, O Lord, we pray, do not let us perish on account of this man's life. Do not make us guilty of innocent blood; for you, O Lord, have done as it pleased you.' And that they would pick me up and throw me in the sea so that the sea would cease from its raging.

But time and time again, the sea was becalmed.

And on November 19th, we saw land at last . . . We fell to our knees and thanked God, crying, praying. William read Psalm 107, which seemed to have been written especially for us . . .

For He commanded and raised the stormy wind,
which lifted up the waves of the sea.
They mounted up to heaven, they went down to the depths;
their courage melted away in their calamity;
they reeled and staggered like drunkards,
and were at their wits' end.

Then they cried to the Lord in their trouble,
and He brought them out from their distress;
He made the storm be still,
and the waves of the sea were hushed.
Then they were glad because they had quiet,
and He brought them to their desired haven.

The last storm had driven the Mayflower many miles north of our intended destination. We were near a cape which we later learned was called Cape Cod. However, the cape was not part of Virginia, the land we had been granted a royal patent for, but part of New England. Our permission to establish a colony was not valid there. We attempted to go further south but were held back by strong currents. And so we were forced to seek refuge here . . .

But the Strangers caused problems: they said that they were no longer bound by our contract because we were outside the bounds of our patent. The Strangers wanted to abandon our colony and set up their own. Chaos loomed: our colony was threatened with collapse before it had even begun.

After discussions between the Pilgrims and the Strangers, we came to a new agreement, a covenant that was signed by all of the male passengers on board the ship: the Mayflower Compact. Together, we would establish good governance and make our own laws, regulations and appointments. Every one of us now had a stake in the success of this undertaking.

John Carver was chosen as our first governor. We put into practice an idea that we had learned about in Leiden and brought with us from the Netherlands: Carver held no religious office, which meant that we could separate the two authorities. Church and government would be two distinct *powers here, each independent of the other, and each respecting the sovereignty of the other in its own domain.*

Once we were on dry land, we explored the terrain. We found a place to build houses. That first winter, the lack of food was a serious problem. We could not yet plant crops for the following year. After all, there is a season and a time for everything. We were dependent on the ship's stores, on the fish that we managed to catch using what primitive means we had, and on the corn that the natives grow which we occasionally found in the area. Some of this we could not eat because we had to save it to use as seed in the spring. And the promised land was not empty. Just as the tribes of Israel encountered the Canaanites after wandering in the wilderness – he that hath ears to hear, let him hear! – we also came upon what appeared to be godless savages. Some were friendly and helped us, others were much more hostile. There have already been violent and bloody confrontations with them. During worship recently, William said that we will struggle to tame these savages and show them that the idols they worship are false. It will be many, many years before these Indians, as they are called, can truly be set free and approach the throne of Christ in humility – after all, it is only through His words that we can truly be set free.

The Mayflower stayed with us and did not return to England until March 1621. So we always had the ship to fall back on. But half of the new settlers died in that first year, and we could do nothing to prevent it. People in the village began to complain. 'If only we had died by the hand of the Lord in Leiden,' they said to John and William. 'There where we sat by the fleshpots and ate our fill of bread. For you have brought us out into this wilderness to kill this whole assembly with hunger.'

John, our first governor, did not survive the first year. William succeeded him.

Luckily for us, more ships arrived carrying new colonists . . . Had they not, our colony would soon have died out.

And if I had died, then I would have made the wrong choice in going to America: all my knowledge would have died with me. I have my own pupil now, just as I was a pupil once myself. This gives me faith that the line will not be broken, even here.

The ships brought more Pilgrims from Leiden, but they also brought people we did not know and who had no connection to us. How providential the Mayflower Compact has proved to be! Because of the good agreements that we had set out in it, we were able to get along despite our different backgrounds and interests.

Because, despite all the difficulties and despite all the setbacks, our settlement, Plimoth Plantation, has survived. So well, in fact, that we can even celebrate by holding a harvest feast every October. We have called it Thanksgiving. The feast reminds us of Leiden, where it all began . . . We have fond memories of the annual thanksgiving service in the Pieterskerk every October 3rd where we gave thanks to God for the Relief of Leiden, for driving away the tyrannical Spaniards who wanted to impose their beliefs and their way of worship on the people of that city, who forgot that every man is ultimately free, neither master nor slave. In the Netherlands, that bastion of freedom, Leiden, these things were engraved on our hearts. And we hold these truths to be self-evident: that all men are created equal, that they are endowed by their Creator with certain unalienable rights, that among these are life, liberty, and the pursuit of happiness.

With these ardent words – words that I had already heard from John's lips and committed to paper – the letter I received from our man in America ended. This was the part intended for the public that I read to the congregation.

But, as I have said, there was another letter. Inside the envelope that was addressed to me was another message that was not meant for me. Of course, I immediately gave it to Josh Nunn. He knows that I have become the Leiden congregation's chronicler in recent years. Tonight, he will give the letter back to me. He has given me permission to reproduce its contents in this account so that what is written in it will not be lost. Josh has told me that I will soon understand the true nature of all that has happened. Who 'the teacher' is, and who 'the pupil'. The true role of our man in America. The real source and nature of the conflict within our group. Why some of us went to America and why such a large group of us stayed here.

Tonight, everything will be revealed.

I already know that . . .

Email from: Piet van Vliet

And there the fragment ends, Peter! Maddening! Either our anonymous writer never found out what was in that letter, or he did find out, but decided against including those revelations in the chronicle. Or someone else made that decision for him . . .

It seems so ironic that the very people who sought freedom in America had such a limited perception of freedom themselves. Just read what he says about William

Brewster – and one gets the impression that he is trying to tell us between the lines that this is not a view that he shares – who told the congregation that they 'will struggle to tame these savages and show them that the idols they worship are false' and that 'it will be many, many years before these Indians can truly be set free and approach the throne of Christ in humility'. The Pilgrims' version of Christ, that is!

They took all the principles that they had learned about in the Netherlands with them on the Great Crossing: freedom of religion, freedom of speech, and freedom of the press. Those principles formed the basis of what eventually became the modern United States: civil marriage, separation of church and state . . . But first and foremost, they were concerned with *their own* personal freedom. It's similar to the way the politicians in the Partij voor de Vrijheid set themselves up as the party of freedom but then wanted to restrict other people's religious freedoms by calling for a ban on the Quran and the closure of mosques. The Pilgrims' freedom, their path to that freedom and the realisation of their desire to be allowed to freely practise their religion without having any restrictions imposed on them from outside, caused the indigenous population to lose their lives and their freedoms. Freedom that costs another person their freedom can never be true freedom!

The people who stayed in Leiden integrated into the wider population of the city. The thing that the Pilgrims were perhaps most afraid of happened, in the end.

But we are left with so many questions. Why did Josh Nunn's pupil, who wrote this letter to our chronicler, go to America after all? What changed his mind? To take his knowledge with him . . . But what knowledge? And he passed that knowledge on to a pupil? What was the 'real source and nature of the conflict within our group'?

The answers to all of these questions are so close, and yet so far. Like a dying father trying to whisper something in your ear, something that will finally answer a question you've had for so many years . . .

But before he can tell you, he breathes his last breath.

Chapter 28

Peter stood next to the Greyhound Bus ticket window at South Station waiting for Tony. He was early, but he had made a habit of always arriving early for appointments.

'I would suggest that you ask him that yourself,' Walter L. Lunt had said the day before in the lobby of the grand lodge.

Walter's two-hour-long torrent of words had seemed to suddenly dry up, and he had bid Peter a terse goodbye before turning around and walking away from him.

Peter had stared after him, but Walter had sat down behind the reception desk and given the impression of being so absorbed in some urgent business that he didn't look up again.

Peter had made the journey back to Harvard with a bad taste in his mouth, wondering if it wouldn't be better to cancel his appointment with Tony.

But then again, Peter had thought, *the man is probably going to be coming over to Leiden regularly. I can hardly avoid him.*

By the time he had arrived at Harvard station, his head had mostly cleared.

His phone battery had been almost dead, but as he'd walked through the campus, he'd typed a quick email to Rijsbergen back in Leiden.

Hello,

Visited the Freemasons in Boston today. Was given a tour by someone called Walter Lunt. He told me about the murder of two Masons four years ago in Jerusalem. Again, an older man and a younger one. You probably know about it already, but I thought I should pass it on, just to be sure. Possible connection to Leiden case? And it gets even more bizarre: the chairman of a Freemason's lodge and his pupil went missing on a fishing trip off the Boston coast. Searches for them have been unsuccessful so far. Flying back to the Netherlands tomorrow. Speak soon.

Regards,

Peter de Haan

It would have been after midnight in the Netherlands when he sent the email, so it was unlikely that Rijsbergen would have seen it straight away.

After eating dinner at the apartment, he and Judith had gone to one of the student bars near the campus and ended up spending the rest of the evening there. Fridays and Saturdays were the busiest nights of the week, but there were always lots of people out and about on ordinary Thursday evenings like this one too.

It had been their last chance to say goodbye over a few drinks before Peter went home. Judith had to give a presentation tonight, and she wasn't able to get out of it. As part of the conditions of her grant, she had to deliver a report about her research at a private event.

Peter had woken early and left the apartment almost as soon as he was dressed, without stopping to eat breakfast or even drink a cup of coffee. He had taken a minute to quickly scan his emails on his laptop. There was a message from Rijsbergen thanking him for the suggestion about the Jerusalem link and letting him know that they were already aware of it. The information about the disappearance of the two men in Boston had been new, however, and they would be closely monitoring the situation from Leiden.

Judith had still been asleep when he'd gently closed the front door behind him. Her bedroom door had been ajar, and he'd caught a glimpse of her through the gap. He'd resisted the urge to go in and pull the covers back over her shoulders.

It was only once he was sitting in a subway carriage that he realised that he had left his phone on the charger back at the apartment. There was no time to go all the way back to Judith's now.

A phone-free day will probably be quite relaxing, Peter had thought. *I usually have it turned off or on flight mode anyway, so I probably won't even notice it's missing.*

Back in Leiden, he often deliberately left his phone at home for the day. Those days were usually so much more relaxed that he often advised other people to try it now and then.

Last night, before he had fallen asleep, Peter had read the seventh – and what so far appeared to be the last – fragment that Piet van Vliet had sent him. He shared Piet's frustration over the abrupt way the manuscript ended just as the real secrets were about to be revealed.

It really is maddening, Peter thought.

But he was thrilled to be visiting the places where the Pilgrims had first set foot in America and to be going to see the reconstruction of Plimoth Plantation – a day after reading the letter that had been written there.

'Peter!' he heard Tony's voice behind him.

'Tony!' he replied, trying to replicate the warmth of Tony's tone.

The bus had already pulled up. The passengers were boarding one by one, showing their E-tickets to the driver on their mobile phones, or like Tony, presenting printed tickets to be scanned.

'Here's your ticket,' Tony said, and he handed Peter a printout. 'I've sent it to you in an email too.'

Peter folded up the ticket and put it in the front pocket of his backpack into which he'd also stuffed an anorak, a notebook and pen, a bottle of water, and his book, which he'd put inside a plastic bag in case the water bottle leaked.

Tony had brought absolutely nothing with him.

As soon as they had found their seats, Peter took out the copy of *Mayflower* that he still hadn't finished reading and put it on his lap. He was genuinely keen to read it, but he also wanted to give Tony a signal that he had no intention of spending the next two hours talking.

Peter wondered if Tony's Red Sox baseball cap was permanently attached to his head. He had been wearing it every time Peter had seen him in the Netherlands.

'Do you ever take your cap off?' Peter asked.

'No, sirree,' he said, like a new recruit responding to a senior officer. 'Never go anywhere without it.'

There were many questions that Peter wanted to ask Tony, but he decided to keep the conversation neutral for now. 'Don't you have a car?' he asked.

'Yes, of course I do,' Tony laughed. 'An American without a car! But we're going for the authentic American experience today: taking a trip on the Greyhound. We'll take a taxi after this, and there are shuttle buses that run between Plimoth Plantation and the town of Plymouth. After that, I have a surprise for you.'

A surprise, Peter thought. *What childish nonsense . . . But we'll see. I can easily find a bus back to Boston.*

'Seventy years old, Plimoth Plantation,' Tony said. 'It was the boyhood dream of an archaeologist, Henry Hornblower II. He wanted to tell the story of the Plymouth Colony, so he started the museum in 1947 with the help of his business partners, and family and friends. They built two cottages and a fort on Plymouth's historic shoreline. Then they expanded it with a replica of the *Mayflower*, a reconstruction of the English village and the Wampanoag tribe's village and so on. It's a wonderful place, it really is.'

The bus had left the subterranean station now, and they were travelling along the quiet road that led to the coast.

'You should visit Archeon next time you come to the Netherlands,' Peter said. 'It's a living history museum near Leiden. They've recreated three periods there – pre-history, Roman, and the Middle Ages. They have guides in period costume who explain everything and answer questions. They call them *archeo-interpreters*.'

'Ah, there aren't any guides here,' Tony said proudly. 'Everyone you'll see walking around the site is an actor. It takes them a whole year to prepare for the role. They read everything they can about the person they're going to be. They even have English accents . . . And they stay in their role the whole time. It's like they just left Leiden a couple months ago. It's fantastic.'

Peter picked up his book and opened it to the page where he had left off.

'How was your visit with the Masons yesterday?' Tony asked, apparently oblivious to Peter's hint that he wanted to read.

Peter gave him a curious sideways look, but it appeared that Tony was genuinely interested and couldn't wait to hear all about Peter's visit to the grand lodge.

'Well,' Peter began, 'it was a very interesting visit. I can tell you that much.'

'Great, great,' Tony said. 'I'm glad to hear it was a success.'

This short answer seemed to be enough to satisfy Tony's curiosity because he asked no further questions.

This would be the obvious moment to ask why he was kicked out of the Freemasons, Peter thought. *But that might get our trip off to an awkward start. And we have an entire day to get through.* He decided to concentrate on his book instead.

Despite the early hour, the bus was soon full and ready to depart. They left the city, and a broad, tree-lined highway took them through a dull landscape of industrial estates and residential suburbs that stretched out into the distance.

Should I ask Tony if he knows anything about the two missing men? And if he thinks the murders in Jerusalem have something to do with the ones in Leiden? Or if all three cases are connected?

Peter suddenly felt reluctant to put those questions to him. Who knew what old wounds they might open up? But just as he had decided that he should ask them anyway, he saw that Tony had pulled his cap down over his eyes. His head was tipped back, and his mouth was slightly open. It looked like he had fallen asleep.

I'll leave it until later. We'll have plenty of other things to talk about.

Two hours later, the bus stopped on a parking lot outside an enormous McDonald's. Tony, Peter and a handful of people got off the bus before it pulled away and headed for its final destination in Hyannis.

Peter and Tony got into the car at the front of a row of taxis opposite the bus stop, and within fifteen minutes, they were at Plimoth Plantation, well before its opening time of nine o'clock.

They sat on one of the benches in the visitor centre and waited for the ticket booths to open.

Lots of people recognised Tony. He introduced Peter to everyone who stopped to talk to him, referring to him as his 'most distinguished' or, sometimes, 'most honoured' guest from Leiden, 'the Netherlands, Europe'.

Only one person responded with interest when they heard that Peter was from Leiden.

He could have told everyone else that I was from Ulaanbaatar for all the difference it made, Peter thought.

They gave the little exhibition and the restaurant in the visitor centre a miss.

'We can get something to drink in the craft centre later,' Tony said, as he marched briskly ahead of Peter.

They left the building via the rear door and went outside. A winding path took them down into an area covered in trees.

'We'll visit the Wampanoag Homesite first,' Tony said. 'It's very interesting. You know, I've heard all the criticism of Mayflower 400. A lot of people are saying, "Yes, but what about the indigenous population?" But I – or rather, we – have always been aware of what a sensitive issue it is. Race is such an incredibly complex thing in the United States. I mean, you can ask someone how much they earn, or what their house is worth. Most people will answer those questions without a second thought. But asking someone where they come from? Well, that's just not done. It's complicated. Although, essentially, of course, if you go back in time far enough, all Americans are immigrants. But it's still not something you can ask people about. It's awkward. It's like you're making a judgement. Who's lived here the longest? Who's the most American?'

'There's a lot of discrimination, of course,' Peter added.

'Yes, very true,' Tony agreed. 'And that's . . . Well, like I said, it's a sensitive subject. So that's why – and this is what I was about to say – that's why, from the very start, we've worked hard to involve the Native Nations, as the indigenous people in America call themselves. Obviously, we realise that the colonists' arrival was a mixed blessing, and that's putting it very mildly. Children have been taught the myth of the empty land in their history classes for far too long. So we're emphasising that it's a commemoration rather than a celebration. We avoid using the word "celebration" as much as we can.'

'I see.'

'We want to present a more balanced picture. We see this as a partnership, not just of three nations – the United States, England and the Netherlands – but *four* nations. In fact, the Native Nations are very much a part of this. They're happy that they have this opportunity to tell their side of the story. Actually, Mayflower 400 will be the start of a decade of commemorations because there are towns all over the country marking a four-hundredth anniversary of some sort, whether it's of a battle that took place there or of the date they were founded.'

According to the map, they had arrived at the Wampanoag Homesite. At the beginning of the seventeenth century, the Wampanoag Indians lived near the shore during the agricultural season. This was where they cultivated their crops, fished, collected herbs and berries, and cut cane to weave mats and baskets.

Peter knew that when the Pilgrims arrived in November 1620, the Wampanoag had moved inland, as they usually did at that time of year. But now and then, they would wander close to the coast, and had these Native Americans not helped the new arrivals, every last one of the colonists would have died. In the end, half of the *Mayflower*'s passengers survived.

The Homesite was a large, open area in the woods with huts made of wood, mud and straw. A path through the trees led to a small stretch of beach next to a lake. A pair of canoes had been dragged onto the sand, halfway out of the water.

On the right, a Native American man stood next to a collection of objects arranged on a blanket. He explained that they were toys and showed them dolls made of deerskin, a dice game made of animal bones, and something that looked like a spinning top.

A little further on, they came across a hollowed-out tree trunk which Tony insisted Peter try sitting in. He gamely obliged and mimed paddling through the water with the wooden oar.

They walked over to a semi-circular hut that was completely open at the front with an open framework of thin tree trunks and thick branches at the back. Three men and a woman sat underneath its straw roof dressed in clothes made of what looked like soft leather. The men wore only trousers and sandals, with necklaces hanging around their necks. The woman's dress left one shoulder bare. They sat on sawn-off tree stumps arranged in an arc around a log fire that seemed to be producing more smoke than flame. One of the men, whose head was shaved bald, turned a rabbit over it on a spit.

The ground in the middle of the Wampanoag Homesite was taken up by crops. A wooden scaffolding structure had been built next to them where the tribe traditionally watched out for birds and scared them away from their fields, Tony explained.

Water was just coming to the boil in an earthenware pot. The woman took a handful of herbs from a pouch at her waist and threw them into the water. She invited Tony and Peter to sit down.

Tony had told Peter that he wasn't acquainted with the people inside. These weren't actors playing a role, but real Native Americans – not necessarily from the Wampanoag tribe, but of Native American descent.

The woman poured the hot water into clay bowls with a large, wooden ladle and handed them to Peter and Tony. The steam that rose from them was fresh and sweet, a combination of mint and thyme.

She left the fire and sat down at a waist loom where she was weaving a long, narrow strip of cloth.

'Where are you from?' the youngest of the three men asked as he busied himself with roasting the meat over the fire.

'I'm from Holland,' Peter said. 'And he's from Boston. I live in Leiden, the city where the Pilgrims lived before they came to America. Leiden . . .' Peter paused dramatically '. . . where Thanksgiving actually comes from.'

The man looked at him blankly. The name 'Leiden' didn't even seem to ring a bell, much less the connection between Leiden and Thanksgiving.

'How do you feel about 2020?' Peter asked. 'The events around the anniversary of the Pilgrims arriving on the coast here four hundred years ago?'

The men exchanged nervous looks.

'Look,' one of the other two men said. 'We want to make it clear that we don't see it as a cause for celebration.'

'That's why we're calling it a commemoration and not a celebration,' Tony said hastily.

'Yes, exactly,' the man agreed. 'No, it's not a celebration . . . You know, for us it's more of a chance to tell our story. Not just about what happened, but to let people know about what life is like for us now. Things have improved, but there's still a lot more to be done in terms of education, economic development, discrimination, unemployment. Whichever way you look at it, it would have been better for the Native Nations if all those people from Europe had never come at all. I belong to the Wampanoag Nation myself. Our territory, Wampanoag territory, stretched from Weymouth to what's now called Cape Cod. Our land included the island of Nantucket – you know, the one in *Moby Dick* – and Martha's Vineyard. It went all the way to Bristol and Warren and the north-eastern corner of what came to be called Rhode Island. You know, it was all ours. The land wasn't empty when they got here. We'd already been living on it for ten thousand years. That's why we Wampanoag are called People of the Dawn or People of the First Light. Because we were the first ones here. There were between fifty and a hundred thousand of us in those days. Now there are only five thousand of us left. Thousands upon thousands died between 1616 and 1618 alone because of the sicknesses that the Europeans brought with them.'

Tony gave a little cough. Then he blew exaggeratedly on his tea before taking a sip.

Maybe this conversation is going in completely the opposite direction to what he was hoping for, Peter thought.

'But even so,' he said, not willing to drop the subject. *This is a unique chance to talk to a Native American about it*. 'You're all sitting here, though. You've decided to be a part of this, of Plimoth Plantation.'

'Yes, that's true,' the second man said. 'But, as my friend here says, that's because it gives us a chance to tell our story. We're grateful for the opportunity to be involved in it all. It means that we can start to change the image of the Pilgrims that's being presented in schools, the mythology that's been created around the Pilgrims. Take the Thanksgiving meal, for example. If you look at the contemporary accounts given in books and letters, they say that the Pilgrims celebrated their first harvest in the fall of 1621, "rejoicing in a special manner together". At that time, Massasoit was the *sachem*, the leader of a village in Pokanoket on Rhode Island, where Bristol and Warren are now. Massasoit wasn't actually his name, by the way. That was his title. It means something like "great leader". His real name was Ousamequin. But I'm digressing. According to legend, he and about ninety other men joined the colonists for this feast. At some point in the nineteenth century, it became known as the first Thanksgiving. That was more than two hundred years later. But it's probably not that simple. Both the English and the Native Nations had long traditions of giving thanks for the harvest.'

'Our stories about the origins of Thanksgiving are completely different.' The third man, who had so far remained silent, spoke up. 'There's a whole other version of its history.'

The man who had been cooking the rabbit muttered something in a language that Peter didn't understand, their native language, he assumed.

A short but heated argument arose that was mostly conducted in whispers.

Afterwards, the man carried on talking, unperturbed. 'What we object to is the myth of the empty land.'

Tony looked at Peter and nodded.

'This image of brave European pioneers conquering America is still being presented far too often in education and the media,' he went on. 'People driving over wide-open prairies in covered wagons, building fences around the land and claiming it as theirs from that moment on. Like it didn't already belong to someone! The settlers might have had trouble with the Redskins from time to time, but in the end, they conquered the land all the way to the North Pacific. How the West was *lost*. That's the real story.'

Peter glanced at Tony again, but he was focusing intently on his bowl, like a Zen master performing a tea ceremony.

'The whole idea of God-fearing, hard-working men and women boldly going where no man had gone before . . . The discovery of America – even just that word, "discovery"! It implies that America didn't even exist until the Europeans first set foot on it, that it wasn't relevant, that it wasn't significant until they arrived.'

'But the Pilgrims weren't the first colonists, were they? The English had already settled in Jamestown in Virginia by then. And the Pilgrims didn't use violence to take the land by force. That was done much later and on a massive scale in the eighteenth century by the English, Germans, Irish, Dutch . . .'

'Yes, that's right, but the Pilgrims were the vanguard of an influx that had disastrous consequences for the culture of the indigenous people of North America. And I should add that people like Captain John Mason came to America from England with the great Puritan exodus, and he was responsible for the slaughter of seven hundred members of the Pequot tribe in 1637. The colonists were angry because a man from the Pequot tribe had killed a trader that they suspected of kidnapping Native American children. So when the tribe gathered for their annual Green Corn Festival, a militia made up of Puritans and colonists surrounded the village and murdered the seven hundred men, women and children inside. They shot them, stabbed them, burned them . . . they even kicked their decapitated heads around like footballs.'

Peter shook his head in horror, his lips pressed tightly together.

'The church declared a day of thanksgiving,' the man continued, 'to celebrate the "success" of the massacre. And *that* is where the modern tradition of a Thanksgiving meal started. They even passed a law stipulating that the day of this huge massacre should be remembered every year from then on, thanking God for their victory and celebrating their complete subjugation of the Pequot tribe. History is always written by the victors, so the story of that bloodbath was replaced with the Thanksgiving myth that's widely accepted today. This is the alternative history that I was talking about. It's been turned into a feast of gratitude for the harvest and so on, with sanitised pictures of whites and natives enjoying a lavish meal together in brotherly love. But the reality is very different. It's what's called an invented tradition.'

'Okay,' Tony said, drawing the word out pointedly. He drank the last dregs of his tea.

Peter realised that he hadn't touched his tea at all, and he emptied the bowl with a few gulps. It was cold now, but it still tasted good.

'Thanks for the story, gentlemen,' Tony said as he got up.

Peter stood up too.

'It's important that this story is told too,' Tony added. 'I'd like to thank you for taking the time to talk with us,' he said. 'And thank you for the tea,' he said to the woman who had sat quietly weaving throughout the entire conversation.

The three men nodded.

Tony and Peter left the hut and went to look inside a large house that, from the outside, appeared to be made entirely of long strips of bark, deftly laid over the top of each other.

I suspect that Tony would prefer not to talk about this subject any more, Peter thought. *The Dutch don't like being reminded of the war crimes that were committed in the Dutch East Indies either.*

Inside the house, a young Native American man was sitting on a dais covered in animal skins and talking to some of the other tourists who had arrived in the village while they had been in the hut. The walls were hung with wooden tools, bows and arrows and animal pelts, and on the floor were baskets filled with grain and beans.

Peter and Tony listened politely for a while as the man told his audience about the Indians' use of herbs and plants, but after a few minutes, they went back outside.

They walked along a path that wound upwards and away from the village.

'The great Puritan exodus . . .' Peter said. 'I'd not heard that expression before.'

'No? That was between about 1620 and 1640. More than twenty thousand English Puritans went to Massachusetts and to the West Indies, Barbados mostly. The unusual thing about the history of the Puritans is that it wasn't just individuals migrating, but whole families. That was something new at the time, as was the fact that they weren't primarily looking for financial gain but for religious freedom. Many Christians, including the Pilgrims, identified with the history of the real Exodus. They explicitly compared themselves to the people of Israel in their writings.'

'Ah, but . . .' Peter began carefully. 'History . . .'

Abruptly, Tony stopped walking.

'Surely you're not about to tell me that you're one of those people who believe that the Exodus story isn't historical fact, are you?' Tony snapped in a tone that conveyed a mixture of surprise and indignation.

Religion and politics. The two topics you were better off avoiding in America. Judith warned me about this on my first day here.

'I think that . . .' Peter said tentatively. 'I think it's more like a *heilsgeschichte*, a salvation history, which describes things as if they really did take place, even though they might not have done. There might be a grain of truth in it, but a bigger story ended up being created around it. Whether or not something happened isn't the most crucial element of a story, at least not for conveying the intended message of the story anyway. I mean, stories by Hans Christian Andersen and the Brothers Grimm can still teach us something about life, about how to get along with each other, about good and evil, even though we all know they aren't true.'

They walked on.

Tony looked like he was conflicted about whether to let this subject lie or continue the discussion. He chose the second option.

'Listen, Peter,' said Tony. 'I respect your opinion, I really do, but the problem for me as a Christian—'

'Christian?'

'Christian, yes. Does that surprise you?'

'I thought that, as a Freemason . . .'

'You *do* know that Freemasonry can be combined with any other faith you choose?'

'Yes, I do know that but—'

'Peter, isn't there actually something else that you want to ask me?'

Now it was Peter's turn to be stopped in his tracks. 'What do you mean? What would I want to ask you?'

'Why I was thrown out of the Freemasons.'

Chapter 29

The day after Van de Kooij had visited Rijsbergen at home to show him an episode of *Unsolved Murder Mysteries*, Rijsbergen had contacted the police in Jerusalem.

The detective who had been in charge of the case at the time was a man called Abner Cohen. He was featured heavily in the documentary – notably, his moustache was the only hair on his head – talking about how the case had developed, the promising evidence they had followed up on, the suspects who had been wrongfully accused, and the leads that had all turned out to be dead ends.

The episode ended with a scene in which the former detective was sitting at a computer in what looked like his home. He had confessed that he often read the entire case file from start to finish, hoping that he would have a sudden flash of insight. But, in the end, he'd had to admit that this was one of those cases that would remain unsolved forever.

But that was about to change.

Rijsbergen had been unable to speak to the detective from the documentary initially. Instead, he'd talked to someone much younger who wasn't familiar with the case. He told Rijsbergen that they were in the throes of a lengthy process of digitisation and were scanning in old case files. They were almost up to date now, so the files from this particular case were available in a digital format.

The man told Rijsbergen that he would send the Israeli police files over and promised that Abner Cohen would get in touch.

Rijsbergen had received an email from Peter in America. At almost exactly the same time that Rijsbergen and Van de Kooij had been finding out about the double murder in the Masonic world in Jerusalem, Peter de Haan had been making the same discovery in Boston.

Peter's email also mentioned two Boston men who had gone missing, the chairman of a lodge and his pupil. The police were treating it as a normal missing persons case for the time being, but this assessment was likely to change once Rijsbergen had called his American colleagues. The link between the cases in Jerusalem and Leiden was still unclear, but it was obviously there: the extreme violence used in the killings and the skin removed from near the victim's armpit. Because the victims in both Boston and Leiden had been an older chairman and his younger pupil, it was easy to conclude that they were linked too.

There's too much here to just be coincidence, Rijsbergen thought.

Although he didn't come from a devoutly religious background, sometimes when he faced a bizarre set of coincidences like this, he almost felt the presence of a 'guiding hand'. It was as though 'something' or 'someone' was leading him in a particular direction. He couldn't think of another way to describe it.

By the time Rijsbergen had replied to Peter's email, it had been 9 a.m. in Leiden, but three o'clock in the morning in Boston; it would be a few hours before Peter would read Rijsbergen's message and learn that the Leiden Police had made the same discovery about Jerusalem that he had made in Boston.

Rijsbergen sat quietly in his office, drumming his fingers on his desk. As he watched the episode for the third time, he added comments to the notes he had made during the first two viewings, jotting down the differences and similarities between the cases and anything else that stood out to him.

He had reduced the size of the media player window so that he could keep an eye on the messaging software that he had been told Abner Cohen would use to contact him. Rijsbergen understood that it employed end-to-end encryption to scramble messages so that they could only be read by the recipient they were meant for, but he had no idea how it actually worked. When Van de Kooij had tried to explain how the messages were sent via multiple computers and servers, Rijsbergen's eyes had glazed over, and he'd had to resort to nodding at what he had hoped were appropriate moments. In short, what it boiled down to was that the software was so secure that it was impossible for third parties to somehow access the messages.

He turned to a blank page in his notepad and made a list of the similarities and differences between the cases:

Similarities
– two murders in quick succession
– severe blunt force trauma to skull
– Freemasons – first victim older man
– second victim younger man
– single men, no family
– murdered on busy evening but no witnesses (except Yona F.)
– multiple people with opportunity but no motive
– murderer(s) still not found
– motive???

Differences
- skin removed instead of tattoo
- heart/hands not impaled
- Yona not (?) Freemason
- Yona asphyxiated
- Yona killed somewhere other than where body found?

Rijsbergen stared at the three question marks he had written after the word 'motive'.

Something in the documentary was bothering him, something he had noticed on the first viewing with Van de Kooij the night before.

He was reminded of the famous psychology experiment in which the subjects were asked to watch a video of a group of people throwing a ball to each other and count how many passes were made. The test subjects were so focused on counting that two-thirds of them missed the appearance of a man in a gorilla suit about halfway through the video, who beat his chest for a few seconds and then disappeared again.

Am I missing something by focusing on something else?

He heard a *ping!* from his computer.

A window popped up on the screen with a profile photo of a bald man with a moustache. Rijsbergen had watched the documentary so many times now that he recognised him as the former detective from the Jerusalem police.

The last time he had watched the video, Rijsbergen had sat with his face just centimetres away from the screen, as though staring deep into the eyes of a suspect, trying to get a confession out of them.

Abner Cohen

You wanted to talk to me about the Freemasons case?

Willem Rijsbergen

Yes, that's right. I appreciate you getting in touch.

Abner Cohen

Happy to help!

Willem Rijsbergen

We happened to see you in an episode of Unsolved Murder Mysteries yesterday.

Abner Cohen

Ah, yes. My fifteen minutes of fame . . .

Willem Rijsbergen

Something similar happened here in Leiden about a month and a half ago: two murders within a short space of time. The older victim had a tattoo in the same place – I'll send you a photo shortly – and the skin had been excised from the same location on the younger victim. Very similar to your two victims. The first victim suffered a fatal pene- trating head injury. There was a Masonic square stabbed through his heart, and a pair of compasses skewering his hands. The second victim was asphyxiated before being dumped in a canal.

Abner Cohen

Wow! That's . . . I've been working on this case for so long! You've no idea how frustrating it's been for me. But this could breathe new life into it. Do you have any leads yet? This is very exciting!

Willem Rijsbergen

Yes, I can imagine! We've had someone in custody for six weeks. He knew things that only the killer could know, but he's been refusing to talk since we brought him in.

Abner Cohen

Has he ever been to Jerusalem?

Willem Rijsbergen

We'll be interviewing him again later today and confronting him with this new information. But, to be honest, my gut feeling is that he can't have done it. I haven't said this to anyone else because, apart from his arrest, we've made no further progress in the case.

Abner Cohen

Gut feeling shouldn't be underestimated.

Willem Rijsbergen

Yes, but the problem is . . . he knew things that he couldn't or shouldn't have known, but he's refusing to say how he knows them. The theory is – and this is the best we've been able to come up with so far – that his wife wanted to be the chair of their lodge, so he killed the current chairman either as revenge for her not being chosen, or to clear the way for her to be chosen.

Abner Cohen

What about the other victim?

Willem Rijsbergen

Ah, yes, exactly. The other victim. There doesn't seem to have been any motive there. It appears that nobody knew him. We've not found a single thing connecting him to the suspect we have in custody. As long as he refuses to talk, we'll never know. But I think it would be very difficult to connect him to your cold case.

Abner Cohen

We'll see. We've not been able to identify any plausible motives either. Both men appeared to be well-liked. There were no tensions or conflicts with anyone, at least not as far as we've been able to determine.

Willem Rijsbergen

But both victims were men with no family, just like the victims in your case. Parents deceased, no siblings. Both unmarried, no children.

Abner Cohen

Yes.

Willem Rijsbergen

Most of our team have been pulled from the case now, but perhaps this will change if the Jerusalem murders can be linked to it.

Abner Cohen

Yes. I'll get in touch with some of my former colleagues here. It seems to me that we have enough grounds to reopen the old case.

Willem Rijsbergen

Great.

Abner Cohen

Can I see that photo of the tattoo?

Rijsbergen looked through his files for the images. It took him a while to work out how to upload them with the messaging software, but he eventually succeeded.

Willem Rijsbergen

This is an illustration of the tattoo. It vaguely resembles the All-Seeing Eye . . . We've shown it to quite a few people, but no one has been able to tell us what it is. We just don't know.

Abner Cohen

This is very interesting, Willem. We never knew what it was that had been cut away. We don't know anything for sure yet, of course, but it seems highly likely that our victims originally had similar tattoos. I don't recognise it, but I'll ask around. The triangle is a universal symbol, of course.

Willem Rijsbergen

We've had experts from the University of Leiden look at it. They circulated it in their network, but nothing came of it. It must be a particularly obscure symbol.

Abner Cohen

Ask Robert Langdon . . .

Willem Rijsbergen

Yes, if only we could . . .

Abner Cohen

Keep me posted, Willem. As you can see, this is a case that has haunted me. I've not been able to let it go. I sincerely hope that the same does not happen to you. And who knows, maybe the progress you make in your case will lead to new insights in the case here in Jerusalem. We'll get things moving again here too.

Willem Rijsbergen

I'll definitely keep you posted. We had assumed – mistakenly, it seems – that our case was unique. It simply hadn't occurred to us that there might be a parallel case elsewhere.

Abner Cohen

These two cases must be connected. They're far too similar for this to be pure coincidence – in my opinion.

Willem Rijsbergen

There was video footage in the episode.

Abner Cohen

Yes, that's right. CCTV images. There are surveillance cameras all over Jerusalem, a sad necessity here. There are lots of people walking in and out of shot, but that can't be helped. We've scrutinised the footage endlessly – I still watch it occasionally, despite knowing how futile it is – but we've only been able to identify a handful of people. As you probably know, Jerusalem is an incredibly cosmopolitan city with many different nationalities. There was a colourful mix of people from all over the world in town that evening. Many of them didn't even live here – they were just visiting as tourists, so they were impossible to trace. Everyone who was positively identified was removed from our list of suspects.

Willem Rijsbergen

Let's stay in touch. I'll keep you informed of any new developments. Actually, I just remembered as I was typing that: there already is a new development. I've been so focused on our two cases ... I got a message from someone in Boston saying that two men disappeared there yesterday while they were on a fishing trip. One of them was the chairman of a lodge, and the other was his young pupil.

Abner Cohen

That's shocking news.

Willem gave him a summary of what he knew about the case so far.

Willem Rijsbergen

As we all know, similarities between cases don't necessarily indicate that they're connected.

Abner Cohen

No, that's true. Let's not jump to any conclusions . . . But it is very strange. Anyway, let's keep each other in the loop. Good luck with the case. Mazel tov, as we say here. I hope I can close this case one day. My poor wife is always chiding me that I spend too much time living in the past when I can't let go of these old cases.

Willem Rijsbergen

Speak soon, and best wishes from Leiden.

Abner Cohen

Best wishes from Jerusalem, too.

Abner Cohen

has left the conversation.

Rijsbergen closed the chat window.

It was almost three o'clock. Tomorrow was Saturday. Officially, he had the next two days off, but it wasn't unusual for him to give up his free time to work on a case.

A message from Jerusalem appeared in his inbox. It was a link to a secure website where he could download the case file. The code needed to access it arrived in a text message. Due to its large size, the file downloaded very slowly.

Rijsbergen was unable to read most of the documents in the file because they were written in Hebrew, but fortunately, it contained regular summaries in English – made for the Discovery Channel programme, as Rijsbergen learned from the notes in the margins. They included tips and pointers for the producers about where the police thought the emphasis should be placed.

The text in the file provided no insights other than what he had already gleaned from the documentary and his conversation with Abner Cohen. He spent a long time studying the photographs of the victims. Some photos were of their entire bodies, while others were only of their heads. They showed that barely half of their skulls had been left intact.

The first victim, the older man, had been killed during an evening event at the Masonic Hall that had been attended by many non-members, Abner had told him. The parallels were abundantly clear: a chairman killed with extreme violence in the presence of a large number of people, which had resulted in a crime scene so contaminated that it had been difficult to make sense of the physical evidence.

Rijsbergen was shocked by the similarities between the photographs of one of the Israeli victims and the photos of Coen Zoutman: both bodies lying on a black and white tiled floor, their heads surrounded by enormous pools of blood.

The second victim had been found in a remote location near the Mount of Olives. The police suspected that he had either been lured there or taken there against his will because no one could think of any reason for him to be in that location so late at night. The murderer had left his body where he had killed him just a few days after the Worshipful Master had been murdered.

Rijsbergen concentrated on the close-up photographs that had been taken of the skin. It had obviously been cut with something like a surgical scalpel because the edges of the wound were clean rather than jagged.

When he compared these photographs to those taken of Yona Falaina, it was immediately apparent that this was the work of someone with the same modus operandi.

It's either the same person or a copycat, Rijsbergen thought. *Perhaps whoever murdered Coen Zoutman didn't have enough time to cut out the tattoo. Were they disturbed before they could finish the job?*

Rijsbergen had promised Abner that he would send him all the material they had gathered so far. Obviously, he would also be dealing with files written in a foreign language, so he would need to have the documents translated.

Rijsbergen started to write an email to a colleague arranging for the files to be sent in the same way that he had received the case files from Israel.

But then he stopped typing, mid-word, and rested his hands on the keyboard like a pianist about to play a concerto.

What had Abner said?

He re-opened the chat app and scrolled back to the point he was thinking of.

As you probably know, Jerusalem is an incredibly cosmopolitan city with many different nationalities. There was a colourful mix of people from all over the world in town that evening. Many of them didn't even live here – they were just visiting as tourists, so they were impossible to trace. Everyone who was positively identified was removed from our list of suspects.

He saved the email as a draft and played the *Unsolved Murder Mysteries* episode for the fourth time, concentrating on the CCTV footage of people going into the Masonic Hall.

This time, instead of sitting close to the screen, he leaned back so that he could see the whole scene.

When the footage ended, he rewound it and played it again.

Then he watched it for the third time, and then a fourth, and then . . .

'There!' he exclaimed.

He leapt from his chair so excitedly that it toppled over and crashed onto the floor.

He had finally seen it.

He rushed out of his office and went to find Van de Kooij. He didn't just want to show his colleague what he had seen. He wanted him to confirm that it was really there.

Van de Kooij looked surprised to see Rijsbergen barge into his office without knocking. He was in the middle of a phone call, but Rijsbergen pressed a button on the phone to break the connection.

'What the—'

'Come with me,' Rijsbergen said simply, and then he turned around and left the room. Van de Kooij had little choice but to follow his superior officer.

Back in his office, Rijsbergen picked up his chair and invited Van de Kooij to sit next to him.

He rewound the video to the right place and held his index finger over the left mouse button so that he could pause it quickly.

Van de Kooij, who could see that something important was happening, stared intently at the screen.

'There,' Rijsbergen said.

They watched the people walking calmly towards the doors of the stately lodge building. They came to a standstill now and then whenever someone left the building, or they got stuck in a bottleneck, but the general atmosphere of the scene was relaxed, and no one appeared to be in a hurry.

Then, a group of people appeared on the right-hand side of

the screen. They approached the doors.

'One . . . two . . .'

Click.

Rijsbergen stopped the video.

'What do we see here, Van de Kooij?'

Van de Kooij leaned forward and peered at the image. His eyes narrowed in concentration and then opened wide in surprise.

'That's . . .'

They looked at each other.

'Well spotted,' Rijsbergen said. 'Then my eyes weren't deceiving me.'

Chapter 30

Peter tried to give Tony what he hoped would pass for a grin, but it was about as effective as nodding and smiling when you realise that someone you've not been listening to has asked you a question.

Tony wasn't going to let him off so easily.

'Come on, Peter,' he said, chuckling when he saw the look of alarm on Peter's face. 'You can do better than that, can't you?'

'Your expulsion?'

'Who showed you around? Dan? Alexander? Walter?'

Peter nodded to confirm that it had been Walter.

'Ah, Walter,' Tony said, in a tone that suggested he was fondly remembering a close friendship. 'Our librarian,' he said, but he was sneering now. 'I'm sure he told you all about my rather unedifying removal from the lodge.'

'Walter wasn't the one who brought it up,' Peter said, taken aback by the audible cynicism in Tony's voice.

He must be bitter about it.

'But how could he have, Tony?' Peter asked. 'Walter wasn't even aware of a connection between us. I asked him if he knew you.' Peter waited for Tony to respond, but Tony only stared blankly back at him. 'I have to say, I thought his response was quite hostile.'

Tony snorted scornfully.

They had arrived at the modern, wood-built craft centre, where demonstrations were given on how the Pilgrims might have made things using seventeenth-century techniques. Artisans in traditional dress were weaving baskets, baking bread, and firing pots, and making cloth on an upright loom.

'And which version of the story did good old Walter tell you?'

'Well,' Peter said, 'to be honest, he didn't tell me very much. He just said, "I would suggest that you ask him that yourself." But I thought: maybe it's an unpleasant episode that Tony would prefer not to be reminded of. And it's actually none of my business.'

'You weren't curious about it? Curious about why a nice guy like me was expelled and given a restraining order?'

'A restraining order?'

'Good God, Peter,' Tony said. He was really incensed now. 'You're a worse actor than I thought. Walter must have told you. He was the driving force behind the whole thing. He even used a whole bunch of false accusations to file a suit against me.'

'I could tell from his reaction that he wasn't pleased when he found out that I knew you, yes. He didn't mention the restraining order, but he didn't want to talk about it at all.'

'So?'

'So what?'

'Are you going to ask me about it or what?' Tony looked genuinely annoyed.

What does he want from me?

'Listen, Tony,' Peter said. 'If you really want to tell me about it, I'm not going to try to stop you.'

Tony seemed to calm down.

They entered a room where two beekeepers stood at a long table laid out with beekeeping equipment. Arranged along the wall behind them were wickerwork hives and what looked like old-fashioned beekeeping suits.

Tony and Peter paused for a moment next to a long cabinet that was just a few centimetres wide and had glass on both sides. They could see a colony of bees inside, industriously building combs and taking care of their young. A transparent tube leading from the cabinet to the wall allowed the bees to go outside to find food. A window that looked out onto the grounds revealed three more cabinets outside with clouds of bees swarming around them.

'I'm still proud of what I did. No regrets,' Tony said. He looked directly at Peter like he wanted to make sure that he was listening. 'Three years ago, our chairman, Joseph Nun died. He was an old man, and he passed away after a short illness. It could be said that an illustrious branch of the American family tree died with him. His line went all the way back to one of the first settlers, Thomas Nunn who settled in Virginia in 1635. No family, didn't have another soul on earth. The brotherhood was his family, his life. Some of his Masonic brothers arranged the funeral and took care of everything else that needed to be done. I asked them if I could speak at the ceremony. And what I said didn't go down well, to put it mildly.'

'What on earth did you say?' Peter asked aghast.

Tony smiled. 'The truth and nothing but the truth. Good riddance, that was the gist of my message. Look, Peter . . .' Tony put his hand on Peter's arm as if he was trying to reassure him, but he appeared to be asking for understanding too. 'I don't know how much you know about the Freemasons. I think this was something we discussed in Leiden. There was all that talk about finding your own way, giving your own meanings to the symbols and your interpretation of them being just as valid as anyone else's, explaining all the traditional stories in an allegorical way. But what sort of society would we have if everyone was just allowed to interpret its history for themselves?'

He looked at Peter earnestly, and then, at last, he removed his hand from his arm.

'History, Peter, factual, verifiable history . . . Historical facts. Just like the Puritan exodus from England. There's nothing mythological about that either! There are sources, written sources, oral histories that have been handed down. Or let's take that other exodus as an example. There *was* a real man called Moses who *did* grow up in the Egyptian court, who *did* lead his people out of Egypt, who *did* wander through the desert for forty years, who *did* enter the promised land, and those battles *did* take place. All those things . . . Archaeology, history, geology . . . They all prove the veracity of these stories. And what do these stories do, Peter?'

He didn't wait for an answer.

'You're a historian. You should know this better than anyone. Stories bring people together, stories give people a common bond, and a shared history gives a community a communal past. A shared view of that past creates unity. What happens if you give everyone the freedom to decide for themselves what a story means? Look at the Protestants. At one time, we only had the Catholic Church. One leader, one interpretation. As an individual Catholic, you sometimes had to compromise, set aside your individuality for the benefit of the community, for something more significant than you could ever be, something that would live on after your death. A community that would still be there long after you were gone. But then look at the Protestants, they all have their own different interpretations . . . What has that led to? They've got as many different denominations as they have opinions. Not even God Himself can keep track of all their churches! If you disagree with your pastor, well, off you go! Just start your own church.

Until eventually, everyone has their own uniquely individual truth, and everyone is alone with their own story, lonely and disconnected from everyone else. But in a real community . . .'

Tony pointed at the beehive.

'Look, take these bees,' he said. 'I've been here a few times, so I know a bit about them now. Listen, each bee lives for six, maybe eight weeks. Her tasks are set out for her from her first day to her last. First, she cleans and polishes the cells to prepare them for eggs. Then, from day three to about day twelve, she feeds the older larvae. After that, she ventures outside for some practice flights . . . Now she can produce honey and help to build the combs. By about day seventeen, her venom glands are well developed, and she becomes a guard bee. On day twenty-one, she starts gathering food for the colony, and she'll do that until the day she leaves the hive and never comes back . . . Bees don't sleep, so for those six to eight weeks, she's entirely devoted to the colony. I think that's incredible. The bee colony moves as one, feeds itself as one, and reproduces as one. None of them can survive for long without their broodmates. And that's what it's all about for me: it's the colony that reproduces, not the individual bee. So it's not about you, but about your community. Sometimes you have to put your own needs and desires aside for its benefit. Isn't that what Christ teaches us? You must know the story about his disciples fighting among themselves about which of them is the most important. Jesus beckons a little child over to him, and then he says to the disciples: "Whoever welcomes this child in my name welcomes me, and whoever welcomes me welcomes the one who sent me; for the least among all of you is the greatest." It's about making yourself less important, being humble.'

Peter looked at an enormous laminated poster on the wall. Thick arrows arranged in a circle illustrated the life cycle of a honeybee, just as Tony had described it.

'But what did Joseph Nun have to do with all of this?'

'In my opinion, he was the biggest exponent of the direction our lodge was taking. So, at his funeral, I said that we were better off without him. I said that I hoped that we could return to a tradition of being connected by stories again, instead of being divided by so many different interpretations of them.'

'Then what on earth possessed you to join the Freemasons?' Peter asked. 'You must know that the spirit that guides the Masons is precisely that of freedom, of finding personal meaning. Why didn't you just join a traditional church?'

'I'm a man with a message, Peter,' Tony said in a tone that made clear that he no longer wanted to discuss the subject. 'There's no role for me in a traditional church, if you see what I mean. I'm a man on a mission.'

Actually, I don't really see what he means, Peter thought.

It reminded him of the conscious choice that some gay people made to remain – or even become – members of a church that rejected homosexuality so that they could fight the battle for acceptance from within.

'But you're not a Freemason any more,' he said.

'I still *am* a Freemason!' Tony said, sounding indignant again. 'A Freemason without a lodge.'

'A rebel without a cause.'

'Yes, something like that.'

'But what about the restraining order?'

'As soon as I'd finished my talk, they ejected me from the building where the service was being held. I have to tell you, it was pretty intimidating.'

Peter found that difficult to imagine, considering that Tony was about two metres tall.

'There must have been about eight of them all crowded

around me. The second I got down from the podium, they escorted me to the exit. I went back to the meetings many times to try to put things right. Until Walter went to a judge and accused me of all sorts of things. The judge believed him. And that's how I got the restraining order.'

'And the threats that were made to the Freemasons? The ones you told me about when you were in Leiden?'

'Threats? Did I say that? I don't recall saying anything about any threats, if I'm honest, Peter. But anyway . . .'

What a strange man, Peter thought. *He really does have issues . . .*

Tony turned around, signalling that as far as he was concerned, the conversation about it was over.

I've probably missed my chance to ask him about the Jerusalem murders and the two missing Masons in Boston too.

'Come on. We'll go to the village,' Tony said breezily. 'You're going to find it very interesting.'

They walked into the English village that lay at the heart of Plimoth Plantation. They climbed the stairs to the top of the fort on the hill so that they could look out over the entire settlement. There were about fifteen houses built within a diamond-shaped enclosure that sloped gently down to the Atlantic Ocean.

The village had been reconstructed as it would have appeared in 1627, seven years after the first Pilgrims landed. The houses had all been built facing the street, and kitchen gardens and crops had been planted behind them.

Once they were back downstairs, they explored the village, visiting the various houses that had been set up like the homes that the Pilgrims would have lived in, with the bedroom, kitchen and living room all in one.

There was a 'Leiden house', full of things that were unmistakably Hollands. An information board – DUTCH OBJECTS IN THE

ENGLISH VILLAGE – gave brief descriptions of the original utensils in the house. They included the ubiquitous Delft blue, a milk jug, glasses, tobacco pipes, a foot stove and chairs with triangular seats, 'as seen in seventeenth-century paintings by artists like Jan Steen'.

A sign titled LIFE IN LEIDEN told the story of the Pilgrims' time in the Netherlands.

In the eleven years before the *Mayflower*'s voyage in 1620, the Separatists lived in the Dutch city of Leiden where they were able to worship in safety. However, life in a foreign country was not without its challenges. The work available to immigrants paid meagre wages, and the standard of living was low. A twelve-year truce between Holland and Spain was due to expire in 1621, threatening a new outbreak of war in the Netherlands. Many of the Separatists were troubled by the hardships endured by their children, who were forced to do backbreaking work. Although living in exile and no longer part of the Church of England, the Separatists wished to retain their English customs. Some young people were assimilating into Dutch culture, leaving their parents and congregation profoundly troubled. Almost half of the *Mayflower*'s passengers lived in Holland before leaving for America, and many of the children had lived in Leiden for most of their lives. It can be very difficult to escape the influence of an adopted home.

It gives all the usual reasons, Peter thought. *But yet again, there's no mention of why half of the original group ended up deciding to stay behind in Leiden. And what about the split that's described in the manuscript Piet van Vliet found? You never come across it in the official history, and there's no reference to it here either.*

They spent more than two hours in the village listening to the actors who were all impressively immersed in their roles, complete with convincing English accents.

They strolled back up the hill, past the fort, and then on to the large gift shop in the craft centre.

Peter bought a few postcards to remind him of his visit. The store stocked a huge number of books, as well as DVDs, clothing, food and wooden utensils.

He was surprised to find that they also sold *stroopwafels* and liquorice in their original Dutch packaging. He bought a packet of each to give to Judith, comfort food that would remind her of home. He put them in his backpack, which he could feel had left a large, damp, patch of sweat on the back of his shirt.

They ate in the restaurant in the visitor centre before taking the bus back to Plymouth village. They got off at a stop on the shoreline, where large colonial houses lined the road.

'We'll visit Plymouth Rock first,' Tony said.

He strode energetically off in the direction of something that looked like a Doric temple, but with its diminutive dimensions of about ten metres by five was merely a miniature version of one. It stood on a wharf on the waterfront. Peter could see a small marina in the distance.

The text on a sign next to the little temple read:

PLYMOUTH ROCK
LANDING PLACE OF THE
PILGRIMS
1620
Commonwealth of Massachusetts

Once they were inside the temple, Peter realised that it was a portico that had been built over a deep, rectangular pit, and at the bottom, on sand as neatly raked as a Japanese Zen garden, was a large boulder with the year 1620 carved into it.

Just as he always did whenever he was near a famous building or artefact, Peter tingled with excitement.

Standing right next to real, tangible history . . .

But soon, and entirely predictably, he was jerked out of his romantic reverie.

'It's not the actual rock, of course,' Tony said. 'Well, actually, they have no idea if it's the real rock or not. They certainly landed here, but whether this rock is the exact spot where they first set foot in America, or whether it was on a rock further up shore or on the beach, nobody knows.'

Folklore and tradition . . . Peter thought. *The longer people tell each other the same story, the more power it has. Eventually, a story becomes so potent, such an irrefutable truth that people are enraged when you call it into question. Point to a tree and say that Siddhārtha Gautama attained enlightenment under it, and people will come from far and wide to meditate there. Point to a place on the banks of the River Jordan and say that John the Baptist baptised people in that exact spot and Christians will come from all over the world to be baptised there. Point to a thorn bush and say that God spoke to Moses from that very same bush and believers will build a monastery there.*

'And anyway, they first landed near to what's now called Provincetown,' Tony went on. 'That's on the other side of Cape Cod Bay, opposite where we are now. The captain would obviously never have steered his ship towards the rocks. But you know, this is the story that's been established, and tradition has decided that this was the site. The power of a place like this only grows over time. I've seen people standing here with tears in their eyes; not just descendants of the Pilgrims, but others too. Of course, in the end, it doesn't matter where it is. You have to choose *one* site, so why not this one?'

'Why are they so often referred to as the Pilgrim *Fathers*, actually?' Peter asked, realising that he had never given this question much thought before. It had only just occurred to him. 'Wasn't the whole point of the Pilgrims,' he went on, 'that – and you actually said this to me yourself – this was the first time that entire families had emigrated. So half of the passengers on the ship would have been women. Leaving aside the children, obviously.'

Tony rolled his eyes.

'Well, that's also . . . tradition. But you're right. Customarily, we talk about Pilgrim Fathers, but of course, there were Pilgrim Mothers and Pilgrim Children as well, but in those days . . . *They* didn't sign contracts or draw up any trade agreements, and they didn't negotiate deals or fight battles. So they more or less disappeared from historical view. Well, from the bigger historical picture, anyway. I'm not making a case for Herstory, as such. That's a big thing here just now, telling the stories of the forgotten and underestimated historical roles that women have played. It's a counterbalance to a History . . .' he emphasised the 'his' '. . . in which the main focus is on men. But the consensus on the Mayflower 400 committee is that, at least in official external communications, we use the gender-neutral word "Pilgrims". But the old name is so ingrained – in me too – that it's going to take a while for it to disappear.'

'What's next?'

'Next, we'll walk a little way along the coast and then up to the Pilgrim Hall Museum. After that, we'll go back to Boston.'

That's good, Peter thought. *Then we'll have seen everything there is to see here.*

Peter looked at the clock on a nearby church and saw that it was after two o'clock.

An hour, maybe an hour and a half in the museum, then at least three hours to get back to Boston . . . Back on campus between seven and eight. Plenty of time to grab something to eat, freshen up, and pack my bag for tomorrow.

They walked along an uninspiring stretch of waterfront lined with parked cars on one side and restaurants, ice cream parlours and souvenir shops on the other.

'As you can see,' Tony said, drawing an arc in the air with his arm, 'Plymouth is on a bay. You can see Provincetown on the other side. It's about twenty miles away over the water.'

Peter did a quick conversion in his head: thirty-two kilometres.

'I swam across it a few years ago with a bunch of other people. Took us about eleven hours. I'm an excellent swimmer, you know. We wanted to make a yearly event of it, a little like you Europeans swimming across the English Channel, but it never really took off. Less than ten people have done it so far.'

Swimming non-stop for eleven hours . . .

Peter was impressed. The hour he spent swimming lengths each week – and even his intensive water polo training sessions and matches – in the public pool in Leiden paled in comparison.

They turned off Water Street and onto Chilton Street, a well-maintained row of carefully preserved colonial houses. It was clear that these homes belonged to people with deeper pockets than the average American.

The Pilgrim Hall Museum was at the end of the street, but it stood out immediately. Peter couldn't help smiling when he saw it.

From the side, the building had looked fairly plain, but its façade was dominated by six enormous columns with a triangular gable on top. At the centre of the gable was a semi-circular window divided into 'pie slices', like half a wagon wheel with glass between the spokes. In contrast to the small town around it, it was quite pretentious.

Here, just like at Plimoth Plantation, there was no need to buy entrance tickets. Tony introduced Peter to several staff members, most of them older ladies.

They both signed the visitors' book that was lying on the reception desk next to the cash register. Peter flipped through it and noted that most of the visitors were from the United States, but there were lots of visitors from other countries too.

'Do you sign the book every time you come here?' he asked Tony.

'Well,' Tony said with a crooked grin, 'it's kind of cheating, if I'm honest. The visitor numbers are calculated at the end of the year. Obviously, they go by the number of tickets sold, but they also look at how many names are in this book, and in particular, where they come from. They want to see an annual increase in the number of tickets sold, and in the number of visitors from other countries. It keeps the museum's funders happy. So yes, my name appears in the visitors' book pretty regularly. I often sign it with a made-up name . . . There's a confession for you.'

After they had hung up their jackets, they took a good look around the exhibit in the basement.

Just as Tony had said, the settlers were consistently referred to as 'Pilgrims'. The first information board explained the origin of the name 'Pilgrims' with a famous quote from William Bradford, governor of the Plymouth Colony:

They knew they were pilgrims, and looked not much on those things, but lifted up their eyes to the heavens, their dearest country, and quieted their spirits.

William Bradford was citing the Epistle to the Hebrews – chapter 11, verses 13 to 16 – in which the Apostle Paul wrote about the Israelites who had left the fleshpots – meaning the good times, when there had been enough to eat – of Egypt and died in the desert in search of the promised land: 'All these died in faith, and received not the promises, but saw them afar off, and believed them, and received them thankfully, and confessed that they were strangers and pilgrims on the earth. For they that say such things, declare plainly, that they seek a country. And if they had been mindful of that country, from whence they came out, they had leisure to have returned. But now they desire a better, that is an heavenly (one).'

The history of the Pilgrims was outlined in neat displays and illustrated with original artefacts like tools, old Bibles and facsimiles of letters and maps.

Peter couldn't help feeling a sense of pride when he read sentences such as:

Seeing themselves molested . . . by a joint consent they resolved to go into the Low Countries (Holland), where they heard that there was freedom of religion for all.

Sometimes Tony appeared to be reading the information boards and labels, but he had told Peter beforehand that he had lost count of the number of times he had visited the exhibition. He could recite some of the information boards by heart now.

All in all, Peter was glad that he had decided to come on this day trip after all.

Tony's a bit of an odd character, of course, he thought. *There's something not quite right about a man who would make such a strange, insulting speech at a funeral. And then there are his rigid opinions about the Freemasons and about taking the stories literally*

. . . People aren't bees. We do have free will. We're not programmed to carry out the same pre-determined tasks day after day without ever deviating from the plan. Quite the opposite. That's what makes us human: our fate is in our own hands.

But their day together was coming to a close.

How likely am I to see Tony when he's in Leiden again, he wondered. *I could always find an excuse to avoid it. I don't owe him anything.*

Peter wondered what the surprise was that Tony had been hinting at.

Perhaps the visit to this museum was the surprise?

Peter read:

The Europeans also believed their colonizing efforts were justified by the introduction of the Christian religion.

It remained a strange fact that there were people who believed that God had promised them a land, and that, on the basis of that divine promise, they had the right to take what didn't belong to them and could even justify wiping out an entire ethnic group in an act of pure genocide.

Peter paused at a text about the religious beliefs of the indigenous peoples that the colonists encountered.

The Wampanoag had a strong and complex spirituality. Many English people did not recognize these beliefs as a "religion".

The arrogance . . .

The labels in this museum were so brief that Peter decided to rummage in his bag for the information booklet that he had taken from a rack in the reception at Plimoth Plantation. Leafing through it earlier, he had noticed a short paragraph about Native American religions at the time of the Pilgrims' arrival. Peter knew from experience that if he didn't read it now, he would probably never read it at all. Once he got home, it would sit gathering dust on his 'to read' pile for a few months before he eventually threw it away.

He sat down on a wooden bench next to the doorway and took a pen out of his bag so that he could highlight significant words and passages here and there.

Most tribes practised a combination of <u>polytheism</u> (multiple gods, including the Great Spirit, Father Sky and Mother Earth) and animism (everything that lives on earth has a soul). The Indians lived <u>in harmony</u> with the plants and animals and never took more from Mother Earth than was necessary.

Native American rituals around death could vary greatly from tribe to tribe and from region to region. However, they were always focused on <u>freeing the spirit or soul</u> so that it could <u>make its way to the afterlife</u>. It was believed that the journey would be long and dangerous. Rituals were vital for guaranteeing the <u>safe arrival</u> of the dead person's soul in the afterlife.

According to many Native Americans, the human spirit has two parts:

1. the <u>transcendent part or free soul</u> that lives on after physical death and journeys into the afterlife;

2. the life-soul that animates the physical body during life and disintegrates after physical death.

After death, the soul goes on a journey to the afterlife, sometimes traversing a wide river in a canoe, climbing a mountain or crossing a desert.

Crossing a desert . . .
Peter circled the word 'desert'.
The dead person's soul travels across the desert . . . Following the trail to a land of milk and honey . . .

The soul's final destination could vary depending on the tribe's beliefs. Some tribes thought that souls lived in the Milky Way. Others thought that the Milky Way was merely the route to a spirit realm on the other side of the universe. A number of tribes saw the afterlife as an idealized version of life on earth: a paradise in a magnificent, lush prairie where people hunted, feasted and danced, otherwise known as the Happy Hunting Grounds.

The concept of reincarnation was not a prominent feature in the spiritual lives of all Native American tribes. For the Plains Indians in particular, the idea was of only minor importance. It was thought that reincarnation took place only when the soul had not been completely developed during life.

Interesting, very interesting . . . Peter thought.
They literally left the fleshpots behind them: the flesh is else-where; the body is left behind. All that remains is the soul that

journeys over mountains, over rivers and lakes and across a desert.

Re-in-carne . . . Back in flesh, born again because there is still more to learn on earth, like the pupil held back for a year and not allowed to move up to the next level. You could read the 'back to the fleshpots' figuratively, back to the flesh, back to the body . . .

Peter gave the leaflet a couple of taps with his pen and then folded it up and put it back in the front pocket of his backpack.

He took the stairs up to the museum entrance on the ground floor, a spacious hall that was mostly given over to paintings.

Peter noticed that his concentration was fading. Whenever he was in a museum – and it didn't matter which one it was – his ability to focus usually lasted less than an hour and a half.

His eye was drawn to a painting of the first Thanksgiving dinner. It portrayed colonists sitting at long tables covered with pristine, white tablecloths. A man with a pointed grey beard stood at the table. The white collar and cuffs of his shirt peeped out from beneath his black clothes, making him look like a clergyman. His clasped hands were pointing towards the heavens.

A group of Native Americans sat on the grass in the background, plainly not allowed to join the others at the table. They had been placed so far to the right of the painting that they were almost falling off it.

Peter left the entrance hall and had a look in the gift shop. While he was browsing the displays, he saw Tony talking to one of the older ladies behind the cash desk.

He went to the toilet and picked his jacket up from the cloakroom on the way back.

'Well, Peter,' Tony said when he got back to the gift shop. 'This is where we part ways.' He grabbed Peter's hand and started to shake it.

The lady behind the desk looked on with interest.

'I've just realised that I have some business to take care of,' Tony said. 'Since I'm here anyway, I ought to do it now. I've called an Uber for you, and it'll take you to the stop where we got off the bus this morning. It's all pretty simple. You can just use your printed ticket. The bus goes straight to South Station, and you can take the subway to Harvard from there.'

This is a bit of an abrupt goodbye, Peter thought. *Hadn't we arranged to travel back together? And what about the surprise he was talking about? Was it this museum, after all?*

Peter didn't mind travelling back to Boston on his own – in fact, it would be good to have some time alone after such a long day – but Tony's sudden departure had come out of the blue.

Tony gave Peter a firm, friendly pat on his shoulder before he went outside. He almost skipped down the wide steps, apparently pleased to be on his own, too.

And I still haven't asked him if he thinks all those cases might be connected to each other.

Peter said goodbye to the lady behind the counter, put on his backpack, and left the museum. He sat down on the low wall that ran around the small garden at the front of the building.

As Tony had promised, ten minutes later, a car pulled up. The driver got out and looked around.

Peter waved at him and walked over to the car.

'Mr Peter?' the chauffeur asked.

'That's me,' Peter replied.

As he got into the back of the car, he noticed a road sign that gave the distance to Boston: 40 miles. A large arrow pointed the way to the bus station on the Pilgrims Highway.

The car drove away in completely the opposite direction.

Chapter 31

The car drove at a leisurely speed along Court Street and onto Main Street. Peter knew that the ocean was behind the houses on his left.

Earlier that afternoon, when he had visited Plymouth Rock with Tony, he had seen Plymouth's marina in the distance.

Soon, they had left the town centre behind them.

'You're taking me to the bus station, right?' Peter asked the driver.

They had turned onto Sandwich Street now. Peter thought it might not be a bad idea to try to remember the street names. He could already see the ocean ahead.

'The bus station?' the driver repeated. 'No, mister, not the bus station. I'm supposed to take you to a boat. We'll be there soon. Don't worry.'

That must be the surprise then . . .

Peter slumped back in the seat. He tried to adopt the confident attitude of the globetrotter who has seen it all and doesn't mind not knowing exactly where he's going.

Should I go back, he asked himself. *Just tell the driver to turn around and take me to the station so I can take the first bus back to Boston?*

He decided to wait and see where he would be dropped off.

If wherever that was didn't feel right, for whatever reason, he could always ask the driver to take him to a bus stop.

He is a bit of a strange man, that Tony, but maybe he really does have a surprise in store for me. And after all, I have really enjoyed today.

The car had turned right onto Ryder Way, a road that ran along a narrow, sandy spit of land. Peter could see water to his left and right, sparkling in the late afternoon sun.

According to the clock in the Pilgrim Hall Museum's reception, it had been almost four o'clock when Tony had left him.

Maybe he wants me to see the bay? Sail along part of the route that the Mayflower *took?*

There were almost no buildings here.

They slowed down but didn't stop. As the car crawled along, the driver leaned over the steering wheel and peered through the windscreen, scanning the coastline on their left.

'It should be here somewhere,' he said, but he didn't sound very sure of himself. He accelerated slightly and shook his head as if he had suddenly realised the futility of his task.

'So who said you should bring me here?'

'Well, uh . . .'

Suddenly, the driver slammed on the brakes, throwing Peter forward. He managed to brace his arms on the seat in front of him just quickly enough to stop himself being hurled against it.

'There it is,' the man said, pointing enthusiastically at the beach.

Peter looked over the man's shoulder at what he was pointing at.

There was indeed a white motorboat in the shallow waters,

keeling slightly as though its skipper had been caught out by the low tide.

A man was standing on the beach, waving energetically with something orange in his hands. He was too far away for Peter to make out his face, but he could tell it was Tony from his baseball cap. He opened the car door and got out, but he kept his right foot on the sill and gripped the top of the door with one hand. He shaded his eyes with his other hand.

'Okay, sir?' the driver asked, making no effort to mask the relief in his voice.

'I think . . .' Peter said hesitantly.

Should I ask him to wait for a few minutes, he wondered. *Just until I know what's going on? Why is Tony waiting for me here? Why didn't we just take a boat from the marina? Why didn't we come here together?*

Peter got out of the car properly and took a few steps away from it. The driver turned the car around to face the other way. And then he appeared to decide that he'd had quite enough. First, he drove forwards very slowly while he performed the acrobatic feat of reaching behind his seat to close the back door, and then he drove off at high speed.

Oh, come on! What on earth is going on?

Peter turned around and saw the long, sandy road behind him. Plymouth, if that was indeed the town he could see in the distance, shimmered in the damp haze drifting in from the sea.

Tony had put whatever the orange thing was back on the boat. Now he held both his arms aloft like a football supporter watching his team score a winning goal.

Despite the strangeness of the situation, Peter started to laugh.

There's something quite endearing about him, he thought. *That enthusiasm . . . Wanting to surprise me like this, like a treasure hunt at a children's party.*

Now Peter finally waved back, and Tony dropped his arms to his sides. Peter decided to go over to the boat. He supposed that the answers to his questions – *Why are we here? Where are we going? When will we be back?* – would be forthcoming soon enough.

'Fooled ye!' Tony hollered when Peter was close enough to hear.

Peter waved again.

'Did you really think I would end our trip so suddenly?' Tony asked, clearly pleased with his little stunt.

Peter had reached the waterline now.

The boat's name, *Sea Breeze*, was painted in ornate letters on the prow, with three horizontal lines of different lengths after it, representing the wind.

Gentle waves washed over the sand bringing little shells and pebbles with them. The endless cadence of the tide's ebb and flow, the rush of the sea and the briny smell of the water always made Peter feel calm. For the first time since he'd got into the car at the museum, he relaxed a little.

'I did think it was a bit . . . unusual, yes,' Peter said. 'But why are we meeting up here? And why didn't we just go to the marina together?'

'Ah, but then it wouldn't have been a surprise now, would it?' Tony said. 'You should have seen your face when I said goodbye! Besides, if we'd gone to the marina together, this would have been no more than an ordinary day trip. But this, my friend, is going to be something you'll never forget. Come on!'

Tony was barefoot, and he had rolled up his trousers. 'Take your shoes off and throw them on board. Then you can help me launch the boat.'

'But what . . .' Peter began. 'What's the plan, Tony? Why are we going on a boat? And what was the deal with the taxi driver? I didn't even get a chance to pay him.'

'I already paid him at the taxi stand.'

'But you *phoned* for a taxi, didn't you?'

'Yes, so he was waiting for me at the stand. It's just around the corner. You'll have gone past it on your way here.'

'But what—'

'I want to give you the authentic Pilgrim experience,' Tony said excitedly. 'From the water, we'll be able to see what the Pilgrims saw when the *Mayflower* sailed into the bay here. Of course, you'll have to imagine all the buildings away. And we'll sail past Provincetown, which is where the *Mayflower* dropped anchor. *And* it's where the Mayflower Compact was signed. We'll be on historic ground, even if it is on the sea. Come on!'

Peter sat down on the sand to take off his shoes. He stuffed his socks inside them. Then he rolled up his jeans and waded through the water to put his shoes on the boat. The water felt pleasantly cool on his hot, tired feet.

This is actually quite nice . . .

'And the best is yet to come, Peter,' Tony said. 'We don't have to take the bus back, because we'll be sailing all the way to Boston Harbor! How do you like that?'

Peter laughed at the childlike and probably very American eagerness with which Tony was looking at him, like a schoolboy inviting his classmate to his birthday party.

He may be a bit of an oddball, and he was thrown out of the Masons because of some very odd behaviour, but on the other hand . . . He is a member of the committee that's organising events for Mayflower 400.

'We're going to Boston?' Peter asked.

They pushed the boat off the beach.

'Isn't that a long way?'

'Oh, it's even further with the bus!' Tony said. 'We'll be navigating close to the shore, no tailbacks, no going the long way around. We can go straight there. It's only twenty-five, maybe thirty miles . . . Oh, sorry! Forty kilometres. It'll take less than an hour.'

The unmoored boat bobbed up and down to the rhythm of the waves.

Tony held the boat steady, and Peter eventually managed to haul himself on board. Tony climbed up after him.

Peter stowed his shoes under one of the plastic benches that were moulded into the sides of the boat and put his backpack on top of them.

Tony was at the helm, sitting on the only chair on board. A low plastic screen divided into three windows protected him from the worst of the wind. The foredeck was so small that it could barely be called a deck at all.

Tony started the motor. It produced a low throbbing sound.

Apart from two life vests and the remarkably large bright orange lifebuoy, there was nothing on the boat. The buoy was so huge that four people would have been able to hold onto it without getting in each other's way.

'Is this your boat?'

'Kind of . . . I share it with some other people. Too expensive for me otherwise. I can't even afford the marina fees!'

The boat skimmed swiftly over the ocean. The wind in his hair felt good. Peter trailed his fingers through the water, feeling the coolness of the air on them each time a wave lifted the boat up and set it back down with a slap.

The two men didn't speak, but the sound of the motor and

the whistling wind would have made normal conversation difficult anyway.

At first, Tony steered towards the Plymouth coast. In the distance on the left, Peter could see the Plymouth Rock Portico. But then they veered right and sailed around the end of the spit. Before long, they were in the open water just outside Cape Cod Bay.

At one point, the boat slowed down and then came to a complete stop. The motor purred softly, as if it was indignantly wondering why it wasn't being utilised to its full potential.

Tony stood up and set his legs wide apart to give himself some stability. Peter stayed where he was on the bench.

'We don't know this for certain either, obviously,' Tony said, 'but the *Mayflower* was somewhere around about here, off the coast near Provincetown when the Mayflower Compact was signed. If you were to look at where we are on a map, you'd see that we're just under the outermost point of the hook of Cape Cod.'

Peter took in the surroundings, already imagining how he could use this in his lectures. Students always liked it when he could liven up a story with his own experiences.

'When the *Mayflower* reached Cape Cod,' Tony said, raising his voice slightly, 'some of the passengers questioned the legitimacy or authority of the group's leaders. They had been given that authority in a patent, a charter that said they could start a new settlement to the north of the Colony of Virginia. But here in New England, that charter was invalid. The passengers said that this meant that the group's leaders had no jurisdiction over them. You can only imagine – or I do, at least – how those leaders must have felt. They were seeking liberty. The freedom to believe what they wanted and practise their beliefs as they saw fit, without any interference from anyone else, without other people telling them what was and wasn't allowed. But just think, they'd crossed an ocean, feared for their lives, survived storms, faced conflicts, deaths, births, tears, laughter, prayers . . . And then . . . then, at last, the coast comes into view. The promised land, the land of milk and honey, the land of all their hopes and dreams. This was the place where they would finally be free. And instead of being thankful to their leaders for bringing them out of Europe, giving them a new future, no less, they started complaining almost before they even saw land. But hey, better to die on your feet than live on your knees, right?'

Peter looked up from his seat at Tony, who had the air of a captain encouraging his demoralised crew.

'The ingratitude . . . the lack of trust . . . Little people with small minds . . . So what do they do then? What do they decide upon? The male passengers draw up a contract, a pact, the first governing document of Plymouth Colony, better known as the Mayflower Compact. The Separatists, the people who had come from Leiden, referred to themselves as the "Saints", the holy ones. The Hebrew word for "holy" literally means "set apart for a specific purpose". They called the others, the adventurers and merchants who had gone with them, the "Strangers". It was only later that both groups were referred to collectively as "Pilgrims". So forty-one of the one hundred and two passengers signed this agreement on November 11th, 1620. Remember, this was according to the Julian calendar that they used then, which, as I'm sure you know, is ten days behind the Gregorian calendar that we use now, so we'd say it was November 21st. The original document is long gone, but we know what was in it because of the writings of William Bradford – just like we know what was in the Ten Commandments because of the Old Testament.'

Tony widened his stance slightly, bracing himself even more securely.

'In fact, they decided between them that they would form a government based on what we call the majority model; it disregarded women and children because they weren't allowed to vote. The compact was actually a social contract. The colonists all agreed that they would follow its rules so that they could preserve order and survive here. A spiritual covenant had marked the beginning of the Pilgrims' Leiden congregation, and now a civil covenant formed the basis of a secular government in America. Because that's . . . Just a few moments, Peter, and then we'll get going again . . . Because ultimately, that's what it's all about . . . Look, Peter, people had come to America before, but they were traders, fortune-seekers, people who made the journey for economic reasons. But this was men, women and children, whole families who came here for something else, and above all, brought something else *with* them. And *that* is where Leiden comes in. That is why your little city played such a vital role in this whole thing. You could say that Leiden was fundamental to everything, fundamental to the principles upon which the whole of the United States would eventually be built. On which, ultimately, all of western civilisation would be built . . . I know you're probably thinking that I'm overstating it, but the ideas that were brought here from Leiden, from the Netherlands: freedom of speech, freedom of religion, freedom of the press . . . Their legacy has proved to be much more enduring than anything the other colonists left behind – if they even left us anything at all. As far as I'm concerned, my dear Peter, this covenant is every bit as important as the Declaration of Independence. Its words should be displayed in every classroom so that pupils can learn its contents. If it was up to me, they would memorise parts of it so that the text becomes as familiar to them as those other famous words: "We hold these truths to be self-evident, that all men are created equal" and so on.'

'And have you memorised the Mayflower Compact?'

Tony looked at him, delighted that Peter had asked this question. 'Of *course* I've memorised it! What did you expect?'

He cast his gaze to the sky and recited the words of the compact with all the poignancy of a Shakespearean actor delivering a monologue. When he was finished, he sat down again. 'And in this too, everything was done for the greater good, working as a single body for the wellbeing of the entire community.'

The boat began to move again, and they navigated along the coastline at a gentle speed.

'There's one thing I don't entirely understand, Tony,' Peter said, 'and I'm hoping you can explain it to me. You're descended from one of the Pilgrims.'

'And very proud of it.'

'As an American, you value your liberty. But at the same time, you talk about community, about unity, about how an individual should go along with the majority, that they sometimes need to practise humility, surrender their free will. Don't those two things contradict each other?'

Tony looked at Peter oddly, as though this was the first time he'd been made aware of the contradiction.

'But, my dear Peter, it's very simple. Charlton Heston expresses it perfectly in Cecil B. DeMille's *The Ten Commandments* when he says that without the law there is no liberty. It's an incredibly profound statement. It seems like a contradiction because how can laws give us liberty? Surely laws are there to limit us, aren't they? A law tells us that we *can't* do something, or even that we *must* do it. You mustn't steal, kill, commit adultery, lie, et cetera.

But people forget that real liberty, total and absolute freedom to do as you please, will ultimately lead to a complete lack of liberty. Because what happens if everyone has total freedom? That's like a class having no teacher or having a teacher who can't control them. It means complete chaos. *Bellum omnium contra omnes*, a war of all against all. Man is a wolf to man. You know Hobbes, right? You'd get a situation of universal fear where the law of the jungle prevails, and nobody is able to realise their full potential. That's the opposite of liberty. It's only within the constraints given to us by the law – the law that regulates our behaviour, in which agreements have been made about which behaviours are permitted and which are not – that we can ever really be free. Only then can people thrive and flourish and become who they truly are inside. By definition, liberty can't be unlimited because your liberty ends where another person's liberty begins.'

He paused for breath and then he continued: 'Almost no one realises this. Many people think that liberty is about having no commitments, having no ties, being independent and going your own way. They don't see that it doesn't work like that, that that's not how we function. That we actually *can't* function like that!'

'This is really an important issue for you, isn't it?'

'Yes, it is an important issue. It should be an issue for more people. You can only be free when you have limits. That's what people just don't get. Sometimes freedom *does* come at the expense of individual sovereignty. You have to surrender a certain amount of control, but what you get in return is worth so much more than that, it's so much greater than your teeny tiny individual self. But Sam and George didn't understand it, either.'

Peter's heart froze, and a chill went through him, as if someone coming in from the snow had laid an icy hand on his neck.

'This is pretty much the place where they went overboard,' Tony said. 'Poor fellas.' He gazed at the water. 'Such a tragedy,' he added, but there was a coldness in his voice that betrayed an utter lack of sympathy.

Oh God, what am I doing here, Peter thought.

He stood up.

The shore had almost disappeared from view. A thin line divided the vast, grey expanse of the sea and the dark blue sky above into two segments, almost as though an artist had tried to make the ultimate minimalist representation of the scene in an abstract piece, *The Coast*.

I've got to get away from here.

'How about we start heading back now?' Peter asked as calmly as possible. 'I really appreciate you giving up some of your valuable time today, Tony, but I'm supposed to be meeting my friend Judith. She's waiting for me.'

It was a lie, of course. Judith was giving her presentation that evening and wouldn't be home until late.

'That's fine, Peter,' Tony said, but there was something in his voice that made Peter feel more uneasy, not less. 'There's just *one* thing . . .'

'And what's that?' Peter asked.

'What was your real reason for coming to the States? Why did you really come to Boston? Why did you want to visit the grand lodge?'

Peter looked at him quizzically. 'What do you mean? I came here to see Judith.'

'Don't lie to me!' Tony roared.

The metamorphosis was so extreme and so unexpected that Peter sat back down in shock.

'What—'

'Do not lie to me! Why did you want to see me? Why did you come and find me? Why did you have to get yourself involved?'

'Involved in what? What on earth are you talking about?'

'Do you think I'm stupid? Do you think I'm a moron or something?'

'Sorry, Tony, but this is . . . ridiculous. I don't know what's got into your head, but this is absurd. Take me back to Boston. Now!' Peter stood up again.

'Did you really think I was going to let you go?'

'What do you—'

Tony laughed, but it was forced and foreboding.

'Did you think I didn't know you only came here to find out what happened to Coen? And to Yona?'

Peter shivered.

'And what happened in Jerusalem?'

'What have you—'

'Jesus . . . Come on! You're a terrible actor, Peter. Do you really think you can pull the wool over my eyes?'

Peter looked longingly at the coast.

Too far to swim. And besides, what's the point of jumping overboard if Tony can just sail after me? Or over the top of me?

'Tony . . .' Peter tried to speak as calmly as he could. 'You're a great guy, really you are, but, honestly, I have absolutely no idea what you mean. Why are you talking about Coen and Yona? And about Jerusalem?'

'Did you really think that Sam and George drowned out here by accident?'

This is going terribly, terribly wrong . . .

'Here!' Tony shouted. He took off his shirt and turned his upper body towards Peter. 'Here!' he shouted again, pointing at the left side of his chest.

When Peter realised what Tony was pointing at, he froze.

He could see the jet-black outlines of a tattoo.

'Did you really think I wouldn't figure out the real reason that you came here straight away?' Tony said in a whisper that was almost infinitely more menacing than when he had been shouting. 'Do you think I'm an idiot?' he said, raising his voice again.

'No, Tony,' Peter said. 'What makes you think that? I don't think you're an—'

'You and your girlfriend just "happened" to find Coen's body,' he said. 'And you just "happened" to go along on that tour with Jeffrey. And you just "happened" to come to Boston to visit your friend at Harvard. And then you just "happened" to visit the grand lodge.'

Tony drew the quotation marks in the air with his fingers, bigger and more angrily each time.

'What are you talking about?' Now Peter was shouting too.

'Did you think I didn't know that you were working under-cover? That your only purpose in coming here was to come after me?'

He really has gone mad.

'But Tony . . .' Peter said. 'I'm just a university lecturer. I teach—'

'You just "happen" to teach about the Pilgrims . . . It's the perfect cover!'

'Tony, you've got it all wrong. I really don't know what you're talking about.'

'Sam and George . . . They had no idea . . .' Tony said with a sudden quietness, as if he considered the subject to be closed. 'They knew me well, obviously. We were members of the same society, the same club. More than three thousand years old, going all the way back to the Exodus, a select group. Secret knowledge.

Boy, if you only knew.' Tony's thoughts appeared to have drifted back to the last time he'd seen Sam and George.

I'm trapped.

Peter frantically tried to work out what to do.

I need to get him talking and keep him talking, go along with his madness, agree with him.

'I just put my boat – this boat – alongside theirs. It was dead simple.' He laughed at his own macabre pun. 'I boarded the boat, knocked Sam out and threw George overboard. Sam was out for a while. George struggled quite a bit when I pushed him down and held his head under the water. That took longer than I'd expected it to. People will try so desperately to cling onto life!'

'But why did they have to—'

Tony carried on talking, unperturbed, as though telling this story was a relief to him, like a penitent at confession glad to be unburdened of the weight of his sin . . .

'George floated away to sleep with the fishes. Sam came round . . . I threw him overboard too, but I wanted him to tell me something first. The poor man barely knew what was going on. Kept begging me to spare him. Didn't want his knowledge to be lost . . .'

'Knowledge? What knowledge? Seriously, what is this about?'

'He did tell me something in the end, but it was almost nothing!' Tony was shrieking in frustration now. 'It's been passed down for more than three thousand years, but orally, only ever orally. It started in Jerusalem, but then after the destruction of the Temple in AD 70, they spread the risk of it being lost by sending people out to the most far-flung corner of the Roman Empire, to England. The Pilgrims eventually brought the knowledge to Leiden, and then one Pilgrim brought it to America on the *Mayflower*, and so it came to Boston. They hid themselves among the Freemasons. I know, I know . . . Officially, Freemasonry began in 1717 when the Masons came out of the shadows and founded the first grand lodge, but in fact, they had been around for three thousand years by then. They go back to the time of King Solomon.'

So it's true! Peter thought. *There have always been rumours that the Masons go back to 1000 BCE, to the days of King Solomon, the son of King David. Solomon was known for his great wisdom, but also for building the first Temple in Jerusalem. The building's architecture was thought to conceal all sorts of secret knowledge, hidden so that it could only be seen by initiates. That's where the essential elements of Freemasonry come from, the square and compasses, the rough stone that has to be turned into a perfect ashlar fit for use in the Temple of Humanity.*

'Philippe de la Noye, Benjamin Franklin, George Washington . . .' Tony went on calmly, 'Paul Revere, Mark Twain, John Steinbeck, Henry Ford, John Wayne, Harry Truman. A long list of illustrious names to which I can add my own, such a great honour.' He spoke these last two words in a sarcastic tone. 'It was based in the cities of Jerusalem, Leiden and Boston, although the people might not always have lived there themselves. There would have been two, perhaps three people in each country who were given the secret knowledge. Their only task was to memorise it and pass it on to the next generation unchanged. They were living books, Peter.'

'Living books?'

My God, Peter thought. *Of course! That's what the author of Piet van Vliet's manuscript was talking about! Boys being initiated and trained, one after the other, to memorise the knowledge and pass it on.*

Despite the absurdity of the situation, for the briefest of moments, Peter was struck by the almost poetic beauty of the idea of a real 'living book'.

What a brilliant way to keep knowledge hidden.

'I'm a living book too,' Tony said.

Peter thought he heard a note of pride in his voice.

'Sam gave the knowledge to George and me so that we could pass it on when the right moment came to reveal it. According to some, that day was approaching, and that's why I *had* to do something. I'd heard the rumours before then. Like lots of other people, I knew the stories about the existence of alternative knowledge, an alternative history. The true story of the Exodus, for example. I never believed it. I mean, I'd always thought that knowledge would be dangerous if it actually existed. But it did exist! For years and years, I searched for it, following tiny clues, poring over old documents, but none of it led me anywhere. And then Sam noticed me. He saw how diligent I was in my search for the truth. George was already his pupil, and I became his pupil too. I was initiated, and I was given my own part of that secret knowledge, Peter. They had no idea. Sam had brought in a Trojan horse, a wolf in sheep's clothing. I only wanted one thing: to have that knowledge so that I could destroy it forever. The hours, the months, the years I spent on it! And it all started in Leiden. A twist of fate had taken the knowledge to Leiden, and another twist of that same fate brought it to Boston. I went to Jerusalem. Two down, four to go. Then there were Coen and Yona. Four down, two to go.'

Peter's chest felt so tight that he could barely breathe.

'Coen was so easy. It was laughable, really,' Tony said. 'There were so many people there that night. I pretended that I wanted to ask him about something in confidence, and I stayed behind in the temple after everyone had left. I pointed at my chest, very discreetly, but there was no need to. He already knew me, even though we'd never met in person. The custodians know about each other. They know who the other books in the living library are. He never saw it coming. It was over in an instant. Putting the square through his heart was actually the hardest part. I had to stab him with a knife first, but my anger gave me the strength to do it. And then the compasses in his hands . . . I was taking a huge risk, I know, but the symbolism was just too perfect. I was going to cut out his tattoo, but I heard someone coming upstairs, so I couldn't finish it. It was a small blemish on an otherwise perfectly executed mission. And then there was Yona. He was in shock, of course, but he wouldn't tell me anything either. I smothered him with a cushion in the end, and then I took him on a little boat trip through your lovely Leiden canals. Water will erase all traces of evidence on a body. It was very unfortunate that he was found so quickly . . .'

'But you'd been back in America for a long time when Yona—'

Tony threw back his head and cackled like a madman.

'I said goodbye to the rest of the delegation at Schiphol airport. "I'll catch another flight," I said. "I still have some business to take care of here." I'm sure that sounds quite familiar. No one questioned it. I went back to Leiden, and then I flew home via Paris. Not under my own name, obviously. Just like the guestbook in the museum this afternoon. I have many names.'

Could it really have been so simple? Wouldn't Rijsbergen have checked that Tony actually was on his flight home? And what did Herman have to do with it all?

'And finally, Sam and George. Six down. Now I'm the only one left. Mission accomplished. And when I die, this heresy will die with me.'

'Heresy?'

Keep the conversation going for as long as possible, Peter told himself. *And let him do the talking for as long as possible.*

He tried surreptitiously to look around the deck, but there was nothing on it except for the lifebuoy and two life jackets.

'Yes, heresy!' Tony said. '*That* was the real reason for the conflict in Leiden. That's why so many of them ended up staying there. The group that stayed in Leiden were the ones who'd congregated around the two living books of *their* time. They were attracted to the liberal interpretations, to letting go of tradition, to the "to-each-his-own-truth" attitude, and to treating Bible stories as allegories. The living books were the only ones who knew what had really caused the split. Eventually, the living books became Freemasons, so there's your connection between the two groups.'

If this is all true . . . Peter thought, *it would be absolutely incredible. The manuscript that Piet van Vliet found in Leiden barely scratches the surface. This means that all of history as we know it will have to be rewritten, not just the history of the Pilgrims. It's all starting to make sense.*

'The people who went to America,' Tony went on resolutely, 'they were the ones who had the *true* faith. That was the real reason that they left. They still believed in the literal truth of the Bible, that the stories in it literally happened, that the Exodus literally happened. They went in search of a promised land, just as the Israelites had once done, to establish a new Jerusalem. But the lie went with them. An initiate, a living book, boarded the *Mayflower* and brought the lie to America, like a parasite hidden inside a healthy body, attacking it from within. The idea was to spread the risk by having living books in the original promised land, in the Old World and in the New World. But I put an end to it. I am the great physician who has provided the cure. And now, at last, it will die with me. Although . . . First, I need to do just *one* more thing . . .'

Could I have seen this coming, Peter asked himself. *Surely there's nothing that indicates that he's really done everything he says he's done?*

'But Tony, I knew absolutely nothing about this. How could I have known? I only came here to visit my friend.'

'Yeah, yeah. Sure . . .' He sounded tired.

'We can work this out, Tony,' Peter said as placidly as possible. 'You've been carrying such a heavy burden.'

'You have no idea, Peter. You really don't.'

'No, Tony, I'm sure I don't. Secrets can weigh so heavily on a man, much more heavily than the outside world could ever understand. Everyone has their own cross to bear. For some people, it's much greater than for others, and yours has just been too much for you, Tony. You did what you thought you had to do, but—'

Tony started to laugh as if he'd been thinking about the punchline to a joke, but now, he'd finally got it.

'Of course, you're thinking,' Tony said, '"I've got to get Tony talking, agree with him, go along with his madness." That might be how it works in movies, but not here, Peter. I'm not an idiot.' He sat back down in his seat.

'No, no, Tony, that's not what I meant. Listen, I've been volunteering in Jeffrey's museum for more than ten years, since long before I ever met you. My girlfriend, Fay, she joined Loge Ishtar three years ago. I just went along with her to the open evening that night. We went to say goodbye to Coen at the end of the evening, and that's when we found him. I called the police and left it in their hands. I'm just a lecturer, Tony. I teach history. My friend Judith got a grant to come to Harvard months ago. I've known her for more than twenty years. I just came to see her, nothing more.'

'I suppose you might have a point,' Tony said, slumping his shoulders and looking at the floor.

Peter got the impression that all of Tony's earlier confidence and conviction was ebbing away.

'Fay asked me to visit the grand lodge in Boston and take some photos for her,' Peter explained. 'I was there for *her*. And obviously I wanted to visit Plimoth Plantation today because that's what you do when you're here, isn't it? Didn't I go whale-watching too? There's nothing suspicious about that, is there? And after meeting you in Leiden, wouldn't it be perfectly normal for me to look you up when I was in Boston?'

Tony heaved a deep sigh.

'That's a load off my mind, I can tell you,' Tony said. His friendly tone was in sharp contrast to his earlier rage. 'But a man's gotta do what a man's gotta do.' He looked at Peter. 'I could recite the texts for you,' he said. 'But you wouldn't understand any of it. It's Ancient Hebrew. I could only memorise the sounds of the words at first. I didn't learn what they meant until later. As an ultimate back-up, there *is* actually a written version of the text. Sam told me about it. Coen wrote it. But Coen wouldn't tell me where it was, not even during our little discussion just before I killed him. It seems he wasn't so fond of life, after all.'

'As if you'd have let him stay alive even if he had told you.'

'Hmm . . . You're right about that. Good point.'

'But come on, Tony. You know yourself that you won't get away with this. Everyone has seen us together. If something happens to me, you'll be their prime suspect.'

'What everyone saw, Peter, was us saying goodbye to each

other at the museum,' Tony said triumphantly. 'It'll have been caught by the security cameras too. People saw me walking away. They saw you getting into a car on your own, going to catch a bus back to Boston. With a ticket that I'm going to scan later on my way back.'

'But . . .'

My God, this was his plan right from the start . . .

'But,' Peter tried again, 'the Uber driver, he's a witness.'

'Uber driver?'

Tony let out a loud guffaw.

'Believe me, that man owes me. He won't report anything. He's got way too much to lose.'

Suddenly, Tony rushed at Peter and gave him a violent shove on the chest.

Peter stumbled backwards and fell overboard. The attack had been so unexpected that he hadn't even had the chance to close his mouth before he fell. He went under, unable to stop the salty water from surging down his throat. He came back up to the surface, coughing and spluttering.

Tony leaned over the side of the boat and grabbed the shoulders of Peter's jacket.

Peter tried to wrestle free, but Tony held on tight.

'Tony!' Peter screamed. 'Come on! This is insane!'

Tony's eyes glowed with an ice-cold hatred, like the eyes of a man who has finally decided to go to the dark side. 'You should have stayed in Holland!' He spat the words out. 'Then none of this would have happened! But you had to—'

'I didn't know anything! This is all in your head!' Peter pulled his legs up and tried to push off from the hull, but his bare feet were unable to find purchase on the smooth surface, and they slid off.

Tony looked like he wasn't sure about what to do next. His grip loosened for a moment.

Now, at last, Peter managed to brace one foot against the boat. He pushed off so hard that he almost pulled Tony into the water with him, but Tony let go.

Peter swam a couple of metres away from the boat. Not that it was going to help him much; they were a long way from the shore and the exhaustion he already felt was made worse by his fear. To make things worse, his waterlogged jeans, shirt and jacket were restricting his movement. He struggled out of the jacket and tried to gather it into a pouch and trap air inside it. He had seen it done on a survival show on the Discovery Channel. But the attempt cost him so much energy that he gave up.

Tony sat at the helm and started the motor.

'Hey!' Peter yelled, but his weak voice was barely audible over the engine's roar.

At first, Tony steered the boat away from him, but a few moments later, he swung it back around. He fixed his eyes on Peter and manoeuvred the boat in wide circles around him.

Peter could tread water for fifteen minutes in his water polo training sessions at the pool, but trying to do that almost fully dressed in cold water was a different thing entirely.

Tony circled closer and closer like a shark closing in on its prey.

As each second passed, Tony felt his legs growing more tired. It felt like something below him was tugging at them, trying to drag him down.

Tony was less than two metres away now. He stopped the boat.

This can't be how I die, Peter thought.

Fay . . .

He sank below the water's surface several times. Out of sheer desperation, he swam over to the boat and grabbed the edge with one hand. He suddenly realised how cold he was. He looked up, almost imploring the heavens for help.

Tony leaned forward and peered into the water, his hands on his hips, and a sardonic smile on his lips. 'You can't keep this up for long, Peter,' he said. 'I'm going to open up the throttle, and then you'll have to let go.'

The salty sea water stung Peter's eyes.

Tony leaned even closer.

I'm so tired . . .

His legs felt even heavier.

They say that drowning is a horrible way to die, he thought suddenly.

Fay, I so want to see you again.

Agapé, I so want to see you grow up.

Judith, I so want to hold you again.

I want to see you all again.

Peter felt hate and rage suddenly burning inside him in a way he had never felt before. For the first time in his life, he experienced what a powerful force these two emotions could be. Strength flowed back into his legs as if they were connected to an invisible source of energy.

He let go of the boat as a still-smiling Tony watched him, leaning so far over that his head was almost touching the gunwale railing now. Peter started to kick his legs, just as he had done for countless hours during water polo matches and training sessions. He moved his body from left to right, and then, in a final burst of energy, propelled himself upwards. His entire torso rose up out of the water. In the same movement, he grabbed Tony's ears and yanked his head downwards.

Tony screamed out in pain and shock and tumbled over into the water. He resurfaced a metre away from the boat.

Now, with the last dregs of his energy, Peter managed to hook one leg over the railing and pull himself on board. He dived towards the control panel to push the throttle lever down, but he missed and banged his head on the wheel. Dizzy with pain and fatigue, he sank to his knees.

He heard a thud behind him. He turned around and saw Tony's hand gripping the side of the boat.

Still on his knees, Peter reached for the throttle. This time he managed to push it down. The boat shot forwards, and then the motor immediately cut out.

Peter looked around him. The hand was gone.

He turned the key in the ignition. The motor rattled and sputtered, but it didn't come to life. He grabbed the lifebuoy. It was surprisingly heavy. Anxiously, he looked over the side of the boat, holding the buoy away from his body, ready to swing it. But he couldn't see Tony.

He walked around the tiny deck, constantly peering over the edge, but there was nothing there. Eventually, he sat down on the seat in the cockpit.

What should I do? I can't pull him back on board – even if he does resurface. And I can't see him anywhere anyway. He's murdered six people. That makes him a serial killer. But I'm no murderer . . .

He threw the lifebuoy into the water. A nightmarish vision of Tony rising out of the water like a phoenix to pull him back overboard flashed through his mind. He tried to start the motor again. Mercifully, it roared back to life. He looked behind him but still saw nothing.

'I'm an excellent swimmer,' Tony had said.

Peter pushed down on the throttle, and the boat catapulted forwards so suddenly that he almost fell over. He grabbed the wheel with both hands.

Less than a minute had passed since Tony had gone overboard.

How long can someone stay underwater?

He pushed the lever down again, and the boat shot over the water.

After a while, Peter lowered the speed until the boat came to a standstill. Then he got up, picked up Tony's shoes with the socks still inside them and hurled them into the water, erasing all traces of him from the boat.

He looked behind him yet again and watched the orange lifebuoy bobbing in the water like a funeral wreath on a watery grave.

What now?

Peter sat back down in the cockpit and opened up the throttle. He steered towards the coast, and then manoeuvred the boat in a wide arc to the right in the direction of what he hoped was Boston.

No one knows that I was here. People saw us say goodbye to each other. There are CCTV images to prove it. They saw me get into a car. The driver has some sort of secret that he can't risk having revealed, so he'll be glad if he never hears from Tony again. If he finds out that Tony has disappeared, he won't contact the police because then he'll have to explain his role in all of this. And I'm leaving for the Netherlands tomorrow. Nobody needs to know anything. What can I actually do? Go to the police? They'll arrest me. In America, you can be locked up for months before you get a chance to prove your innocence. It would be easy for a prosecutor to turn a jury against you. A foreigner goes on a boat trip with an American citizen, a member of the Mayflower 400 committee – he has a small stain on his character because of being kicked out of the Masons, perhaps, but that was a private matter. A model citizen, a patriot . . . Who would believe me over him?

At last, the outlines of the city of Boston came into view in the far distance. But he couldn't moor the boat in the marina. There would be security cameras everywhere, and he'd probably have to report to the harbour master first.

Peter decided to head for the coast and find somewhere to put ashore.

The closer he got, the more determined he became.

He was going to kill me. For no reason. Because of something he thought I knew. What a sick mind . . . Playing God like that . . . Perhaps I played God too, but that was in self-defence. It was him or me . . .

He piloted the boat carefully towards a small beach and stopped when he felt the soft sand chafing at the hull.

There was a small cloth like a chamois leather lying on the dashboard. He used it to wipe down the steering wheel and throttle lever. Then he wet it and ran it along the entire length of the railing around the gunwale. When he was done, he picked up his backpack and shoes and carefully lowered himself onto the beach.

He gave the boat a push to free it from the sand and allowed it to drift away. Peter realised that he was still holding the cloth in his hand. He dropped it into the water.

If they found the boat, it would probably lead them directly to Tony – or it would if it really was registered in his name. And if his body was found, the police would almost certainly go looking for the killer within the Masonic community, since his departure had been so acrimonious. *And,* if the police turned up at Peter's door, he could tell them truthfully that he and Tony had parted ways at the museum because Tony had some business to attend to in Plymouth.

'No,' he would say. 'He didn't tell me what that business was.

I was surprised because I thought we'd agreed to go back to Boston together. Something seemed to come up unexpectedly, something urgent. I took the bus back to Boston. I got on at the terminus on Pilgrims Road. The bus was late, so the driver told me to hurry up and get on board. He didn't check my ticket.'

Peter took his shirt off and wrung it out onto the sand. Surprisingly little water came out of it. His clothes had already started to dry in the strong winds out at sea.

He put his shirt back on, followed by his shoes and the socks that he had stuffed inside them before boarding the boat. He checked his backpack and made sure that his wallet and everything else was still inside. Suddenly feeling cold, he took out his anorak and pulled it on.

Only someone observing him very closely would realise that his jeans were still quite wet. Anyone else would probably think that they were just a very dark colour.

As if anyone would be paying attention to that . . .

He took a moment to appreciate the pleasure of having dry socks on his feet and solid ground beneath them again.

Then, the realisation struck him: *I killed someone.*

No, I might have killed someone, he corrected himself. *Will I get away with it? Can I live with it?*

He trudged along the deserted beach, looking for the nearest road. He felt like the student, Raskolnikov, in Dostoevsky's *Crime and Punishment* as he descends the stairs after killing a despicable old moneylender. Raskolnikov appears to have got away with the perfect crime . . . Initially, he feels no remorse. But, eventually, his conscience starts to get the better of him.

Peter laughed when he saw the name of the beach on a sign: EGYPT BEACH.

The knowledge, the ancient secret knowledge, has disappeared beneath the ocean's waves. In that respect, Tony has achieved his goal. But what about the document he was talking about? Where could that be?

He left the beach and found himself on a street called Egypt Beach Road. Peter wasn't exactly sure where he was. Or how he would get home. The best option was the one that avoided being seen by anyone as much as possible.

Then again, how many people would remember a face that they had only seen once?

He took a chance and turned right onto Hatherly Road. The roadside was thick with trees, and on his left was what looked like a wood, but soon the trees thinned out, and houses began to appear.

He followed a completely random route and went into the first street he came across, turning left this time.

About two hundred metres along the road, he came to a Catholic church. There was a large sign outside:

CATHOLIC CHURCH
Friends of St. Frances Xavier Cabrini
Patron Saint of Immigrants

As he stood outside and wondered which way he should go next, a truck pulled into the church parking lot.

Peter realised that he must have looked helpless – or the car's driver was a good Catholic who had been brought up to help those in need – because the car stopped. The driver's side window opened with a soft whir.

No point trying to run now.

'Can I help you, sir?'

'Well,' Peter said, 'to tell you the truth, I'm a little bit lost.

I've been to Egypt Beach. I got a ride in with friends this morning, but now I need to get back to Boston by public transportation.'

'Public transportation?'

The man, a friendly-looking fifty-something, gave Peter a look that suggested that he was on the verge of delivering a long rant about the state of American public transport.

'At this hour, sir . . . Sir, it's after five o'clock.'

'I know. Is that going to be difficult?'

'You know what? Why don't you hop in? I'm going that way anyway. I can drop you off at JFK/UMass subway station.'

Peter walked around the car.

This man is definitely going to remember my face, Peter thought. *But running away would look even more suspicious . . . By the time Tony is found – if Tony is found – I'll be safely back in the Netherlands.*

Before he got into the car, he took a plastic bag out of his backpack and laid it carefully over the passenger seat.

The man nodded approvingly.

'Been swimming?'

'Yes. I've still got my trunks on, and everything's a bit wet.'

He recognised the name JFK/UMass. He had seen it often enough – it was one of the subway stations on the line he took from Harvard to South Station.

'That's the Red Line, right?' he asked.

'That's right,' the man agreed. 'So you know your way around here. Where are you staying?'

'At . . . Wait, let me think.'

When he and Judith had gone on the whale-watching trip, they had passed some large hotels that looked out over the bay.

The less this man knows, the better.

'Sorry, it's just that I've stayed in so many hotels recently,' Peter said. 'Something Waterfront.'

'Oh, you mean the Westin Boston Waterfront?'

'Yes, that's it.'

'That's a beautiful hotel. Or so I've heard.'

'It is,' Peter replied. 'This is so kind of you, by the way. I don't know what I would have done if you hadn't come along.'

'We always try to help those in need, right?'

They spent the rest of the journey in silence. Peter was too worn out to talk.

Less than an hour later, the man dropped Peter off at the subway station.

Peter thanked him heartily, grabbed the plastic bag from the seat and closed the car door. As he walked towards the subway entrance, he fished around in his bag for his cap. He pulled it down over his eyes before he opened the fare barrier with his ticket. The gates swung open with a beep. When he got to the platform, he leaned against a pillar to wait for the train to Harvard. He folded his ticket over a few times to make the thin card easier to tear in half.

I won't need this tomorrow, anyway. And for all I know, my ticket could tell them exactly when and where I got on and off the subway.

When the train arrived, Peter put the two halves of the ticket into separate bins before he got into one of the carriages.

So, there was a manuscript.

And Tony had been dying to know where it was.

Literally.

Strangely, Peter was vaguely aware that he actually knew where he needed to look for it. What he didn't know was how to bring that knowledge to the surface of his mind.

If all that secret knowledge is lost, then Tony will still have won, and he'll be able to claim his victory from beyond the grave. And then everyone – Coen, Yona and all the others – will have died for nothing. If I can find this manuscript, then I can save the knowledge that they devoted their lives to. And ultimately sacrificed them for.

The puzzle pieces whirled around in his head like a hurricane. Then, as if someone had pressed a slow-motion button, they began to settle down. Soon, slowly but surely, they would all start to fall into place.

Chapter 32

L iving books . . .
Peter tried to process all the information that Tony had revealed to him.

Can this really all be true, he wondered. *Or was Tony crazy? Just a man with a very sick mind?*

After all, Tony's belief that Peter had only come to America to unmask him was hardly rational. On the other hand, his tattoo was real, and his confession had seemed so . . . genuine.

Peter always found it difficult to suspend his disbelief whenever a murderer in a book or film took the time to exhaustively explain his motives or brag about his other murders to his prospective victim. It was a well-known trick used by writers and directors to give their audiences crucial information. But now Peter realised that it did actually work like that. The killer confessed his crimes to his latest victim because he was confident that they would shortly take his secrets to their grave.

So, these living books had been around for centuries – three thousand years, Tony had said – passing on some sort of secret knowledge. Tony hadn't revealed what that knowledge actually was, but considering his repeated references to the Exodus, it *had* to be something to do with that. What was more . . . Christians believed that the Israelites had left Egypt around three thousand years ago, somewhere around 1400 or 1200 BCE. And the secret knowledge had been preserved within the community that would later come to be known as the Freemasons.

There were three important places. Jerusalem – it always came back to Jerusalem – and England, and then, because of the Leiden Pilgrims, America. Six living books were now gone, and their knowledge would never be passed on. If what Tony had told him was true, Tony was the last living book.

Or had been the last living book.

But the knowledge still existed in a written document. Somewhere.

I have to tell Rijsbergen about this. But not . . . not until I've left America. Rijsbergen isn't likely to say: 'Excellent work, my man. Nicely solved. Why don't you come back to Leiden and we'll discuss all the details here?' As an upstanding officer of the law with a firm belief in due process, he would insist that I reported it to the Boston Police.

But Peter knew the police made mistakes – how many news stories had he read about suspects who'd spent decades on death row before being exonerated by DNA evidence?

He would tell Rijsbergen everything when he got home. Then they could decide what steps they should take next, once he was safely back in Leiden and protected by Dutch law.

To what extent could they prosecute me for this? Would it be seen as an act of self-defence? Or was leaving someone in the water two kilometres away from the coast a criminal act?

In his defence, he could offer the fact that he had thrown the lifebuoy into the water. Everyone would understand his reluctance to haul Tony back up onto the boat when the man had been so determined to kill him.

The subway car lurched and rattled from side to side, jerking

Peter back to the here and now. He realised that he was only a couple of stops away from Harvard.

When he got off the train, he tried to be as unobtrusive as he could. But he was sure that at any moment, he would hear a rough voice yell, 'You're under arrest. Put your hands where I can see them,' followed by the famous words, 'You have the right to remain silent. Anything you say can and will be used against you in a court of law.'

Once he was back up at ground level, he realised that he was ravenously hungry. According to the station clock, it was almost 8 p.m.

It had been well before noon when he'd eaten lunch with Tony at Plimoth Plantation, and it had been a light meal at that.

It all seemed so incredibly long ago.

It's bizarre to think that Tony was already planning to get rid of me then, Peter thought. *How sick do you have to be to spend an entire day with someone before you kill them, toying with them like a cat playing with a mouse?*

His jeans were no longer soaking wet, but they were still quite damp. He decided to leave his anorak on.

It was already getting dark. He considered going back to Judith's, but she wasn't at home, and he didn't want to be alone. He was almost afraid of his own thoughts.

But above all, he was hungry.

Peter set off along Massachusetts Avenue and headed for the Starbucks. He stopped at the Harvard Coop on the way. He had seen a book there a couple of days earlier, *The Bible Unearthed*, by the Israeli archaeologists Israel Finkelstein and Neil Asher Silberman. He knew that they had written extensively about the Israelites' journey out of Egypt and the apparent total lack of archaeological evidence to support it. Everything that had happened recently seemed to point to the Exodus, including the texts that had been found on Coen's body.

He decided to buy the book. It would give him something to read over dinner later.

Peter had never found it easy to sit passively and just stare into space, except perhaps when he was smoking a cigar. But smokers were so in the minority these days that there was almost nowhere where he could enjoy one in peace. He'd only found the opportunity to do so once or twice over the last few weeks.

The enormous bookstore spanned multiple floors, and during his time in Boston, he and Judith had literally spent hours here. They had roamed the stacks separately, each selecting piles of books before meeting back up in the store's café to make their final choices over coffee.

But today, Peter headed directly for the floor that housed the theology and archaeology books to find and buy one specific book.

There's no such thing as too many books . . .

He paid with his credit card, something he rarely did in the Netherlands except for booking flights and buying concert tickets. But here in America, he'd used it to pay for even the smallest things, like cups of coffee.

I'm probably going to be in trouble as soon as they start to question me. If I tell them that I got on that bus, then I'll have to account for a couple of missing hours somehow. Although . . . I could say I was in Judith's apartment, and she wasn't home so, 'unfortunately', there aren't any witnesses. Then, I could say that I went out later to buy this book and get something to eat at Starbucks.

He left the bookstore with the book tucked under his arm and crossed the street to the coffee shop, which was busy as usual. He ordered two sandwiches and a medium latte and took them up to the first-floor seating area. Two people got up to leave just as he arrived, freeing up a comfortable two-seater sofa with a view over Harvard Square.

He unzipped his jacket, releasing a musty smell, like the stink of wet laundry left in the washing machine for too long.

He ate his sandwich unhurriedly, drinking his coffee between bites.

Each time he closed his eyes, his mind replayed the scenes of his struggle on the water with Tony.

He noticed that his breathing was shallow and high in his chest. He gripped his coffee mug to control the trembling in his hands. He remembered the feelings of hate and rage that had given him just enough energy to lift himself out of the water, like an invisible force had been pushing him upwards. He saw the dumbfounded look on the deranged Tony's face as he'd realised what a huge mistake he had made by leaning so far over to watch him. Grabbing Tony by the ears had been a smart move. The outer ear was very sensitive, and he had been rendered completely powerless. There was a good reason that teachers used to drag their troublesome pupils out of class by the ear.

How could I have just left him there? How could I abandon someone like that? And where was that maniac anyway? How long can a person actually stay underwater?

Peter had to force himself to think about something else.

Fay.

It had been a good idea to spend some time apart. They had emailed each other every day and texted too. And although their tone had been somewhat formal, it had been nice to stay in touch with her while he was away. They had skyped a few times, and it had been great to see her face, but they had both found it slightly awkward. There was something artificial about having a conversation that way. At home, you could comfortably say nothing for ten minutes while you both read the paper, for example, but in a video call, you were obliged to chat continuously. So there had been lots of small talk, but they had also talked about themselves and their relationship . . . They had resolved to make a fresh start when he got home. Agapé had wandered into view a couple of times during their calls; she had waved at him so cheerfully and looked so happy when Peter waved back that his heart had melted on the spot.

Peter had brought up Fay's emails with Coen again and explained that her secrecy about them had made him feel distanced from her.

Fay had apologised, but not entirely convincingly. In her opinion, everyone had a right to keep some secrets, even within a relationship. The idea that you had to be absolutely open and honest about everything was an outdated '1960s idea', she had said. A partner who told you everything would be impossible to live with. If every irritation, every thought and idle fancy was spoken out loud, where would it end? Every fantasy that you had about someone else, every daydream about a life without your partner, or a life with someone else . . .

'I think it's good that you don't know everything about me,' she had said. 'And that I don't know everything about you.'

And she was right.

She had told Peter that the email conversation with Coen had been frustrating because Coen had died before whatever he'd been hinting at in his messages could be brought to fruition. Something monumental had been about to happen. He'd wanted to tell her things, make her a part of something historic. But he had expressed his thoughts in vague terms without ever explicitly saying what he meant. She had reread the emails again and again and concluded that they actually said remarkably little.

But Peter now had a strong suspicion that he knew exactly what Coen had wanted to share with Fay.

Something that would have involved a visit to a tattoo studio . . .

His coffee mug was empty. It was completely dark outside now, but Peter still felt reluctant to go back to Judith's. He would be going back to an empty apartment, so he might as well stay here.

He picked the book from the table and read the back cover.

Searching for the rightness of the Bible, two Jewish archaeologists found a different reality.

Finkelstein and Silberman have written a fascinating book based on the most recent archaeological research into early history as we know it from the Bible. It was not the intention to test the reliability of the Bible texts, but to place the relationship between those texts and the archaeological finds in the right light. Finkelstein and Silberman show the story the stones tell, but that is a different story than we find in the Old Testament.

This book shows that the descendants of David rewrote history for political and ideological reasons. The remains found in the soil tell the real story. Without sensationalising, Finkelstein and Silberman describe how biblical fiction and historical reality became interwoven.

There is no evidence that Abraham existed; nor is there any other patriarch. And the same goes for Moses and the Exodus.

He found the chapter on the Exodus and started to read. It was a well-known story, for him at least, about how, after more than a century of digging, archaeologists had not found a shred of evidence for the presence of such a large group of people at the time and location that the Exodus was supposed to have taken place. There was nothing in the Egyptian annals about thousands of slaves departing en masse, and furthermore, research had proved that, genetically, modern Jews were identical to Palestinians, so the idea of them as a separate people was highly disputable. The people of Israel had simply been one of the dominant tribes in the area at the time. To cement their dominance and to create more national unity, they had invented a mythological history around the storm god Yahweh – his wife Asherah was left out of this story but still appeared in surnames like Asscher – and the religious rites and rituals in the Temple in Jerusalem.

Having a story in common, a shared history, is essential for forging a mutual bond among a country's inhabitants. That's as true today as it was in ancient times, Peter thought. *A nation needs stories and myths. They don't necessarily have to be true as long as they highlight the character and identity of its people. For us in the Netherlands, that's the story of the Batavian revolt against the Romans, the Dutch revolt against the Spanish Empire, the suffering and resistance of the Dutch people during the Second World War. But it's also the celebration of King's Day, watching the Dutch squad play in international football matches, remembering those who died in the two World Wars on May 4th, and celebrating Liberation Day on May 5th.*

Time passed, and the more absorbed he became in the book, the calmer he felt. The thoughts of his terrifying ordeal at sea faded into the background.

He tried not to think of Tony's body and how it was probably floating in the water, rising and falling on the waves as it was carried along by the tide. He tried not to think of the boat that had probably run aground on Egypt Beach by now and would surely be found in the morning.

He was due to check in at 9 a.m. the next day, and his flight would leave two hours later, first to New York, and from there to Amsterdam.

If only it were tomorrow already . . .

He closed the book. He had been so engrossed in it that he hadn't noticed that almost all the other customers had left. The staff were already tidying up around him.

It was almost 11 p.m. Judith would surely be home by now.

Peter left the coffee shop and followed the tall, wrought-iron railings that led to the Harvard yard entrance gate. The next day, he would leave the campus via the main gate.

From below, he could see that there were lights on in Judith's apartment, but in the hallway rather than the living room. That meant that she was probably in bed already.

Slightly crestfallen, he let himself in and went upstairs. He turned the key in the lock as quietly as he could, and carefully opened the apartment door. The light in the hallway was on.

Judith's bedroom door was ajar again, but this time, he saw that she was tucked up under the covers.

He silently closed the front door.

Laboriously, he peeled off his clothes and hung them up around the bathroom. He would make sure to wash them all thoroughly when he got home. He took some dry underwear from one of the shelves that Judith had cleared for him. The T-shirt that he had been sleeping in while he was here was hanging on a hook on the bathroom door.

The noise is bound to wake her up if I take a shower . . .

He considered resorting to a strip wash at the bathroom sink, but he desperately wanted to rinse off his entire body, as if it might wash away his sins.

It didn't take long for the water to heat up. He stepped under the shower and felt the familiar comfort of hot water flowing over him. He soaped himself up thoroughly and scrubbed his body so vigorously that his skin turned bright red.

Oh God, what have I done?

He rinsed the suds away, turned off the shower and dried himself off.

He brushed his teeth, and then he tiptoed back out of the bathroom, wearing only his T-shirt and boxers.

Judith had kicked off her bedsheet in her sleep, and now most of it was on the floor. She was lying on her side facing the bedroom door, wearing a long T-shirt that reached almost to her knees. He watched her chest calmly rise and fall.

Peter couldn't stop looking at her. He held his breath, afraid that it might break the spell.

I should go to my own room now, he told himself. He exhaled slowly.

Just as he was about to move, Judith opened her eyes.

'Hey, you,' she said sleepily and smiled.

'Hey,' he said back. 'I was . . .' He felt himself turning red, caught standing there at her door in his boxers, staring at her.

Dirty old man . . .

Instinctively, he sucked his belly in.

Judith laughed. 'You don't need to hold your tummy in for me, you know.'

She was wide awake now. She sat up and pulled the sheet loosely back around her. 'Come and sit down,' she said. 'Tell me about your day.'

Peter went into her bedroom, trying to act like this was a perfectly normal situation.

What can I tell her? It's all in the past now . . . The fewer people who know about this, the better . . . I'll be on a plane back to Holland tomorrow.

He sat down on the edge of the bed. 'How was your presentation?' he asked. 'Did it go well?'

'Yeah, it was good. Interesting. Good questions afterwards, good discussion. I think they were happy. Happy that they got their money's worth, I mean. That they gave the grant to the right person. They're going to get two papers out of it. So yes, it was a lovely evening. But what about you? You're back late.'

'It's been a long day,' Peter said. 'You should visit it, you know, Plimoth Plantation. It's really worth the trip out there. You could go with Mark when he's here.'

She nodded. 'Was it exhausting, spending the whole day with Tony?'

Peter swallowed. 'No, it was okay, actually. He was on his own turf, and he was clearly in his element. He knows a lot of people there, so he was constantly shaking people's hands, introducing me to everyone we met. He ended up having to take care of some business in Plymouth, so I got the bus back on my own. I grabbed a coffee and a bite to eat in Starbucks, and then I bought a book at the Harvard Coop.'

'Don't you have enough books already?' she said and smiled. She lay down again. 'I'm glad you had a nice day,' she went on, without waiting for a reply. 'Tell me more about it tomorrow? I'm a bit tired,' she said. 'Sorry.'

'No, no,' Peter said quickly. 'Don't worry. I'm going to go to sleep too. I just need to make up the sofa bed.'

She slid an arm out from under the bedsheet and patted the mattress.

'Why not come and sleep next to me?' she said without opening her eyes. 'Save you the bother of sorting your bed out.'

Peter swallowed awkwardly. 'Yes,' he said, his voice suddenly hoarse. He cleared his throat. 'All right.'

How often have I fantasised about this?

Judith opened her eyes and smiled. She held the sheet up invitingly. Peter lay down and pulled it over him.

'So. There we are,' Judith said.

Yes, here we are, Peter thought. *Now what?*

He lay on his back with his hands folded behind his head, smiling awkwardly. He lay still, trying to avoid touching her.

But Judith moved closer to him.

Without thinking, he stretched out his right arm so that Judith could put her head on his shoulder.

I'm so glad I took that shower, he thought.

Judith threw her arm over him, and a few moments later, she rested her right leg on his thigh. 'Goodnight, dear Peter,' she said and pressed a kiss onto his chest.

Peter felt the heat from her hand spreading over the skin on his torso, the softness of her breasts pressing into the side of his body, the warmth of her belly touching his thigh. He gingerly moved his arm so that he could stroke her back.

She responded to his touch with a low 'mmm'.

Peter could only think of how natural this all seemed. *This feels so good.*

'It's so nice, lying here next to you, Judith,' he said quietly.

'Yes, nice,' she murmured, already half asleep.

'I've wanted this for so . . .'

Judith slowly opened her eyes. 'Long?'

'For so long, yes. Sorry. From the very first time you walked into my office twenty years ago.'

She smiled, and drowsily closed her eyes again. 'Oh,' she said. 'Haven't you?'

'Sometimes . . .' she said. 'Well . . . Maybe, yes. But this, what we have now . . .'

'What?'

'Imagine that there *had* been something between us. If it hadn't worked out,' she said, 'we'd probably not want to have much to do with each other now. But instead, we have this lifelong friendship. And that's better than . . .' She left the words unspoken.

Better than what, Peter wondered. *Better than having a one-night stand or a relationship that hits the rocks after two years? Maybe she's right . . .*

But there had been plenty of moments when he would have chosen the one-night stand or the relationship that eventually hit the rocks, given the option.

'Or maybe, just once, we could have . . . Ah, well . . .' she said wryly. 'Now it's too . . .'

'Now it's too what?'

'Now it's too late for that, isn't it? That ship sailed years ago. Now you have Fay, and I have Mark . . .' She snuggled closer to him. 'But this is lovely. It really is.'

He moved his hand down from her back to her bottom, felt its fleshy softness and the firm muscles beneath. He fought the urge to squeeze it.

'Goodnight, dear Peter,' she said again. She gave him another kiss on his chest, and he replied by kissing her hair.

'Goodnight, dear Judith,' he said. He hardly dared to move. He gently pressed his lips to the top of her head and breathed in the smell that had become so familiar to him.

438   *Jeroen Windmeijer*

What if . . . he thought. *Was 'Now it's too late for that, isn't it?'*
a statement or a question?

What would it be like to reach over and pull her on top of
him now?

We would lie quietly in each other's arms, at first, he imagined.
Then, shyly kiss each other's necks, moving higher and higher . . .
kissing all around the ears, my lips brushing her cheeks . . . one
careful kiss on her lips, then we hold each other close again . . .
And then, our mouths meet at last, like two magnets, inevitably
and irresistibly drawn to each other. Gentle first kisses, teasing bites
on the lips, tongues tentatively probing. And then which of us would
give in first? Give in to kisses so passionate that we almost devour
each other, stopping now and then to gaze at each other. Is this
really happening? To us? Finally, after all these years! Laughter
that turns into soft moans. My hands under her T-shirt, over her
back, on her bum. She rises up slightly, tries to take off her T-shirt
with her lips still pressed to mine . . . so delightfully awkward . . .
red blushes on her neck . . . She helps me to take off my T-shirt
before lifting her own over her head. She's wearing a thong, embroi-
dered with flowers . . . So sweet . . . Then, at last . . .

Two bodies, one desire. She lies on top of me, and her beautiful
breasts feel soft and warm against my chest . . . Then she sits up,
and I see her, glorious in the moonlight. I feel the weight of her
body against mine and the heat between her legs. My erection is
undeniable now . . . I hear a soft 'mmm' in my ear. 'Well, that
seems to be working just fine,' she laughs. She teases my crotch
with her fingertips . . . Almost painful, but what a wonderful, deli-
cious pain. And there's no embarrassment between us . . . How
beautiful you are, my friend, my love. Your lips are like a crimson
ribbon, and your mouth is lovely. Your cheeks are like the halves
of a rosy pomegranate when you smile. Your breasts are like two

fawns, twins of a gazelle. You have ravished my heart. You have ravished my heart with a glance of your eyes. Come here, my darling . . . I bury my face in her breasts, and she entwines her fingers in my hair. I cup her breast with my hand, take her nipple between my finger and thumb and pinch it gently. It hardens instantly. She leans even closer into me, pressing her pelvis into mine . . . We roll slowly from one side of the bed to the other and back again like we're lying in the waves on the waterline as the surf plays with our bodies . . . My hand on her bottom, inside her knickers, on her bare skin, firm and muscular but still soft . . . I gently squeeze . . . I reach down with one hand to take off her knickers, and she helps me with one hand . . . Then we take off my boxers . . . She rolls off me and lies next to me. I trace her belly with my fingers and see a small tuft of hair . . . She grabs my hand and moves it downwards . . .

Then, at last, she rolls on top of me again, straddling me, just as I imagined her doing in my wild fantasies. Wordlessly, we become one as we gaze at each other, so full of love, hardly able to believe that this is finally happening. After so many years. And so naturally . . .

If time were to stop at that moment and he died right there and then . . . Well, he could think of worse ways to go.

Peter heaved a deep sigh.

Judith had fallen asleep.

I'm driving myself crazy, lying here next to her, Peter thought.

He hoped that the restless rising and falling of his chest wasn't disturbing her, but soon, he began to calm down and his breathing returned to normal.

Peter thought about Fay.

And Mark.

Now I'm starting to have secrets too . . . But nothing actually happened, did it, he asked himself, trying to push away the rising feeling of guilt.

But it's still wrong . . .

Peter knew that, of course.

If Fay or Mark were to walk in now . . .

He carefully slid his arm from under Judith's head. Her eyelids fluttered briefly, and then she turned over onto her other side and slept on.

He felt guilty, not so much about Fay or Mark, but about Judith. He had allowed himself to be carried away by his fantasies while she had invited him into her bed out of pure friendship.

But her saying, 'Or maybe, just once, we could have . . .' had naturally set him off. In all these years, it had never occurred to him that she might have the same feelings or desires for him that he'd had for her.

But that ship has sailed . . .

Peter lay awake, listening to Judith's breathing. In his head, images from his fantasy fought for attention with images of his tussle with Tony earlier that day.

Eventually, the image of himself and Judith proved to be the most powerful, and he fell asleep too.

When he woke up again, it was already light. The other side of the bed was empty. He saw Judith's crumpled nightshirt lying on the floor.

The sound of percolating coffee drifted down the hall from the kitchen.

Peter leaned over to check the time on the clock radio: 7 a.m. Either he had slept through the alarm, or Judith had cancelled it before it had gone off.

His taxi wasn't due to arrive until 8.30, so there was plenty of time to get ready. His suitcase was almost packed. All that was left to do was pack yesterday's dirty clothes, some books and his toiletries.

'Hey, sleepyhead,' Judith said. Despite the early hour, she looked radiant.

'Hey,' he said, getting out of bed and following her.

He gave her a quick hug. She returned it warmly, but she let go before he did.

'I'm just going to pack up the rest of my things,' he said.

'All right. The coffee is nearly ready. And then we'll have breakfast together one last time, okay?'

'Okay,' he replied. 'Let me just get my phone. I forgot to take it with me yesterday.'

'I forgot to take mine with me yesterday too,' Judith said. 'When I got back from the library, I just grabbed something to eat and went straight back out to the meeting.'

Peter unplugged his phone from the charger.

His screen was filled with notifications. There were texts from various people, including Fay of course, whose tone had grown increasingly impatient the longer she had waited for an answer.

And there was a message from Inspector Rijsbergen:

Willem Rijsbergen

Many thanks for your message about the murders in Jerusalem. We eventually made the connection ourselves too. We had initially confined our investigation to Leiden, but we're now looking into the Jerusalem case. We will also be closely monitoring developments regarding the two missing men in Boston.

16:56

The message had been sent at around five o'clock in the afternoon.

It would have been around eleven in the morning here . . . Tony and I were still at Plimoth Plantation.

Peter looked at the clock. 7.16 a.m. in Boston, which would make it 1.16 p.m. in the Netherlands.

He sent a reply.

That's good to know. I hope that it proves to be a useful lead. My flight leaves at 11 am. Once I'm back in Leiden, I'll come to the station as soon as I can to find out more.

Kind regards, Peter de Haan

7:16

I'll tell him the whole story when I get home, Peter thought.

'Do you want to pack first?' Judith asked. 'Or have breakfast first?'

'I just want to send Tony a quick message,' Peter blurted out, almost without thinking. 'To thank him for yesterday. He left so suddenly.'

That's not a bad idea, actually . . .

Peter opened the email from Tony that had his bus ticket attached to it and pressed 'reply'.

'Dear Tony . . .' he typed.

What do you say to a dead man?

Dear Tony,

I just wanted to thank you for such an interesting and educational day in Plimoth Plantation and Plymouth yesterday. It was a shame we had to say goodbye to each other so suddenly, but I hope you were able to successfully take care of the business you said you had to attend to. The bus journey back to Boston went smoothly. Thanks for the ticket!

When do you plan to come back to Leiden? It would be great to see you again. Fay and I would love to have you over for dinner.

Best wishes,

Peter de Haan

'Actually,' Peter said, 'I think I'll pack first. It won't take long.'

It took less than ten minutes. His suitcase was heavier than it had been when he had arrived. He was leaving behind the gifts he had brought with him for Judith, but he had bought quite a few books during his visit.

He put *The Bible Unearthed* in his backpack.

They drank coffee in the kitchen together, their now-familiar ritual.

'Glad you came?'

'Yes, very. It's been so good to be able to spend so much time with you. I've really enjoyed it. It's deepened our friendship, I think.'

'Yes, that's true. It's been lovely having you here.'

She took his hand and squeezed it. 'Right then,' she said, 'I have to be at the library for eight. I've got an appointment with that professor from Chicago I was telling you about.'

'Oh, yes,' lied Peter, who had completely forgotten about it. He felt a sudden pang of jealousy. 'You did tell me. It's great that you're meeting so many interesting people out here.'

'You can manage on your own, can't you? You know where the taxi stand is. Your taxi should be there at half eight.'

'I'll be fine.'

Judith disappeared into the bathroom to brush her teeth. Peter cleared the breakfast table and put everything neatly back where it belonged.

When she had put on her coat, Judith came in and wrapped her arms around him. She gave him three kisses, alternating cheeks in a way that suddenly felt very formal to Peter, like she was no more than a colleague or an acquaintance.

'I'm really glad I came, Judith.'

She turned around, picked up her bag from the table in the hallway and gave him a final wave.

'Have a safe trip home!'

'I will!'

But Peter was not entirely convinced that he would.

I'll be so glad if I can just make it onto that plane, he thought.

Peter pulled his jacket on. With Judith already gone, there was no reason to stay. With a bit of luck, the taxi would be there already, and he could leave sooner.

He sent a text to Fay.

> Hey, darling, just said goodbye to Judith. About to get a taxi to the airport. And then I'll be on my way home, flying 1,000 kilometres an hour right back to you. ♥ ♥ ♥

8:02

Fay and Mark have placed so much trust in us. Neither of them made the tiniest bit of fuss about me staying with Judith for so long. And neither of us have broken that trust. How could we have done?

Peter left Judith's house keys on the kitchen table. He took one more look around the apartment he'd called home for the last few weeks.

Then he went outside and closed the outer door behind him for the final time.

As he walked across the campus to the taxi stand, the words from Jesus' Sermon on the Mount in the Gospel of Matthew came into his head:

Everyone who looks at a woman with lust has already committed adultery with her in his heart. If your right eye causes you to sin, tear it out and throw it away . . .

The taxi was indeed already waiting for him. The driver put Peter's bags in the boot while Peter got into the back of the car.

The driver pulled away without another word. The airport was less than twenty minutes away in good traffic, so he would be well on time.

'Flight to Europe, sir?' the man said a few minutes later.

'Yes, to the Netherlands,' Peter said.

'That's Terminal A,' the man said.

To pass the time, Peter took *The Bible Unearthed* out of his bag. He turned to the bibliography to see which books the authors had consulted. It was only then that he realised that there were appendices at the back of the book with biblical maps of Egypt, Sinai, Palestine and Israel.

The map of Sinai showed the route that the Israelites had taken on their journey out of Egypt – based on what was written about it in the Book of Exodus. They had gone in the direction of Mount Sinai, also known as Mount Horeb, in South Sinai, where Saint Catherine's Monastery had stood since the beginning of the fourth century.

Peter looked at the map, poring over it like an art historian scrutinising a canvas.

Is that what I think it is?

A feeling of excitement flooded through his body, not so very different from the excitement he had felt the night before.

Yes, that is what I think it is.

The puzzle pieces in his head were no longer whirling but starting to float down and slot into place.

Peter closed his eyes.

The driver looked at him in the rear-view mirror. 'Tired, sir?'

'No,' Peter said. He opened his eyes. 'There's been a change of plan.' He tried to speak calmly, but he was finding it difficult to hide his excitement.

I know what it is.

'Excuse me, sir?'

'I'm going to take a different flight. Take me to the terminal that the flights to North Africa leave from. I'm going to Egypt.'

If the man was surprised, he managed not to let it show. 'As you wish, sir.'

Peter rested his mobile phone on his lap and stared out at the landscape that flew past his window.

Of course . . .

He almost felt stupid for not having realised it earlier.

It was hidden in plain sight.

The driver dropped him off outside the terminal.

Inside, Peter followed the signs to the EgyptAir desk.

'Good morning,' he said to the woman behind the counter.

'Good morning to you too, sir,' she replied. She was a stunningly attractive woman with tawny skin and striking brown eyes. Her mascara made them look even bigger than they already were.

'How can I help you?'

'When is the next flight to Sharm el-Sheikh?'

'Well now, let's take a look,' said the woman, whose name was Faarouz according to the badge on her lapel. A moment later, she had found the answer to his question. 'There's a flight leaving in two hours, sir,' she said. 'You'll have two transfers: one in New York, and another in Cairo. That's quite a long journey. Altogether, it's going to take you twenty-four hours. The flights themselves are just over sixteen hours.'

Her perfectly manicured nails flew over the keyboard. She clicked the mouse a few times, then said, 'There are some seats left. You still need to go through passport and security, so you'll need to hurry. But it's not very busy today. May I see your passport?'

Peter gave her his passport and took out his credit card.

She entered his details, holding his passport with the long slim fingers of her left hand and typing with her right hand.

A deep furrow appeared on her brow.

'Is there a problem?'

'I just need to check something,' Faarouz said.

Peter felt like an invisible hand was gripping his throat.

Keep breathing, keep breathing . . . he thought, and he tried to smile as casually as he could. *Look like you completely understand, like this is the most normal thing in the world. Just a routine check* . . . *This gentleman has nothing to hide.*

She picked up the telephone and pressed two or three buttons before saying simply: 'Could you come here, please?'

That does not sound good.

Peter fought the urge to grab the passport out of her hand and walk away.

His hands trembled. He clasped them together so that it would be less noticeable.

'Come with us please, sir,' a stern voice behind him said.

He felt like a second invisible hand was wrapping its fingers around his neck. He slowly turned around and found himself staring at the impassive faces of two State Police troopers. Their right hands rested on the holsters of their guns.

He gulped, but then quickly regained his composure. 'Of course. No problem. What's the matter?'

'Come with us please, sir,' the man said again.

Faarouz handed Peter his passport. She avoided looking at him, but she made eye contact with the troopers. Peter could see the enormous relief and gratitude in her eyes.

'Standard procedure, sir.'

Peter walked between then, pulling his wheeled suitcase behind him.

They took him to a small room with large windows. The blinds were closed.

Peter sat down. He put his backpack on his lap and rested his hands on top of it, still firmly gripping his passport. 'What seems to be the problem, gentlemen?' he asked. *Take the initiative*, he thought. *Don't take the offensive, but don't be defensive either.*

The officers were young, perhaps in their mid-twenties, Peter estimated.

One of them had taken up position next to the door while the other sat at a table with a computer on it.

'Your passport, please.'

'Could you please first tell me . . .'

This must be about Tony. What else could it possibly be?

'If you give me your passport, I can explain it to you,' the officer said. He didn't even sound weary or irritated. 'I don't know what the problem is either, sir. We're going to find out . . .'

Peter handed over his passport, and the man typed in his name and passport number before swiping it through a machine.

A second later, Peter's passport photo appeared on the screen.

'You're on a watchlist, sir.'

'A watchlist? But . . .'

The trooper held up his hand to signal to Peter that he should stop talking.

Another image appeared on the screen. It looked like a document made up of various sections, with each box containing a few lines of text.

The trooper took the time to read it carefully.

'Okay,' he said, finally. He looked at the screen expressionlessly.

Here it comes.

An extraordinary feeling of calm came over Peter as if a protective cloak of impunity had been draped around him.

'Do you know a Tony Vanderhoop?'

'Yes, I know him,' Peter said.

Keep looking at him. Don't do what liars do and get caught up in the details. Don't widen your eyes. Sit still. Don't lean back in the chair . . .

'I went to Plimoth Plantation with him yesterday. Why?'

'What is your relationship to him?'

Peter told him that they had met in Leiden, and when he'd come to visit his friend at Harvard for three weeks, he had contacted Mr Vanderhoop. They had visited Plimoth Plantation together and then taken the bus to Plymouth to see Plymouth Rock and the Plymouth Hall Museum. And that was where they had said goodbye to each other because Tony had said he had some business to take care of. Tony had arranged for an Uber to take Peter to the bus terminus, and he'd caught a bus back to Boston from there.

The trooper nodded.

Peter's story seemed to match the one he had been expecting. 'Did Mr Vanderhoop say what that business was?'

Stick to the story, stick to the story . . .

'No, he didn't tell me.'

Now smile . . .

'I don't think he'd been expecting it,' Peter said. 'We'd originally planned to travel back together. But may I ask what this is about? And why my name came up?'

'Well,' the officer said, flicking up his eyes to look at his colleague as if he was asking for permission to reveal this information.

'The police, particularly the police in Leiden, are very keen to speak to him. Let's just leave it at that. I'm sure you'll understand that I can't go into the details.'

'Absolutely,' Peter said reasonably.

So the police in Leiden know too! But how did they find out?

'They've been looking into Mr Vanderhoop's recent movements,' the trooper said. 'Our colleagues in the Netherlands heard that he was visiting Plymouth with a foreign guest. To cut a long story short, your name was in the museum guestbook. The museum staff confirmed that Mr Vanderhoop arranged a taxi for you and that you both went your separate ways.'

Peter nodded.

'Have the Dutch police contacted you?' the officer asked.

'Yes,' Peter said. 'I got an email, but that was about something else. The police didn't know that I was on a day trip with Tony, uh . . . with Mr Vanderhoop.'

'And you've told them that now?'

'No, to be honest, I haven't. I wasn't aware that they wanted to talk to him.'

Now the two troopers nodded.

'I was quite disappointed yesterday, I must admit,' Peter said.

'What do you mean?'

'We had arranged to spend the day together, and I thought we would travel back to Boston together too. But then, in the museum entrance hall, he told me he had to go and deal with some business, and suddenly, he was gone.'

'And you really have no idea what that business was?'

'No . . . But it must have been something urgent, something that couldn't wait.'

'Yes, it must have.'

The officer typed a few short words or commands on the keyboard and then clicked the mouse a couple of times. The expression on his face was much friendlier now than when he had been asking Peter questions.

Peter got the impression that he was off the hook.

'You're free to go, sir,' the trooper said. He held out Peter's passport, but he kept hold of it when Peter tried to take it from him.

Peter smiled, but the man didn't smile back.

'If we look at the video from the security camera on the bus from Plymouth to Boston, we're going to see you on there, right?' he asked.

'Yes, of course,' Peter replied. He was amazed at the ease with which he told this lie. 'People were getting on and off, and the driver was getting bags out of the compartment under the bus. He was behind schedule, so he told me just to get on.'

'Did you get on in front or in back?'

Don't hesitate.

'At the back. The doors were open, and I saw two empty seats.'

There's probably only a camera at the front of the bus.

The trooper smiled – a little apologetically, Peter thought –

and let go of the passport. 'You're going to Egypt?' he asked as he stood up.

'Yes, I am,' Peter replied.

'Why Egypt? You have a ticket for Amsterdam, right?'

'That's right, I do,' Peter said. 'But I'm a lecturer at Leiden University. I teach History and Archaeology. I have a few weeks off. And I bought this book yesterday.'

He took *The Bible Unearthed* out of his bag. The till receipt that he had been using as a bookmark was sticking out of the top. 'I was reading it, and I thought: what the heck, why not? I'm going to go to Egypt. I've dreamed of going there my entire life, but I've never been . . .'

The man nodded in a way that said he knew everything about unfulfilled dreams.

'You're free to go, sir,' he said. 'Enjoy your flight. Whatever your destination might be.'

His colleague opened the door.

'And if Mr Vanderhoop contacts you, we'd like to know about it.'

'You'll be the first to know,' Peter promised.

Back at the EgyptAir desk, he had to listen to Faarouz's profuse apology before he could buy a ticket. She'd had a legal obligation to call the police and so on.

Peter forgave her graciously and received a beaming smile in return.

She checked in his suitcase, gave him his boarding passes and pointed him towards the gates.

Just as Faarouz had said, the lines at the border control desks were short, and it didn't take long for him to reach the front.

The man in the kiosk scanned his passport and stared at the

screen just long enough for Peter to start feeling uneasy again. But, eventually, he flipped to the right page in his passport, picked up a stamp and brought it down with a loud thud.

Peter almost cried with relief.

What a stroke of luck it was that they didn't ask me what time my bus left Plymouth.

He reached the gate before the flight had started boarding.

Once he was installed in his seat on the plane, Peter took *The Bible Unearthed* out of his bag again and thumbed to the map of the route that the Israelites were supposed to have taken from Egypt to the promised land.

Then he opened the images app on his phone and scrolled through his photos. The last three weeks flashed before his eyes, just as they say images of your whole life do at the moment of your death.

Like when you're drowning, for example . . .

Eventually, he found the image that Rijsbergen had shown to him and Mark: the tattoo that Coen Zoutman and Tony Vanderhoop had both had.

He pressed 'edit'.

Rotate.

Ninety degrees to the right . . .

The top of the triangle was now pointing to the right.

He rotated it again.

Ninety degrees to the right . . .

Now the top of the triangle pointed downwards, like a wafer in an ice cream sundae.

He held his phone next to the map in the book. The similarity was blindingly obvious. They matched so perfectly that he was amazed that he hadn't seen it before.

How could even Tony have missed this? . . . But you wouldn't see it unless you were actually looking for it.

The tornado in his head had stopped completely now, and the puzzle pieces had tumbled gently to the ground, each piece landing in exactly the right place, all the parts of the puzzle combining to form a complete picture.

Each individual piece was almost insignificant on its own. It was only when it was put together with the other pieces that it became meaningful.

Tony would have liked that metaphor.

The image that had now emerged was astounding.

The tattoo wasn't the all All-Seeing Eye or two pyramids or the sun over a mountain.

It was simply a map of Sinai that showed the route of the Exodus.

The outer edge represented the borders of Sinai itself, with the inner line showing the path that the Israelites were thought to have taken through the desert. Peter was on his way to the little circle, Mount Horeb, where God had given Moses the stone tablets.

At the foot of the mountain was a monastery that had been built on the site where God had spoken to Moses from the Burning Bush, commanding him to lead his people out of Egypt and take them to a new land, a land overflowing with milk and honey . . .

This was where the whole story had begun.

In Saint Catherine's Monastery.

PART THREE
THE PROMISED LAND

SINAI

Chapter 33

Rijsbergen's eyes hadn't deceived him.

He had recognised Tony Vanderhoop on the CCTV footage on *Unsolved Murder Mysteries*: the same build, the same curls poking out from under a baseball cap. Once the image had been cleaned up and enlarged by a whiz kid from digital forensics, there had been no doubt that it was him.

However, in reality, the Leiden Police Department still had nothing concrete. There was no evidence against Tony Vanderhoop other than that he had been in Jerusalem at the time of the murders. But when it was added to the fact that Tony had said nothing about it when Rijsbergen had spoken to him, it made him a very likely suspect. And even more suspiciously, he had turned up four years later in Leiden at the scene of another murder.

What are the odds, Rijsbergen wondered. *Admittedly, it would* be a hell of a coincidence, but we can't assume that this makes him a murderer.

And there was still nothing to link Tony Vanderhoop to Yona Falaina's death because he had already left the country when the young man had been killed.

Rijsbergen's investigation unit had immediately been reinstated and fully staffed so that new leads could be followed up. They had found out which flight Tony and his delegation had been booked onto and looked into whether he had actually flown back to Boston that day.

Rijsbergen questioned himself constantly. *Was it my fault?*

Although he was always the first to critically examine his own performance and the mistakes he might have made, he felt that in this case, he could hold his head high. When all was said and done, there were no clues that he had overlooked. Tony Vanderhoop hadn't been in the picture at all until now, so nobody had thought to check whether he had been on the flight with the rest of his group.

And we already had someone in custody: Herman van der Lede. The evidence against him is weak, but he knew that a square and compasses had been used in Coen Zoutman's murder and his refusal to reveal how he knew about them made him a prime suspect.

They had informed the police in Boston, and now Rijsbergen was in direct contact with them.

Just today, they had found out that Vanderhoop had been to Plimouth Plantation with a foreign guest the previous day. He'd had no mobile phone with him, so they had been unable to trace his location that way. They had found out about his movements indirectly, by asking around in Vanderhoop's network.

That was how they knew that he had been to the Pilgrim Hall Museum, where a foreign name had been found in the visitors' book.

Peter de Haan.

And yet again, Peter de Haan's name comes up, Rijsbergen noted with amazement. *Had he and Tony Vanderhoop really not known each other before the open evening in Leiden? Were Peter de Haan and his girlfriend involved in some way after all?*

Now, a completely different hypothesis was forming in Rijsbergen's mind. *Vanderhoop, De Haan and Spežamor murder Zoutman. Afterwards, De Haan and Spežamor give Vanderhoop an opportunity to escape. And finally, Peter calls 112 to report that he and Fay have found the body.*

If De Haan and Spežamor were involved, Vanderhoop could indeed have been back in the USA by the time Falaina was killed. Peter could have killed him – with or without Fay.

We can't rule anything out, Rijsbergen thought, *but it's not a particularly plausible hypothesis. The Jerusalem murders were four years ago, and Judith wasn't even a member of Loge Ishtar then. Her lodge didn't exist.*

On Saturday, at 10 a.m. local time, the police had paid a visit to the Pilgrim Hall Museum, where the ladies at the reception desk had confirmed that Vanderhoop and his guest had left the museum separately after saying goodbye in the entrance hall. It had been clearly visible on the CCTV video that they had shown to the police. Afterwards, a car had pulled up, presumably to take the Dutchman to the terminus on Pilgrims Road so he could take the bus back to Boston.

Their immediate priority was to arrest Tony Vanderhoop, but he appeared to have vanished from the face of the earth. The Boston Police also wanted to speak to Peter de Haan since he had been the last person seen with Vanderhoop. They hoped that he would be able to tell them where Vanderhoop might have gone. De Haan hadn't answered his phone when he'd been called.

The Boston Police had visited Judith Cherev's apartment where De Haan had been staying for the last few weeks. The officers had eventually found Cherev in the library, but De Haan, it turned out, had already been on his way to Boston Logan airport.

De Haan's name had been put on a watchlist. As soon as he checked in at the airport, the agent at the desk would have received an alert with instructions to call the police so that he could be questioned.

Rijsbergen knew that there was nothing he could do right now to expedite the situation in America.

As soon as De Haan set foot on Dutch soil, he would be apprehended and taken to the police station in Leiden. Rijsbergen wanted another chance to interview him, more rigorously this time, about the events of that fatal evening. And about the exact nature of his connection to Tony Vanderhoop.

Fay Spežamor would also be picked up for further questioning the next day.

But first, Rijsbergen and Van de Kooij were going to go to the Haaglanden Penitentiary in Zoetermeer, the prison where Herman van der Lede had been in pre-trial detention for the last six weeks.

Herman the Silent, Rijsbergen thought.

It was a short drive to the prison, less than half an hour usually, but this time it felt like it was taking much longer.

We're so close to solving this case now, I can feel it . . .

They had already visited Herman several times, and each visit had been just as pointless as the last. The man had only sat and stared at the wall, looking right through Rijsbergen and Van de Kooij as if they were invisible.

He had remained silent during his preliminary hearing as well – at one point, the magistrate had asked, quite earnestly, if Van der Lede was perhaps hard of hearing.

Herman's determination not to speak even extended to his wife Jenny who had visited him every week; he had never said so much as a 'hello' to her.

The visiting room in the prison was bare except for a table and the four chairs around it. Van de Kooij sat down, but Rijsbergen was too agitated to sit still.

Rijsbergen got straight to the point. 'Today is your last day here,' he said as soon as Van der Lede was brought into the room.

It was hard to tell who looked at Rijsbergen with the most surprise, Van de Kooij or Van der Lede.

'What does that mean?' Van der Lede said, ending six weeks of self-imposed silence.

'Take a seat,' Rijsbergen instructed him, although he didn't sit down himself.

The guard brought the prisoner to the table, then left the room and waited in the hallway.

Well, I've managed to get a response out of him, at least.

'I'm convinced that you're innocent,' Rijsbergen said. 'And I'm going to explain why.'

Van der Lede looked at him expectantly, as though he was watching the conclusion of a thrilling crime series on television.

'When was the last time you were in Jerusalem?'

'Jerusalem?' Herman asked, looking bewildered. It was clear that this wasn't a question he had been expecting to be asked.

'I've never been to Jerusalem,' he replied. 'Jenny and I have wanted to go for a long time, but—'

'Exactly,' Rijsbergen said, cutting him off. 'Listen, there's a new suspect in the case. We expect him to be arrested very soon. It's just a matter of time.'

Pure bluff, Rijsbergen thought. *But let's see how he reacts.*

'We can link this person to two murders. We also have strong evidence linking him to Coen Zoutman's murder and possibly Yona Falaina's as well. That would completely exonerate you of any involvement in their deaths.'

Van der Lede nodded.

Van de Kooij tried to adopt a solemn expression that would say that he knew precisely what Rijsbergen was talking about. But Rijsbergen could tell from his furrowed brow that he wasn't entirely sure what was going on.

'Yes,' Van der Lede said.

You're going to have to say a bit more than that.

'So, now that we're sure that you're not guilty . . . Right, Van de Kooij?' Rijsbergen looked down at his colleague, who immediately nodded back. '. . . We would just like to know how you knew that a square and compasses had been used in Coen Zoutman's murder when nobody but the killer could have known about them. And the person who found his body, obviously. If you can explain that convincingly, then there's probably nothing to stop you leaving this building shortly, as a free man.'

'It was me,' Herman said.

'What do you mean?' Rijsbergen asked genially.

'I was the one who found Coen.'

Rijsbergen opened his mouth to speak but found himself unable to say anything.

'You *what?*' Van de Kooij asked.

'I found him first.'

'And why didn't you tell us that?' asked Rijsbergen, finding his voice again.

Van der Lede sat up straight and folded his hands together as though he was about to pray. 'I didn't think it was . . .' he began, but then he stopped.

'Important?' Van de Kooij suggested. 'All that bad? Serious enough? Worth the hassle?'

'Bad. I didn't think it was really all that bad,' Van der Lede replied, as though it had been a multiple-choice question with only one answer. 'Don't get me wrong,' he went on, suddenly giving the impression that he was about to take control of the conversation. 'It's always terrible when someone dies.'

'Dies!' Van de Kooij exclaimed.

'Easy there,' Rijsbergen urged his colleague. 'Let's hear what Meneer Van der Lede has to say.'

Van de Kooij pressed his lips together so tightly that they started to turn white.

'Let me put it this way,' Van der Lede said. 'It's always sad when someone dies. I . . .'

Rijsbergen decided to sit down after all. Over his long career, he had interviewed more people than he could count, and he had developed an intuition about the moment when a suspect was about to reveal the truth. It was something in the tone of their voice, their posture, a clarity in their eyes . . . It was a confession, ultimately, and confession always brought relief. In a way, it was comparable to walking home carrying an increasingly heavy load, and the relief of finally being able to put it down when you got there.

'The event was nearly finished, and I was about to go home,' Van der Lede said. 'But Jenny wanted to stay behind. I went upstairs to get the CDs that we had been using that evening. The temple door was open, and when I went in, I saw Coen lying on the floor. There was a spotlight shining on him. It made him look like a performer on a stage. Really bizarre. I don't think there was anyone else in the room, but I can't be certain. Although someone could have been hiding behind the curtains. I went over to him, and I could see that he was already dead, and that's when I noticed the square and compasses.' Then, as if he had reached the end of the story, he stopped talking.

'And what were you thinking then, Herman?' Rijsbergen asked. 'What was going on in your head?'

'Can I be frank with you?'

'This would be the time to do just that, Herman.'

'To be very honest, I felt relief.' Van der Lede's face flushed pink. 'This is the man who saw to it that Jenny could never be chairwoman. If you knew how much that hurt her! I don't know how often I've had to hear about it, about how frustrating it was for her. Yet another man in the chair, and in a co-Masonic lodge! As if that wasn't already bad enough, it was someone whose ideas about interpreting the symbols and the stories and everything else that Jenny told you about were far too liberal. I saw him lying there, and I thought: now the way is clear for Jenny. Sorry, but that's what I thought. I backed away from his body, but I kept looking at him, and then . . .' he looked at Rijsbergen and Van de Kooij in turn, as if he was telling an exciting story to his mates in the pub.

Rijsbergen slammed his hand down hard on the table. 'Come on!' he bellowed. 'We don't have time for this!'

'I heard footsteps behind me, someone leaving the room. They were very quiet, but I definitely heard footsteps. I stood there for about ten, maybe fifteen seconds until I heard the function room door close. I didn't turn around, partly because I was scared and partly because I thought: what you don't know can't hurt you . . . Then I went downstairs, got my coat, got on my bike and went home. Peter de Haan and Fay Spežamor must have gone upstairs shortly afterwards.'

'He's not off the hook yet,' Van de Kooij said to Rijsbergen.

Rijsbergen nodded. 'Why didn't you tell us about this weeks ago?' he asked. 'My colleague here is right. This doesn't let you off the hook – you still had the opportunity to murder Zoutman, and you had a motive as well. So why did you stay silent for so long?'

Van der Lede's bottom lip trembled. His face contorted into the ugly grimace of someone trying very hard not to cry. But he couldn't stop himself. 'I was so ashamed!' he managed to blubber before he lost his resolve and gave into uncontrollable sobbing.

All traces of his cool indifference and good-riddance-to-bad-rubbish attitude had vanished.

The two detectives gave him time to pull himself together.

He wiped his teary eyes and runny nose on his shirt sleeve and then spoke again. 'I was just so terribly ashamed,' he said. 'And I'm still ashamed. Because his death made me happy. Because I didn't have the courage to turn around. Because I didn't tell anyone about it afterwards. Because innocent people might have been arrested for it. Because I obstructed the case . . . and it was all because of the stupid chairmanship . . .' He started to cry again.

Rijsbergen heaved a deep sigh.

All the time we've lost . . . The investigation being put on the back burner after he was arrested . . . On the other hand, the investigation had stalled anyway. It only got moving again because Van de Kooij discovered the Jerusalem connection.

'Well,' Rijsbergen said, 'even if you are telling us the truth, we can't let you go now, as I'm sure you'll understand. But that's no longer up to us. Someone else will have to make that decision. They'll also be looking into what sort of consequences you'll be facing for withholding such crucial information.'

Van der Lede buried his face in his hands.

Rijsbergen and Van de Kooij got up and left the room. The guard was still standing outside.

'What do you think?' Van de Kooij asked when they were back in the car park.

'I think it all happened just the way he says,' Rijsbergen said. 'What a fool . . . He's never been to Jerusalem, he says. We'll have to see if that checks out. But if he's right, and he did hear someone leave the temple and go downstairs to the function room, it leaves us with a much smaller pool of suspects. There were only about twenty-five, possibly thirty people left at the end of the evening, and we have all of their names.'

'And it means that De Haan and Spežamor probably did go upstairs shortly afterwards and find the body.'

They drove back to Leiden.

'I think it would be a good idea to contact the Freemasons in Boston,' Van de Kooij said. 'Peter de Haan took a tour of their building, didn't he? They might be able to tell us more about Vanderhoop.'

'I was already planning to,' Rijsbergen lied.

When he turned on his computer back in his office, he saw that he had a message from his contact in the Boston Police Department.

Dear Inspector Rijsbergen,

We briefly interviewed Mr De Haan at Logan airport, but unfortunately, he was unable to provide any further information about Mr Vanderhoop's intended plans after they left Pilgrim Hall Museum. Matters have been complicated by the fact that Mr Vanderhoop appears to have vanished into thin air. The last sighting of him was 24 hours ago. So it looks like we might have a missing person case on our hands. He has a boat moored in Boston, *The Pilgrim*, but we have been able to confirm that it has not left its usual berth. A motorboat called *Sea Breeze* was reported stolen from Plymouth Harbor, but we are so far unaware of a potential connection to our case. No reports have been made of Tony's disappearance. It would appear that nobody is missing him – he is unmarried, has no brothers or sisters and both parents are deceased. There is no other family. We are stepping up our efforts to find him.

We'll keep in touch.

Inspector Luigi D'Amico

Rijsbergen replied with a short email thanking Inspector D'Amico for keeping him informed. Then, he entered the search terms 'Freemasons' and 'Boston' into Google. The top search result was precisely what he was looking for: massfreemasonry. org.

Rijsbergen clicked on the 'Contact Us' link, and a form appeared. But with those things, you never knew where your message would end up and how long it would be before you got an answer. There was a tiny search box at the top of the page. He typed in 'Walter Lunt', the name of the man Peter de Haan had mentioned in his email. This produced a few results, mostly the minutes of the lodge meetings in which Lunt had been involved.

Then, he noticed a telephone number, with the words 'within MA' after it in brackets, meaning that it could only be called from numbers within the state of Massachusetts. It took him and Van de Kooij a while to work out how to call the number from the Netherlands, but once they knew how, they managed to get Walter Lunt on the line surprisingly quickly.

As a librarian, he was, of course, likely to be somewhat tied to his place of work and quite easy to find.

'Walter Lunt speaking.'

In a few short sentences, Rijsbergen explained who he was, that he had been given his name by Peter de Haan, and his reason for calling. When he mentioned Tony Vanderhoop, Rijsbergen could almost feel the frostiness coming through the wires from the other side of the ocean.

Walter Lunt said that he would only be prepared to talk to Rijsbergen after he had sent him an email with his own telephone number, his police identification number and the name, address and telephone number of his contact person in the Boston Police.

Rijsbergen had no choice but to oblige him. He hung up and immediately sent Lunt an email with all the information he had asked for.

Within seconds, he received a reply from Lunt informing him that he would check the details and get back to him.

'Pfff,' was all Van de Kooij could say.

'Indeed,' Rijsbergen said. 'He, uh . . . He wants to make sure it's safe to talk to us, apparently.'

While they waited for him to respond, Rijsbergen googled 'Walter Lunt' and found out that he was an author who wrote science fiction and thrillers about secret societies and unsolved mysteries.

His most recent book, *A Song in Stone*, was about 'the mystery of Rosslyn Chapel and the demise of the Knights Templar'.

'Ah,' Rijsbergen said. 'He's a thriller writer. That explains it. Maybe he thinks he's somehow got himself mixed up in one of the conspiracies that he writes about.' He clicked on some of the links in the search results.

Ten or so minutes later, the phone rang, making Rijsbergen jump. He turned the speaker on so that Van de Kooij could listen in.

'This is Walter Lunt,' the voice on the other end of the line said, sounding much friendlier now. 'I understand that you would like to ask me some questions.'

'That's correct, Mr Lunt.'

'Call me Walter.'

'Excellent, thank you. My name is Willem Rijsbergen.'

'A pleasure to make your acquaintance. How can I help you?'

'As I told you earlier, we're investigating two murders that took place about a month and a half ago in Leiden. Two local Freemasons were murdered within a very short space of time. One of them was an older man, a lodge chairman, and the other was a younger man.'

'Yes, Peter told me about it. Did he also tell you that two members of our lodge have gone missing?'

'Yes, we're aware of that case. It's all very troubling.'

'It certainly is,' Walter said. 'I've already called the Boston Police to inform them of the cases in Jerusalem and Leiden. At the moment, they don't have any reason to suspect foul play in Sam and George's disappearance, but it is remarkable that all three cases concern a chairman and his young pupil.'

'The obvious conclusion would be that the three cases are connected in some way.'

'I would be inclined to think so too, yes. But right now, all we can do is wait.'

'The Boston Police have promised to keep me informed of any developments.'

'Peter drew a picture of a symbol and asked me if I recognised it. I do have some knowledge of symbols, but I can't make anything of this one, I'm afraid.'

'That's quite all right. That's not actually what I wanted to speak to you about. I was calling about some similar murders in Jerusalem.'

'All I know about that,' Walter said, 'is that two of our brothers were killed there. Needless to say, I don't know the details of any other similarities. We assumed that you would be aware of those.'

'We are now, yes,' Rijsbergen said. 'But Tony Vanderhoop's name came up during our investigation, and that led us to you. We've found out that Tony Vanderhoop was in Jerusalem at the time of the murders there.'

'That's correct. I was with him.'

'You were there too?'

'Yes. That's not a secret. We were part of a small delegation visiting our brothers there. We travelled quite extensively in Israel.'

Rijsbergen digested this new information. 'But the point is,' he said, growing slightly nervous under the watchful eyes of Van de Kooij who had been staring at him throughout the entire call. 'that Tony Vanderhoop was also visiting Leiden with a delegation when the murders were carried out here.'

'Yes, that is rather curious.'

'The police in Boston are looking for him, but there's been no sign of him since yesterday afternoon.'

'Would you like me to make some enquiries in my network?'

'If you would, yes. Thank you. But I was hoping that you could tell me more about Tony. Was he a member of your lodge?'

'He was a member, yes,' Walter said. 'But he was expelled three years ago. He's no longer a Freemason.'

'Expelled?'

'Yes, expelled. What can I say? Vanderhoop is a rude . . . Actually, it might be best if I don't finish that sentence.'

'So what happened?'

'That's a very long story and also a very short one.'

'Then tell me the short version.'

Walter let out a mirthless laugh. 'Tony spoke at our chairman Joseph Nun's funeral. He'd died of cancer . . . It was dreadful. Tony gave the most appallingly inappropriate speech. He told us how fortunate we were that our chairman had passed because it gave us the opportunity to go in a new direction and other such nonsense. He said that the stories and symbols should bring people together rather than divide them, which is what he felt would happen if people were allowed to find their own meanings in them.'

'Wow. That's—'

'He didn't get to finish his speech. Let's just say that a few people stopped him and escorted him outside. Afterwards, he came to the lodge on numerous occasions, trying to seek redress. That became very unpleasant. Intimidating, even. I reported him to the police, and it went to court, which resulted in a restraining order.'

'Wow.'

'You know, people like Tony Vanderhoop have no place in our fraternity. The whole purpose of our meeting together is that we can exchange views with each other, openly and freely. Someone gives a lecture, and we discuss it. Nothing is set in stone, and we don't judge anyone whose interpretation deviates from the one that's generally accepted. Although "deviate" isn't really the right word because we're non-dogmatic. We have no orthodox interpretations, so there's nothing to deviate from.

Heterodoxy, holding unorthodox opinions, can only be possible when there's a single interpretation imposed by a higher authority, and it's seen as the only correct interpretation by the entire organisation. So if one's opinion differed from that, then it would be a deviation. But we don't have anything like that.'

If this is the short version of the story, what's the long version like?

'Anyway, Willem . . . What I mean to say is that people like Tony can't cope with this, with such fluid interpretations of the symbols and stories. Of course, the rest of the world has trouble with it too. The churches are full of people who want their priest or pastor to tell them what to think. Here's what happened in this Bible story, and this is what it means. There are a lot of people who prefer not to think for themselves, let me just put it that way.'

'But Tony's speech . . .'

'Oh yes, exactly, his speech. Our chairman thought that the emphasis in Freemasonry should be on the "free" and that nothing should be set in stone. In contrast, Tony's view was that there could be no fraternity, no society, if you didn't commit to a set of agreements about how certain things should be understood. Of course, he had a Christian background – or has, I should say – which is usually a good combination with Freemasonry. But, in the end, he simply didn't belong here.'

'What do you think, Walter? Is a man like Tony capable of murder?'

'What can I say? I think that everyone is capable of murder. To be honest, I've felt like murdering people myself at times. On TV shows about serial killers, they interview the murderer's neighbours and colleagues, and they always say that he was "such a nice, ordinary man", and that they never noticed anything unusual about him. Tony *is* a man with a great deal of anger inside him. And yes, he was in Jerusalem, he was in Leiden, and he was in Boston. He had the opportunity in every case, but did he have a motive? He didn't even know those people in Leiden and Jerusalem. And I can't imagine that he would have killed Sam and George simply because they didn't share his views about the stories in the Bible.'

'I see your point, Walter.'

'So . . .'

He's right that the likeness between the cases doesn't necessarily indicate a link. But one plus one is increasingly starting to look like it adds up to two.

'I'd like to thank you for taking the time to talk to me, Walter,' Rijsbergen said, bringing the call to a close.

And I'd also like to organise a welcoming committee at Schiphol airport for Peter de Haan.

'My pleasure,' Walter said.

After exchanging a few more polite pleasantries, they ended the call.

'Six murders,' said Van de Kooij.

'Well, four deaths, in any case,' Rijsbergen corrected him, although he was inclined to think the same thing.

'You're right,' Van de Kooij admitted. 'Four dead, two missing. Although the chances of them being found alive get smaller by the hour. The two men in Jerusalem were bludgeoned to death, just like Coen Zoutman. But Yona Falaina was suffocated with a cushion or something similar, and the two missing men were probably drowned. If they were all killed by the same person, then the murderer doesn't have a modus operandi.'

Van de Kooij rolled the 'r' of the word 'operandi' in his thick Leiden accent.

'I'll send the Boston Police an email now,' Rijsbergen said, 'and give them an idea of where our thinking is headed.'

Fifteen minutes later, he had typed up a concise report on the latest developments and sent it to his opposite number in Boston. He copied the text into his own case file.

'Well,' Van de Kooij said, 'it's starting to look very clear to me that all signs point to Vanderhoop, don't you think? And Tony Vanderhoop apparently doesn't want to be found.'

'Yes,' Rijsbergen said pensively. 'Or he could have been involved in an accident. But if not . . .'

'Then?'

'Then we've got nothing.'

'Hmph. If he really wanted to disappear . . . Well, that's a piece of cake in America. You just assume another identity, move out of state . . .'

The telephone rang.

'Rijsbergen.'

A voice came over the speaker. 'Hello, this is Fay Spežamor.'

'Mevrouw Spežamor, I'm so glad you called.'

'I've just had a very odd message from Peter,' she said. 'He sent it just before his flight left New York. I've tried calling him, but I couldn't get through.'

'An odd message?'

'Yes. He's not coming back to the Netherlands tomorrow at all. He's taken another flight.'

'Another flight? Where to?'

'To Egypt. To Sharm el-Sheikh.'

Chapter 34

The Boeing 737's tyres hit the runway with a loud thud. Peter had watched Sharm el-Sheikh airport come into view as the plane was landing. It was a surprisingly modern complex with two enormous terminal buildings but just two runways; they curved around to meet each other at either end like an enormous karting track. There were drifts of sand here and there, blown onto the runway from the desert that surrounded the airport. Two aeroplanes were waiting on the tarmac with their noses pointing at the terminal, both about the same size as the plane that Peter had boarded more than an hour ago in Cairo. Three small Cessnas stood nearby.

There was room for almost two hundred passengers on board the Boeing, but it was less than half full. Peter's fellow travellers seemed to be mostly Egyptian, probably people who lived here or who had come for a holiday. There was also a group of men who were obviously travelling together. The moment the aircraft had levelled out after take-off, a few them had unbuckled their seatbelts and congregated in the aisle next to the other seated members of their group, all holding cans of beer that they seemed to have acquired almost magically. Despite the heat, they were impeccably dressed in suits and ties. Peter predicted that they would take their ties off the second they left the aircraft and entered the searing heat of the Sinai desert. They appeared to be businessmen, perhaps people with interests in one of the many hotels along the coast that now stood empty.

Tourism in the area had declined heavily since Al Qaida and other fundamentalist groups affiliated with the Islamic State had started to appear in the Sinai Peninsula. There had been fighting between these loosely organised factions and the Egyptian army. There had been attacks on army bases too, sometimes resulting in many deaths. At the end of October 2015, ISIS had claimed responsibility for a bomb attack on a passenger plane that had blown up over Sinai, killing all two hundred and seventeen of the mostly Russian passengers and the seven crew members on board.

While it was easy to assume that it would be simple to track down these militant groups in the desert, it was a vast area – twenty-five times the size of the Netherlands – with geographical features like canyons and caverns that offered more hiding places than one might expect. Moreover, it was impossible to tell from an airborne drone whether a group of men sitting around a tent were terrorists or just members of the Bedouin tribes who had lived in this area for centuries.

The handful of western tourists who joined Peter when he stepped out into the blistering desert heat – it felt like walking fully clothed into an infrared sauna – were all young, and they happily accepted the heat as part of their holiday experience.

They walked in a long line to the terminal where their passports were given cursory glances by the border officials. Inside the terminal building, even away from direct heat and blinding light of the sun, it was still very warm.

Soon a baggage tug arrived, pulling a convoy of open cages full of suitcases and backpacks that the baggage handlers dumped in a large pile next to a broken carousel.

Peter picked up his suitcase and was about to head towards

the exit when a young couple caught his eye. They were friendly-looking twenty-somethings who gave the impression that they were somewhat overwhelmed by the adventure they had embarked upon. They were both dressed in the universal hippy uniform of baggy trousers and colourful shirts faded by bright sunshine and overwashing. The young man's cheerful face was framed by curly hair that reached his shoulders, and he had a two-day growth of stubble that made him look scruffy and unkempt. The girl with him had dreadlocked hair pulled back with a red scarf.

Peter decided to offer to share his taxi with them. He remembered how lost he'd felt at their age whenever he got off a plane, bus or train and entered a strange new world. The no-budget nature of his travels had always meant that he'd never been able to afford the luxury of just jumping in a cab.

'Would you like to share a taxi?' he asked them, forgoing the polite introductions.

The delighted reactions told him that his suggestion had hit the mark.

The young German man launched into a story about a man they had met at their hotel in Cairo. He'd seemed very nice at first and had offered to arrange cheap flights to Sharm el-Sheik for them. They had accepted his offer, but when they got to the airport, the same nice man had suddenly demanded more money. He'd threatened to call the police and tell them that the young pair had refused to pay him at all. 'I have many friends here,' he'd said menacingly. Naturally, they had handed over the extra money, but it had almost completely wiped out their funds. Since they already had the now very expensive tickets in their pockets, they had decided to go to Sharm el-Sheikh anyway, intending to live as cheaply as possible for the next few days, perhaps by sleeping on the beach.

Peter offered to pay for the taxi. The girl flung her arms around his neck, while the young man clapped him heartily on the back.

The man, who was called Melchior, sat next to the taxi driver with his little backpack perched on his knee. Peter shared the back seat with Katja. As they left the airport's grounds, Katja grabbed Peter's hand and didn't let go until the taxi dropped them off on a street that ran parallel to the shore. On the beach, there was a colourful collection of small thatched huts with clothes pegged out on washing lines strung between them.

When they pulled up, Peter paid the driver, and Katja hugged him again. Melchior shook his hand profusely. They were both clearly relieved to have been helped out of their predicament.

'In the guidebook it says that there are places where you can sleep on the beach without anyone bothering you,' Melchior said. 'And everything is cheap here, so I think we'll be able to manage for the next five days.'

'Good luck!' said Peter.

'We really want to visit Saint Catherine's Monastery and climb Mount Sinai,' Katja went on. 'That's why we accepted that man's offer in the first place. Getting there is going to cost us most of the money we have left.'

Peter had been hoping to avoid having to deal with other tourists by taking a taxi to the monastery as early as he could the next morning, so he judiciously chose to remain tight-lipped about his plans.

He would have preferred to leave for the monastery straight away, but the man sitting next to him on his flight had advised him that he would have trouble finding a driver willing to make the trip so late in the afternoon. By six o'clock, it would be completely dark, and considering recent events, everyone tended to avoid the empty desert roads at night because you had no idea what sort of people you might run into.

Peter said goodbye to Katja and Melchior and made his way to the first hotel that he saw, more or less exactly where the taxi had dropped them off.

When he left the bright sunlight outside and stepped into the lobby, it took some time for his eyes to adjust enough for him to be able to make out his surroundings. But once they did, there was no one to be seen.

He pressed the reception bell a few times until a young man jumped up from underneath the desk. He had clearly been taking a nap on a mattress on the floor, and he looked at Peter sleepily. He leafed through a large book to see if there were any rooms available, but Peter could see from the rows of keys hanging on the board behind him that this was purely for show.

While the young man copied his passport details into the ledger, Peter looked around him. There were no lights on in the lobby, but he could see that there were rugs on the floor and paintings made on papyrus hanging on the walls. It looked like it had been decorated by someone with great taste and an eye for authentic Egyptian details once upon a time, but now it looked shabby and neglected. When his eyes had adapted to the gloom, he saw couches arranged in a U-shape around a coffee table with people lying on them, all asleep. A fan turned above their heads, but too slowly to cool the air at all.

The room that Peter was given, however, was spotlessly clean and smelled fresh, with white bed linen that looked like it had just been changed.

When he tried to plug in his phone to charge it, he discovered that the charger he had brought with him didn't fit in the Egyptian socket. Then he realised that the travel adaptor he'd bought at Schiphol was still plugged into the socket in Judith's Harvard apartment.

What an idiot. I'll see if I can buy one somewhere. I doubt I'm the first foreigner here to be caught out like this.

Even the shower worked perfectly, he realised with relief when he stood under its warm jet to wash away the dust and sweat of travelling. The muscles in his neck, back and shoulders relaxed as the hot water flowed over his body.

He put on a loose cotton shirt and long Bermuda shorts. When he went back outside, it was still very warm, and he almost felt like he was on holiday. The lights of the seafront bars twinkled invitingly in the twilight, and the waves washed gently over the sand.

The atmosphere in the shop next to the hotel was as languid as the lobby had been. The shopkeeper gave the impression of having given up all hope and sat watching a football match on a small television with the sound turned off.

When Peter showed him his mobile phone cable, the man sprang into action. He strode purposefully to one of the shelves and came back with a universal adaptor plug.

'Dollar?' Peter asked.

The shopkeeper held up both hands. He waggled all ten fingers and grinned horribly, revealing a nearly toothless mouth.

Peter paid him with a crisp, new ten-dollar note that he'd withdrawn from a cash machine at Boston Logan shortly before his flight.

The shopkeeper handed him the plug, and then patted his chest with his hand, saying, '*Shukran, shukran.*' Thank you, thank you.

Peter went back to his hotel room where he 'put his phone to the teat' as Fay so amusingly liked to put it. He realised straight away that he had no network coverage at all here. Maybe he could find an internet café with Wi-Fi later.

At the airport in New York, he had texted Fay to tell her that there had been a change of plan and that he had decided, on a whim, to fulfil a long-held dream of going to Sharm el-Sheikh. He hadn't even been lying.

Saint Catherine's.

Now he was certain that the little circle on the tattoo was a reference to the monastery. The outer triangle represented the Sinai Peninsula, the inner lines stood for the route the Israelites had taken. Now that he could see it, it was inconceivable that he hadn't realised it before.

If he was right, that was.

In any case, Tony hadn't seen it. Otherwise, he would have come here long ago.

The monastery held a collection of thousands of manuscripts that were so unique as to be genuinely priceless.

Even if it was likely to be useless, his phone was at least charging up now.

Peter left the hotel and went to a deserted bar on the beach. It was little more than a few tables and chairs arranged on a wooden deck with a narrow bar running along its length. The four men standing behind it were visibly bored. He ordered a beer and took it to one of the chairs closest to the water's edge. Droplets of condensation ran down the bottle, leaving trails that looked like little rivers on a glassy landscape. He took a couple of long, satisfying swigs of the cold beer.

It's not really surprising that nobody ever considered Tony Vanderhoop as a possible suspect, Peter thought. *He's a nice enough guy, and he seemed to be as shocked as everyone else about what had happened. And he was literally out of the picture in Leiden because his delegation had gone back the USA.*

The day before Yona Falaina was murdered.

He was a man with a mission who had granted himself a licence to kill. A consummate actor, a conman who managed to pull the wool over my – and everyone else's – eyes.

Could he really have drowned? Had he really been swallowed up by the ocean's cold, black depths? How ironic . . . To meet the same fate he'd inflicted on Sam and George.

Peter had been nervous when he'd boarded the plane at Boston Logan airport, inwardly cursing the pilot when the aircraft was kept standing at the gate. When the flight from New York's JFK had been delayed too, Peter had been convinced that a team of heavily armed police was going to storm the plane and arrest him for murder. And even when the plane's wheels had left American soil, he'd still been unable to completely relax. When the plane banked to change direction for the first time, Peter had been sure that it was about to take him back to New York where he'd be thrown straight into an American jail cell.

It wasn't until the screens in the cabin had shown that the aircraft was flying far from the coast that he had finally dared to think he was safe.

This must be how Tony felt when he was on his flight from Amsterdam to Boston.

Peter finished his beer in no time at all and motioned to one of the men at the bar who hurried over with another bottle.

He saw two people walking along the shoreline and recognised them as Melchior and Katja. He beckoned them over, and they veered away from the path they had been taking along the water's edge and headed towards him. Katja flung her arms around him like a long-lost friend and planted a warm, slightly wet kiss on his neck. Melchior embraced him in a strong, brotherly hug.

'Come and sit down,' Peter said. 'Do you want a beer?' They

hesitated, and Peter remembered their precarious financial situation. 'My treat. Let's have something to eat, too.'

'No, no, Peter,' Melchior protested earnestly and held up his hands in polite refusal. He spoke English with a typically German accent. 'We wouldn't want to take advantage of your kindness.'

'Listen,' Peter said adamantly. 'You had a bad experience with that man in Cairo. Let me restore your faith in humanity by buying you a meal and a few drinks. You can repay me by sitting with me and telling me your stories. I'm all alone here, and I could do with some company.'

Ultimately, their objections were no match for how hungry and thirsty they were, and they gave in.

Without having to be asked, the barman brought over two more bottles of beer. They ordered extra-large portions of shawarma and salad.

'What are you doing all alone in a place like this?' Katja wanted to know.

'I teach history at Leiden University,' Peter told her truthfully. 'I've always wanted to visit Saint Catherine's Monastery. I was taking a week off anyway, and I thought . . .'

'It's now or never,' Katja said.

'Yes, something like that,' Peter said. 'My . . .' He hesitated and found his own hesitation troubling, like he wanted to deny Fay's existence.

'My partner, my girlfriend, had other commitments, so she couldn't come with me. She has a young daughter too, so it's not easy for her to get away from home.'

It was a watertight story, almost without a word of a lie. You could have a memory like a sieve if you always told the truth: you just had to keep telling your story exactly as it had happened. Only liars needed to have perfect recall.

Katja told him that she and Melchior – not her boyfriend but a fellow student – were both studying Egyptology. They had been on a dig for six weeks in Saqqara, a village about thirty kilometres from Cairo. The University of Leiden had led digs there every March and April since 1975. Peter even knew some of the people Melchior and Katja had been working with. When that year's Saqqara excavation project had ended, they'd decided to go travelling together, but then they'd ended up being tricked by the villain in Cairo.

As the plates of food and more bottles of beer were brought to the table, they told Peter about how wonderful it had been to start work early each morning, excavating Egypt's history centimetre by centimetre the old-fashioned way with a trowel, bucket, sieve and brush. They'd been happy to work for long hours because they knew that at any moment, they might uncover a find, the sort of discovery that they'd dreamed of since they were children. When they looked up from their work and gazed at the horizon, their view had been of Pharaoh Djoser's famous step pyramid. It was such a fantastic place to work! And so many spectacular finds had been made at the site, like the double statue of the high priest Meryneith and his wife Aniuia that had been found there in 2001. Katja and Melchior had seen it in the Egyptian Museum in Cairo. The desert near the village of Saqqara had been used as a burial ground for senior Egyptian officials and other important people in Ancient Egypt for thousands of years.

'Personally, I'm most interested in Pharaoh Akhenaten's period,' said Melchior brightly, clearly revived by the food and beer. 'I'm hoping to make it the subject of my thesis, maybe even a PhD, if I can.' He paused as if this was a confession that he suddenly regretted, as if speaking the wish out loud might spoil his chances of making it come true.

After a moment, he continued. 'Akhenaten was the pharaoh who tried to transform religion in Egypt. He wanted to replace its traditional polytheism with a religion that worshipped only one god, the sun god Aten. It's incredibly interesting.'

Of course, Peter had heard of this pharaoh and his attempts to reform the Egyptian religion, but he didn't know much about the finer details. He did know about the theories that suggested that the pursuit of monotheism during this period had influenced the change to monotheism in Judaism, which originally had many gods.

In fact, there were still references to multiple gods in the Bible that had never been removed, particularly in the Psalms. For example, in Psalm 88, David sings: 'There is none like you among the gods, O Lord.' Or in Psalm 82, where Asaph writes: 'God has taken his place in the divine council; in the midst of the gods he holds judgment.' Centuries later, the storm god Yahweh won the battle for pre-eminence and was promoted to supreme deity.

'My thesis focuses on the "Great Hymn to the Aten",' Melchior went on. 'Do you know it?'

Peter shook his head.

'You should look it up when you get home,' Katja said, joining the conversation again. 'The text was found on the wall of the tomb of the courtier Ay. He was the father of Akhenaten's wife, Queen Nefertiti. It's really fascinating. It says: "How manifold it is, what thou hast made! They are hidden from the face of man. O sole god, like whom there is no other! Thou didst create the world according to thy desire."'

'And when you compare it with Psalm 104,' Melchior said, taking over from her, 'you see that both the "Great Hymn to the Aten" and the Psalm proclaim the glory of God's creation with a sense of ecstatic joy and wonder. The whole cosmos basks in divine light. They describe a world of abundance and order where man and beast are engaged in a sort of adoration of what God has made. There's an obvious and deeply felt feeling of religious awe at the heart of the hymn.'

It was easy to see that Melchior was well-versed in the subject.

Peter always enjoyed listening to people talk about the things they were passionate about. It didn't really matter to him what those things actually were. He had once attended a dinner where he had spent the entire evening sat next to a man who was studying frogs. His enthusiasm for the creatures had been so infectious that Peter had gone to Boekhandel Kooyker the very next day and bought a book about them.

'The hymn describes the first sunrise,' Melchior continued enthusiastically. He was in full flow now. Perhaps it was the relief of knowing that their trip to Sharm el-Sheikh wasn't going to be the disaster they had been imagining. 'It goes like this: "Thou appearest beautifully on the horizon of heaven, thou living Aton, the beginning of life! When thou art risen on the eastern horizon, thou hast filled every land with thy beauty." And then night falls and darkness comes, and Aten's absence is felt like a death. When Aten reappears in the morning, the world is reborn. "All the world, they do their work. All beasts are content with their pasturage. Trees and plants are flourishing. The birds fly from their nests." Many people are convinced that Akhenaten's ideas about worshipping one god, about monotheism, had an influence on Judaism. According to the most accepted chronology, Akhenaten's reign coincides with the time that the Israelites were slaves in Egypt, so we can't entirely rule it out.'

'That's a pretty big coincidence, right?' Katja chimed in.

She seemed to enjoy being able to tell Peter something that he appeared to know little about. She kept putting her hand on his leg, and the sudden warmth of her hand through his thin cotton shorts caught Peter by surprise each time he felt it, but it was quite pleasant, nonetheless. However, the alcohol was now taking its toll. He wanted to get up early the next day to visit the monastery, and he regretted having downed four beers in such quick succession.

Let me tell them something they've probably not heard before, he thought.

'But what if the Exodus never actually happened?' he asked them. 'What if the whole story is completely untrue, not even the slightest bit true? What if the Israelites were never in Egypt at all? Then the Old Testament story would lose much of its meaning and significance, wouldn't it? It would just be one more text like so many others you can find all over the world in which a supreme god – one who doesn't even deny the existence of other gods – is praised for the splendour of his creation. You can probably find similarities between them all, as you just did with the "Great Hymn to the Aten" and Psalm 104. Although a likeness doesn't necessarily mean a link, of course.'

Melchior and Katja went quiet, as though they had never considered this possibility.

'Well, yes,' Melchior said cautiously. 'But what if the story didn't happen exactly as it's described in Exodus, but it *does* contain a grain of historical truth? Namely that we believe in one god because a pharaoh came up with the idea and the Israelites took that idea with them to Palestine?'

'Personally, I think,' Peter said, 'and a lot of serious academics agree with me, that the Israeli Jews are actually just descended from tribes that lived in Palestine. The Israelites weren't a separate people that came from somewhere else and conquered Canaan. They already lived there. The Exodus story was cut

from whole cloth, invented to reinforce the Israeli national identity and back up the claim to the land. It's true that when they
were writing the Bible stories, they borrowed from neighbouring
cultures and possibly the Egyptians as well, so could have got
the idea of monotheism from Akhenaten, but you'd have a hard
time proving it. They probably brought it with them from
Babylon where they'd been in exile. It was only after then that
they started to write the Bible stories down. I'm reading a book
at the minute by two leading Israeli archaeologists. It's called
The Bible Unearthed. You should read it. It's eye-opening stuff.'

'Yes, but . . .' Melchior started to argue, but then he suddenly
stopped and let out a long yawn. 'I'm really tired,' he said.
'Shouldn't we be getting off to bed, Katja?'

Peter couldn't tell if Melchior really was tired or just tired of
the conversation.

'Have you found somewhere to sleep?' Peter asked.

'Yes,' Katja replied. 'One of the hotels is letting us sleep on
their roof. It's actually pretty romantic. It's a flat terrace with a
wall all around it, and you can lie there and look up at the stars.
It only costs about two euros a night. For both of us!'

'Well, that doesn't sound too bad at all,' said Peter, feeling
oddly relieved that they wouldn't have to risk sleeping on the
beach.

They said goodbye, and Katja hugged him again, even tighter
and for longer than she had done before.

'You will be careful tomorrow, won't you?' she whispered in
his ear.

It sounded like a warning.

Chapter 35

'*Allahu akbar!*' The message echoed from the speakers on the minaret near the hotel.

God is great.

The call to prayer began just before the alarm on Peter's phone went off. He had slept poorly, and he'd had to get up to go to the bathroom a few times too. With a headache pounding at his temples and his eyes screwed up with sleep, he dragged himself into the shower. He turned on the cold tap, hoping it would wake him up, and leaned on the wall with one hand for support.

You will be careful tomorrow, won't you?

Katja's parting words were still making him feel uneasy. He turned off the tap, dried himself off and got dressed.

He bought some bread, fruit and two large bottles of water in the shop next door where he had bought the adaptor the night before.

The early morning air was slightly chilly, but Peter knew that it would be hot by seven o'clock.

He walked along the street to where a line of yellow taxis stood waiting for customers. They all looked empty, but when he looked through the dirty window of the car at the front of the row, he saw a man asleep on the back seat. He had contorted himself into a strange position that allowed him to fit most of his body on the seat.

Peter tapped on the window.

The man woke up, and with what looked like a considerable amount of effort, emerged from the car.

'Katrîne, Katrîne,' the taxi driver said before Peter could say a word.

Peter nodded.

They agreed on a price. Peter had no idea if it was a good deal or not – he just wanted to get going.

As he was about to get into the car, he saw the now familiar figures of Melchior and Katja walking towards him and waving enthusiastically. His first impulse was to get in the taxi and tell the driver to go, but he couldn't bring himself to do it. He waited for them to reach the car.

Katja hugged him again.

'You're going to Saint Catherine's too, right?' Melchior asked.

Peter realised that it was going to look very odd now if he didn't offer them a lift. Besides, he'd already agreed on a price with the driver.

'They're coming too,' Peter said to the taxi driver. The man objected theatrically but backed down as soon as Peter pressed an extra twenty dollars into his hand.

'We'll pay our share,' Melchior said, clearly for form's sake because he didn't ask what the fare would be. He got into the passenger seat, leaving Peter and Katja to share the back seat again.

The driver turned on the radio, filling the small car with loud Arabic music. It was about a two-hour drive to the monastery, so if all went well, they would arrive by 8 a.m.

Suddenly, Peter felt a pang of doubt.

Why didn't I just go home? Why am I getting myself even more

mixed up in this when Tony's death has already brought the whole
affair to an end? Not a very satisfying end, it's true, but still . . .

But he couldn't let go of the idea that if he found the hidden
manuscript, Coen and Yona wouldn't have given up their lives
for nothing. Nor would the two men in Jerusalem. And in a way,
even Tony's death wouldn't have been in vain.

Apart from that, Peter had naturally grown curious about
what the secret knowledge was. What sort of information could
be so important that it had been handed down through the
generations for thousands of years via 'living books'?

What if I'm wrong and don't find anything at the monastery?
How would I even go about looking for it? It's not as if I can just
walk in and say: 'Hello, I'm looking for a document containing
secrets that have been hidden for thousands of years. Could I come
in and have a little look?'

It was no more than a hunch, an inkling, a gut feeling.

It had all gone so quickly that there had been no time or
room for doubts. He'd not even had a chance to rest since arriving
in Sharm el-Sheikh because of meeting Melchior and Katja at
the bar, drinking too many beers, going to bed too late and then
having to get up so early.

He looked down at Katja, who was resting her head on his
shoulder. Her eyes were closed, and she looked like she had
fallen asleep, although Peter couldn't imagine how that was
possible because the back of the car was so uncomfortable, the
music was so loud, and an increasingly warm wind was blowing
through the windows.

Before long, they had left Sharm el-Sheikh and were driving
along a wide, flat stretch of road. There were no road markings,
and the verges erratically appeared and disappeared, half
obscured by the sand that had drifted onto the asphalt.

Is that someone's job, Peter wondered. *Is someone employed to clear off the sand every day with a road sweeper? What an endless, Sisyphean task that would be.*

They zipped through the desert at high speed. It was much more colourful than Peter had expected. There was sparse vegetation here and there – shrubby bushes that were more brown than green – but in the constantly changing light, the sand and rocks took on new hues: yellow, orange, pink, sometimes even purple, and dark brown, like an experimental painter's palette.

Melchior appeared to be using the journey as a meditation exercise; he stared out of the window, watching the landscape as it flowed past.

Katja was fast asleep now. Her head lolled heavily on Peter's shoulder.

So far, they hadn't seen anyone else on the road.

'There aren't many tourists?' Peter shouted at the driver, trying to make his voice heard above the noise of the music, the wind, and the car's engine.

The driver twisted around to look at him, and the car swerved dangerously across the road. 'No tourists!' he shouted back, stabbing the air emphatically with his index finger. Fortunately, he soon turned his attention back to the road. 'No one! They say terrorists in Sinai, but no terrorists here. Only good people here. Good Muslims.'

More to check the time than anything else, because obviously, there was no signal out here at all, Peter took his phone out of his backpack. He saw that it was almost 7 a.m.

He scrolled through some photos that reminded him of home, of Fay and Agapé in the *hofje*'s courtyard, him and Fay together in Leiden's botanical garden, a photo of Judith.

He put the phone back in his bag.

A herd of camels wandered over the road ahead, seemingly without anyone leading them.

The car began to slow down, and Melchior seemed to perk up.

'Could you stop for a minute?' he asked the driver. 'I want to take some pictures.'

The driver drove slowly towards the camels and then stopped on the side of the road.

'Come on,' Melchior said to Peter enthusiastically, like a National Geographic photographer finally spotting an animal long thought to be extinct.

Peter moved away from Katja as carefully as he could, but she woke up anyway. She groggily asked if they were there yet, but kept her eyes closed. She stayed in the car while Melchior and Peter got out.

Peter was glad to be able to stretch his legs after almost an hour scrunched up on the cramped back seat. He decided he might as well follow Melchior over to the increasingly large herd of camels.

The taxi gradually caught up with them and then manoeuvred carefully around Peter, Melchior and the camels before pulling up again to wait for them further along the road.

I suppose this is no different to tourists in the Netherlands stopping their cars to take photos of the cows.

As Melchior walked back to the taxi, Peter closed his eyes and enjoyed one last long stretch before getting into the car again.

All of a sudden, he heard tyres screeching on tarmac.

The taxi pulled away at high speed, and judging by the noise the engine was making, it was doing it in the wrong gear. The wheels skidded in the sand on the road but soon recovered their grip. Katja waved at him from the back seat. Peter thought he saw her smiling and sticking both her thumbs up at him.

At first, he was too shocked to react, like someone seeing an accident happen and not knowing what to do. Then he burst into a panicked sprint. This was an utterly pointless exercise, he soon realised, because ten or twenty seconds later, the taxi was no more than a tiny yellow dot on a long, straight road stretching endlessly away from him.

Is this . . . Is this some kind of terrible joke?

He stood in the middle of the road, half expecting the car to turn around and come back for him in a twisted display of German humour. But it quickly became clear that he shouldn't count on it.

They had been in the car for an hour, so they were about halfway to Mount Sinai. That meant it was at least a hundred and twenty-five kilometres in either direction, so walking there wasn't an option and nor was walking back.

His bag was still in the car, so he had no food or water with him. His short sprint had left him sweating and thirsty. All he had with him was his passport, some money and a credit card, stashed in the money belt around his waist.

'You will be careful tomorrow, won't you?' Katja had asked him the evening before.

What did she know then that she didn't want to tell me? Couldn't tell me?

Peter suddenly wondered how coincidental their meeting at the airport had been. The feigned helplessness, the plausible story about a conman, the pleasant evening together with food and beer.

Had this all been part of a sophisticated ruse? Had he walked into a trap with his eyes wide open? But he had approached them at the airport, hadn't he? Or would they have found another way to make contact with him? And whose orders were they acting on?

Peter started walking back in the direction they had come from, but he knew it was futile and soon gave up. The few kilometres he'd be able to cover by walking would only make him exhausted and dehydrated. In this environment, the sun would finish him off in no time.

He recalled the tragic death of the manager of the 013 concert venue in Tilburg. He and his girlfriend had been visiting the Joshua Tree National Park in North America when their car got stuck in the soft sand. They had tried to walk to find help, only to be overcome by dehydration and the forty-degree heat. Their bodies had been found just a few kilometres from their car.

I'm so thirsty!

His tongue already felt like an old chamois leather rag, which wasn't helped by last night's salty food and this morning's hangover.

There was no shade anywhere here, and the sun was growing stronger with each passing minute. He had left his cap in the car, so he had nothing to protect his head or his eyes. He was overcome by a feeling of despair.

Why? Why? Why? Surely this isn't how my life ends? But then, that's probably what anyone would think if something like this happened to them.

In Plymouth, too much water had almost killed him. Here, the lack of it would do the same if he didn't find help soon.

He decided to walk to the first bend in the road in the hope of finding some sort of shade. It turned out to be a vain hope. All he saw was a pathetic little shrub with just a couple of leaves on it. He walked on.

This is not good, Peter thought dispiritedly.

His head started to throb with pain.

I should have taken some aspirin for my hangover this morning.

The tiredness from travelling, the fight with Tony, his narrow escape from America, and most of all, this betrayal by Melchior and Katja and the dire situation they had left him in, it all came out now. For the first time in many years, Peter broke down and wept.

He screwed his face into a strange grimace in a desperate attempt to catch the precious moisture in his tears in his mouth, but it was useless.

He saw a small bush that cast a pale shadow on the ground.

A headache, exhaustion, stress, thirst, and a hangover . . . I can't imagine a worse state to be in in this situation.

He lay down on his side in the sand and did his best to position his head in the shrub's thin shade.

Maybe another car will come along.

He covered his face with his arm to protect it from the relentless heat of the sun.

Have to save my energy as much as I can now . . . he thought before he slowly slipped into unconsciousness.

Chapter 36

Peter's eyes fluttered.

I'm still here, was his first thought. *I haven't seen a tunnel of light. My life didn't flash before my eyes. There weren't any dead relatives or radiant, benevolent beings telling me to return to my body because I still have work to do on earth.*

The fact that his soul was still firmly attached to his body was made abundantly clear by his pounding headache. He opened his eyes. Wherever he was, it was dark, but not entirely. The light was being filtered somehow.

The skin on his cheek felt raw from the rough material he had been lying on for who knew how long. He tried to sit up, but the violent thumping in his head forced him to fall back again. After a few more attempts, he eventually succeeded. He was lying on a simple cot made of what looked like an animal hide stretched over a wooden frame. Someone had taken off his shoes for him, but he was still fully clothed.

He saw that he was in a large tent made of a rough black material that was indeed filtering the light. It was sparsely furnished. There was another cot like the one he was sitting on. There were two big bales of what looked like carpets bound up in a large, thin cloth. The ground was covered in carpets too, with sand and rocks visible through the gaps. An artfully decorated silver-grey jug stood on a large tray, surrounded by about ten small tea glasses and a pile of roughly shaped cubes of sugar.

The tent flap was flung open, and a sea of light flooded in.

Peter instinctively shielded his eyes from the piercing brightness with his hand. He slowly removed it again, but the bright light behind the figure in the tent opening made them hard to see. The flap fell closed, and Peter was plunged into darkness again.

Whoever it had been, they were gone again.

Where am I?

Peter noticed a jug of water at the foot of the bed. He put it to his lips and drank so thirstily that he choked and coughed, and the water spilled over his chin and onto the floor. Exhausted, he put the jug back on the ground and fell back onto the bed.

He heard the tent flap being opened again. He could see the light increasing even with his eyes shut; a pink glow moving over his eyelids.

I was lost, but now I'm found.

Someone approached him, cautiously, like he was a wounded animal and they weren't sure how he would react to being touched. Then there was silence. Peter turned his head to the side and slowly opened his eyes. A man was crouched down beside the bed, staring at him intently. He had a rugged, weather-beaten face, a stubbly beard and dark eyes. He wore a loose-fitting djellaba that looked like it was made from the same fabric as the tent.

A Bedouin.

A long white scarf was draped around the man's head just like Peter had seen on photographs of desert nomads.

The man put his palm flat on his chest and tapped it gently.

'Bilal,' he said. 'Bilal.' He gave Peter a wide smile that revealed missing front teeth and molars.

Peter copied him. 'Peter,' he said. 'Peter.'

The man repeated it, but it came out as 'Bater'.

Peter nodded.

Bilal picked up the jug of water.

'You drink,' he said in English. Peter couldn't tell from his intonation whether he was asking a question or making a demand.

Peter took the jug and swigged from it a couple of times.

'You Katrîne?' Bilal said, pointing at Peter emphatically, as though he wanted to avoid any misunderstanding about who he was referring to.

Peter nodded.

'Katrîne, yes,' he said and pointed to himself.

'I bring,' Bilal said, jumping up energetically, evidently happy that he had worked out where this stranded stranger had been trying to get to. 'You eat?' he said, obviously asking a question now.

It was only now that Peter realised how ravenously hungry he was. He hadn't had a chance to eat any of the bread and fruit he had bought that morning.

Bilal went back outside. He uttered a few sharp sentences in what sounded like Arabic, apparently giving someone orders. The gentleness with which he had spoken to Peter in English had vanished in an instant.

Why on earth would they leave me, Peter asked himself.

His hand flew to the money belt at his waist to check that it was still there.

That couldn't have been what they were after, could it?

He heard camels grumbling outside and the scrape of metal on metal, probably cutlery on plates.

Peter slowly heaved his legs over the side of the cot so that he could sit up. He suddenly realised how full his bladder felt. He eased himself up and hobbled over to the tent entrance, not quite steady on his feet.

He threw back the large tent flap and blinked hard. He heard the blood rushing in his ears, pulsing hard then soft. When he opened his eyes, for a moment, he thought he had stepped into a travel documentary on the Discovery Channel or National Geographic. To his right, a group of veiled women dressed in brightly coloured robes stood around a cooking pot hanging over a wood fire. Two young girls glanced at him for a brief second, but they averted their eyes as soon as he looked at them. They nudged each other and giggled.

A few metres away was a large, half-open tent, like the beach tents that bathers might use to shelter from the wind but many times bigger. Inside, the ground was covered with overlapping carpets. Cushions had been arranged into two u-shaped seating areas with enormous silver-grey serving trays in the middle. Two camels lay next to the tent in the blinding sun. They appeared to be chewing something, although Peter couldn't see anything in their mouths. They stared impassively ahead.

Bilal dashed over to him. 'Bater,' he exclaimed. 'Bater!'

Peter didn't bother to correct his pronunciation.

Bilal grabbed Peter's arm and led him over to the seating area.

'I need to . . .' Peter tried to think of a way to tell him he needed to urinate. 'Pee pee,' he said, hoping that baby language might somehow be international. He pointed at his crotch. 'Pee pee,' he said again.

Bilal understood immediately. He took Peter's hand and led him away from the tent to an area where, to Peter's surprise, two thorny bushes were somehow growing in this otherwise barren patch of desert. Bilal waited until they had reached the bushes before he let go of his hand, and then he went back to the camp.

With great relief, Peter emptied his bladder, taking care to aim at the bushes as much as possible.

For I will pour water on the thirsty land, and streams on the dry ground . . .

The moisture was drawn into the ground so quickly that, before he had even zipped up, all that was left of his deed was a dark patch in the sand.

He heard a noise in the distance coming closer. He held his breath and listened carefully, but it was soon obvious that it was a car. His immediate impulse was to walk towards it, thinking that he might be able to get a lift. But after taking a single step, he froze.

What if it's Melchior and Katja?

The sound grew louder. There was a row of sand dunes about fifty metres away from him. They looked like they were protecting an invisible coast from the crashing waves of a cruel sea. He heard the car speed past without slowing down, and then the noise faded away.

It's only a car, only a car . . . It doesn't mean anything.

Peter walked towards where he had heard the noise coming from. As he reached the top of the sand dune, he saw not only the road he had been on but also the bush where he had tried in vain to seek shelter. When he turned back around, he realised that if he had just climbed the sand dune then, help would have been less than fifty metres away.

He returned to the tent where Bilal was waiting for him, waving his arms in the air as though he was worried that Peter would get lost on the short walk back.

He hadn't been able to catch a glimpse of the car.

They sat down on the hard cushions, and Peter noticed that he was sweating profusely. He gratefully accepted a large tin mug that was filled to the brim with cold water.

How do they keep the water so cold here?

Almost as soon as he had sat down, the two girls he had seen earlier came in. One of them carried a steaming plate piled with rice and some sort of stew, and the other brought in a roughly torn piece of bread. They gave these to Peter and then stood and watched him curiously. Bilal snapped at them to leave.

'You eat,' he said to Peter with a friendly smile. He took a cigarette from a packet lying on a tray in front of him.

How long was I lying on the roadside? How long was I asleep?

Peter pointed at his wrist, hoping that the gesture also meant 'What time is it?' here too.

He was surprised to see that Bilal was wearing a watch. He held his arm up to show Peter the time.

Almost midday. It had been five hours since Melchior and Katja had, for whatever unfathomable reason, abandoned him in the desert.

The stew was chickpeas and chunks of meat in a sauce. It didn't take long for Peter to finish it all. He mopped up the remaining sauce with the bread until the plate was completely clean.

'Good,' Bilal said approvingly and took the empty plate out of Peter's hands.

'You family?' Peter asked him, drawing a large circle in the air with his hands.

Bilal nodded and parroted back, 'You family.'

He didn't seem to have understood.

'You live here?' Peter asked.

'You live here?' Bilal parroted again, like an eager student at his first English lesson.

'I Katrîne,' Peter said. 'You bring? Katrîne?'

Bilal's face lit up.

'Yes. Bring Katrîne.'

He sucked aggressively on his cigarette a couple of times and then shouted something in the direction of the large tent. A boy who Peter hadn't seen before appeared. He stood still while Bilal barked a few short commands at him.

Peter wanted to explain to him what he was doing here, but their lack of a shared language made it impossible.

So here you are then, with all your education and knowledge, reduced to the ineloquence of 'You family' and 'You bring.' A sort of 'Me Tarzan, you Jane.' It's amazing how strongly language is linked to who you are, to your whole personality. All your jokes and anecdotes, all your clever wordplay. It all disappears without language, and who you are disappears along with it.

He heard the camels bleating again, and the boy clicking his tongue at them reassuringly. Peter heard clanging bells and then he felt the ground shake.

Surely we're not . . .

'Camel,' Bilal said. 'You camel. Katrîne. Camel.'

Before Peter had a chance to say anything, a woman came in carrying a dark brown robe that trailed on the ground, leaving a track in the sand. She gave it to Peter along with a large, white headcloth made of coarse fabric.

Bilal pointed at them and said, 'You.' Then he pointed upwards. 'Sun.'

Peter stood up with the surprisingly heavy clothes in his hands and wondered how they could possibly ever be comfortable. They would protect him against the blazing sun, but he was worried that they would also be unbearably hot.

On the other hand, there's a reason they've been wearing these things for centuries.

Bilal took the robe and headcloth from him. He threw the robe over Peter, which disoriented him for a second, but he quickly found the hole at the top and poked his head through.

Then, with a few deft movements, Bilal draped everything around Peter's body so that it all sat comfortably. The woman tied a belt around his waist, and then fastened the headcloth around his head, leaving just a narrow gap for his eyes.

For a brief moment, he imagined himself as Lawrence of Arabia about to embark on a grand and exciting adventure. For the first time since he had been left behind on the desert road, he forgot what a precarious situation he was in.

The boy came around from the back of the tent holding a pair of reins in each hand, by which he was leading two camels. The camels' saddles were richly decorated and hung with copper bells. The boy ordered the camels to kneel.

The beasts sank down on their front legs. It all looked so awkward, as if they were doing it for the first time. When they had finally settled, the two girls came over and tied a water bag to each camel's flank with ropes.

'Come,' said Bilal, taking Peter's hand.

Meanwhile, Bilal had wound a cloth around his own head, just like Peter's. He led Peter to one of the camels, and after a few clumsy attempts, Peter managed to clamber onto it, eliciting more giggles from the girls. The saddle was a tight fit, and Peter shuffled around to try to give his pinched privates some room. He needed to pee again already, but he had just found a comfortable position, and he didn't want to lose it.

Bilal spoke some encouraging words to his camel, and it stood up. Peter's camel got up too, almost throwing Peter out of the saddle, much to the amusement of Bilal's family.

'You okay?' Bilal asked when everyone had stopped laughing.

'I okay,' Peter replied, although the pressure on his bladder felt incredible now.

The boy slapped the camel's backside, and it started to move.

It only took a few steps for Peter to realise why the camel was called 'the ship of the desert'. Within minutes, he felt seasick. It had also started to grow very hot underneath the heavy robe he was wearing over his clothes. The intense light from the sun reflected back from the sand, forcing him to squint until his eyes were thin slits.

Good Lord, please don't let this take too long . . .

He vaguely recalled that a camel could easily run faster than sixty kilometres per hour, but only an experienced jockey would be able to stay in the saddle at that speed. However, even at twenty kilometres an hour, it would take them at least six hours to reach the monastery. But perhaps the route across the desert was shorter than going by road.

As time passed, his need to go to the bathroom strangely disappeared. He tried to fix his gaze on the horizon as they rode through a monotonous landscape of sand, weather-beaten rocks, and the thorny bushes that somehow managed to cling onto life in this harsh environment. Sudden twinges of cramp in his thighs and lower back forced him to adjust his position every few minutes.

The camels' initial burst of speed had given way to a steady trot now, which meant they could make faster progress, but surprisingly, it also made the ride even more uncomfortable.

They appeared to be following a completely random path. How Bilal could find his way in a place where there were so few landmarks was a total mystery to Peter.

After an hour, or possibly even two hours – Peter had lost all sense of time – they stopped near a rocky outcrop that had seemed to be the same distance away for so long that Peter had thought they would never reach it.

The camels knelt down again, and Peter had to grip the pommel tightly to stop himself falling out of the saddle. His legs had gone numb, which made it difficult to keep his balance when he dismounted.

Bilal spoke to him for the first time since they had left the camp.

'You drink,' he said, and took a drink from the water bag himself.

They shifted their head coverings aside and gulped down greedy glugs of water.

'Camel drink?' Peter asked, pointed to the animals who stood calmly looking around them with their usual blank expressions.

Bilal shook his head.

He tied the water bag back onto the saddle and scaled the rocks, as though he needed to check where they were. He fished inside his robe and produced a packet of cigarettes. He held it out invitingly.

It had been a while since Peter had smoked his daily cigarillo, but it had been years since he had last smoked a cigarette.

He was overcome by a great longing to be back in his little office in Leiden.

And a great longing for Fay.

Peter felt himself choking up but walked over to Bilal and took a cigarette. After they had lit their cigarettes, they both sat down on the sand to smoke them.

If you didn't know any better, you would think I was a rich tourist who had paid hundreds of dollars for an authentic desert experience with a real Bedouin.

The air was still, and the smoke from their cigarettes rose up in almost perfectly vertical plumes. Something was bothering Peter about all of this that he couldn't quite put his finger on, but he was too tired to think deeply about it now.

It was absolutely quiet.

Peter stared out over the endless, open plain.

Any Christian or Jew who believed that the Bible should be read literally would need to spend just a minute in this environment before they realised that nobody could wander around here for forty years. According to Exodus, manna rained down from heaven, and God provided quails in due course – quite a lot of manna and quails would have been needed to feed three million people each day – but the amount of water necessary to quench the thirsts of such a multitude would require the sort of water sources that weren't found anywhere in the desert.

'You Muslim?' Peter asked, breaking the silence.

Bilal looked at him as if he had forgotten there was someone else with him.

Bilal nodded. 'Muslem.' He pointed at the sky and said, 'Allah. Muslem.' Then he pointed at Peter. 'You?'

'Isa,' Peter said, managing to remember the Arabic name for Jesus. This wasn't the time or the place to explain that he thought of himself as an agnostic. Experience had taught him that in the Middle East – and other parts of the world too – you couldn't just come out with the fact that you didn't believe in God, so he always told people that he was a Christian.

'Isa good,' Bilal said approvingly.

That, apparently, was as far as the theological discussion was going to go, because Bilal got to his feet. Peter got up and walked over to a spot a few metres away from the camels, but after he had struggled to hitch up his robe and unzip his shorts, he realised that he didn't need to go at all. He took a few more large gulps from the water bag, then he fastened the white cloth around his head again.

It only took a few minutes in the saddle for Peter to rediscover the position that was the least uncomfortable. He regretted having forgotten to ask how long the journey would take. If they had left at one o'clock, it would be getting on for three o'clock now.

He looked at the sun. It had sunk closer to the horizon, so they only had a couple of hours of sunlight left. Peter assumed that Bilal wouldn't want to travel in the desert at night, although the light from the moon and stars meant that it wouldn't be completely dark.

They rode on for a long time, much longer than they had on the first leg of the journey, Peter thought. Then, to his great surprise, a black ribbon of asphalt appeared in the distance. As they got closer, he could see the hot air shimmering above the road. Bilal steered his camel to the other side of the road and followed the sandy verge. Peter's camel followed meekly behind.

After a while, they came upon a faded blue road sign half scrubbed away by sand and covered in rust spots. There were about ten perfectly round holes in the metal that must have been made by bullets. The sign read:

دير سانت كاترين

Dair Sānt Kātarīn
Km 40

Either the camels had been walking faster than Peter had thought, or he had been dumped closer to Saint Catherine than he thought. Or maybe they had just been able to take a big shortcut through the desert.

We could be there in less than two hours, before it gets dark.

The camels set off again at a brisk trot, moving faster than they had done before. It took a great deal of effort and considerable strength to keep his balance, but the thought that they would be at the monastery within an hour and a half at this speed gave Peter renewed energy. His knuckles were white from gripping the reins so tightly, the muscles on his inner thighs ached, and he could feel another headache coming on.

About an hour later or perhaps even as little as three-quarters of an hour – in any case, much sooner than he had expected – they passed a sign that said the monastery was only twenty kilometres away.

The light was fading almost imperceptibly, and every few minutes, Peter found himself having to squint a little less. The sun was close to the horizon now, and it was noticeably less hot. He had heard that the desert could be freezing cold after the sun went down, and now he realised that the clothes the Bedouins wore during the day could serve as warm blankets at night.

He heard a car coming up behind them. The driver beeped his horn a couple of times to make sure they had heard him.

The yellow taxi passed them at high speed at first, but then abruptly skidded to a stop about a hundred metres away. The car reversed and came to a standstill about twenty metres from them.

The driver got out and yelled something at Bilal, who shook his head in reply. He started to get back into the car, but then changed his mind, slammed the door shut, and walked over to Peter.

'*As-salamu alaykum,*' the man greeted him in a manner that was much more friendly than the way he had spoken to Bilal.

'*Wa alaykum al-salaam,*' Peter replied, which was about the full extent of his knowledge of Arabic. The man fired some questions at him – or at least, Peter assumed they were questions – and Peter shook his head.

The man narrowed his eyes as if he was squinting at the sun.

He came a few steps closer. His face radiated anger and suspicion, and he motioned aggressively at Peter to take off his head covering.

What's going on?

The man stood on his tiptoes and grabbed Peter's arm.

'Scarf!' he screamed.

Well, he's at least worked out that I don't understand Arabic.

'Put away. Scarf,' the man hissed.

Peter was about to heed his command when Bilal shouted something at them. Then he nimbly turned his camel around and, in a flash, he had manoeuvred it between Peter and the taxi driver.

Even for someone who didn't know a word of Arabic, it was clear that the two men were not engaged in small talk about the weather or the price of bread.

The man tried to walk around Bilal's camel, but before he even got halfway, Bilal reached out with his foot and kicked him hard in the chest. As the man fell backwards, Bilal snatched Peter's reins, urged his own camel forward, and they took off at full speed.

Bewildered by what had just happened, Peter looked behind him. The man scrambled to his feet and ran back to the taxi. The passenger door opened. A man got out and stood next to the car. He shaded his hand with his eyes and stared at Peter and Bilal.

Peter recognised him immediately. His height gave him away. And so did his red baseball cap.

Chapter 37

Terrified, Peter took another look behind him, but his camel was swaying violently from side to side, and he needed to focus his attention on staying in the saddle. When he looked back a few moments later, he saw that the taxi was moving again. Even the fastest camel stood no chance of outrunning a car.

Bilal seemed to realise this too. As soon as they reached a point where the sand dunes were lower, he steered his camel away from the road. He had let go of the reins of Peter's camel now, and after a few attempts, Peter managed to grab hold of them again, which helped him to sit in the saddle more securely.

They galloped on for what felt like a long time, even after they had reached safer terrain where no car could follow. Eventually, they slowed down to a gentler trot, and Bilal came and rode next to him. Peter wanted to ask a thousand questions, but that was impossible without speaking Bilal's language.

'Not good,' Bilal said, perfectly summing up the situation.

'Not good?'

'Bad man. Not good,' Bilal said again.

He seemed to have plenty of questions too. He stared into Peter's face as if he hoped he might be able to fathom the answers by reading his mind.

'Katrîne?' Peter asked hopefully, pointing at the horizon. He was afraid that Bilal wouldn't want to continue after such an alarming encounter.

'Katrîne,' Bilal confirmed, and Peter could hear the grim determination in his voice. He spread out the fingers on both hands and showed them to Peter. Peter couldn't tell if he meant ten minutes or ten kilometres.

As they made their way across the sand, Peter wondered if it hadn't just been the stress of the day's events that had made him think he'd seen Tony in the figure staring back at them.

Was it really Tony? Yes, it had to be. The same height, that ever-present baseball cap. And who else would be coming after me? Nobody except Fay even knows I'm here. But then, how the hell did he survive in the ocean? I know he 'said, 'I'm an excellent swimmer,' but I was sure he hadn't come back up to the surface.

Peter was convinced that he had definitely just seen Tony. He must have managed to get back to the shore somehow.

After that, it would have been easy for him to watch me and follow me to the airport. That nutjob was convinced I was an undercover agent who had come to America to expose him. As if I would be able to go after him on my own . . . But how did he get past the border when I didn't even manage to check in unnoticed myself?

Peter shook his head in the vain hope that he could erase the mental image of a resurrected Tony.

He looked around. The afterglow of the setting sun had provided some light for a while, but now it too had disappeared. It wasn't as dark as he had expected, and he could already see the first stars.

According to the Bible, when the Israelites travelled through the desert, they were guided by a pillar of fire by night and a pillar of cloud by day. This had led many writers to suggest that the Exodus had taken place in the Minoan era between 1650 and 1600 BCE, the time of a massive volcanic eruption on the island of Thera in the Mediterranean – one of the largest volcanic eruptions ever recorded on earth. The resulting tsunami was more than twenty-eight metres high and reached as far as Crete, where it caused tremendous devastation. The evidence that half of Thera had been blasted away by the volcanic eruption can still be seen today; the island, now called Santorini, is shaped like a crescent moon.

From a distance, the tower of ash and smoke from the eruption would have been clearly visible during the day, and at night, the molten lava would have given off an intense glow.

Mark had once explained to Peter how the smoke and ash from the volcano could have caused the Ten Plagues of Egypt. The ash cloud would have prevented rainfall and turned the Nile into a foul, slow-moving river of mud in which algae would thrive. Pollution would eventually have caused the abundant algae to die off, turning the water red. This could also have driven the frogs out of the water to the safety of dry land. They would have died very quickly in the arid desert, and the absence of this natural predator probably allowed flies and lice to multiply unabated, spreading diseases that were fatal to cattle. People would have been bitten and stung on a massive scale; scratching the bites would have led to open sores. The ash in the air collided with thunderstorms, and the resulting hail pelted the earth. This would have created a humid climate in which locusts could breed more rapidly. The ash particles blotted out the sun, plunging the land into darkness. Because of the humidity, the Egyptians' food would have begun to rot; the grain grew mould. According to Egyptian custom, the eldest child in a family was always the first to be given the newly harvested grain to eat, and this would have brought about the deaths of all the first-born children.

This still assumes that the events in Exodus actually took place, Peter thought, *but for different reasons. So while a volcanic eruption could explain the stories of the Ten Plagues and the pillars of cloud and fire that the Israelites saw, in the Bible's version of the story, Egypt was blighted by disaster because God wanted to punish the pharaoh for refusing to let the Israelites go. And afterwards, He took on the forms of smoke and fire to lead His people through the desert.*

They rode on for another half hour or so, and then Bilal stopped and held up his arm, like a commanding officer on a mission giving his troops an order to halt. He told the camels to kneel so that he and Peter could dismount.

Peter was so stiff and tired from the bumpy ride over rough terrain that he sank to his knees too.

Bilal knotted the camels' reins together so that they wouldn't run off during his brief absence. He patted their rumps and whispered softly to them.

'Katrîne,' he said to Peter.

They climbed to the top of a rocky hill, and at last, Peter saw Saint Catherine's Monastery. It looked like they were approaching the rear of the building rather than the front. In the distance, Peter could vaguely make out a large area that was dotted with parked cars. The moonlight glistered on their metal and glass.

If this was a film, Peter thought, *I would be shouting at the screen: 'Don't go inside! Go to the airport and take the first flight home!' Tony must have been on his way to the monastery. Because where else would I have been going? He knows. Does he know what the tattoo on his chest means now too? I just need to get inside the monastery. I can't go back to Sharm el-Sheikh. Tony might have paid people to keep an eye out for me there. Just as he must have paid Melchior and Katja. And I'm so close now! The safest place for me is in the monastery. The monks will protect me. The law of the desert says to offer hospitality and protection to anyone who knocks at your door. And if the secret manuscript has to be found by someone, please don't let it be Tony!*

The monastery was surrounded by a tall wall that was at least twenty-five or thirty metres high in places.

Peter and Bilal headed directly for it. When they reached the monastery, they went left, skirting around the perimeter. Peter held onto the wall, trailing his hand over the rough stones as they went. Just as they were about to turn left again, Bilal, who had so far remained silent, stopped. He stuck his head around the corner, then decided that the coast was clear enough for them to go further.

Peter couldn't see a taxi in the car park, although that didn't necessarily mean that Tony wasn't hiding here somewhere. It was very likely that he had arrived before them; it was probably no more than a fifteen-minute drive.

Tony could be hiding behind the rocks right now, watching us.

As they walked across the open space of the car park towards the entrance, Peter suddenly felt very, very vulnerable.

The entrance door was made of thick oak with ironwork fittings. It was closed. Bilal knocked on it a few times. Seconds later, a little hatch opened, and the bearded face of a monk appeared.

Peter knew that Saint Catherine's Monastery was one of the oldest in the world and that it had remained almost unchanged since it was built. It belonged to the Greek Orthodox Church, and its monks had always been of mostly Greek origin. This particular monk apparently also had a good command of Arabic because, after a short, whispered explanation from Bilal, Peter heard bolts sliding and the sound of keys being turned in various locks.

When the door opened, Bilal stepped aside and invited Peter to go in. As he was about to step over the threshold, Bilal grabbed his arm. He shook Peter's hand, and they embraced each other. The smell of sweat, cigarette smoke and camel assaulted Peter's nose. It all happened so quickly that Peter could only mumble, 'Thank you, thank you.' Before he knew it, Bilal had turned around and was gone.

Peter went inside, and the monk locked and bolted the door again. Peter unwound the scarf from around his head and removed the heavy clothing. He wouldn't need them here.

The monk spoke good English, which made the conversation much easier.

'Come, come. I'm Brother Antonius. Let's get you registered. It's required of every guest who stays here.'

Brother Antonius led him down a wide, well-lit corridor and stopped in front of an open door. The walls of the room beyond it were lined with bookcases crammed full of books, maps and bundles of paper. It looked like they were all covered in a thick layer of dust.

Peter sat down, and Brother Antonius gave him an English-language leaflet about the monastery. Peter read the front page while the monk was busy with his paperwork.

Saint Catherine's Monastery lies at the foot of Mount Sinai and was built between AD 548 and AD 565 by Emperor Justinian I. The monastery was built around the traditional site of the Burning Bush.

The monastery's library is home to one of the largest and

most important collections of holy manuscripts in the world – only outnumbered by the Vatican Library. The library preserves approximately 4,500 religious, scientific, medical and other documents in Greek, Coptic, Arabic, Armenian, Hebrew, Slavic, Syrian, Georgian and other languages.

Saint Catherine's Monastery is the oldest working Christian monastery in the world and is also the smallest diocese in the world. The Chapel of the Burning Bush was originally commissioned somewhere around AD 330 by Empress Helena, the mother of Constantine the Great. The monastery itself was built in the sixth century by Emperor Justinian to protect the monks and glorify the site of the Burning Bush. Five hundred years later, monks discovered Saint Catherine's remains on the mountain that now bears her name. Her body was believed to have been transported to Mount Catherine by angels. The relics of Saint Catherine are kept in a marble reliquary in the monastery's basilica.

Until the twentieth century, the only access to the monastery was via a small door set into the wall at a height of nine metres to which provisions and people were hoisted up via a pulley system.

'What's your name?' asked Antonius, who was finished with his paperwork. A huge book was open on the table in front of him, and his pen hovered over a page that was divided into columns. He noticed Peter's reluctance to answer his simple question. 'We register all visitors who spend the night with us,' he said encouragingly. 'Where are you from?'

'Leiden, the Netherlands. L-e-i-d-e-n,' Peter said.

Brother Antonius wrote this down and then looked at Peter gravely.

Is something wrong?

'And your name?'

'Peter . . .' he said hesitantly.

It can't do much harm to give away my first name, Peter thought. *And if I use a made-up name, I might forget to listen out for someone calling me by it.*

'De Rots. Peter de Rots,' he said, but as he spelled out the letters of this invented surname, he realised that a monk who worked in a multilingual library was very likely to know how to say a name as significant as 'Peter the Rock' in several languages and recognise it as an invention. He decided to keep talking. 'I teach. At a university.'

Antonius tutted approvingly as he wrote down these details in a beautiful, neat hand.

'Do you have many guests here?' Peter asked.

'Some. Not many. A few people stay here on a long-term basis to learn, to study the manuscripts. But it's not like it used to be,' the monk said, clapping the book closed.

Fay said that Coen had been here many times on retreat. It's the perfect place to hide away and devote yourself to learning. Or to hide secrets.

'Tourists came here by the coachload at one time. They'd climb to the top of the mountain at two in the morning to see the sunrise. It's very beautiful. Would you like to do that?'

Peter hesitated.

'It really is beautiful. I could arrange a guide for you if you like, someone who'll go with you as far as the steps.'

'Isn't it dangerous?'

'Dangerous? No, why would it be?' Antonius asked, and waved his hand dismissively. 'They leave us in peace here. I've lost count of the number of times I've been to the top. You could go up on your own. There's only one path, so it's impossible to get lost.'

'I'll think about it,' Peter said. 'Have any other guests arrived today?'

'No, you're the first we've had in weeks.'

'Okay,' Peter said with relief.

I made it. I'm safe.

For now.

'Come. I'll show you to your room,' Antonius said. 'Then you can have something to eat. If you'd like to climb the mountain tonight and need a guide, just let me know.'

They left the office, but halfway down the corridor, Peter realised that he had forgotten to pick up the clothing he had borrowed from Bilal.

How stupid of me not to have taken it all off while he was still here so I could give it straight back to him. I don't think I'd be able to find the exact location of his camp again, even if he and his family are still in the same place.

Back in Brother Antonius's office, he hurried over to the desk to look in the big book. He flipped anxiously through it until he got to the page where the monk had recorded his details.

The only name next to today's date was his own, and the previous entry had been made five or six weeks earlier.

For now, he was safe.

Chapter 38

Dear God, what's just happened?

Peter stared at his bloody hand in shock. He leaned his back against the massive oak door as if not even the combination of its cast-iron lock and large bolt were secure enough.

The gentle flame of a large candle cast a soft glow evenly around the room. The spartan monk's cell would have made a beautifully atmospheric photograph: the simple bed with its thin mattress and rough woollen blanket, the wooden table and chair, the writing implements and paper on the tabletop, the ceramic water jug and mug. In a small niche in the wall was a simple statue of the Virgin Mary with an infant Jesus in her arms.

Peter put his ear against the rough wood of the door. He couldn't hear anything behind it, but that told him little. This door was his only route outside. There was no window in the cell. Its sturdy walls had been built to last an eternity and were impenetrable. But staying here was not an option.

Earlier that evening, after Brother Antonius had shown him to this cell, Peter ate a simple but nutritious meal in the deserted refectory.

He imagined it in better days, bustling with large groups of tourists sitting convivially together at the long tables, enjoying the soup and the traditionally baked bread before retiring to their rooms in the guest wing. At two o'clock in the morning, a large caravan of people would go up the mountain, Antonius had explained to him. The first stage of the journey stopped at the foot of the steps that had been created by a monk as an act of penitence, carved out of the granite by hand. Many people chose to do the first stage by camel, providing a major source of income for the local Bedouins. On the busiest days in summer, the line of people winding their way up the mountain was kilometres long, and their lamps and flaming torches made them look like a glowing snake. When they reached the top some four hours later, they would discover that taking a quiet moment to reflect was out of the question. Hundreds of people would be squashed together on the plateau, all seeking the best position from which to watch the sun rise over the mountains of Israel and Jordan in the east.

Peter and Antonius sat at an empty table, but shortly after they had begun to eat, they were joined by one of the other brothers. He said very little but looked up repeatedly to fix Peter with a penetrating stare. He introduced himself as Brother Milan. Like all the other monks Peter had seen so far, Milan had a full beard. His age was hard to guess; he was obviously over sixty, but Peter couldn't tell more accurately than that. Laughter lines crinkled around his eyes and he looked friendly but radiated a stern, meticulous intelligence. For some reason, Peter found it easy to imagine him in a rage.

Peter had been careful to keep the purpose of his visit vague, and Antonius hadn't questioned him too closely about it. It was almost as if Bedouins turned up at the door every evening with a stranded foreigner in tow.

They talked briefly about Leiden, a city that, much to Peter's surprise, both Antonius and Milan had heard of. Dutch scholars had visited their library on numerous occasions to study the manuscripts.

Coen Zoutman.

Some of them had even stayed for months. One of them had been from Leiden and repaid their hospitality by bringing copies of manuscripts from Leiden University's library to add to the monastery's collection.

Peter couldn't put his finger on what it was, but as soon as the conversation turned to Leiden, he noticed a change in Brother Milan's mood. The monk narrowed his eyes as if he was furiously turning something over in his mind.

Antonius excused himself – the sound of ringing bells had sounded in the distance, signalling the start of evening prayers – and Peter was left alone with Brother Milan, who evidently wasn't obliged to go to the service.

A few other monks passed through the room, including one who seemed unusually tall, all hurriedly making their way to the church.

Even when the last brother had closed the refectory door behind him, and it was clear that they were now completely alone, Brother Milan looked furtively around the hall before he spoke. 'You know Coen Zoutman?'

Peter nodded slowly.

It was odd to hear the name of the man whose tragic death had been the catalyst for this adventure spoken here, thousands of kilometres from home.

'You know Coen Zoutman,' Milan said again, and it sounded like statement this time rather than a question.

'You knew Coen?' Peter said, amazed.

'Knew? You don't mean to say that he's . . .'

'I'm sorry,' Peter said. 'He's dead, but . . . how did you know each other?'

The monk was visibly upset by the news of Coen's death. His lips moved silently as if he was saying a prayer, beseeching God for a blessing. 'That's . . . That doesn't matter now,' he said, regaining his composure.

'I saw in the guestbook that you're from the Netherlands, from Leiden. I'm always inclined to be particularly alert whenever I see that. And now, with this terrible news . . .' Brother Milan stared into space, lost in thought for a moment. 'Did Coen die naturally?'

What should I say?

'I'm sorry, no. He was murdered. The police don't know who did it yet.'

But I do.

'I think I may have been waiting for you,' Milan said.

'Waiting?'

For me?

'Come with me.'

Brother Milan led him out of the refectory. His long, black habit swished over the floor. It covered his feet entirely, making him look as though he was floating above the ground.

They walked down a series of long, empty, terracotta-tiled corridors, crossed a courtyard and eventually entered a small chapel.

When Peter saw what was inside it, he gasped in horror.

Piled up in the chapel's large alcoves were hundreds upon hundreds of human skulls. The gaping holes where their eyes had been seemed to be staring blindly back at him. Many of the skulls' jaws had slipped crookedly downwards, making them look like they were trying to scream something from another realm, a reproach or a warning.

'Why are we here?' Peter asked. He clenched his fists, ready to fight his way back outside if he had to.

'Don't be afraid,' said Milan, who could see that Peter was confused and on the edge of panic. 'I'm on the same side as you. The same side as all of you. Look . . .' he said, sweeping his arm in an arc towards the skulls, almost like a guide telling a story to an attentive tour group.

'I'm also . . . Coen and I . . .' he began, but then changed his mind. 'This is what remains of us when we're gone, isn't it? These are the skulls of all the monks who've lived here since the monastery was founded. Many of them have completely turned to dust. This is all that's left. This is our fate. Do you agree? Our bodies are only temporary vessels for the soul. The earth is only our temporary home. We weren't supposed to be here. We have a higher calling. Our true home is in the Garden of Eden that we were once cast out of.'

We got to get ourselves back to the garden . . . So far, Milan hasn't said anything that I didn't already know about or that contradicts Christian doctrine, Peter thought. *Doesn't every Christian believe that life is merely a long test of faith? Earth is the laboratory that God uses to decide which of us will be with Him forever after death and which of us will be separated from Him.*

'We must break free from our bodies,' Milan went on. 'Break free from the physical matter that keeps us shackled to the earth. Otherwise, we'll keep coming back for as long as it takes for us to learn our lessons.'

What is he talking about? Keep coming back? Reincarnation? That's not part of Christian dogma . . .

'That's why I'm here. That's why we're all here in this monastery, to focus on the eternal through study and prayer, and to turn away from the temporal. But I . . .' He paused. 'But I discovered that . . . Coen came here sometimes to do research, as a . . . He was an initiate . . . We had many long conversations together. He showed me that we need to read the Old Testament stories in Genesis and Exodus in a way that's quite different from our previous understanding of them.'

Peter got the impression that Brother Milan wanted to tell many different things at once but didn't know where to start. Large beads of sweat were forming on his forehead. A hush had fallen over the small chapel, as if everything had come to a standstill.

'What does Coen have to do with all of this?'

'When he was here, he confided in me . . .' the monk said, looking more composed now. 'Coen told me that his death would be unnatural and violent, and that he would send someone to . . .'

Send someone? But I hadn't planned to come here at all, Peter wanted to shout. *Was Coen going to send that young man, Yona Falaina? Did I really end up here by chance? Have I come here of my own free will? Or am I being directed by a higher power? Was I destined to come here?*

'Coen was a living book,' the monk said. When Peter nodded to show that he understood what this meant, he continued. 'There were six living books spread over three different places. The tides of history determined that those places would be Jerusalem, Leiden and Boston. One living book for each city, each with a second book in training. I've heard rumours that there was sometimes even a third pupil. The pupils are usually young, but sometimes older people too . . .'

A second and sometimes even a third pupil? In Boston, that was George with Tony as the third. Does this mean that there's another living book alive still in Jerusalem? If that's true, then Tony slipped up . . . Or did he murder that person as well? And who could Leiden's third living book be?

The idea had fleetingly occurred to him in America. He hadn't given it a great deal of thought then. But now, that possibility had bizarrely become a very likely probability. Peter was dumbfounded.

Fay? Had Coen been about to initiate her so that she . . .

'It went terribly wrong in Jerusalem with those two murders. And now Coen in Leiden . . .'

'Someone else was killed in Leiden shortly after Coen,' Peter said. 'A young man, Yona.'

Milan shook his head, aghast.

And two people were drowned in Boston, Peter almost added. *But how much shocking information can a person process at once?*

'But are you also—'

'No, no,' Peter said. 'I've not been initiated, but I have learned something about it. I know about the history of the living books. I think I know who the third person in Leiden was going to be. And I know who the third person in Boston was – or is. And I know that he's responsible for the murders. He fooled the chairman of the Boston lodge into trusting him, but his only goal was to erase the secret knowledge forever.'

The look of shock had not yet left Milan's face.

I've got to ask him.

'But what is this secret knowledge? What is it about?'

'It's about . . .' Brother Milan leaned forward and whispered so softly that Peter could barely hear him. 'It's about the Torah. Or, in other words, it's about the first five books of the Old Testament. The books as we know them are . . . there's another tradition, an oral tradition, a different version that explains the original meaning of the books. The books aren't an accurate historical account, nor were they ever intended to be. The stories are ultimately all about . . . the journey inwards. Not the Ex-odus, the outward journey, but the Eis-odus, the inward journey. *Gnothi seauton*, Know thyself . . . It's about the Christ within us, the journey of the soul. It's too complicated for me to be able to explain everything to you here now.'

'And how does Coen fit into this?'

'Coen visited us here a few times. He said . . . The last time that he was here, he was very, very worried. He knew what had happened in Jerusalem, of course, and he was convinced that the murderer would eventually come for *him*. So, Coen made the decision to write some of the knowledge down for the first time in history, the first time in more than three thousand years. Doing so was absolutely forbidden, but he chose to write a synopsis of the second book. He chose Exodus because he considered it to be the most important book. Everything springs from Exodus. It's in Exodus that God makes his promise to the people of Israel, telling the Hebrews that they will have their own land, a place of safety. Their journey through the desert and the crossing of the Red Sea represent the soul's journey after death. Before the soul can reach heaven, the promised land, a host of enemies must be vanquished and inner demons defeated. Man longs for the flesh-pots of Egypt. Our fleshly desires keep our souls trapped in our bodies. The mind is willing, but, ultimately, the flesh is weak.'

What Brother Milan was telling him was astonishing, but it made sense.

All the puzzle pieces were slotting together . . .

This is what Tony was telling me, although he explained it differently. His obsession with sticking to a strictly literal reading of the stories is purely a reaction to the existence of these living books. If everyone started interpreting the Bible in different ways, its stories would lose their power to bring people together, and who knows what the consequences of that would be?

'But what now?' Peter asked.

'I have it,' Milan said. 'I have the document that Coen wrote.'

I'm going to have to tell him.

'Two men were drowned in Boston earlier this month. Sam and George. They were living books too.'

Milan's eyes began to fill with tears.

'Then there's no one left! The knowledge is almost entirely lost. All we have left is what Coen wrote down. And I'm afraid that it's not safe, not even here. Please, take it! It's the only way that a small piece of the knowledge might be saved. It's the only way we can stop it all being lost.'

What are the chances of someone getting caught up in a situation like this? Or was this fate? Is this a role that I was predestined to play?

'Come,' Brother Milan said. 'Let's go to my room.'

They left the chapel and walked past a bush that was growing over a two-metre-high wall, like a houseplant in a giant flowerpot. It wasn't the actual bush from which God was supposed to have spoken to Moses, but according to legend, it had been grafted onto a branch of the original bush.

It doesn't matter if a story is true or not as long as people believe it could be true . . . I must come back here one day, Peter thought with a pang of regret. *It's so beautiful.*

They walked past the famous basilica, and Peter felt another pang of regret because he wouldn't have an opportunity to go inside. They crossed the courtyard and came to the building that housed the monks' cells. They stopped at a door that was indistinguishable from all the other doors they had passed.

The monk reached inside his habit and took out a bunch of large, antique-looking iron keys. Seamlessly, he inserted the correct key into the lock and turned it twice, producing a grating, metallic creak.

'This is my room,' said Milan, who hadn't spoken since they had left the ossuary.

The cell was the mirror image of Peter's except for the addition of two sturdy bookcases tightly packed with books.

As soon as they were inside, Milan closed the door behind them and then locked it.

'Sit down,' the monk told Peter. He stood in front of one of the bookcases and counted the books on the top shelf, starting at the left, touching each of the spines with his index finger.

'You need to understand, Peter, that this knowledge has been passed down for thousands of years, since a time before the Bible even existed. And it didn't start with Moses. Moses is a myth. There was someone like him, but the Moses in the Bible was an amalgamation of various figures, some historical, some fictional.'

When Milan turned around again, he was holding a book in his hands.

'In principle, the secret knowledge may not be written down. To do so would be to desecrate the divinely inspired text. If you were to capture what it reveals in something as banal as a manuscript, then people would be able to copy its sacred words, and they would make mistakes . . . it would be a defilement. The text that Coen and the others had memorised was too sacred to make into an ordinary book. The words would take on a life of their own. You'd no longer know who had access to it. People would change words, whether unintentionally or deliberately.

'So by various twists of fate, three groups of living books were created to preserve the text. To reduce the risk of the knowledge being lost, two living books from Jerusalem were sent to England after the destruction of the Temple in AD 70. And as you're aware, at the beginning of the seventeenth century, two more went to Leiden. But there were disagreements and divisions in the Leiden group, and that's why only some of the Separatists went to America. A number of those who stayed behind in Leiden joined the Freemasons. It was the safest place for them then – and now. Their ideas didn't attract much attention there. The ones who went to America were the literalists, the hardliners who argued that everything should be taken literally and believed that the Bible should be read as a factual historical account. But one living book secretly joined them on their ship. He passed the knowledge on to others, and those others eventually joined the Freemasons, as their successors have continued to do to this day.'

He opened the book. The pages had been hollowed out and hidden inside it was another book. Although 'book' was too big a word to describe something that was more like a small portfolio. It was a parchment cover that contained just a few sheets of paper.

Brother Milan removed it from the hollowed-out book.

Peter couldn't help feeling a deep disappointment when he saw it. Now he understood what Milan had meant when he said that a holy text could be defiled by writing it down.

It makes it so . . . ordinary, and it's vulnerable to decay too. Paper doesn't last forever. It degrades, grows mouldy, gets eaten by silverfish.

'It's only a small part of the complete text that Coen had memorised, and a summary at that, so not even the actual words themselves. But Coen made me promise to hide it. He said that I was to take the secret of its existence to my grave,' the monk said solemnly, holding the six or seven pages in his hand.

'And nobody else knows . . .'

'Brother Antonius, who you just met, is my confessor. He

knows that I have "something", something important, but he doesn't know what it is. I made a promise to Coen . . . but now the moment has come for me to break the promise, or rather the moment has come for me to keep a promise that I made to him. Coen told me that if something went wrong, he would send someone for this text. Someone who was intelligent enough and would somehow be guided by someone or something . . .' Milan raised his eyes heavenward '. . . and find his way here. You may not have been sent here, at least, probably not in the way that Coen expected, but you are here now. And that's all that matters.'

Peter nodded silently.

'You found the map?'

'The map? Oh, the map, yes . . . The tattoo.'

Milan smiled like he was enjoying a private joke. He put a page on the table in front of Peter and held out a pen. 'Here,' he said. 'Draw it for me.'

Peter stood up, took the pen and drew the symbol as accurately as he could remember it: the triangle inside a triangle with a small circle on the top of the smallest shape. He gave the pen back to Milan, who traced over the inner triangle with the nib, emphasising the line that led to the circle.

'This is where we are now,' he said simply. 'They wanted the tattoo to show that, although the story isn't literally true, it began here, just as every story must begin somewhere. Coen used this ancient symbol to place the document precisely here, where the story began.' He handed Peter the pages from the portfolio. 'And if you rotate it,' he went on, 'you can see Sinai, and inside that, Mount Horeb. The circle represents God, the sun. According to the story, He appeared to Moses here on the mountain. God is truly the eternal light that shines forever.'

Peter looked at the sheaf of paper. 'But,' he said in amazement, 'this is in . . . Dutch!'

'Yes,' the monk smiled. 'It's ingenious, isn't it? How many people can speak your language? I doubt that anyone who went looking for the text would be able to make much sense of this. They would probably be looking for something written in ancient Hebrew. Of course, the words of the living books were "written" in a sort of proto-Hebrew. But this text, the Dutch version, would probably be overlooked.'

Unable to contain his curiosity any longer, Peter began to read . . .

Eisodus

This is the secret knowledge, the oral teachings handed down by Moses, a Son of Light, to guide Man on his eis-odus, his journey inward, and to bring him into the safe haven whence he should never have departed, the Promised Land, his true home.

We must find our way back to the garden.

There are two stories.

The story of the ex-odus, the outward journey, is for those who have eyes but cannot see, who have ears but cannot hear. They are like ones who swim in the sea, thinking that the surface of the water is all that there is to see.

The second story, the eis-odus, the journey inward, is for those who have been awoken, those who have gained access to the secret knowledge that is hidden from others. They are like swimmers in the sea who dare to dive beneath the water and discover the wonderful world hidden beneath that seemingly smooth surface. They will know the secrets of the Kingdom of Heaven that are forbidden to others. For to those who

have, more will be given, and they will have an abundance;
but from those who have nothing, even what they have will
be taken away. The reason I speak to them in parables is that
seeing they do not perceive, and hearing they do not listen,
nor do they understand.

We must all follow the road that leads from the flesh to the
spirit, for know that death can be defeated by seeking the
path to the Light.

1

Moses – 'he who is drawn out of the water' – and Aaron – 'the
Enlightened One' – the brothers. Aaron speaks for Moses, who
is slow of speech and slow of tongue. Is it not written: 'Your
brother Aaron shall be your prophet. You shall speak all that
I command you, and your brother Aaron shall tell pharaoh'?
Moses, the physical leader, Aaron, the spiritual leader. God
commanded them to deliver the Hebrew people from slavery.

Aaron was high priest in Heliopolis, the city where the sun
was worshipped in the Temple of Ra-Atum, the god who
created himself. He carried the souls of dead pharaohs up to
the starry heavens – as Aaron himself directs souls to the
Promised Land.

Aaron, Aharon . . . Only someone who has discovered within
himself the light of the invisible sun that cannot be extinguished
is capable of guiding others on the path to the Light, from the
flesh to the spirit. Because he is in contact with the spiritual
world. He resides below the water's surface that separates the

hidden spiritual world from the visible world above. He is an initiate, a faithful servant of God, who intercedes on behalf of mortals and helps them to find their way back to the garden.

2

How the soul suffers under the yoke of its human form! It seeks deliverance because the soul longs to be free, like a captive bird struggling to escape its cage. The body is Man's prison. But the soul was meant to be free, without limits, without constraints.

The soul goes through three stages: from young soul to mature soul to old soul. Similarly, the incorporeal soul, which undergoes a temporary ensnarement in the corporeal with each new life, must go through the three stages of humanity – from child to adult to elder. To what end? To return to the divine parental home that Man was forced to leave. But God keeps watch every day, looking along the path to see if His lost son or daughter is returning to Him. He is ready to welcome them home, to embrace them and never let them go. We are all Lost Sons and Lost Daughters.

If he is to return home, Man requires knowledge. But not the knowledge that can be gleaned from books, not the knowledge that comes from outside, but knowledge that is already within us. The enlightened helper is like a midwife. Just as the midwife helps the pregnant woman to give birth – giving new, corporeal life to an incorporeal soul – so the Aharon guides Man through the birth of the ideas that were always inside him from the very beginning. That is why we are reborn again and again. That is why we are forced to return in human form to the vale of tears, over and over, to learn, to gain knowledge so that the soul can ascend to greater heights and finally free itself from the mortal chains that repeatedly pull it back into the mire. But then, one day, the journey ends. Our mortal and spiritual desires have done battle. The soul has fought to overcome all that is mortal, overcome all that is corporeal. But what a triumph when the soul is victorious. For this perishable body must put on imperishability, and this mortal body must put on immortality. When this perishable body puts on imperishability, and this mortal body puts on immortality, then the saying that is written will be fulfilled: 'Death has been swallowed up in victory. Where, O death, is your victory? Where, O death, is your sting?'

3

In the desert, the Hebrews were accompanied by a pillar of smoke by day and a pillar of fire by night. The pillar of smoke accompanies Man in the daytime, indicating the way he should go. A pillar of light guides Man at night. This pillar of light is the light at the end of the tunnel that every soul passes through when it leaves the body at the end of this corporeal existence. A guide or angel leads the soul into the light where it prepares for a new birth, for a new existence, for a new phase in the learning process.

4

Just as the waters of the Red Sea receded when Moses touched them with his staff, so the lifeblood recedes from the body when the soul leaves its temporary home. The Egyptian army could not follow the Hebrews, because where souls go, mortal man – still full of lifeblood – cannot follow.

5

When the soul leaves the body behind, it feels abandoned, alone – like the Hebrews in the desert. The ties with the past have been severed … The soul still feels alive, but at the same time, it is invisible, no longer able to communicate with loved ones. The desert is a purgatory, heaven's antechamber, and the soul must pass through this domain before it can enter into the light. Here, it will be purified and brought back to its essential nature.

6

Hence forty years in the desert. The number forty is associated with trials and tests, but also with the spirit realm. It takes the soul forty days to finally free itself from physical matter, to free itself from the body, to free itself from all mortal, earthly family ties before it goes into the light. And in Egypt, the body was embalmed for forty days to remove all moisture before it was wrapped in linen.

7

In the desert, the antechamber, the soul has no need for earthly food but, instead, for heavenly food. The manna from heaven provides insight and divine knowledge. It was not Moses who gave the Hebrews bread from heaven, but God who provided the soul with true sustenance. The tribes of Israel wandered in the desert for forty years. The clothes on their backs did not wear out, nor did the sandals on their feet. They did not eat bread, and they did not drink wine or strong drink. And so, when Man passes over, the soul leaves the body and needs neither earthly food nor earthly clothing.

8

The people tell Aaron that he must make them a golden calf because God seems too far away, invisible. They smelt down their rings, their bracelets, their earrings, and their necklaces, and they create an image that they can see, an image that they can worship. This is the crisis of the soul when it has reached the deepest point. The soul is confused and is all alone in the dark – or so it thinks . . . This is the ultimate test of strength.

The ego longs to return to the flesh. The body wants to become flesh once more. Is it not written: 'The whole congregation of the Hebrews complained against Moses and Aaron in the wilderness. "If only we had died by the hand of the Lord in the land of Egypt when we sat by the fleshpots and ate our fill of bread. For you have brought us out into this wilderness to kill this whole assembly with hunger."

What is the soul's true intention? Will it go on or will it give in? The ego resists with all its might. The ego takes on the form of a god, a deity to be worshipped. It is the last phase of the soul's journey through the realms before it finally awakes. The desert is the land of the 'night-sea journey'. It

was in the desert that God issued his laws and rules and put
his people to the test.

9

The Ark of the Covenant was a symbol of the covenant made
with God. It contained the two stone tablets of the Decalogue,
the Ten Commandments. This is a reminder of the importance
of having faith in God. If we are to pass through the twilight
zone, the no man's land from which no one has ever returned,
only one thing matters: faith in God. In addition to this, one
other thing is needed to ensure a safe journey: knowing who
you are. Imagine an unfortunate sailor who falls overboard
and is swallowed by a big fish. Only when he prays to God
will the fish spit him out, like the body releasing the soul.

10

In Egypt, the Law is called Ma'at. She brings order to the
cosmos – she shines like a jewel. Opposite her is Isfet, chaos.
Does not a righteous person act according to the Ma'at? Act
according to the law of the cosmos? Is not the heart of a
person weighed in the Hall of Two Truths after death according
to the Egyptians? After death, the person's soul appears before
Osiris and forty-two judges. The soul's heart is placed on a
set of golden scales in the middle of the Hall. The feather of
Ma'at is placed in the other scale under the watchful eye of
Anubis, the God of the dead. If the heart is lighter than the
feather, the soul is allowed to pass on to the Kingdom of
Osiris. If not, the heart is devoured by the monstrous god
Amut.

What is the soul's destiny? Has it followed the divine law? Has it finally found the path to within? Or must it go back again, like the pupil given a second chance, a third chance, infinite chances, until its lessons have all been learned?

11

And finally, the soul reaches the Promised Land! But first, it must wade across the River Jordan. Crossing the River Jordan means to descend, to go down into the river of death. Here, the old self is immersed in the water and dies and comes back up again as a new person. Truly, I say to you, no one will enter Paradise, no one will go into the garden unless he is born of water and Spirit. That which is born of the flesh is flesh, and that which is born of the Spirit is spirit. Do not marvel that everyone must be born again.

In the Jordan, Man loses his life to find it again. For those who want to save their life will lose it, and those who lose their life will save it. For what will it profit them to gain the whole world and forfeit their life? Indeed, what can they give in return for their life?

And so, Man enters the Promised Land at last. This is where Man belongs. This is where Man can be with his creator in an eternal, indivisible moment of happiness. The soul is free from sickness and suffering because God is the great physician.

Man is no longer in the land of Egypt, where he had to sow the seed and irrigate the land like a vegetable garden. Instead, he is now in the Promised Land, a land of hills and valleys, watered by rain from the sky, a land that God Himself takes care of. Out of the ground, God makes to grow every tree that is pleasant to the sight and good for food. His eyes are always on it, from the beginning of the year to the end.

12

But Moses may not enter the Promised Land. He stays behind on Mount Nebo on the edge of the Jordan Valley. His faith in God was not strong enough to convince the Hebrews to trust that His goodness and knowledge would take them to that remote place. If only he had not failed to reveal to the Hebrews that it was not he but God who made water come out of the rock, letting them think that Moses himself had exceptional powers. At the very end of his journey, Moses falls short because of his pride and his lack of faith in God.

But there is always a new chance, a new life . . .

Joshua is the son of a widow and comes from Nun. The Son of the Widow, just as Horus is the son of the widow Isis, he who guides souls through the Underworld to lead them to his father, Osiris.

Joshua, the Son of the Widow, none is more fit than he to shepherd the wandering soul on its way to the Promised Land.

Chapter 39

Peter had read the text so fast that he didn't yet entirely grasp the full extent of its contents. Nor did he fully comprehend the devastating effect it would have on the official history of Judaism and Christianity if they were revealed.

He wondered if it would have made more sense to him if he had been able to read it more slowly. There were so many dark passages in it: the Ma'at . . . the fish spit him out . . . Joshua, the Son of the Widow . . .

The way out, the outward journey . . . but the Exodus is actually an Eisodus, the way inward . . . How ironic.

'You'll never read the Bible in the same way again, will you?' Milan said, taking the pages from Peter and putting them back inside the parchment folder.

'But,' Peter said, 'if you know this, if you have this knowledge too, even if it's just the tip of the iceberg and the rest was still hidden inside Coen's head, why are you still here? If you know that it's not only possible to read the story allegorically but that it was originally *intended* to be read allegorically?'

Milan thought for a moment. 'Look at me,' he said. 'I'm in my seventies. I've lived here for fifty years. Everyone I knew back in Greece is dead. Where would I go? How would I support myself? This is my home. This is where I live, and this is where

I will die. One day, my skull will be added to the mounds of other skulls I showed you earlier this evening.'

'But what now?' Peter asked. 'What do we do now?'

Once I get home, I have to let the world know about this. Publish the manuscript and find people who can help me make sense of it.

'Now you go back to your room,' Milan said flatly. 'Tomorrow, a large van will arrive with our weekly supplies. The driver will load the empty crates onto it, and you will hide among them. No one saw you arrive here, and no one will see you leave.'

Milan gave Peter the manuscript.

Peter thought it all sounded very simple.

Too simple.

However, this was identical to the ruse that Hugo Grotius had famously used to escape from Castle Loevestein after he had been sentenced to life in prison by the Synod of Dort. The brilliant jurist and follower of Professor Arminius had made his escape by hiding inside a chest that was used to deliver books to the castle.

But right now, Milan's instruction to go back to his room seemed like a good idea. He returned to his cell – once he eventually managed to find his way back there – with the parchment folder in his hand. He sat down on the bed and read the entire text again.

What a terrible shame it is that Coen only wrote down a small part of his knowledge, that he didn't share everything he knew about the allegorical interpretations of the Bible stories. This is just a summary. It's a comprehensive summary, but no more than that. What could the living books have told us about Adam and Eve in the Garden of Eden, about Cain's murder of Abel, about Noah and the Flood, about the construction of the Tower of Babel?

On the wall next to the door of his cell, there was a rucksack hanging from a simple hook, probably left behind by a previous guest. Peter put the manuscript inside the front pocket and slung the bag over his shoulder. Although for some reason – most likely an awareness of the enormous value of what he now had in his possession – he was reluctant to leave the safety of his room, he knew he would have to sooner or later. And right now, he had two very good reasons for doing so: firstly, he was very hungry and secondly, he badly needed to go to the bathroom.

Peter opened the door a fraction and peered through the gap. There was neither sight nor sound of anyone in the corridor, not even when he opened the door wider and poked his head outside.

He closed the door behind him and headed down the corridor towards the refectory and kitchen. He was relieved to find a surprisingly modern and well-maintained toilet in one of the corridors and made grateful use of it.

Afterwards, he scanned the corridor again before making his way to the refectory.

It's mind-blowing to think that the text that I'm carrying now could have such an earth-shattering effect on the world if it was published. There's no historical basis for flight from Egypt; Moses and Aaron were fictional characters; the Ten Commandments – the bedrock of Judeo-Christian civilisation – weren't laws carved into the stone tablets by the Creator on Mount Horeb, but just rules created by ordinary people; there are no divine promises that justify Israel's claim to the Palestinian territory because no one ever promised anything to anyone . . . It's all just the writings of mortal men who never intended for the stories to be taken literally . . .

A completely new insight burst upon him.

According to the New Testament, Jesus himself believed that the events described in the Torah, the Christian Old Testament, had actually taken place. Like other Jews of his time, he believed that the stories of Abraham, Isaac and Jacob, Joseph and his brothers, Moses and Aaron were historically accurate. If this document shows that those stories aren't true after all, what does that say about Jesus? What does it say about the omniscience that Christians ascribe to him if he didn't know that it was all pure fiction?

Peter walked across the refectory and into the kitchen.

On the other hand, he thought, *it's clear that this text was only recently written down. It would be easy to suggest that it's the work of a mystical fantasist and that he based it on an original source that can't be examined because it doesn't exist in physical form . . . and now that Coen and the others are gone, it doesn't exist at all.*

The kitchen was entirely deserted. He assumed that the brothers were all at the evening prayer service that Brother Antonius had been hurrying to earlier. Or, since the monastic day started so early in the morning, perhaps they had gone to bed already.

Peter opened one of the refrigerators and found it packed with large bottles of water. He decided to take two and put them in his bag for later. You could never have enough water in this environment. Another refrigerator contained small, flat loaves of bread. He took a couple, tore a chunk from one of them, then put them in his bag along with some apples and plums.

He returned to his cell, chewing hungrily on the bread. Once inside, he locked the door, sat down at the table and took Coen's papers out of the bag.

Just as he was about to read them for the third time, he was assailed by a strong feeling that he needed to leave.

Not tomorrow . . . Now! Now! Now!

No amount of rationalising and reasoning with himself could make the feeling go away.

There are lots of cars in the car park. There must be someone who can take me back to Sharm el-Sheikh right now.

The room's thick walls no longer felt like those of an impregnable fortress but of a prison.

No wonder they're called cells . . .

He opened the door and checked that the coast was clear before going back into the corridor to look for Brother Milan.

No sooner had he closed the door behind him than he heard someone shouting in the distance. No . . . not shouting . . . These were screams of panic.

Still clutching the manuscript in his hand, Peter ran outside and followed the sound of the screaming and shouting.

Across the courtyard, he caught a glimpse of a habit disappearing into the monk's dormitory building.

What's happening?

Without thinking twice, he followed the figure into the dormitory, where he found everyone gathered around the door to Brother Milan's cell.

The brothers were clearly in great distress. Three monks stood in the doorway, clutching the wooden crosses that hung from their prayer beads as if their lives depended on it.

Peter shoved them aside, more roughly than he had meant to. What he saw a second later was the bloodiest scene he had ever witnessed in his entire life – even bloodier than the one he and Fay had encountered in the Masonic Hall on the Steenschuur.

Brother Milan was lying on the floor with an enormous, sticky red pool spreading beneath his head. His skull had been crushed. His confessor, Brother Antonius, was kneeling at his side.

Tony! Did he find a way to get inside the monastery without being seen?

Antonius turned around, and when he saw Peter, he began to shout.

'Get out! Get out!' he yelled at Peter as he tended to the lifeless body of his fellow brother. His hands dripped with gore from his futile attempts to piece the shattered shards of Milan's skull back together. The unfortunate monk had already crossed the Jordan, but Brother Antonius seemed not to have realised it yet.

Or not to have accepted it.

'Go up the mountain. Go to the top and stay there for three days,' he hissed through his teeth. His blood-soaked fingers gripped Peter's hand, and for a brief moment, both men held onto Coen's manuscript. 'I know everything . . . Go up the mountain! Until that devil is gone from here! He won't be able to find you there. Go now! Save yourself!'

It took a few seconds for Peter's body to heed the monk's words. But when he eventually turned around, it was not to the mountain that he fled, but back to his room, where he locked the door behind him in a blind panic.

Dear God, what's just happened, he asked himself again.

Two giant strides took him from the door to the table. He grabbed the water jug and poured the dregs onto his bloody hand, not caring that it was splashing all over the floor. He ran his fingers through his hair to dry them.

I can't stay here.

He cautiously opened the door.

Everything seemed to be quiet again, but it was an illusory quietness, he knew now.

Like a roaring lion your adversary, the devil, prowls around, looking for someone to devour . . .

He looked right, then left, but saw no one. Staying close to the wall, he took the shortest route he could remember to the door that led outside.

The door was secured with a large bolt, but it shifted easily. Peter looked over his shoulder to make sure that he wasn't being followed, but again, he saw no one.

Could Tony really have killed Milan?

He turned right, running through the gate and onto the path that led to the mountain.

If it was Tony, why didn't he come straight to me? Why did he have to bludgeon poor Milan to death? Was he lying in wait, watching me to see if I would lead him to what he was looking for?

Peter kept running as the sandy path turned to bare rock. He looked over his shoulder now and then, but he couldn't see anyone following him.

Would I be better off going back to the road instead? Or following the route I took here with Bilal? But I'm bound to get lost, and I wouldn't last long out there with only the water I've brought with me. Going up the mountain seems like the best option. I'll hide there for three days and then come back down. The storm will have blown over by then.

The path was easy enough to see. There wasn't really any other way you could go. He was surprised by how clearly he could see everything, even though the only light came from the moon and stars. But Mount Sinai still formed a sharp, black contrast against the night sky, like a piece torn out of the heavens.

Peter was out of breath now, and he slowed down to a walk. He could hear the water bottles sloshing in his bag, but he resolved not to drink anything until he had made more progress. His shadow was visible on the ground in front of him.

With each step, he was plagued by doubts about whether this really was the wisest course of action. But there was every chance that Tony was still hiding inside the monastery, waiting for an opportunity to strike. When he realised that Peter had left the compound, he would probably assume that he would try to get back to Sharm el-Sheikh as fast as possible.

Going up the mountain increasingly seemed like the safest option.

After a while, when he felt brave enough to look back again, he saw the small, dark postage stamp of the monastery in the distance, much further away than he had dared to hope. The mountain, however, didn't seem to be getting any closer.

Peter stopped to catch his breath and drink some water. He felt overheated, but the water brought some relief as he poured it down his parched throat.

No more water until I reach the stairs, the Steps of Penitence.

The stairway had been carved into the mountain by a monk who had given himself the arduous task to teach himself the meaning of humility, Brother Antonius had told him.

It took just an hour to climb to the summit via the steps.

Eventually – Peter couldn't tell whether he had been walking for an hour, an hour and a half or even two hours – the foot of the mountain came closer. Soon the meandering path began to take him upwards, with the mountain on his left, and a slope that led downwards on his right.

He rewarded himself with another swig of water, swishing it around in his mouth before he swallowed. He took one of the plums from the bag and ate it, taking small bites. Its flavour was intense, like eating a plum for the first time.

And then, just as he had started to believe he would never reach the steps and was giving serious thought to turning back, he was suddenly there. The Stairway to Heaven.

He sat down on the first rough step and looked out over the

landscape. He felt like he could have been an astronaut on the moon, or the last man on earth. He had never felt so far away from the rest of the civilised world.

The summit is just an hour away from here. Come on, man up. Hide up there for three days, and then you can go back down. And Antonius said that there was always someone keeping watch up there, night and day, changing guard every few days.

He stood up and started the trek upwards. At first, he counted the steps to keep his mind occupied, but he soon lost count. Instead, he concentrated on his breathing, trying to keep it calm and controlled.

So many people have made this journey before me. And so many of them believed that they were following in the footsteps of Moses who climbed this mountain while the people of Israel waited down in the valley below. This is where he was supposed to have been given the Ten Commandments on two stone tablets while the Israelites grew so impatient that they melted down all of their gold jewellery and made themselves an idol to worship. But none of it is true. Zip, nada, zilch. The story doesn't contain even the tiniest grain of historical truth.

As he climbed higher and higher, Peter's pace settled into a comfortable rhythm, but soon he began to feel the long day taking a toll on him.

I can collapse when I get to the top if I need to . . . But right now, I have to keep going.

After what felt like barely an hour, the steps ended, and Peter realised that he had almost reached the top of the mountain. He found himself in a narrow pass that eventually led to a rocky plateau where a small guardhouse stood.

Peter knocked on the closed door, but there was no answer. He banged on it a few more times but heard nothing but silence in reply.

Scattered on the ground outside it were some sturdy-looking sticks, probably left behind by people who had hiked up here before him. He noticed some blankets stacked neatly in front of the building and took a few from the top of the pile. Although he felt hot, the air around him was cool.

He went around the back of the guardhouse, out of sight of anyone who might come up the mountain and folded two blankets in half to create a reasonably soft mattress on the ground. Using his rucksack as a pillow, he lay down and covered himself as best he could with the other blankets.

His legs ached with tiredness. But as he stared up at the majestic canopy of stars above him, the words of the old Psalm echoed in his mind.

> *When I look at your heavens, the work of your fingers,*
> *the moon and the stars that you have established;*
> *what are human beings that you are mindful of them,*
> *mortals that you care for them?*
> *Yet you have made them a little lower than God,*
> *and crowned them with glory and honour.*

It really is a wonderful book when you think about it. A work of pure fiction, but its ancient wisdom and timeless beauty still speak to us. And even if the stories in it aren't true, we can find truth in them. They're about the universal human experience, so they remain powerful, even today.

A few minutes later, he was completely unconscious.

Chapter 40

It wasn't the dawning light that woke Peter, but the sound of footsteps. Thinking that the guard had ventured out of his hut at last, he stretched his stiff limbs and stood up. Perhaps the guard had pretended not to hear him. He was probably fed up with having his sleep disturbed by the fool-hardy tourists who climbed the mountain ahead of the organised groups.

Peter picked up his rucksack, folded up the blankets and carried them around to the front of the building to put them back where he had found them.

When he rounded the corner, he realised that he had been mistaken. The guardhouse door was still shut, and there was no sign of the guard. But he saw the man whose footsteps had woken him up. The man who had read Peter's mind and climbed up the mountain after him.

A man wearing a baseball cap.

Peter recoiled in fright and dropped the bundle of blankets on the ground.

What can I do? I'm no match for Tony physically. I know that from experience.

They were alone here. There was no chance of anyone coming to help him.

Tony smiled at him in the way one might greet a colleague at work every day, absently, and without much emotion.

'Mr De Haan, I presume?' he sneered.

Peter took a few steps away from the guardhouse, keeping his eyes fixed on Tony. Behind him was the only way down from the plateau.

Tony walked towards him, matching Peter's steps to maintain the distance between them.

'How?' was all Peter managed to say, his voice loud and panicked.

How is this possible? How did he survive falling into the sea?

Tony's smile was gloating now.

'How the hell did I survive?' Tony said, making a complete sentence of Peter's desperate wail. 'Is that what you're trying to ask me?'

'What do you want from me?'

'Let's start with your first question,' Tony said, and he looked very much at ease, like a chess master who knows he is playing from a winning position and can take his time.

'I've got to hand it to you, Peter, you really surprised me. Getting yourself out of the water like that. Very impressive, Peter, very athletic. But I dived under the water and swam away. Of course, I figured you wouldn't want to let me back on board after our little tussle. But then I saw that orange lifesaver floating there, and I thought: what a good man that Peter is. No "Eye for an eye, tooth for a tooth" for him. It was a little lesson in humility for me. You literally threw me a lifeline. So I swam over to it and held my face just above the water inside the ring so I could breathe. Aaah, oxygen . . .'

He took a deep breath and held his arms out wide.

'You see, if you'd just come a tiny bit closer, Peter, you'd have

seen me. But, well, what would you have done then? You're not
the type to give me a whack on the head, so your only option
would still have been to just sail away. But thanks anyway! It
was a hell of a long way to swim, but hey, I'm an athlete too.
The lifesaver even gave me a chance to have a little rest now
and then. You really are a lifesaver, Peter! I guess the boat has
already found its way back to its owner by now.'

Peter considered laying all his cards on the table.

*What if I just show him Coen's manuscript? That's what he
wants. I could even throw it on the ground behind me and then
run like mad. Try to find somewhere to hide on the way down.
But he'll probably make sure he puts me out of action first before
he picks it up.*

Instead, he screamed: 'What do you want?'

'Not so fast, Peter! I have the good fortune to know a lot of
people, Peter. I'm truly blessed. A good friend of mine lives on
the beach just outside of Plymouth. He's the sort of friend who
. . . How should I put this? Who won't ask any questions if you
turn up unannounced on his doorstep in soaking wet clothes.
The kind of friend who'll go to your house and pick up some
dry clothes for you, pick up some passports.'

'Passports?'

'Of course. You don't think I travel as Tony Vanderhoop, do
you? America is a land of endless possibilities, Peter, the land
of the free and home of the brave. To cut a long story short: I
watched you leave the Harvard campus and take a taxi. You were
supposed to be going home, but then things took a different
course when you got to the airport, didn't they? You got the taxi
to drop you off at a different terminal to the one that the
European flights leave from. My curiosity was piqued. EgyptAir
. . . Faarouz, what a lovely lady she is. Totally fell for my story

about wanting to join my Dutch friend. "In Sharm el-Sheikh?" she asked me. I can't believe you didn't see me there, buddy. But it's easy to hide from someone who isn't expecting to see you. Amazing, how that works. And then there were our German friends, Peter . . .'

Peter was listening intently now.

'What cash-strapped people won't do for five hundred dollars. I had them convinced that I just wanted to scare you . . . But rescued by Bedouins! I wasn't expecting *that*.'

'That's enough, Tony. Whatever it is that you want, I don't have it. Leave me alone!'

'Well,' Tony hissed. 'We'll have to see about that. And I think you do have something I want, something that poor, unfortunate monk gave you. And if he didn't give it to you, then I'm sure he told it to you.'

Peter responded with silence.

'Exactly,' Tony went on. 'He gave you something, or he told you something – or both. Something about Coen, who visited the monastery a few times and was just a little too candid and shared his secret knowledge with Brother Milan. So then Brother Milan knew far more than was good for him. Knowledge is power, you know that. And sometimes, as the good brother learned, it can be deadly.'

Peter tried to move towards the steps, but Tony bounded over and blocked his path in a couple of long strides.

Play for time. I've got to stall him somehow . . . Wasn't there supposed to be a permanent guard here?

'But how . . .'

'. . . did I get inside?' Tony said, finishing Peter's question. 'Ask, and it will be given you; search, and you will find; knock, and the door will be opened for you. The law of the desert,

Peter. That's why the Bedouins saved you. If a weary traveller appears at your door, you must *always* invite them in. The trickiest part was finding a monk's habit in my size. I saw you, you know, sitting in the refectory. The monks lead such a beautiful life.'

Tony appeared to be thoroughly enjoying this game of cat and mouse.

'It's a pilgrimage,' he said placidly. 'Nothing more, nothing less. In the end, we're all Pilgrims. As the words on the plaque on the Pieterskerk so eloquently put it, "But now we are all, in all places, strangers and pilgrims, travellers and sojourners." Passers-by, that's what we are. And on our pilgrimage, we go searching for who we really are. We travel into the unknown, and we all end up where we are right now, in the wilderness.'

He held his arms out wide, emphasising his words.

'A no man's land,' he went on. '*Hic sunt leones*. Here be lions! Dangers lurk around every corner, waiting for a moment of weakness so they can lead us from the straight and narrow road, away from the path of righteousness. On our pilgrimage, we try to remember who we actually are.'

Tony was pacing now, like an animal. The more he spoke, the less he seemed to be aware of the world around him, like a professor so deeply absorbed in his lecture that he forgets that he's standing in front of a room full of students. Even his language took on a more formal tone.

'We're confronted by our own selves,' he continued, 'but also by the realisation that another reality exists: that of the soul. Our existing values disappear and are replaced by new values, spiritual values, and these values are not temporal but eternal. It's a voyage of discovery, if you will, a voyage on which we become aware of a Higher Power, an eternal being who has had many names.

Every age, every people, every religion has called it by a different name. This Power is a god of forgiveness and second chances, like the Father in the parable of the Lost Son. Like someone who doesn't strike back when they're struck, but instead turns the other cheek and gives the offender another chance, a chance not to strike again. This Power is a god of mercy and of love. He wants us to do the right thing, just as a mortal father wants to see his children do the right thing. He longs for His children to return home, simply because that is where they belong.'

If Tony really believes all of that, then maybe I can get out of this. This is very different from the way he was talking last time.

'But this is fantastic news, Tony! This is wonderful, isn't it?' Peter said enthusiastically. His excitement was genuine. 'Together with what I learned from the monk – and he only told me a few small details – this is an amazing message. It should be shared with the whole world. Why keep it hidden? Why not reveal it so that everyone can benefit from it? If you can give people definitive proof that the whole Bible is a collection of allegorical stories, that there's barely a trace of historical truth in it and they don't have to interpret it literally any more, then doesn't that create room for everyone to understand it in a way that's more personally meaningful to them? Then—'

'Listen,' Tony interrupted him sharply. 'This knowledge will mean nothing to people if they aren't ready for it. It would be like reading a book to a baby. It'll hear noises, and it'll coo and smile, maybe fall asleep, perhaps be delighted by the sound of your voice, but it won't understand a word. It would be like giving your first-year students a lecture from the last year of their course. Pointless. And besides, this knowledge is already available in other forms and in other traditions for anyone who goes looking for it.'

'So why not share the knowledge with others?'

'I just told you. It would be pointless. Pearls before swine. But there's a much bigger problem than that. Don't you see the dilemma here? The real dilemma?'

Peter looked at him with incomprehension.

I'm not getting out of this just yet, then.

'It's so obvious, Peter. Look, the stories were never meant to be taken literally. Everyone used to know that, but that knowledge was lost. For most people, anyway. But then everyone knew that there was something else hidden in the stories, wisdom that wasn't supposed to be given to everyone. When Jesus told the parable of the sower, he said to his disciples: "To you it has been given to know the secrets of the kingdom of God; but to others I speak in parables, so that looking they may not perceive and listening they may not understand." What good would it have done those people who came to Jesus, the simple farmers, the labourers, the tax collectors, the prostitutes and lepers, if he had explained those hidden meanings to them? It would have gone in one ear and out the other! Simple people need simple stories. You can tell a child a hundred times to stay on the right path, watch out for the bad guys, and above all, to do as their mother tells them. They'll listen, but the message won't really sink in. But tell them the story of Little Red Riding Hood over and over and the message sticks. Do you see?'

'I see what you mean, Tony. I really do. You have a point, but . . .'

Keep him talking, tell him he's right, agree with him . . . And what he's saying does make sense. But that doesn't mean that he gets to decide who should be given this knowledge and who shouldn't.

'This is why people tell each other stories. This is why we wrap messages up inside stories. It's so that people can understand them on their own level and in their own time. We know that the Exodus story is actually about the journey inwards. That's the irony of all this: the story about leaving is really a story about coming home!'

'So what's the dilemma?'

'If the Exodus story is a true historical account, at least in terms of our general understanding of history, then how can the Bible still be considered to set the moral standards for western civilisation? The Bible is the cornerstone of all of western civilisation. It's been used to legitimise the conquest of worlds, the subjugation of peoples – so that we could trade with them, obviously, or take their resources. But it was so that we could civilise them too, and bring them the gospel. Love, forgiveness, a return to God, whatever. But then when you really read the Bible, particularly the story of the Exodus, the story of the conquest of the promised land . . . With God's blessing and help, the Israelites murdered hundreds of thousands of people, six hundred thousand, maybe even more. Then another ten thousand were thrown off of a cliff by King Amaziah who "did what was right in the sight of the Lord". Men, women, children, cattle . . . They slaughtered everything and everyone to cleanse the land. It was actual genocide. If the stories in the Old Testament are historical truth, then how can we, even for a single second, entertain the idea that the Bible sets the moral standards for our civilisation?'

These are the stories Coen Zoutman wrote down. This is why he had them with him!

'Those people weren't even given a chance to leave,' Tony continued. 'They weren't even allowed to exist. They had to be wiped out, exterminated as if they were an infestation. And why? What act of sin had been committed by these people, people who had, after all, also been created by God? They lived in the promised land! That was their crime! Their religion was destroyed, their culture destroyed, their villages and towns burned to the ground and obliterated, their temples and idols burned. Their virgin daughters were taken from them as the spoils of war and divided among Joshua's brave warriors for God. Good God, how was that any different from the atrocities committed by the Islamic State fighters today? The barbarity and intolerance . . . how were they any different from ISIS, who blew up the ancient Buddhas of Bamiyan statues, destroyed churches? Who will slaughter anyone who doesn't share *their* one true path, *their* one true faith? Who even kill other Muslims if they refuse to join their ranks? Who massacre Yazidi men and take their wives and daughters as their own personal property to be used as sex slaves? Who burn people alive, decapitate them, throw them off of towers? Who will not be satisfied until their caliphate is cleansed of everything that's been forbidden by their god? A god who is on their side alone, a god who rejoices every single time one of His fighters blows himself up and sends an unbeliever to hell? How is that any different?'

Maybe he's not as crazy as I thought . . .

Peter was lost for words. 'But . . .' he eventually managed to say. 'But then surely you must let the world know that you have solid, conclusive proof that the story of the Exodus was never intended to be read as history. That it's a parable with a deeper meaning that can only be understood by those who've been initiated.'

'That's not possible! If this is brought out into the open, everything falls apart. And it will only get worse. I doubt that most people even care about this anyway. There are plenty of believers who won't care much, and the non-believers won't care at all. No, most people already understand that it obviously wasn't possible to fit every single animal in the world on Noah's ark. How could there have been koalas in the Middle East when they depend on the leaves of the Australian eucalyptus tree for food? How would they have survived? There are more than ten million species of insect alone, and each one lives in a specific habitat like a plant or a tree, often in symbiosis with another animal. And then what about the flood waters rising until they covered every mountaintop? Mount Everest is nearly ten kilometres high. Any living thing that didn't freeze to death at that altitude would have died from lack of oxygen . . . Not to mention where all the water went after the flood. And it doesn't stop there: if the story of Adam and Eve isn't true, then there was no fall, no original sin, no separation between God and man. So Jesus' death, the sacrifice that reconciled man and God, wouldn't have been necessary. Do you understand what that means? What the consequences are?'

Tony was as breathless as someone who had just run a hundred-metre dash.

'If we take the Bible literally,' he said, 'it loses its moral authority. Because its stories are full of hate, intolerance, murder and rape, all authorised by God because the victims weren't Jewish. But if people are told that we don't need to take those stories literally, what will happen then? Well, just to name one thing, the State of Israel's legitimacy vanishes. There would be no story, no book that people could invoke and say: this land is ours because it was promised to us by God! And if the State of Israel falls apart, then everything falls apart. It's been said for years that Israel is a role model for the rest of the Middle East, the only democracy, the only country where peace and security reign. America's foreign policy, the west's foreign policy, the unconditional support given to Israel, the tens of thousands of young people who've worked on the *kibbutzim* helping to develop the land, the United Nations Blue Helmets who were supposed to protect the young state from Arab aggression. Imagine what will happen if people knew that all of those things were based on a lie, a myth! That will only add grist to the mill of the anti-Semites. The State of Israel's right to exist would vanish, and so would the divine promise that Jews still invoke to defend it. If Exodus is a fable . . . Jesus himself believed in it, spoke about it often . . . Must we then say that even Jesus, the Son of God, was wrong? That even he didn't know that none of it really happened?'

That's what I was thinking yesterday!

'What becomes of Jesus' omniscience then?' Tony said. 'His omnipotence? His divinity? Don't you see? Nothing, absolutely nothing in the world will be stable after that. And it won't just be unstable; it will topple and eventually all collapse . . . Imagine the chaos, Peter, if this is revealed. Don't you see? Judaism, Christianity, Islam . . . they're all based on these stories. So many conflicts are based on religion. Or rather, religious justifications are often given by those who wage wars over land and resources. People will always find something they can use to divide the world into "us" and "them". Where everyone is a Christian, it's Catholics against Protestants. And where everyone is a Catholic, it's the people who speak Dutch against the people who speak French . . . But religion brings people together too, gives millions of people a sense of purpose and meaning in their lives. Religion encourages people to try to be good, to try to do good. Imagine a world without these three Abrahamic religions. Imagine what would happen if they collapsed. It would be the end of the world as we know it.'

'I do understand what you're saying,' Peter said carefully, 'but—'

'For pity's sake, let's just leave things as they are, Peter. The world can't cope with the truth. People can't cope with the truth.

Especially not right now . . . There's going to be a huge focus on the Pilgrims soon.'

Of course. I was wondering when he'd get to them . . .

'That story will fall apart too. The Pilgrims came to a new land, too, God's own country. They were convinced that their venture was blessed by God. They compared themselves to the Israelites, and their leaders said to James I, "Let my people go." And when he refused, just like the Israelites, they had to flee. They had to emigrate too, leave behind the fleshpots of England and Holland and cross a sea to reach their promised land with their Bibles in their hands. That land was inhabited already, but they cleared it so that it would be fit for *their* way of life. If the Book of Exodus isn't historical fact, then the legitimacy of the Pilgrims' whole endeavour crumbles, and so do the very foundations of the United States of America . . . But enough of that.'

Tony looked at him blankly, and the hollow look in his eyes was more terrifying than when they had burned with hate.

I have to get away from here. Give him what he wants. I can't win . . . He won't let anything stand in his way.

'Here,' Peter said, and he opened the rucksack. He kept his eyes fixed on Tony. 'You're right, Tony. You've convinced me. There aren't many people who could cope with knowing this. It should stay between you and me. Here.' He grabbed the pages that Brother Milan had given him. 'I've not been completely honest with you,' he said. 'Brother Milan did give me these. But you've convinced me, Tony, you really have. These are Coen's papers, the texts he wrote down. You can do whatever you want with them. You've got more right to them than anyone else. This knowledge was entrusted to you, so it should be left in your hands.'

Peter took a step towards Tony, but he carried on staring at him expressionlessly.

Surely he'll be happy now that he's got the manuscript.

But Tony didn't seem to be interested in Coen's manuscript at all.

'Well, here's the thing, Peter,' Tony said, picking up one of the abandoned walking sticks that were lying in front of the guard-house. He moved towards Peter, adjusting his grip on the stick like a baseball hitter getting ready for a pitch.

'The only people left who know about this are me and you,' Tony said menacingly. 'The living books are gone. There's nothing left to prove that this knowledge exists. And there's nobody else who could bring about the end of the world as we know it. So . . .'

Completely unexpectedly and with a speed that Peter didn't see coming, Tony had swung the stick back, ready to strike. Peter instinctively raised his arm to ward off the blow, but the stick smashed into his left wrist. He heard a dry crack as the bone broke. A burst of searing pain surged through his body as if his nerves had been electrified.

He heard his own shriek of agony echo in the mountains.

His right hand flew to his wrist in a vain attempt to soothe the pain, but that left him unprotected against the next blow that landed heavily on his skull.

Peter felt blood from the wound stream over his forehead. A moment later, he realised that he could see nothing out of one eye. He tasted metal on his tongue.

'Stop!' he screamed desperately, falling to his knees. His instinct told him that this was the wrong thing to do because it would make him more vulnerable. But he was in too much pain to do anything else.

Still gripping the stick, Tony bent to pick up the papers that were now scattered on the ground. He shook the rucksack upside down until it was empty.

'Were you planning to stay up here for a while?' he said snidely when he saw the bread, the fruit and the bottles of water. He stood up again and read the first lines of the text that Coen had written down. '*De "Eisodus"*? But that's . . .'

Tony laughed maniacally.

'Is this *it*? This is *all* there is?' He scanned the pages. 'This is Dutch, right? Genius. Sam only taught me "Genesis", and I only learned the sounds at first. You don't know what it means, so the words go past your mind and straight to your heart without you translating them. It's only later that their meaning is explained to you. It's about man's lifelong search for the garden he was cast out of. But that story is really nothing more than the primal experience of every human being: at first, you're one with your mother, safely cradled in her womb, but then you're banished.'

Tony didn't even bother to look at the other pages properly.

'Our whole life is really a search for that same sense of security, for the feeling of oneness that we've lost. The womb is the real Garden of Eden. In the end, we're all refugees. We humans have been pilgrims from the very beginning, all searching for our true home. All the way back to Adam and Eve, who were banished from Eden, sent away because they disobeyed God. And mankind has been on a journey ever since, looking for the lost garden, trying to find our way back to the lost paradise where we actually belong.'

And we've gotta get ourselves back to the garden . . .

'Mary, Joseph and Jesus were refugees, of course,' Tony said, more quietly now, as if the thought had only just occurred to him. 'They stole away from Bethlehem like thieves in the night to escape the Massacre of the Innocents. They found asylum in Egypt, and they could only go back to Bethlehem when Herod was dead.'

He walked over to a pair of spindly-looking bushes that were growing on the rocky plateau. They stood side by side like two people desperately holding onto each other for comfort after a disaster. He kept his eye on Peter, although there seemed to be little chance of Peter posing any kind of threat to him now.

'Excellent,' Tony said, like a teacher about to hand back an A+ essay to his top pupil.

One by one, he crumpled the pages of Coen's notes into balls and poked them into the thorny branches. When he was finished, he took a cigarette lighter out of his pocket.

Like a priest about to make an offering, playing on the emotions of the devotees who are watching him with bated breath, Tony sparked up a flame. He held his arm outstretched as Peter observed him from a few metres away.

I've got to get away from here.

Never in his life had Peter been in so much pain. He felt nauseous. He tried to get back on his feet but abandoned the attempt almost as soon as he had started.

Everything makes sense now: the Bible stories that Coen wrote down, the murders, Coen and Yona, the living books. And not just that: everything I've ever read about the Old Testament too . . .

Tony crouched down next to the bushes and lit the paper on the lowest branch. It ignited almost instantly and, seconds later, the bone-dry thorn bushes went up in flames. Peter could feel the heat from where he was sitting.

'I really ought to take my shoes off,' Tony said, 'since this is holy ground. But let's not make the situation any more dramatic than it already is.'

A dark cloud of smoke rose up from the burning bushes, but the flames didn't last long. Once the paper had been reduced to black flakes of ash, the fire burned out.

A few glowing embers dropped onto the stony ground and were quickly extinguished.

'*Voilà*,' Tony said, pronouncing the French word with a strong American accent. 'That's that.'

He approached Peter again now, looming over him with the stick raised menacingly in the air.

At first, Peter didn't realise that Tony was there. He had closed his eyes in the hope that the darkness would reduce his splitting headache.

But then he heard a whoosh nearby warning him that Tony had swung the stick back ready to take another slug at him. Peter lunged for Tony's legs and wrapped his arms around them like a rugby player in a scrum. An excruciating bolt of pain shot through his arm.

Peter's unexpected tackle caught Tony by surprise. He lost his balance and fell backwards. He lay motionless for a fraction of a second as clouds of dust from the dry ground scudded up around him.

Peter scrambled to his feet, clutching his injured wrist with his hand.

But now Tony was on his feet again too.

Peter reached for the stick that lay between them, but before he could grab it, Tony kicked it away. Peter was still bent over when Tony took a hard swipe at his neck with the side of his hand. He fell flat on the ground.

Peter's already parched mouth filled with sand, drying it out even more and scouring his tongue. He tried to spit it out and saw that the sand was a pinkish red colour. He blinked. His eyes were blurred with blood and sweat, making it hard to focus. He slowly raised his head.

Tony picked up the stick again and leaned on it like a weary traveller. He paced back and forth across the plateau. He seemed unsure about what his next move should be.

Just as Peter was wiping the blood and muck from his eyes, he heard the sound of moving air again. A fraction of a second later, the stick landed with a loud crack on his back, and once again, he collapsed to the ground. He couldn't believe that this was how his life was going to end. He closed his eyes and listened as the dull, sand-dampened thud of Tony's footsteps moved away from him.

Judith, he thought.

And then: *Sorry, Fay.*

Moments later, he felt hands grabbing hold of his feet. He tried to kick himself free, but he could make no more than a feeble attempt.

He was dragged roughly away, like a dead bull after a bullfight in a Spanish arena. The heel of his left foot slipped out of his shoe, but the shoe stayed on.

Still holding his broken wrist, he pressed his face into his arm to protect it from the hard rocks and coarse sand.

A light gust of wind rushed up, cooling him off despite its warmth. His feet were dropped to the floor. With a great deal of effort, he managed to raise his head a couple of centimetres to see where he was.

To his horror, he found himself staring into an abyss.

Surely he's not going to . . .

Very carefully, Peter moved away from the edge of the ravine.

Where's Tony? Why hasn't he already . . .

He managed to sit up. Blood, sweat and tears muddied his vision, but it looked like Tony was already getting rid of the evidence. He was sweeping the sand with a rough besom that was barely more than a bunch of twigs tied to a stick. He swept the broom wildly back and forth, erasing the drag marks that Peter's body had made.

Why is he doing that now? Does he just want to torture me? Make me watch him so I know that he's going to get away with this? That no one will ever find out what happened here?

Peter tried to get up but failed miserably. He was already feeling dizzy, and a throbbing headache was making it worse. His ears rang with a pulsating thrum that faded in and out as if he was driving past parked cars with the window down.

Tony was just a few metres away from him now. He raised the broom in the air like a javelin and hurled it towards the guardhouse. Then he rubbed his hands together. Peter wasn't sure whether this was to remove the dust or in satisfaction at a job well done.

'So, Peter,' he said in the same warm, friendly tone he had used when they'd first met. 'We have to get through this together, old boy.' He picked Peter up by his armpits and dragged him back to the edge of the abyss.

Peter tried to resist, but his feet found no purchase on the rocky, sandy ground beneath them. He thought he might black out from the pain in his wrist. His mouth was as dry as cork, and his head felt like it was about to explode.

'We're both in the same boat here,' Tony said, panting from the effort of carrying Peter. 'I know everything, and you know too much, so if we disappear together, the knowledge disappears with us.' He paused for a moment. 'Come on,' he said.

No.

Gathering every last ounce of strength he had left, Peter turned his head until his mouth made contact with Tony's upper arm. With all the force he could muster, he sank his teeth into the soft flesh. He felt Tony's muscles contract as he bit through the fabric of his shirt and then broke through his skin.

For a moment, the deafening sound of blood rushing in his

ears gave Peter the sensation that he was standing next to an enormous waterfall.

Now it was Tony's turn to scream in pain. He yanked at Peter's hair with his right hand, but when Peter's teeth stayed clamped onto his arm – like a dog refusing to give up a tennis ball – he began to punch Peter's head.

Peter let go.

When he felt Tony's grip weaken for a moment, he launched himself backwards with all the force he could muster, throwing Tony to the ground.

I can do this . . .

He lay on his back on top of Tony, who was gasping for breath now from exertion and pain.

'You son of a . . .'

Peter pushed off with one foot and managed to propel himself over Tony, landing just behind him. Holding his injured wrist, he tried to shove Tony over towards the ravine with his shoulder. Tony leapt up, which sent Peter flying forward. He ended up with his head close to the cliff edge.

No, no, no . . . Dear God, please, no.

Tony started to push Peter towards the edge.

And war broke out in heaven. Michael and his angels fought against the dragon, and the dragon and his angels fought back.

The solid ground beneath him disappeared. As Peter fell, his loose shoe slipped clean off his foot and stayed behind on the plateau.

But they were defeated, and there was no longer any place for them in heaven.

For a fraction of a second, time stood still. Adrenaline surged through Peter's body. He imagined that this was what bungee jumpers felt just after they stepped off the platform.

But bungee jumpers have ropes.

Peter and Tony plummeted into the depths of the ravine.

The great dragon was thrown down, that ancient serpent, who is called the Devil and Satan, the deceiver of the whole world.

A brief burst of warm wind blew through their clothes.

He was thrown down to the earth, and his angels were thrown down with him.

But then, much sooner than Peter had been expecting, they crashed onto a hard surface, a small ledge protruding less than a metre and a half out from the cliff face, just two metres below the plateau.

Peter landed on his back and Tony came down on top of him with his lower body dangling over the ledge.

He will command his angels concerning you, to protect you, and on their hands they will bear you up so that you will not dash your foot against a stone.

'Damn it!' Peter heard Tony shout.

Tony scrabbled around behind him with his right hand, trying to get hold of Peter's shirt. When he eventually managed to grab it, he pushed himself away from the cliff face with his feet. Peter felt both of their bodies shift over the edge. His backside was already halfway over it. Tony had already almost completely disappeared now, but his grip on Peter didn't weaken. Centimetre by centimetre, they moved closer to the fathomless depths below them. Peter was paralysed by the pain in his wrist. He was afraid that he might pass out at any moment. He watched the knuckles of Tony's hand turn white from the strain of holding onto him.

A primal, animal instinct to survive welled up in Peter, just has it had done in the water in Plymouth. Tony's fingers were next to Peter's mouth.

If Tony fell now, he would drag Peter with him.

Peter lifted his head once more and bit into one of Tony's fingers as hard as he could. Tony let out a bloodcurdling scream.

There was a barely audible but nauseating ripping sound, and then . . . Tony let go.

Peter tasted blood. He spat out the chunk of raw flesh in his mouth. He had bitten off most of Tony's finger, just above the middle joint.

He quickly swept the bloody stump into the ravine.

Then he closed his eyes and sank into a deep, black oblivion.

Epilogue

The ice cube that Rijsbergen had added to his whisky had completely vanished. He had been staring at the glass without taking a sip, wondering if he would see the ice melt. But its slow disappearance had been imperceptible.

The Zoutman–Falaina investigation had finally been closed that afternoon. Although he knew with certainty who had murdered the two men, in many respects, the resolution of this case had brought him no satisfaction.

Those little grey cells had failed him after all.

In the end, it hadn't been old-fashioned detective work that had led to the solution but a series of dramatic events, events that had almost claimed an eighth innocent victim in the form of Peter de Haan.

Six 'living books', as Rijsbergen had learned, and an elderly monk in Saint Catherine's Monastery had been unable to escape the murderous hands of Tony Vanderhoop.

Only Peter had managed to narrowly avoid being killed by the madman who had eventually taken his own life.

But is Peter a victim? Is there such a thing as a 'guilty victim'?

At last, he took a sip of whisky.

That afternoon, he and Van de Kooij had sat silently in Rijsbergen's small office where, over the last few weeks, they had spent far more time together than was good for their professional relationship. Their little plastic beakers of coffee – or what passed for coffee – had gone stone cold.

How I would love, just once, to be able to bring a case to a close by giving a speech, Rijsbergen thought. *Knowing that the killer was in my audience, I would lay everything out in exquisite detail, explaining how the murderer had initially managed to throw me off the scent. What an idiot I had been – I, Rijsbergen! – to allow him to deceive me. The murderer would nervously shuffle his feet and try to keep a straight face. I would name a few other suspects first, and he would relax a little, thinking he had got away with it. Until! 'Until . . .' I would say. 'Until that one clue that had seemed so insignificant at first, that no one, including myself – because even a great mind such as my own can be mistaken, can it not? – had paid any attention to, turned out to be of enormous significance.'*

'In that one clue,' he would tell his spellbound audience, 'we found the key that unlocked the case.' And then, in the triumphant culmination of all his meticulous detective work, he would point his finger at the murderer.

One must seek the truth within – not without.

In reality, Rijsbergen and Van de Kooij had been playing a constant game of catch-up. The moment they had established that Tony Vanderhoop was involved in all three cases, the man had vanished into thin air. Their American counterparts had been unable to catch him. Only after his death had they discovered that he had left the United States travelling under a false name, and that he had been on the same flight to Sharm el-Sheikh as Peter de Haan. A man had been spotted on CCTV at Logan airport with the same unmistakable build as Tony Vanderhoop. The authorities in Egypt had not picked up the alert that had been put out for Peter de Haan's arrest. Even now, Rijsbergen had received no response from the Egyptian police.

Vanderhoop had indeed failed to board the flight to Boston with the rest of the American delegation, inventing an excuse and parting ways with them at Schiphol.

This did not let Van der Lede off the hook, however, since his long silence had obstructed the case.

A few days after De Haan had arrived back home in the Netherlands, Rijsbergen and Van de Kooij had spoken to him in Fay Spežamor's little almshouse. His left wrist had been in a cast, and the wound above his eye was a deep, purplish blue, almost black. He had looked like a boxer after an epic fight.

Spežamor's daughter, who had been sitting on De Haan's knee when Rijsbergen and Van de Kooij arrived, had been sent upstairs. Her mother had wanted to spare her the gory details of what had almost been De Haan's final hour.

'The guards found me,' De Haan had told them, his face contorting with pain now and then. 'It turned out that there was someone in the guardhouse. The man was dead to the world. Maybe he was in a drunken stupor. Lord knows, but he heard absolutely nothing. Not a single thing, from my arrival in the night to my fight with Tony the next morning.'

It was only when his colleague had gone into the hut to take over from him the next day that the guard had returned to the land of the living. Outside, the two guards had noticed a single shoe on the edge of the plateau that hadn't been there earlier. Taking a closer look around, they had found evidence of a struggle and peered over the edge of the ravine where they saw De Haan lying on a ledge, apparently dead.

One of the guards had tied a rope around his middle and fastened it to a rock, then lowered himself onto the ledge. He had discovered that De Haan was still alive but unconscious. With the rope tied under De Haan's arms, the guards had eventually managed to haul him up onto the plateau and move him into the protective shadow cast by the guardhouse. They had tried to give him water, but most of it had trickled back out of his mouth. De Haan's broken wrist would have been obvious to any layman. They had splinted it with reeds, then strapped him onto the stretcher that had stood in the corner of the hut since time immemorial but never been used.

The guards had carried him down the mountain together, an impressive feat on the uneven steps and under the harsh sun that had already grown very hot.

At the bottom of the steps, they'd been met by the Bedouins who congregated there every morning hoping to take tourists back to Saint Catherine's Monastery by camel.

The Bedouins took De Haan to the monastery where he'd spent the rest of the day in a cool and spartan cell regaining his strength under the care of a bearded priest.

By the next day, he had been well enough to take a taxi back to Sharm el-Sheikh and had asked the driver to take him to the hospital so that his wrist could be set in plaster.

When he'd returned to his hotel to pick up his suitcase, he'd been surprised to find Melchior and Katja waiting for him. Katja had thrown herself into his arms, so happy to see him alive. They had told him that Vanderhoop had offered them a huge sum of money, an amount that far exceeded the loss they had suffered in Cairo.

Vanderhoop had shown the pair some photographs of De Haan and himself together – presumably taken during Willem Hogendoorn's Pilgrims tour in Leiden – and convinced them that he and De Haan were old friends. He had spun an elaborate yarn about how they had been playing jokes on each other for years to keep their wits sharp. 'Never anything that would cause any real danger, obviously,' he had told them, putting his hand on his heart to show how sincere he was. He'd promised them he would be along in another taxi to rescue De Haan less than five minutes after they had driven off without him. He had even told them convincing stories about some of the tricks they had already played on each other. Supposedly, during a trip to the rainforests of Borneo, De Haan had instructed their guides to break down their camp while Vanderhoop was asleep and move it a hundred metres away. And he had tricked De Haan on a trip to Paris by getting off the train one stop early with all of their luggage and passports while De Haan was in the bathroom. These tests of wits had served to deepen the long-standing bond of friendship between them. Together with the five hundred dollars in cash that Vanderhoop had paid them on the spot, this strange but convincing tale had been enough to persuade Melchior and Katja to go along with the plan to leave De Haan in the desert.

That explained why Katja had smiled and given him two thumbs up as the taxi had sped away. She had been wishing him luck on his latest exciting adventure, one that would give him entertaining anecdote to tell back home.

After his visit to the hospital, De Haan had been taken to the police station in Sharm el-Sheikh to be interviewed. He had told them that Vanderhoop had attacked him but had claimed not to know why the man wanted to kill him. And of course, Vanderhoop was no longer available for questioning.

He hadn't been able to stop thinking about poor Brother Milan . . . After spending more than fifty years in the monastery, the monk had been denied the dignity of having his skull laid in the charnel house intact.

The Egyptian police officer who wrote up the interview on an old-fashioned typewriter had looked delightedly up at De Haan, obviously pleased at having been able to wrap the case up so soon.

'The sun does strange things to people here,' he'd said. 'We will inform the gentleman's family in America. We don't have the resources to go looking for his body. The terrain is dangerous and mostly inaccessible. Perhaps he'll be found one day if his body is not eaten by animals. But if he's in an area that the animals cannot reach, then . . .'

'Then what?' De Haan had asked.

'Then he will become a mummy,' the officer had said. He had wound the report out of the typewriter, pounded various official stamps onto the paper, and signed it in a conspicuously elaborate hand. 'Case closed,' he'd said with evident satisfaction.

'We wish you a safe and pleasant journey home,' he'd said to Peter afterwards, like a tour guide bidding farewell to his group after a wonderful day trip. 'We hope to see you again in our beautiful country.'

Peter had shaken his hand.

The next day, Peter had taken a direct flight from Sharm el-Sheikh to Amsterdam Schiphol airport where he was met by Spežamor and her daughter Agapé. De Haan had told no one but Spežamor about his return.

The young girl had been holding an enormous helium *Dora the Explorer* balloon with the word WELKOM printed on it, although it was probably more of a gift for herself than a welcome-home surprise for De Haan.

Rijsbergen wondered if he would ever unearth all of the details in this case.

It had begun with the brutal murder of Coen Zoutman,

followed soon afterwards by the equally senseless death of Yona Falaina. They appeared to be connected to two earlier murders in Jerusalem and two more that followed in Boston. Supposedly, there was an obscure relationship between the Pilgrims and the Freemasons that Rijsbergen didn't fully understand. Apparently, all would become clear after the publication of a document that a researcher called Piet van Vliet had found in the Leiden Heritage Organisation's archives.

Rijsbergen had a strong suspicion that De Haan and Spežamor still had unresolved issues to work through. They might have been sitting next to each other on the sofa, but she had barely spoken, and they had seemed to be trying very carefully to avoid touching each other. Somehow, Fay's manner gave Rijsbergen the feeling that she was burdened with a deep secret, as if she needed to tell Peter something but hadn't yet found the right moment.

However, De Haan's last words to him had sounded hopeful.

'When I walked into the garden here,' De Haan had said, as he finished telling Rijsbergen and De Kooij his story, 'and I was back in our little paradise again . . . That's when I really knew: I'm home.'

In a corner of the Church of the Holy Sepulchre in Jerusalem, the Church of the Resurrection where it is said that Christ was both crucified and buried, a young man of no more than thirty sits on a simple wooden chair with his eyes closed and a peaceful expression on his face. He moves his hand now and then to a place on his chest that still smarts a little. When the Worshipful Master had taken him under his wing, he had been a young boy, all alone in the world, and the man had become like a father to him. He had entrusted the ancient texts to him. And now the devil had been defeated and had met his end in the desert. His plan had been thwarted on Mount Horeb . . .

They'd had enough time together for him to learn the five books . . .

But only now that the danger has truly passed has he dared to put the sign on his chest.

He opens his eyes, eyes so bright that light seems to shine from them. His lips move as he murmurs the sacred words, quietly enough that no one nearby will hear . . .

This is the secret knowledge, the oral teachings handed down by Moses, a Son of Light, to guide Man on his eis-odus, his journey inward, and to bring him into the safe haven whence he should never have departed, the promised land, his true home. We must find our way back to the garden.

Fragment 8 – The End of the Pilgrims in Leiden

After they had waved off the Speedwell, the remaining Pilgrims returned to their homes. Many of them hoped that they would be able to emigrate to America one day, and as we read in the manuscript, some were eventually successful. In the early 1620s, around a hundred members of the Leiden Pilgrim congregation made it to the New World. They included the wives, children and other relatives of those left behind, and new families too. Among them was Thomas Willet, a man who rose to great heights in America, first as Peter Stuyvesant's assistant, and then as the first English mayor of New York.

John Robinson would never reach the American colony. He stayed in Leiden at the request of the remnant congregation. It was agreed that he would go to America when the group's affairs were all in order, and he was no longer needed in Leiden. It was not to be. Robinson died in 1625 after a short illness and was buried in the Pieterskerk. Only his son, Isaac, eventually went to America in 1632.

Robinson maintained regular contact with the congregation in the New World. His letters provided them with useful advice and religious guidance, and he remained the Pilgrims' spiritual leader in both Leiden and America until his death.

After he died, it became very clear how important he had been for the group. Robinson had been the glue that held the community together, and without him, the Leiden congregation quickly fell apart. Its members joined the English Church and the Dutch Reformed Church. They gave up their English customs and even their English names and integrated with the people of Leiden.

Sooner or later, everyone who reads the manuscript gets the impression that they are not being told the whole story. That is why it is so very disappointing that the last few pages appear to be missing. In the last fragment, the author hints at the imminent revelation of certain secrets, for example, the role of the 'teacher' and his 'pupil'. I have set these words in quotation marks because we cannot know their roles for certain, but it does seem likely that the younger one was being initiated or schooled in some knowledge.

The larger group that stayed in Leiden was apparently at odds with the smaller group that set sail for America. At the time, a clash between two groups was often explained in religious terms. Disagreements were fought out as religious disputes, but often – as is also the case today – these were a smokescreen for something else, like a power struggle, access to resources, money . . .

The dissolution of the Leiden congregation and its eventual integration into the English Church or the Dutch Reformed Church seems, then, to be only half the story. We know from the historical record that the congregation suffered a gradual decline, but it tells us nothing about what the group's leaders – including the teacher, his student and the people around them – might have done that was not detailed in their official history.

I cannot help feeling that secret knowledge, handed down from generation to generation, was somehow a factor in the split. It came to the Netherlands from England and then travelled across the ocean to America. The custodians of these secrets died centuries ago, but if they too passed them on, there may still be people among us who possess this knowledge today. What an exciting thought! Speculation about this – and now, of course, we are leaving the realm of strictly scientific methodology – is, in my opinion, one of the charms of historiography: reasoned theorising about what might be written between the lines. Perhaps it is just as well that we do not know the full truth, that we are, in a sense, looking through a glass darkly. Now our knowledge is still limited, but perhaps, we may one day know the full story.

All that remains now is to tell you what happened to John Robinson's house after his death. De Engelse Poort or 'English Gate', as the house became known when the Pilgrims moved into the compound around it, fell into disrepair and seemed destined to come to a sad end. But the Walloon merchant Jean Pesijn left money in his will to build almshouses, and his wife, Marie de Lannoy, bought up the houses around the Engelse Poort for this purpose. Construction of the Jean Pesijnhofje began after her death in 1681. A stone set into the façade of the gatehouse reads: ON THIS SPOT LIVED, TAUGHT AND DIED J. ROBINSON 1611–1625.

Other traces of the Pilgrims' time in Leiden can be found on, in and around the Pieterskerk. There is a memorial stone for John Robinson on the wall of the Pieterskerk opposite the Jean Pesijnhofje. A second memorial is located inside the church on the same wall, and there's also an informative display about the Pilgrims.

On the corner of the William Brewstersteeg, a plaque above the archway leading to the Pieterskerk-Choorsteeg marks the site of the Pilgrim Press.

In the Beschuitsteeg near the Hooglandse Kerk, you'll find the Leiden American Pilgrim Museum, where the stories of the Pilgrims truly come to life.

Piet van Vliet

Acknowledgements

"**K**nock and the door will be opened to you."
It's great to see how willing people are to help when you approach them. For a writer it is easy to open doors: a request for answers to a particular question, permission to quote or a conversation over a cup of coffee. So many people have contributed to this book by offering up their time and knowledge. Maarten Dessing suggested back in 2016 during one of our countless film evenings, which always began in the café Van Engelen, that I do "something" about the Pilgrim Fathers in anticipation of the 400 year commemoration in 2020. André van Dokkum, who is starting to gain a permanent place in my words of thanks, was an engaged reader of the primeval version of this book all the way from Macau, and he offered countless suggestions about interesting Bible passages that were useful for this story. Of inestimable importance has once again been Lisanne Mathijssen, whose extremely sharp and inspiring editing chops away everything that is superfluous – like a kind of Michaelangelo from a piece of marble, so that the image underneath eventually comes to the fore. And of course Lidia Dumas, the dream editor-in-chief, who not only finds innumerable mistakes and flaws, but also always comes up with good alternatives.

This is also the place to express my gratitude to the other

people at HarperCollins Holland: to Jan-Joris Keijzer, Miranda Mettes and Jacqueline de Jong. Their great confidence gives me the peace and quiet needed to be able to write. And, of course, to the tireless Annemieke Tetteroo, who literally drives around town and country to bring my books to men and women; to Marianne Prins, who maintains telephone contact with the bookshops; to the always alert Chantal Hattink, who sees opportunities to bring my work to public attention time and again; and to the creative Nanouk Meijer, who knows how to reach younger readers through social media.

And then, in more or less alphabetical order, I would like to thank the following people. Jeremy Bangs, initiator and director of the Leiden Pilgrims Fathers Museum, who gave me an extensive tour of his small but fine museum. Co Berendsen and Jeroen Deen of the Loge Concordia Res Parvae Crescunt no 40 of Freemasonry Grootsneek, who provided a video recording of a lecture on Chief Seattle. Annie Houston, the program officer of the Massachusetts Cultural Council, who during our visit to Boston and Plymouth, helped organise the logistics of several meetings. Executive director Michelle M. Pecoraro, who found time in her busy schedule to tell me extensively about the memorial year in the US and the significance of the arrival of the (Leiden) Pilgrims to America, drawing my attention to the ideas that the Pilgrims brought with them from the Netherlands, such as freedom of speech, religion and the press, civil marriage and the separation of church and state. Anita Walker, who I unfortuantely didn't meet in person, but who took care of the tickets for Plimouth Plantation and the Pilgrim Hall Museum. Nancy Gardella, the executive director of the Martha's Vineyard Chamber of Commerce, who was kind enough to pick me up from the ferry on Martha's Vineyard and give me a whole tour of the island. Durwood Vanderhoop, an important and proud spokesman of the Wampanoag tribe, who showed me around the Aquinnah Cultural Center and told me about the significance of '2020' for the Indian population: the Native Nations, in addition to the US, England and the Netherlands are in fact the fourth nation involved in this year of remembrance. Jan-Bart Gewald and Trudi Blomsma, who checked and improved the Afrikaans in Chapter 2. Annette ter Haar, the 'Leiden Bridge Builder' of the Technolab Leiden, who tries to make young people enthusiastic about nature and technology, but also has an eye for the alpha and gamma sciences. Like a real spider in the web, she brought me into contact with various people and organizations and helped me think about how my books could be used in an educational project. Mieke Heurneman, History and Education advisor at Landscape Heritage Utrecht, who gave me permission to quote extensively from their website www.entoen. nu/en/regiocanons about Arminius and Gomarus. Former detective, philatelist and city guide, Willem Hogendoorn, for his enthusiastic recommendations about which places related to Leiden Pilgrims should not be missing from my book, and for introducing me to the wonderful walk that brings 400-year-old history back to life.

Director of the Pieterskerk Leiden, Frieke Hurkmans, who I already described in this book as 'an almost unstoppable speech waterfall, in which the new plans and ideas constantly tumbled over each other while talking'. Her love for Leiden and her enthusiasm for my books are heartwarming. Wouter Hollenga, who is my always responsive contact at the Pieterskerk. Annabel Junge, for generously granting me permisson to have my characters quote from her website: www.eeuwigheidvandeziel.nl. The Hague rabbi, Shmuel Katzman, who gave important information about the celebration of the seder meal, which was a scene unfortunately cut from the Prologue. Frank van Leeuwen of http://www.prokwadraat-groepswijzer.nl, who ensured that the walks designed by Sijbrand de Rooij ('Petrus', 'Paulus') and Willem van Hogendoorn ('Pilgrims') were available in both print and digital format. Mayor Henri Lenferink, who made his beautiful lecture, from the Diets celebration of the Historical Society of Oud-Leiden in the Hooglandse Kerk on Saturday, November 5, 2017, on the identity of Leiden available, and documents from this lecture can be found in Chapter 23. Nadia Mouaddab for the translation of some English fragments into flexible Dutch.

Marjolein Overmeer, Humanities editor of NEMO Kennislink, who gave permission to quote from the website about the significance of Thanksgiving as an important part of Dutch legacy. Michaël Roumen for the enthusiastic conversations we had about the Pilgrims, my book and its use during the Leiden memorial year. Tanneke Schoonheim of the Historical Society of Oud-Leiden, who is always willing to sort everything out for me immediately, from facing bricks to Pilgrim surnames. As an extension of that I would like to thank Hans de Sterke, who edited and sent me the beautiful photo of the facing brick 'In t nieuwe lant' by photographer Wilbert Devilee. Huub Pragt, who manages kemet.nl, which supplied me with all the information I needed about Aton and the Atonhymne. The small gem of a booklet, *Voor de Grote Oversteek* by Piet van Vliet, which describes the history of the Pilgrims in Leiden in a beautiful and compact way. This booklet forms the spine of my novel and I want to thank Van Vliet for his selfless and enthusiastic cooperation, and I hope that a possible reprint of *Voor de Grote Oversteek* will reach a large audience. Van Vliet's book appears in the text as the "manuscript", which is supposedly found by him in the archives of Erfgoed Leiden en Omstreken, but this so-called manuscript is of course entirely the result of my imagination.

I would like to thank journalist Rien van Vliet for his nice article in De Leydenaer about the discovery of the Pilgrims manuscript, as well as Annelies Spanhaak and Ariela Netiv of Erfgoed Leiden en Omstreken for their cooperation on this article. Leo van Zanen, who pointed me to numerous important websites concerning the Pilgrim Fathers. I am grateful to the always hospitable Cees van Veelen and Jenneke van Reemst, who allowed me to stay in their beautiful farm in Gelderland again, and granted me undisturbed days for a week to write the second version of my book. And the Freemasons of Leiden of course! Chris Beresford's statement is that the Freemasons do not form a secret society, but they do have secrets. During the open evening in 2017 I spoke to him extensively, just like Gerlinde Vliegenthart, who was my very helpful contact. I would like to thank Ingrid de Bonth for the extremely interesting lecture she gave that same open evening, which supplied me with most of my current knowledge about Freemasonry, and large parts of which also ended up in the book.

And then of course Hamide, my rock and my castle, with whom I always find peace and quiet. To remain in the terms of Freemasonry: through her, slowly but surely the pure cubic material emerges from the rough, unprocessed stone. Finally, this book is dedicated to our lovely daughter Dünya.

Consulted literature

Armstrong, K. _ De Bijbel: De Biografie. Mets & Schilt, Amsterdam, 2007 _ Bangs, J. _ Strangers and Pilgrims, Travellers and Sojourners. Leiden and the Foundations of Plymouth Plantation. General Society of Mayflower Descendants, Plymouth, 2009 _ Barthel, M. Wat Werkelijk in de Bijbel Staat: Een Nieuw Licht op het Boek der Boeken. Elsevier, Amsterdam/ Brussel, 1981 _ Bartlett, S._ De Geheimen van het Universum in 100 Symbolen. Librero, Kerkdriel, 2015 - Berents, D. _ Adam At Geen Appel. Uitgeverij Aspekt B.V., Soesterberg, 2016 _ Doane, T.W. _ Bible Myths and Their Parallels in Other Religions. Kessinger Publishing's, Whitefish Montana, Reprint, 1882 _ Feiler, B. _ Walking the Bible: A Journey by Land through the Five Books of Moses. Perennial/ HarperCollins, New York, 2002 _ Finkelstein, I., N.A. Silberman _ De Bijbel als Mythe: Opgravingen Vertellen een Ander Verhaal. Den Haag, Uitgeverij Synthese, 2006 _ Freke, T., P. Gandy _ The Jesus Mysteries: Was the "Original Jesus" a Pagan God? Three Rivers Press, New York, 2001 _ Hart, M. 't _ Wie God Verlaat Heeft Niets te Vrezen. De Schrift Betwist. Amsterdam, Arbeiderspers,1997 - Hart, M. 't - De Bril van God. De Schrift Betwist II. Amsterdam, Arbeiderspers, 2002 _ Hilton, C. _ Mayflower: The Voyage That Changed the World. The History Press, Gloucestershire, 2005 _ Horst, P.W. van der _

Mozes, Plato, Jezus: Studies over de Wereld van het Vroege Christendom. Prometheus, Amsterdam, 2000 _ Hulspas, M. _ En de Zee Spleet in Tweeën: De Bronnen van de Bijbel Kritisch Onderzocht. Fontaine Uitgevers, 's Graveland, 2006 _ Kardux, J., E. van de Bilt _ Newcomers in an Old City. The American Pilgrims in Leiden 1609-1620. Serie: In den Houttuyn, Burgersdijk & Niermans, Leiden, 1998 _ Kirsch, J. _ De Ongehoorde Bijbel: De Betekenis van Schokkende Verhalen uit het Oude Testament. Servire Uitgevers, Utrecht, 1997 _ Kirsch, J. Mozes: Een Nieuwe Visie op de Grote Bijbelse Wetgever en Profeet. Becht, Haarlem, 2002 _ Kovacs, J. _ Shocked by the Bible: The Most Astonishing Facts You've Never Been Told. Thomas Nelson, Nashville, 2008 _ Leeuwen, M. van _ Van Horen Zegen: Geschiedenis en Uitleg van de Bijbel. Uitgeverij Balans, Amsterdam, 2004 - Lenferink, H. _ Over de Identiteit van Leiden. Toespraak bij de Diësviering van de HVOL, 2017. Historische Vereniging Oud-Leiden, 2017 _ Morison, S.E. _ Of Plymouth Plantation 1620-1647 by William Bradford. Alfred A. Knopf, New York, 2006 _ Raymondt, S. _ Mythen en Sagen van de Griekse Wereld. Haarlem, Fibula-Van Dishoeck, 1982 _ Schaik, C. van, K. Michel _ Het Oerboek van de Mens: De Evolutie en de Bijbel. Uitgeverij Balans, Amsterdam, 2016 _ Seattle, L. Couvee _ Hoe Kun je de Lucht Bezitten? De Rede van Seattle. Jan van Arkel, Utrecht, 2018 _ Seltzer, R.M. _ Jewish People, Jewish Thought: The Jewish Experience in History. Prentice Hall, Inc: New Jersey, 1980 _ Steiner M.L. _ Op Zoek Naar . . . De Gecompliceerde Relatie tussen Archeologie en de Bijbel. Uitgever MijnBestseller.nl 2016 _ Toorn, K. van der _ Wie Schreef de Bijbel? De Ontstaansgeschiedenis van het Oude Testament. Uitgeverij Ten Have, Kampen, 2009 _ Vliet, Piet van _ Voor de grote oversteek: De Pilgrims in Leiden. Serie: Leidse Verhalen, Leiden Promotie VVV, 2001.

Consulted websites (March 2017-March 2018)

Boston

https://nl.wikipedia.org/wiki/Paul_Revere
http://www.thefreedomtrail.org/freedom-trail/official-sites.shtml
https://www.harvard.edu/
https://www.boston.gov/

Exodus

www.debijbel.nl
http://www.chicagonow.com/an-atheist-in-illinois/2013/05/
moses-the-celebrated-baby-killing-psychopath-of-the-bible/
https://eeuwigheidvandeziel.wordpress.com/reincarnatie/rein-
carnatie-en-religie/de-metafysische
http://janbommerez.createsend1.com/t/ViewEmail/t/
EB53F4ADE6DFF676

Indigenous People of the Americas

https://www.verenigdestaten.info/americana-de-wereld-der-
indianen/
http://wampanoagtribe.net/Pages/index

The Netherlands/ Leiden

http://www.oudleiden.nl/
https://www.visitleiden.nl/nl/landingpage
https://www.pieterskerk.com/nl//
http://www.shuttleworthdesign.com/gallery.php?boat=MARS
https://nl.wikipedia.org/wiki/Republiek_der_Zeven_
Verenigde_Nederlanden#Religie
http://www.regiocanons.nl/utrecht/zuidwest/arminius-contra-
gomarus

https://www.medischcontact.nl/nieuws/laatste-nieuws/artikel/
te-dom-voor-specialist-te-lui-voor-huisarts.htm

The Pilgrims
https://www.plimoth.org/
http://www.leidenamericanpilgrimmuseum.org/index.htm
http://www.mijnstambomen.nl/leiden/pilgrim.htm
http://www.gutenberg.org/ebooks/24950
http://people.brandeis.edu/~dkew/David/Marsden-
Mayflower-1904.pdf
https://archive.org/details/lastofmayflower00harriala
https://archive.org/details/findingofmayflow00harruoft
http://www.pilgrimhall.org/

Sinai/ Egypt
http://www.info-egypte.nl/sint-catherina-klooster/ – https://
www.oneworld.nl/mensenrechten/is-er-precies-aan-hand-sinai/
https://www.unesco.nl/erfgoed/sint-catharina-klooster#zoom=
3&lat=28.5562&lon=33.9754&layers=BT
https://kunst-en-cultuur.infonu.nl/geschiedenis/40248-het-st-
catherina-klooster-in-de-sinai.html
http://www.kemet.nl/de-grote-atonhymne/

Thanksgiving
http://www.rense.com/general45/thanks.htm
https://www.nemokennislink.nl/publicaties/thanksgiving-een-
nederlandse-erfenis#

Freemasons
https://www.vrijmetselarij.nl/
http://www.vrijmetselaars-leiden.nl/

https://massfreemasonry.org/
https://www.leidschdagblad.nl/leiden-en-regio/vrijmetse-larij-leiden-wordt-gemengd
https://www.leidschdagblad.nl/leiden-en-regio/open-huis-bij-de-vrijmetselaars
https://www.erfgoedleiden.nl/component/lei_verhalen/verhaal/id/488
http://hetuurvandewaarheid.info/2010/11/04/sinistere-plaatsen-het-amerikaanse-capitool//

Other
http://www.van-de-baanhoek.nl/bijen/de-levenscyclus-van-de-bij/

Wikipedia
Searchterms: Achnaton/ Aton, All-seeing Eye, Arminius/Gomarus, Bible, Bees, Boston/ Harvard, Chief Seattle, Egypt, Esotericism, Exodus, Indigenous people, Israel, Judaism, John Robinson, Leiden, Lodge Ishstar/ La Virtu, Mayflower, Mayflower Compact, Mozart/ Die Zauberflöte, Moses, Old Testament, Paul Revere, Pilgrim Fathers/ Pilgrims, Plimouth Plantation, Plymouth, Sinai, St. Katharina Monastery, Remonstrants, Sharm El-Sheik, Thanksgiving, Freemasons, (History of the) United States, South-Africa/ Orania.

Afterword by Piet van Vliet

First and foremost, I would like to sincerely thank the author Jeroen Windmeijer for providing this platform for my work. Discovering the Pilgrim manuscript in Leiden City Archives is – and will no doubt remain – the absolute highlight of my career.

Usually, the discovery of such a document, however special it may be, causes no more than a ripple in the academic pond. It may lead to the recalibration of our understanding here and there, an article or two will be published, and historians will discuss among themselves the details that are of little interest to the outside world.

I am delighted that, on this occasion, things have proceeded in a less conventional way. I could have chosen to publish the translation of the manuscript in a history magazine. However, I thought that such an unusual find warranted something a little less ordinary. Furthermore, with events to commemorate the four-hundredth anniversary of the *Mayflower*'s voyage taking place in Leiden, Plymouth and Boston in 2020, it seemed to me to be the perfect moment to take a different approach.

I did not know Jeroen Windmeijer personally, but I am

Leidener born and bred, and I had read his books *The Confessions of St Peter* and *St Paul's Labyrinth*, which both take place in Leiden.

At a book-signing in a local bookstore, I decided to take the plunge and introduce myself to him. I told him about my discovery. As a writer, he immediately recognised the manuscript's potential. To cut a very long story short: after a few meetings, we decided to embark upon this journey together. I would translate the manuscript into modern language, and he would weave an exciting story around it.

A fruitful collaboration ensued. Jeroen consulted me for feedback on each new draft of what eventually became this novel. I must say that this has been an exciting adventure from start to finish, one which I have not regretted for a single second!

Naturally, as a researcher, I find it incredibly frustrating that the last few pages of the document are missing. Perhaps they are still hidden somewhere . . . The fact that they have not yet been found does not mean that they do not exist. Archaeologist Peter de Haan would probably quote that famous axiom: 'Absence of evidence is not evidence of absence.'

What makes it especially frustrating is that in the manuscript's final sentences, we are promised that certain things will be revealed, particularly about the mysterious boy and the older man. Their relationship appears to be one of a teacher and pupil engaged in the transfer of knowledge. But what was this knowledge? The first boy eventually grows into a young man, and he goes to America. But the group that he joins on the voyage to the New World appears to have split away from the group in Leiden. Why does he go with these 'enemies'? The Leiden group then apparently reorganises itself around the same 'teacher' and a new boy.

And what does that reference to builders mean? One would assume that this was at least a century too early for Freemasonry . . .

As for the conflict, in those days, it could only have been a theological dispute. Although, at that time, the struggle for power was often hidden behind the mask of religion, just as it is today. But what was the conflict about? Why did such a large group stay in Leiden?

These are all questions which may never be fully answered. Although we might find this unsatisfying or frustrating, perhaps something can also be said for not having a clear view of what actually took place. This leaves room for us to speculate, to form theories that stand the test of time, that can actually be verified or eventually even disproved. And that, I think, also has a certain charm.

This is why I am so pleased that Jeroen Windmeijer has used the manuscript to form his own imaginative and meticulously researched theory about what might have happened. And of course, a novelist has the advantage of not being limited by scientific conventions which demand that every claim is backed up with evidence, quotes from other authors, footnotes and endnotes.

Now that I have read his book, I am almost unable to imagine that events unfolded in any other way!

I would like to end with something that I have written myself. This time, in a reversal of roles, I consulted Jeroen for feedback on *my* work.

I have called the resulting text 'Fragment 8', although, obviously, it was not part of the original manuscript. I thought it would be interesting to use the facts that we do have about the Leiden Pilgrims and add an ending to their fascinating story.

In co-operation with Leiden City Marketing, the manuscript

fragments have been published as a small book with a foreword and afterword. *Before the Great Crossing* seemed like a fitting title. It is, of course, a reference to the Pilgrims' voyage over the ocean, but *The Great Crossing* also happens to be the title of one of my favourite *Asterix and Obelix* adventures in which they voyage to America . . .

Keep Reading . . .

Enjoyed *The Pilgrim Conspiracy*? Make sure you've read *St Paul's Labyrinth,* Jeroen Windmeijer's previous thriller!

A shocking secret that has been buried for centuries . . .

When university professor Peter de Haan attends a library event, he has no idea of the dangers that await him. As an area outside the library collapses, a hidden tunnel is revealed. Inside cowers a naked man, covered in blood. Then Peter receives a mysterious text message – *the hour has come . . .*

When Peter's colleague Judith disappears, he realises he has been drawn into a plot with consequences deadlier than he could ever have imagined. He has twenty-four hours to find her, otherwise she will be killed.

As Peter investigates, he uncovers mysteries that have been hidden for years. But following his every footstep is an underground society who will stop at nothing to keep their secrets hidden. Will Peter save Judith in time, or will his quest end in disaster?